When the Stars Align

JEANETTE GREY

New York

Forever Yours
Hachette Book Group
1290 Avenue of the Americas
New York, NY 10104

www.HachetteBookGroup.com

Printed in the United States of America

First edition: September 2015

10 9 8 7 6 5 4 3 2 1

OPM

Forever Yours is an imprint of Grand Central Publishing.

The Forever Yours name and logo are trademarks of Hachette Book Group, Inc.

The Hachette Speakers Bureau provides a wide range of authors for speaking events. To find out more, go to www.hachettespeakersbureau.com or call (866) 376-6591.

The publisher is not responsible for websites (or their content) that are not owned by the publisher.

ISBN 978-1-4555-6270-1

To all the summer students staring up at the stars wondering what they're doing with their lives.

Acknowledgments

This story never would've been told without the help of a lot of incredible people:

My editor, Megha Parekh, who always knows exactly what to tweak.

My agent, Mandy Hubbard, who safeguards my sanity at every turn.

Brighton Walsh, for believing in this story in its infancy and keeping me from giving up on it.

Heather McGovern, whose feedback and inspirational photos helped it all come together.

My partners in crime at Bad Girlz Write and Capital Region Romance Writers of America, with their constant support and commiseration.

My incredibly patient husband and family, who put up with my crazy writer eyes even on Christmas Eve.

And Darik and Justino, for getting me out of a bind a very, very long time ago.

Chapter 1

You don't ask, you don't get. It was one of the very first lessons Jo's father had ever taught her—right after "stop existing" and "be a boy."

She chuckled darkly to herself and wiped some of the sweat from her brow, leaning an elbow out the open window of the van and staring at the rows of palm trees lining the road.

She might not have been able to fulfill all his wishes for her, but at least there were a few of good old Dad's teachings she'd taken to heart. She was going to ask all right. She just had to *get there* already, before she lost her nerve.

Twisting around in her seat, she glanced at the clock and worried her lip ring with her teeth. "How much longer?"

The driver, Roberto, tapped his finger against the steering wheel. "Ten minutes?"

Ugh, that still sounded like forever. After eight odd hours in airports and planes—and getting on near forty minutes in an un-air-conditioned van—Jo was more than ready to be done with travel for the day. Nodding to herself, she turned to face the window again, staring out at the little clusters of tiny, pastel-colored houses set off from the road, with their clothes-lines, satellite dishes, and what seemed like unending swaths of overgrown green.

She took a deep breath, trying to let the scenery zipping past calm her down. Obsessing over what she was going to do and say when she arrived wasn't going to get them there any faster. It was only making her more anxious and pissed off.

How could she not be agitated, though? She'd been bust-ing her ass at school for ages. Had snagged decent internships after her freshman and sophomore years, and now here she was: one of nine undergraduates getting to spend the summer work-ing in Arecibo, Puerto Rico, doing research at the biggest radio telescope in the world. It was her dream job. The capstone for her CV—the thing that was going to propel her into a top-level graduate school. Make her dad stand up and finally take notice of everything she'd managed to achieve.

Anger and disappointment echoed in her chest. She'd thought it would be all of that and more. Right up until she'd found out she was being shunted off into a second-tier project. Again.

Curling her hands into fists, she shook her head, pent-up rage sending fire and ice down her spine. Whoever this P.J. Galloway person was who had divvied out the assignments had a lot of nerve. If the guy thought she was going to sit back and be side-lined and *coddled* just because she was a girl, trying to hack it in the sciences...well. He had another think coming.

Just as her simmering frustration threatened to boil over, a sign appeared over the crest of a hill, pointing the way to the observatory, and Roberto put the blinker on.

Okay. Go time.

He looked to her as he took the turn, gesturing to the left. "I take you to where you are staying."

"Actually…" She swallowed hard and channeled all the lessons she'd learned over the years. Making her voice as authoritative as she could, she insisted, "I need to go to the main building first. I have an e-mail." She patted the pocket of her cargo shorts, reassuring herself with the crinkle of the printout she'd stashed there. "From Dr. Galloway."

He frowned, lines appearing between his eyes. "I think you meet Dr. Galloway tonight."

"Everybody else will," she agreed. "But we have things to discuss before that."

He gave her a sidelong glance, and she held her breath. But after a long moment, he shrugged. "If you say so."

She exhaled long and slow. She *had* said so. She'd asked, and she'd gotten what she wanted. Now she just had to do it one more time.

Without saying anything else, Roberto drove them straight up to the observatory gates, where he got waved through by the guard on duty. Jo blocked out the sights around her, concentrating on psyching herself up for this. Channeling all her righteous indignation and all the times people had tried to pass her over in the past.

Because it wasn't going to happen. Not today. No way.

As soon as the van pulled to a stop, Jo unhooked her seat belt and shoved open the door. Behind her, Roberto protested, "You sure you don't want me to take you to the house?"

"I'm good." She waved him off, her focus intent on the closed door in front of her. On flinging it open.

The second she was inside, it was like she went blind, the humming fluorescent lighting overhead no match for the brilliance of the sun outside. She blinked to get her eyes to adjust, staring down a series of corridors, all painted cinder-block walls and propped-open doors. She had no idea where she was going, but she didn't let that stop her. She knew the drill: walk around as if you own the place, and most people will assume you do.

"Miss? Miss!"

Sighing, Jo called over her shoulder, "Give me just a second."

Roberto wasn't letting her off that easily, though. He called after her again, and she swore beneath her breath as a couple of faces turned to give her curious stares. Yeah. Turned out the whole "walk around like you own the place" thing didn't work quite so well when everyone knew you didn't.

For the first time, a little prickle of doubt made her stomach twist. This entire plan of hers had the potential to be a disaster. She was tired and sweaty and disgusting, and it felt like her hair was plastered to her head. She was going off half-cocked, and in the kind of mood she was in, she was probably going to burn a bridge or two.

She hadn't gotten as far as she had in life by being nice, though. In a man's world, a girl never did. Not unless she had a hell of a lot bigger tits than Jo did.

The thick soles of her boots thudded against the tile floor as she rounded the corner, turning to enter a hallway lined by open doors. She scanned the numbers beside each one until finally she spotted it. Office number 109. She screwed up her confidence and tugged the hem of her top down. Shoved her hair out of her face and rubbed the studs in the shell of her ear for luck.

She knocked once before stepping right in, keeping her voice strong as she said, "Dr. Galloway?"

And then she did a double take as the chair of one Dr. P.J. Galloway slowly rotated, spinning to face the door, revealing—

Not the pot-bellied, middle-aged man Jo had been expecting. But a sixty-something-year-old lady in a lilac dress.

Fuck. So, *so* many layers of fuck.

The woman who was apparently Dr. Galloway raised one silver-hued eyebrow, peering over her glasses at Jo, and Jo was not the type to demur, but she shrank just a little inside. "Yes?"

"I'm—" Jo snapped her mouth shut when her throat made a wobbling sound. She swallowed and tried again. "I'm Jo Kramer, and I'm—"

"One of the delightful members of our Research Experience for Undergraduates program, yes. Yes, I know."

As long as she didn't know who else Jo was.

Before she could say another word, Roberto caught up with her. Breathing hard, he skidded to a stop in the middle of the hallway, and Jo glanced to find him sending a pleading look at Dr. Galloway over Jo's head.

Dr. Galloway made a withering sort of noise but smiled as she shook her head. She refocused her attention on Jo, who hadn't felt this much like a butterfly pinned to a specimen tray in years. "Is this regarding the matter about which you e-mailed me earlier this week, Ms. Kramer?"

Fuck it. Jo wasn't about to back down now. She squared her shoulders and lifted her chin, crossing her arms over her chest and planting her feet. "It is."

"Did you not receive my reply?"

"I did, but—" But what? But she'd thought she might be able to get her way through sheer force of will and personality. Thought she'd butt her head against the problem at least a few more times, because people got tired of dealing with her. They *always* got tired of dealing with her, and being exhausting and tenacious was how she got things done whenever someone slammed a door in her face. Whenever someone tried to tell her no. "But I'm here to argue my case in person."

"Well, then." Dr. Galloway tugged her glasses off and folded them before setting them down on her desk. "Please. Be my guest."

All the words she'd rehearsed on the plane and in Roberto's van seemed to shrivel as she called them forth. "I am...I... You've assigned me to a female advisor."

"That I have."

"And I'd like to request that I be switched to a different one."

"Do you find yourself uncomfortable working for women, Ms. Kramer?"

"No! No, of course not." It was ridiculous to think about. Almost as ridiculous as the idea that she'd be trying to make this case to a woman. A woman named *P.J.*

Seriously. How was she supposed to have seen that one coming?

Dr. Galloway tapped one short-cropped nail against the arm of her chair. "Because our nondiscrimination policy is quite clear on this point."

"Nondiscrimination?" she croaked. As if *Jo* were the one trying to discriminate? It was laughable, and if this woman knew an iota of her history, she'd never dare suggest it. "I'm happy to work for a female advisor. Only..." She trailed off, uncertain how to say this.

How to explain the look that had been in her tenth-grade counselor's eyes as she'd suggested that Jo should consider a field of study more suited to her sex. The way her physics teacher had never learned her name. The way the department chair at her university had scowled as he'd told her that maybe the lone female professor in their group might be able to find some work for her when he couldn't be bothered to.

The way her father had always looked at her whenever she'd asked him for anything. Anything at all.

"Only...?" Dr. Galloway prompted.

Fuck it. There wasn't really any way Jo could mess this up any worse than she had so far. "Only, I wasn't sure if you were assigning me to a female advisor on account of my being female myself."

It had happened before, and it burned, every time.

Dr. Galloway's expression was one of very, very thinly veiled amusement as she arched her brows higher. "Ms. Kramer. You are one of six women enrolled in our undergraduate research assistant program this summer. Four of the nine resident scientists who were kind enough to take on students happen to be women. It would sadly be mathematically impossible for at least one of our female students *not* to be paired with an advisor of the same gender."

The breath Jo sucked in made a whistling noise, a sound that echoed the one currently happening inside her head.

Six women. She was one of six women here this summer, and the very thought of it made something loosen in her chest.

Three years of undergraduate physics and astronomy and math and computing courses, and not once had there been *six* girls. Hell, in general, there had never been more than one. She'd only ever had one female professor in all that time, and now there were going to be at least four.

She wasn't about to let her guard slip—it was entirely too tightly ingrained in her for that. But for the first time in a decade, the armor she surrounded herself with seemed to lighten. It made the junction of her shoulder and her neck pinch a little less hard, and her lungs filled in a way they rarely did as she let herself inhale.

Seeing Jo's posture relax, Dr. Galloway smiled, her lips teasing upward with a knowing look that wasn't about derision. No, Jo recognized derision entirely too well, and this was something else. Something Jo didn't know exactly what to do with, but something that felt...safe, almost. It was a novel concept.

"Will there be anything else?" Dr. Galloway asked.

"I...um...no. Just that."

"Well, thank you for being so accommodating with accepting your assigned advisor. Now, if you'll excuse me, I do have some work to finish up before our welcome session this evening."

"Right. Of course."

"Roberto?"

"*Sí?*" he said, stepping forward.

"If you would be so kind as to deliver Ms. Kramer and her belongings to the girls' residence?"

"Yes, ma'am."

"Thank you."

It was a dismissal if ever Jo had heard one. Her cheeks felt warm, embarrassment at the way she'd acted—at what she'd assumed—almost as hot as the climate.

But that was how things had gone for her—how things had *always* gone for her. You could only be discouraged or shunted aside so many times before you learned to expect the worst of people.

It burned to admit that she was wrong. But a person did what she had to do. "I apologize for—" she started.

Dr. Galloway waved her off. "Not an unrealistic presumption, unfortunately. I've been there a time or two myself, as you can imagine."

"Um. Yes."

Dr. Galloway started to spin around to face her computer screen again, and Roberto stepped to the side, holding out a hand for Jo to go ahead of him. Gritting her teeth, Jo nodded and plotted her retreat.

She'd only just turned away when Dr. Galloway called after her. "Oh, Ms. Kramer?"

Jo paused. "Yes?"

"Do try not to accuse Heather of sexism the first time you meet her. I think you'll find she's not quite as understanding about that kind of thing as I am."

Jo's stomach churned. "Right."

With that, she put one foot in front of the other and let herself be marched back to the van they'd left waiting at the front of the building. The whole time, her neck tingled, shame and anger both twisting her up.

Shame at her behavior. At her presumptions and the way she'd let her temper get away from her. Anger at all the people who'd made her feel like she had to go in swinging every time—at her professors and her father. At herself.

"The other girls are already here," Roberto said. He visibly stopped himself from getting her door for her.

"Great." It wasn't, though. She was in no mood to play nice with other people right now.

But maybe that was for the best. There wouldn't be any hiding or mistaking. They'd know right off the bat what kind of bitch they were dealing with, and they could skip right over that awkward moment when people tried to be her friend.

She had neither the time nor the inclination to be anybody's friend. She was here for ten weeks, and she was here to do her job. In her first five minutes, she'd managed to make a bad first impression on the person running the program and on the guy she'd have to talk to any time she needed a ride off-site for any reason. But that was fine. Totally fine.

Gazing out the window at the mountains in the distance, she sucked her lip ring tight between her teeth. The first impressions she'd given them weren't wrong. They were just irrelevant.

And she'd work as hard as she needed to prove it.

* * *

Adam McCay was lucky. So, so lucky. He just had to keep reminding himself of that.

Mopping sweat off his brow, he folded up the last of his shirts, tugged open a drawer, and dropped them inside. He straightened back up and surveyed his room. Four white walls and a couple big, screened windows with clunky wooden shutters. A closet and a dresser.

And it all looked unbearably empty. None of his usual posters or prints. None of his usual anything, but there hadn't been space in his suitcases for much except books and clothes. It didn't really matter, though. Just ten short weeks here, and then he would get to go home.

He frowned at himself for even thinking it. If he started romanticizing home on his first day, he was going to be wallowing by the end of the week. And it was so damn shortsighted and selfish, anyway.

He was here, in sunny, beautiful Puerto Rico. He had a summer research job that any physics or astronomy major in the country would kill for, mapping out galaxies using a giant radio telescope. He was getting paid, and he was getting valuable experience, and he was living someplace exciting and interesting.

And all he could think about was that his phone still hadn't rung.

Even though he'd sworn to himself he wouldn't do it—

wouldn't keep worrying at this like a scab about to bleed—he pulled out his phone and glanced at the screen. No messages, no missed calls. Nothing. He put the thing away with a sigh. Shannon was probably busy with whatever she was up to back at home, and he didn't begrudge her that. Their mismatched schedules were part of why they'd decided to take a break this summer, after all. Part of why she'd wanted to take a break. And he hadn't thought she was entirely wrong.

He had thought he'd hear from her occasionally, though.

Not that standing around obsessing about it was going to do him any good. He shook it off, giving himself a couple of quick slaps on the cheek for good measure, because honestly, this mood of his was starting to piss him off.

He gave the room another quick once-over, but there really wasn't anything left for him to do. Coming from his parents' place in Florida, he'd managed to be the first one here by a long shot, arriving early enough that it had warranted the observatory's driver, Roberto, making a special trip out to San Juan just for him. It had been a good chance to pick the guy's brain about how things operated out here, and an even better chance to get first dibs on the room of his choice. An extra couple of hours to work on getting settled in, but now he was restless, and really, really in need of a distraction.

Normally, this was the kind of energy he'd prefer to burn off by going for a run or lifting some weights, but the heat made him think twice about it. He'd have to get used to fitting in his exercise routine in the early mornings if he didn't want to die of heat stroke. Didn't help him much right now, though.

At a loss, he pointedly did not reach for his phone, but instead wandered out into the hall and stuck his head into the room next door.

"Hey." It took him a second, but he remembered. "Tom?"

"Yeah?"

Tom was sitting on the floor, suitcase barely touched, with a book in his lap and a fan pointed right at his head. Adam chuckled at the sight, plucking at the damp fabric of his own T-shirt in sympathy.

"A summer without AC is gonna be killer, huh?"

Tom shrugged. "Labs are all air-conditioned, and it won't be too bad out here at night."

True enough. Changing the subject, Adam gestured at his bags. "You need any help getting unpacked or anything?"

"Nah."

Okaaaaay. Adam was plenty accustomed to dealing with the antisocial types who ended up in the sciences, but this was going to be a very long summer if everybody was like this. "All right. Well. Just let me know."

"You could go ask one of the girls. Girls usually like…" Tom trailed off, giving Adam an assessing look. "…*Help* from guys like you."

Adam frowned at the "guys like you" comment. And at the inflection to the way Tom had said "help." Really, the whole sentence kind of bugged him, but he didn't want to go taking offense for no good reason. Whatever Tom was implying, the fact of the matter was that Adam did get his fair share of attention from women. Shannon'd always used to make fun of him for it—used to ruffle his hair and tweak his nose and tell him he was going to get himself in trouble someday.

A pang echoed dimly through his ribs. She wasn't the reason he hadn't headed over to the other house to lend a hand. It wasn't. He just didn't need any complications this summer. His life was messy enough as it was.

He forced a weak approximation of a smile. "Well. I'll...leave you to it, I guess."

"Okay."

Yeah. With Tom not exactly inviting him in, he moved on. The other guy sharing the house with them—Jared—had seemed a lot more sociable, but as Adam approached his room, it was to find the door closed, music ringing out from within. He was tempted to knock regardless, but hesitated.

In the end, he sighed and kept walking, meandering through their minimally stocked kitchen for a glass of water before soldiering on.

Outside, it was even stickier and muggier, and the itch beneath his skin only deepened. Fresh air usually made him feel better, but the density of it pressing on his lungs was claustrophobic. He set down his glass, then clasped his hand to his chest and dug his thumb in hard.

All at once, it dawned on him the situation he'd gotten himself into. He was lucky to be here, sure, but he was also cut off from all his friends and from the girl he'd been seeing on again and off again since he was seventeen. His cell phone reception was mediocre, and he was stuck in the middle of nowhere without a car. It was too hot to run, and his housemates didn't have any interest in keeping him company.

And...and the van that had brought him there that morning was pulling into the drive.

For one single, heart-stopping second, he imagined leaving all his shit behind and making a run for it. Telling Roberto to take him to the airport, that he'd made a terrible mistake. But that wasn't who he was. It wouldn't be—not anymore. Dropping his hand from his chest, he sucked in a deep, hard breath. Curled his fingers into his palm and squared his jaw.

Rather than heading his way, the van veered off toward the house where all the girls were staying, lurching to a stop right in front of their door. Roberto stepped out and headed around to the rear, but there was a tension in his shoulders. Before the guy could get over there, a girl tugged open the doors at the back. A girl in heavy boots and cargo shorts that hung low on slim hips and a long-sleeved shirt that made him feel even hotter in his tee. Her face glinted with metal, piercings in the shells of her ears and in her lip and her brow, and her chin-length hair shone a deep jet black, except in the front. Where it had been dyed blue.

He swallowed, his mouth suddenly dry. She was…something. That was what she was. Everything about her said to stay the fuck away, but as she beat Roberto to unloading her things, Adam took a single step forward. And then another. And another.

Because it didn't matter if she was tough as nails. He'd treat her the same as he would anyone else, and that meant offering to help. And if his palms got even damper just watching her as she turned toward the house, well…that was no one's business but his own.

Roberto and the girl were saying something to each other, but Adam couldn't quite make it out. He kept moving, crossing the space between the two houses as Roberto held up his hands, then turned and walked toward the front of the van. Adam frowned at the expression on the man's face, but before he could call out, the engine started up, and the gravel churned beneath the tires as the van peeled out.

Adam stepped aside as it rumbled past, peering beyond it to watch the girl's shoulders slump. She was faced away from him, looking brittle in a way he hadn't entirely anticipated. Black ink peeked above the collar of her shirt, curving along the base of her neck, and his hands itched as he stared. Maybe it had just been too long—maybe it was that he'd never touched a girl who looked like that—but for a second all he could think about was tracing the lines etched in her skin, following them down, down, down. Soothing the brittleness away with his lips against her nape.

He shrugged aside the guilt that threatened to boil over at that thought and walked a little faster, because he *could*, damn it. He could touch and kiss and sleep with anyone he liked. Because—if the way she had spoken the last time he'd gotten a hold of her was any sign—Shannon wanted him to.

And he didn't know exactly what got into him at that point. It was clear the girl didn't hear him coming, and for some reason he wanted to show off a little. Make an impression. Get noticed.

He stole across the last few feet of gravel, sneaking up behind her and getting close as he leaned in for the handle of her suitcase, a flippant hello and a flirty smile on his lips. And he was just about to use them, too, but before he could do a single damn thing, a steely grip closed around his wrist.

"What—"

All his weight went out from underneath him, and he was rolling. He choked, lungs empty as his back impacted with the ground, and then he was just lying there, mouth agape and gasping for air, looking up at dark eyes and fair skin and pale, soft lips. Blurry eyes and blurry lips.

He squeezed his eyes shut before blinking them open. Squinting at the face above him, he watched it swim into focus, bringing with it glints of metal from the girl's piercings, the dark furrows of angry lines between her brows, and...Jesus. Everything hurt. He groaned and shifted just to make sure he could still feel all his fingers and toes.

And, wow, he thought he'd gotten himself into a shitty

situation before? Contending with it all while feeling like one giant bruise was going to be *awesome*.

The girl drew his attention from the sharp rocks digging into his shoulder blades by shaking him. "What the fuck do you think you're doing?"

Well, he had been trying to make an impression. Mission obviously accomplished, if not exactly in the way he'd been hoping.

He blinked a few extra times for good measure and lifted a hand to shield his eyes from the sun. "Um." His voice sounded gritty and raw and like he'd just been flipped by a girl who weighed a hundred pounds. "Hi?"

"You have got to be fucking kidding me," she mumbled under her breath before stepping away and extending a hand.

He eyed her warily and decided maybe he'd just pick himself up off the ground after all that. Holding his palms out to show he meant no harm, he sat up with a groan. The back of his head twinged, and he lifted one hand to grab at it, wincing.

She'd crossed her arms over her chest by that point. "Who are you?"

"Adam." He jerked one thumb toward the guys' house across the way. "I live next door. Was going to offer to help you with your bags, but I'm guessing that won't be necessary."

"No. It won't."

And he didn't miss the fact that there wasn't the slightest hint of an apology to her tone, nor any hint that she might be thinking about offering one. It was a little presumptuous to expect one, but saying you're sorry was pretty de rigueur for attacking a guy who'd come in peace. Or at least that's how he'd always assumed this kind of thing was supposed to go.

"Okay."

"Okay." Her expression held, firm and impassive and living up to the promise of all the ways she presented herself. A beat passed, and then another. For the first time, something in her eyes flickered, and the set of her lips cracked. "You really shouldn't sneak up on people like that."

"Yeah. Got that."

"People get the wrong idea, and instinct takes over, and—"

"Right. I said I got it."

Her mouth snapped shut, and any quiver of vulnerability he might have thought he'd glimpsed disappeared. "Fine. Asshole."

She had *got* to be kidding him. "I was *trying* to be nice!"

"Well, you failed."

"Sorry?" He waited, but she clearly wasn't about to reciprocate, and okay, sure, whatever. Except it bugged the hell out of him. Rubbing his neck, he grumbled at her, "Least you could do is apologize for trying to cripple me."

Her eyes narrowed. "Hardly. I'd have to be an idiot to cripple you using a move like that. It was pure self-defense."

"Used on someone you didn't need to defend yourself against!" Ugh. He was just blurting stuff out at this point, and that never went well. Nothing he'd tried today had gone well, and he laughed darkly to himself. He just shouldn't try. "Fine, fine, I get it. You don't apologize. I hope that works out super well for you."

"Always has."

"Great."

No further insults seemed to be forthcoming, so he ignored her as he stood, dusting off both himself and his pride. God, this whole day—this whole summer—was a mess. If he'd just stayed in Philly, he'd be hanging out with his friends right now, and maybe he'd be working a crap job stocking shelves or something, but he'd be able to go to Shannon's apartment tonight, and maybe she wouldn't exactly comfort him or anything, but she'd let him be near her. Feeling not nearly so alone and bruised and useless as he did right now.

Gravel crunched beside him as the psycho started wrestling with her luggage. He rolled his eyes, because the bags were clearly heavy, but before he could take too much satisfaction in her struggle, a tiny plastic wheel rolled over his toe, and he just... *lost* it.

He jumped back, rounding on her and kicking at the gravel, ready to spit, because this was ridiculous. "Jesus Christ, what is *wrong* with you?"

All she did was laugh, though, and it was hollow and awful, and for half a second he felt bad. "You don't even want to know."

His empathy didn't last long. As she turned around and stormed away, he shook his head. "You're right," he called after her. "I don't."

Only there'd been something in her expression just then. Something real.

Something that made him wonder if maybe he did.

Chapter 2

"Excuse me?" Jo put her hands on her hips, bristling with the effort it took to keep her voice restrained. Between Roberto, Dr. Galloway, and whoever that meathead had been outside, she'd already fucked up three first meetings today, and goddammit if she was going to overreact and make a mess of this one, too. Especially if the girl standing in front of her really was going to be her— "Roommate?"

"Sorry." The girl—Carol, she'd said her name was—shrugged. "Six of us and only three bedrooms here, so we don't exactly have a lot of choice. You could try your luck over at the guys' house, but I doubt that would fly with anyone."

She gestured toward the window and the other house across the way. The one that guy was slinking his way back to, and Jo had to force herself not to watch him. Even with the fake little limp he was probably putting on for her benefit, he had an amazing ass. And really broad shoulders, and a trim waist, and she always had been a sucker for the blond-haired, blue-eyed, all-American look on a man. She was even more of a sucker for the chance to mess that kind of perfection up—get that skin all nice and hot and sweaty between the sheets.

She probably would have tried to tap that, too, eventually. If she hadn't, you know, accidentally flipped him when he snuck up behind her. Or run over his foot.

Fuck.

"Listen," Carol said, drawing Jo's attention back. "It's really not so bad. I know you're the last one here and didn't get your pick of rooms, but they're all about the same, and I'm easy. I sleep like the dead, I promise I don't snore, and it's just ten weeks. It'll be fine."

Right. Just ten weeks, in a tiny little room in a sweltering house on the edge of what looked like a jungle, rooming with a blonde who apparently thought a sundress was good moving-in-day attire. A blonde who Jo was pretty sure had Katy Perry streaming out of her earbuds.

This was going to go *great*.

"No. I mean, sure." Jo forced a little smile, but it might have looked more like a grimace. "I'm just not used to sharing space with someone." She hadn't, not since freshman year. What a fiasco that had been. Both she and the poor girl who'd gotten stuck with her had kissed the ground once it was over. But this would be all right. Like Carol had said, it was only temporary. "Besides, we'll probably be spending most of our time in the lab, right?"

That was Jo's plan, anyway. If she played her cards right, she could probably get another paper or two to add to her CV this summer, and then she'd be all set when it came time to get her grad school applications ready in the fall.

Carol arched an eyebrow. "A bunch, sure. But we are in Puerto Rico, you know."

"So?"

"So, how often do you get to visit here? And in all those e-mails we got from P.J., she said they had a bunch of trips planned."

Oh, great. So this girl was on a first-name basis with Dr. Galloway, then?

"I don't know. I'm not a big field trip kind of girl," Jo hedged.

"Suit yourself. I mean, I'm all about getting my job done. But life is about more than that, you know?"

"If you say so."

Because life hadn't ever been that way. Not for her. Not when she was a kid, desperate to live up to expectations that always seemed right about to crush her. And definitely not now.

"I do," Carol said. She smiled, and it wasn't mocking or pitying or any of the other hundred belittling responses Jo had received over the years. "Just you wait. I bet you'll end up having a great time in spite of yourself."

"Weirder things have happened," Jo muttered. Louder, she sighed and gestured around the room. "So where should I put my stuff?"

"Right-hand side of the closet is empty, and I left that whole dresser for you." With that, Carol dropped to perch on the edge of her bed and pulled her laptop closer.

Jo could work with that.

Aware the whole time of the potential for eyes on her, she hauled her suitcases over toward the window and squatted down to tug the zippers open. She hadn't really had a clue what she was packing for. Already, she could tell she was going to die of the heat, but she hadn't worn anything but boots in years and wasn't inclined to stop now. Somehow or other, she'd make do. She dumped her two extra pairs of Docs on the floor of the closet, then started loading socks and underwear and bras into the top drawer of the dresser. She checked over her shoulder to see Carol seemingly immersed in whatever was happening on her computer screen before slipping her vibrator in there, too.

She *really* hadn't been planning on having to share a room when she'd decided to bring that.

Before long she was pretty much unpacked. She glanced at the closet to see her array of black and gray and brown hung side by side with Carol's pink and yellow and purple. Cargo pants and canvas shorts against frilly skirts. It made a weird tangle unfurl in her gut—that mix of superiority at her own utilitarianism and uncertainty. Not for the first time, she wondered how her life would've differed if anyone had ever taught her how to be a girl.

"You're welcome to borrow stuff if you ever want to," Carol said from behind her.

Jo choked back a laugh. "Thanks. But I don't think your stuff would really fit me."

"I don't know. I'd say we're about the same size."

That wasn't what Jo had been talking about at all. "I'll keep it in mind."

"Okay." Carol was clearly waiting for reciprocity, but Jo didn't see much point in offering. Jo's clothes really wouldn't fit Carol, either.

Sometimes, Jo wasn't even sure they fit her.

* * *

Adam was sitting on his bed, leaning against the headboard, writing a letter to his grandmother of all the ridiculous things when a knock came on his door. He pulled out one of his earbuds and looked up to see Jared standing in the hall.

"Hey," Jared said. He jerked his thumb behind him. "Welcome

session is down at the main building in half an hour. I was thinking about heading over and maybe poking around a little. Wanna come?"

Do I ever, Adam thought gratefully. Capping his pen, he shrugged. "Why not?" He took a quick second to set his things aside and unhook his headphones before pocketing his (still-silent) phone and hopping off the end of the bed. "You ask Tom?"

"Yeah. He passed." Jared raised one eyebrow meaningfully, and Adam chuckled.

"Shocker."

"Pretty much." They headed out the front door and down the path toward the road. Jared glanced over at the other house as they passed it. "You been over there yet?"

"Kind of?" Adam wasn't sure exactly how much to say. "Met one of the girls when she got dropped off."

"Yeah?"

"She, uh, made an impression." An impression on the back of his skull, mostly. And his toes.

"Good impression or bad impression?"

Adam rubbed at his neck. "A little of both. It was…weird. I'll let you make up your mind when you meet her."

"*Okay*," Jared said, drawing out the last syllable. "Was she cute at least?"

"Yeah. Sort of. No." Not cute, exactly. "Hot," he eventually decided on. "But kind of in a might-just-fuck-you-up type of way."

Jared made an appraising noise. "That'll be something, huh? Six of them and three of us?"

"Unusual, anyway." Astronomy wasn't as bad as physics, but there were still typically a lot more guys than girls in his classes. Being outnumbered would be a novelty. That probably wasn't what Jared was asking about, though, considering the first thing he'd wanted to know was if crazy-girl was cute or not. "Why, you looking?"

"Isn't everybody?"

"I'm not." Not really anyway, no matter how he'd reacted at the first sight of those piercings and that hair and hint of ink. The way he was still reacting to the thought of it. Even after the way their meeting had gone—*especially* after the way their meeting had gone.

After the past year of tepid sex, the idea of a girl who got up in his face like that, got physical with him...it had its own appeal. In another world, if he'd been another guy, he might have pushed right back when she had pushed him. She'd have looked so good shoved up against a wall. Felt so good pressed up against him, and he bet she would *bite*.

All of a sudden, the walk was getting a little uncomfortable, and he tried to think of other things. Like the fact that Jared had just asked him a question. "Huh?"

Jared chuckled. "You got a girl at home or something?"

"It's...complicated."

"I've heard that story before. How's 'complicated' working out for you?"

His silent phone felt like it was burning a hole in his pocket. "I guess I'll have to let you know." He really didn't want to get into the specifics right now, so he redirected. "How about you? Single?"

"Free as a bird."

"Well, enjoy it."

"I always do."

The road rose up into a pretty steep hill that was going to be a lot of fun on his morning runs, but it was less exciting now, with the late afternoon sun beating down. His damp hair kept falling into his eyes, and he brushed it aside, only to have it slip right back down. After what felt like an awfully long time, the hill crested, and just like that, both of them stopped at once.

"Damn," Adam let slip.

"You got that right."

The whole of the observatory campus spread out before them. In one way, it was like any facility he'd been to before, with clusters of buildings linked by asphalt paths, but in other ways it was a sight unique unto itself. There was no doubting they were in the tropics, with palm trees and lush greenery taking up all the unoccupied space. And that was just the beginning.

Because beyond all of that, far off in the distance through the haze, lay the reason they were there. The biggest radio telescope in the world. From this angle, he couldn't see the giant receiver dish nestled into a crater in the earth, but all the trappings of it were plain as day. The three columns rising from the edges of the dish, soaring umpteen stories into the sky, all connected by cables and walkways, and suspended from the center of them, a half dome of shining metal. Intellectually, he knew it was big enough to house equipment and full-grown men, but from here it looked like it could fit into the palm of his hand. And held inside it were all the optics and receivers and antennae a person needed to look into the vastness of the universe. Into an invisible world of darkness and stars.

Adam gulped, making his throat work against the lump there. It was an inspiring sight. He was lucky to be here, seeing it in person. And yet he couldn't help the little pang that went through him as he stared.

He wished he had someone to share it with. Not Shannon, necessarily, because she wasn't really into all the science stuff. But someone.

Jared clearly had no such reservations. "Well, what are we waiting for?"

Adam really, really didn't know.

They took the downward slope a lot faster than they had the upward one. At the gates, they had to stop and sign in. Adam checked his watch and saw they had a little time to kill. He pointed at a path to the right. "Wanna take the long way around?"

"Sure."

As they walked, he kept track of the places they were passing, cross-referencing them with the campus map he'd grabbed at the guard station. Cafeteria, guest rooms for visiting scientists, maintenance building. A series of stairs leading up to more on-site housing and research facilities.

The path eventually looped back around, depositing them near the main building where they'd been heading. Ahead, a few girls were walking along, talking amongst themselves. They were all about Adam's age—probably part of the same program. Beside Adam, Jared whistled.

Adam's breath hitched a little, too. The girls were dressed in shorts and skirts and lacy tanks, and there was no denying the quality of the view. It didn't quite get his blood boiling, though, not the way—

And then he saw her. She was taking up the rear, a good five feet separating her from the rest of them. The front locks of her hair shone even more brightly blue in the sunlight, and unlike the rest of them, all involved in conversation, she was clearly taking in her surroundings, gaze piercing. Like she was missing nothing.

Not even him, he realized, as she jerked her head forward, looking away from where he stood.

It was a splash of cold water, pulling him from wherever his mind had been wandering to. Grinding his teeth together, he forced his gaze elsewhere, too, because he wasn't a sucker. She'd been unpleasant and callous, and she was one of only four people he'd even met here so far, and she didn't want to *look* at him.

What the hell was he doing here?

Apparently, following Jared, for the moment. The guy had moved to meet the girls, and Adam took a couple of quick jogging steps to keep up, swearing under his breath as he did.

"I thought this was a Research Experience for Undergraduates program," Jared whisper-yelled. "Not a modeling convention."

A couple of the girls ahead giggled and slowed, but the crazy one glowered, continuing to stalk forward and past the rest of them when they paused to wait for Jared and Adam.

Jared leaned in closer and whispered, "That the one you were talking about before? The one that 'made an impression'?"

"What gave her away?" Adam asked drily.

Jared shook his head, then turned on a hell of a smile as he spread his arms in welcome to the ladies. "Well, hello, hello."

"Hi, there," a pretty redhead said, insinuating herself at the head of the pack. Her gaze was just as openly appreciative as Jared's had been. "You guys here to do science, or did you get lost on your way to a surfing competition?"

"Touché," Jared said, and oh wow. Those two were going to be trouble.

Rolling his eyes, Adam stepped forward. "Hey. I'm Adam."

The redhead smirked. "Kim."

"Jared." Jared held out his hand, and if Adam had believed in such a thing, he would have said he actually saw sparks fly as Kim reached forward and accepted it.

A blonde cleared her throat and stepped around them. "Carol."

"Nice to meet you," Adam said.

Adam smiled at each of them as they introduced themselves, reciting all the names over and over in his head, but without a whole lot of hope. Remembering names had never been his strong suit.

"Shall we?" Jared asked, extending a hand toward the door.

They filed in one after another, and as the last of them slipped through, Tom caught up with them, which prompted a whole new round of introductions, which at least was a chance to hear all the names again. All of them but one.

As they wound their way through the hall, he ended up next to the girl he was pretty sure had said her name was Anna. "Hey," he said, tipping his head. "That other girl who was with you before. What was her name?"

"Jo? I think?"

"Jo." A man's name on a hard-as-nails girl's body. Fitting.

The girl in question was already sitting in the middle of the rows of chairs set up in the library by the time the rest of them filtered in. A bunch of other people were milling around the edges of the room, all of them older and casually dressed, but no one else had sat down yet, leaving that one lone seated figure looking all the more isolated. For just a second, she looked up, and her sharp, dark eyes seemed to bore straight into Adam's.

He was the one to look away first this time.

There was a little bit of chitchat and some snacks, but before long, an older woman in a light purple dress called everyone to attention and invited them to find a seat. Adam ended up in a corner toward the back, next to Jared and Tom, with a good vantage point to see not just the lectern but also the rest of the people looking on.

The same woman moved to stand before them all, clasping her hands in front of her as she raised her voice above the chatter to say, "Good afternoon." Once everyone quieted down, she smiled. "It's so wonderful to have all of you here. Welcome to Arecibo Observatory. As you may or may not know, my name is P.J. Galloway."

Huh. So this was the person he'd been e-mailing with for the past few months. She wasn't quite what he'd been expecting, but then again, he hadn't exactly had a lot to go on. While the rest of the staff scientists had photographs of themselves on the place's website, P.J. Galloway was represented by a cartoon picture of a turtle looking through a telescope.

Then again, as he squinted, he supposed he could see the resemblance.

"While you're here," she continued, "you'll be working with some of the premier astronomers active in the field today. Many of you will be performing direct observations using the telescope, and all of you will have a chance to get to know the ins and outs of our facility. But that's not all. We also hope you'll form life-long friendships with your peers, and we're looking forward to introducing you to this magical island we call our home.

"Most weekends, we'll head out to explore a different part of the island, including some of our beautiful beaches and the only national park that is also a tropical rain forest. While the trips are not mandatory, they are highly encouraged." She gave them all a knowing smile. "It's going to be a busy summer, and a productive one, but we hope it's one you'll remember for the rest of your lives."

With that, she introduced one of the staff scientists, who stepped forward and asked for the lights to be lowered, then launched into a PowerPoint presentation, reviewing the history of the lab and the summer research program. Most of it was stuff Adam already knew, but hearing it like this made it feel real in a way it hadn't before. It also brought back that pang, because this was all so *cool*, and he was going to be itching to tell someone about it later on.

The lights came up once the guy was done, and P.J. took the floor again. "Now, I know you're all excited to meet the people you'll be working with, so we'll go through some quick introductions. Then you'll have an hour or so to talk to your advisors before you're all invited to meet in the cafeteria for dinner."

One by one, she called off names, pairing up students with the research supervisors. With each name she recited, the person in question stood or raised a hand. They were almost at the end of the roll by the time she got to Adam, and it didn't escape his attention that there was just one other student she had yet to call.

"Mr. Adam McCay? You'll be working with Dr. Lisa Hernandez."

Adam stood and looked over at the small, middle-aged woman raising her hand.

"And Ms. Josephine Kramer has the privilege of working with Lisa's research partner, Dr. Heather Simms."

Adam's stomach lurched as Jo—or Josephine—stood. If their advisors were research partners, odds were good their projects would be at least tangentially linked. Which meant they'd probably end up working together. The tender spot between his shoulders twinged, but he managed to keep his expression neutral. This would be fine. Peachy, even.

As P.J. moved on, Jo sat back down. The whole time, she never looked at him. Not once. But somehow, her lack of attention felt almost more intentional than a backward glance could ever have been. Like she was ignoring him so hard he could feel it in his bones.

Chapter 3

This day was never going to end.

Jo stared down the choices in front of her in their steam trays, each less appealing than the last.

The man behind the counter smiled at her, his accent thick but comprehensible as he asked, "What can I get for you, miss?"

"Is there a…a vegetarian option?" At his frown, she clarified, "No meat?"

He shook his head. "Sorry, miss."

She probably should have known this was going to be an issue, and she had some contingency plans, but the stash of protein bars in her suitcase was going to get old fast. "Um. Just the rice and the vegetable, then."

She resolutely ignored the way each of them shone with what was probably lard. Not something she could be picky about right now if she wanted to eat at all.

He passed over a plate full of just what she'd requested, and she gritted out a smile of thanks as she accepted it and placed it on her tray. She grabbed a carton of milk from the fridge to round out her feast and got in line to pay, looking on in both

disgust and envy at the girl in front of her, whose plate was swimming in some sort of greasy-looking gravy.

"Vegetarian?" the girl asked, eyeing Jo's food.

"Yup."

"Ouch. Sucks to be you."

The girl had no idea.

Fortunately, her meeting with her advisor—who'd insisted on
being called Heather, as opposed to Dr. Simms—had gone well
enough. Mostly because Jo had made an effort to keep her trap
shut before she made any more shitty first impressions. Her project seemed interesting, and when she'd expressed her hopes about
getting something publishable out of the experience, Heather
had been receptive. She'd been clear that it would require some
extra work, but that was one thing Jo had never shied away from.

Unlike awkward social situations. Which she'd more than
had her fill of at this point.

Keeping a stiff upper lip about how annoyed she was to be
forking over money for a plate of rice and broccoli, she paid for
her meal, then followed the girl who'd been in front of her out
the door of the little cafeteria, toward the picnic bench outside
where all the other people from her program had assembled.

As the last one there, she had about as many options in her
choice of seating arrangements as she had in her menu. Or her
room. Taking the open spot on the end, she set down her tray
and looked around. She remembered her roommate, Carol's,
name, and she was pretty sure the girl who'd spoken to her in
line was Anna. The asshole who kept checking out everybody's
tits was definitely Jared, and the one who never made eye contact
was...Tom? Tim? She wasn't sure.

And two seats down from her was the guy who'd snuck up on
her when she'd arrived. The one with the pretty blond hair and

the dimples and the shoulders of a god. The one whose advisor was BFFs with hers. Adam. She sure as hell remembered him. He glanced over at her as she settled in but didn't linger long enough to actually make eye contact, and *that* didn't bother her at all. At least he didn't seem to have mentioned their less-than-awesome meeting to anyone else, because no one had given her any shit for being a total sociopath who couldn't handle a guy getting within two feet of her without her self-defense training kicking in.

Thank fuck for small favors.

The others were all involved in some sort of conversation, and as she dug in, she kept half an ear open, trying to pick up the thread.

"Dude," the hornball, Jared, said. "I don't know anything about astronomy. I don't even know much physics. I'm an engineer."

Excuse me?

The redhead at the end of the table seemed to have the same thought, crinkling her brow. "Then how the hell did you end up here?"

Jared shrugged. "My advisor back home was college room-mates with P.J. I didn't have anything going on this summer, so she managed to snag this for me."

Oh *hell* no. Indignation rose up, hot and volatile in Jo's chest. The sciences were supposed to be a meritocracy, but there wasn't any getting away from all the BS of politics and connections, was there?

It was almost enough to make her regret severing her very best one. Almost.

"Wow," Carol said. "That was lucky."

"I guess so," Jared said.

"I mean, this program is really hard to get into," Carol argued.

Jared held his hands up in front of him. "As long as it looks good on my résumé. That's all I really care about."

Great. Just great. Jo was plenty mindful about the credentials she was building up for herself, too, but you didn't come to one of the best observatories in the world *just* for a line on your CV. Not if you didn't care about the work they were doing there.

Swallowing down the hundred comments she could have made, she concentrated on her food. She just had to sit through this crap for a little while, pretend to be part of the group for as long as it took to finish her dinner, and then she could go back to the lab. Start digging into the binder full of articles Heather had assembled for her. Prove that she was here to do her job.

"It'll definitely look good on a résumé," the redhead said after a long pause. "I'm still a little surprised they took you if you don't have any background in astronomy."

"My major is physics," one of the other girls said. "I like astronomy, but we don't really have a separate department for it, so I haven't taken any classes in it."

"Still, though." The redhead pointed her fork at the girl. "You're open to the idea of going into it."

"Sure." She frowned for a second. "Though I wonder if I would have gotten in if I hadn't had a connection, too. I met Marcos— the guy I'm working with this summer—at a conference last spring, and we got to talking, and I told him I was looking for a summer thing. He told me to apply here."

Antisocial boy piped in, "I did my last summer research position at a collaborating university. That probably helped me."

A beat of quiet passed before another girl said, "The professor I got to write my letter of recommendation used to work here a few years ago. I'm sure it's not the only reason I'm here, but connections do help."

"I don't have any." *Not anymore.* Jo heard the words before she'd fully decided to chime in. But then all the faces around the table were pointing at her, and the base of her neck flashed hot. She stared at her last spear of broccoli like it might have the power to turn the clock back a minute or two, but the time stream stayed intact. Stupid broccoli. She clenched her jaw. "I just filled in the application."

And then she'd cried when she'd gotten her letter, because this was exactly what she'd wanted. This summer here—this was succeeding beyond her wildest dreams. This was getting somewhere on her own blood, sweat, and tears. Long hours in the lab and going half blind from reading textbooks and hunching over a computer screen.

This was light-years beyond what her father would have ever led her to believe she could achieve.

The longest, most awkward pause followed her words, until there was the sound of a throat clearing from the middle of the table. She dared a glance up to see Adam putting down his utensils.

"I'm sure we're all here on our own merits," he said, his voice all quiet certainty and peacemaking, and everyone just seemed to hang on his words. "But they had a lot of applicants." He shot his gaze over at her and then away, looking at each of the other people around the table in turn. "It only makes sense that they would give some weight to references from people they can trust."

In other words, it wasn't nepotism. It was just good sense. Right.

"And who vouched for you?" Jo asked.

For the first time since that afternoon, their gazes met, and *Christ* his eyes were blue. Clear and frank and deep, and for all that she was steel, cold and tempered, there was something in her that went molten in her core.

Keeping his chin high and his gaze steady, he admitted, "My stellar astronomy professor. He co-wrote a paper with Lisa last year."

So he was making excuses for why it was okay that apparently *everyone* here except her had secured their place through some kind of connection, and he was just as bad as the rest of them.

And she didn't know why that was the final straw. Today already, she'd embarrassed herself in front of P.J., made stupid assumptions, accidentally inflicted actual, physical violence on the most attractive man here, been forced to eat rabbit food, and now she was drowning in the consequences of how inbred this whole field of study was, and this *guy*—this perfect-looking, deep-voiced, peacemaking guy was looking at her like that. Like he had nothing to be ashamed of and like she was being ridiculous. And maybe she was.

Finished with her greasy rice and her overcooked vegetables and this whole conversation and this entire day, she gritted out, "Well, good for you."

She rose without another look back, just needing some quiet and some space and a minute to think. She dropped her tray off at the window where the same man who had served her was loading dishes into the machine. And she did what she always did.

She retreated to the lab. To where she was safe.

* * *

"All right, you guys." Adam put his hands on his knees as he levered himself up—mostly steadily—to standing. "I'm out."

The whole gang, except Jo and Tom, had spent the evening in the girls' house, sitting around their living room, sipping off a smuggled-in bottle of rum and generally just shooting the shit. They were good company, funny and smart in turns, but he wasn't tipsy and he wasn't sober, and it was late.

And he shouldn't, but he had to give it one more try.

"Lame," Jared said. His head was leaning against Kim's thigh, and Adam was suddenly really glad he'd happened to pick the room that didn't share a wall with his.

"I know, I know," he conceded. He gave a general wave to the room as a whole as he picked his way toward the door. "See you in the morning."

A couple of the girls were starting to look a little droopy, and they all had big days tomorrow. He felt sort of bad about starting the exodus, but he didn't doubt things would have wound down soon regardless.

Low murmurs of conversation followed him outside, receding but not quite disappearing when he shut the door behind himself. He took a deep breath and stretched his arms up over his head. It felt good to fill his lungs, good to be alone for a second after a long day. Good to feel the cool, damp air.

Then he looked up at the sky, and "good" fell out of his vocabulary.

Holy *shit*. He'd been living in the heart of Philly for the past few years, and Tampa before that, and wow. If he'd ever seen a sky like this, he'd forgotten it. The darkness of it seemed to stretch out into infinity, and everywhere were stars. Stars and stars and the brighter lights of satellites and planets, and then this thin, misty wisp of a stripe streaking its way across the center of it all...

He laughed out loud when he realized it was the Milky Way. Their very own galaxy. He'd never lived somewhere with so little light pollution that he could actually see it before, and he ran a hand through his hair as he gazed up at it, staring until his neck started to crick. Christ, all the constellations were different. He picked out the Southern Crown and Delphinus, and then just about smacked himself when he saw what he'd overlooked.

Scorpius. It took up almost the whole damn sky, a perfect, looping spiral of stars, and part of him thought this whole mess of a trip might have been worth it just for this. For *feeling* like this, out in the night air, looking up at a sky so brilliant it made his chest ache.

This time he had to share it with someone.

He'd known he was going to break down and do it anyway, but it was with less heavy of a heart that he pulled out his phone and scrolled through to Shannon's contact info. He pressed the button to dial and put the speaker to his ear, strolling over to sit on the bench between the two houses, out of reach of the front porch lights of either. Cloaked in that darkness and gazing upward at the countless points of light, he held his breath for the first two low-pitched rings.

By the third ring, he knew she probably wasn't going to pick up, but that was okay. He collected himself the best he could. It was good just to hear her voice, even if it was a recording. When it was time to leave his message, he cleared his throat.

"Hey. Hey, it's me. I know I already texted to tell you I got in okay, but I just…I wanted to say hi. See how you're doing. Tell you how things are over here. It's…" How did he describe it all? "It's good. Hot as balls during the day, but there are some really great people here, and the facility is amazing. I got to meet with Lisa for a bit, too, and I just…" He paused for a second. "It's so beautiful. I wish you could see it." And then he broke down— said the thing he wasn't supposed to say. "I miss you. If, ah, if you don't have time to call me back, just shoot me an e-mail or text sometime, if you get a chance. Just to let me know you're all right."

It was too much concern, considering, but he'd never really been able to stop himself from worrying. Never been able to stop himself from caring, even when it would've been easier not to.

"Okay. Well. Good night." He didn't say "Talk to you later" because he didn't know if he would. Instead, he took a breath and hung up.

He leaned back and scrubbed a hand over his face. "Well, that's done," he said to no one. To himself.

Movement from over near the girls' house drew his attention. He looked over, and Jared was spilling out from the open door. He stumbled along and almost tripped over Adam before he seemed to spot him there.

"Oh." Jared squinted in the darkness. "Hey."

"Hey."

"What're you doing out here?" Jared glanced around, as if he were going to find some hidden source of entertainment he'd missed until then. He looked everywhere except up.

Adam chuckled and pointed at the sky. "Just taking a moment."

Screwing up his face, Jared followed his direction and almost lost his footing in the effort. He righted himself and shot Adam the strangest expression. "Stargazing? By yourself?"

Adam shrugged, remembering Jared's comments from earlier in the day about how he was an engineer and didn't really know what he was doing here. "Maybe it's an astronomer thing."

"Whatever gets you off," Jared said, shaking his head.

"I wouldn't go that far."

"Good." Jared shot him finger-guns. "Because that would be super weird."

"Right."

With a sloppy salute, the guy set his attention back to walking in a straight line. He mostly succeeded, even. But he didn't look up again. It made that wistfulness resettle in Adam's chest.

Jared made it over to the guys' place, and Adam stayed there, gazing upward, looking over occasionally as one by one, the lights in both houses went out. The tightness behind his ribs eased a little with every one, until he was well and truly alone.

And it was a strange thing, solitude. Back at home, there'd been him and his parents and his brothers, and in college, he'd always had a roommate. Being all alone for any significant length of time had been a rarity, but when it had happened, it'd been both incredible and terrible. Stifling. Like a really nice jacket that never managed to fit quite right.

It fit better than usual right now.

He wasn't sure how much time passed like that, and he should've been bored. Should've been exhausted. But there was something about the cool relief of the night and the company of the stars.

And then there were footsteps, crunching on the gravel.

Intellectually, he'd known Jo was still on campus, but looking out toward the road to see her approaching was a jolt. An unexpected interruption to his vigil. She had a binder hugged close to her chest, and there was a certain easiness to her gait he hadn't seen on her before.

The idea of solitude came back to him as he watched her. It clung to her like a second skin, molding to her every curve, and he hadn't thought her *pretty*, necessarily, by light of day. Attractive, sure, but her jaw had been too square and her edges all too sharp. Now, though, she was walking slowly, limbs loose.

Face full of wonder as she stared up at the stars. Unaware she was being observed, and all the more relaxed for it.

And she was beautiful.

He let the silence linger, let himself remain undetected for as long as he dared. Only when she reached the point where she was bound to notice him if she kept going did he clear his throat.

"Quite a view, huh?"

She startled, and yeah, just like that, some of the edges returned, as hard and harsh as they had been before. But earlier he hadn't known what she looked like when she thought she was alone.

"Yes," she said, curt as anything, and her gaze darted toward her front door.

"I think they've all gone to bed already. You should be safe." It was like when he'd left the message for Shannon, revealing more than he wanted to.

Her fingers tightened on her binder. All day long, he'd been avoiding looking at her and avoiding her gaze out of...what? Some misplaced sense of pride because she'd gotten the jump on him when he'd tried to show off, helping her with her bags? Because she'd looked away from him first? Well, they were staring right at each other now, and he didn't know what she saw. He wasn't even entirely sure what *he* saw.

But whatever it was, it made him feel less alone.

She blinked first, turning her head to glance toward the girls' house. "Thanks. I'm going to—"

"Yeah, it's late."

"Okay." She lingered with one foot planted and the other edging away for half a beat. Then with resolve, she turned and stalked off. When she got to the door, she didn't gaze back at him. But she did take one last, longing look up at the stars.

The door closed behind her, leaving him by himself again.

For the second time that night, he gazed at the galaxy above him. And murmured, "Good night," to a woman who wasn't listening.

Chapter 4

Jo shoved her pencil between her teeth, balancing her binder on her knees as she leaned forward and typed another set of coordinates into the terminal window on her computer screen. She glanced at the calendar on the desk beside it. One week to go until her first observing run on the telescope, and she had a lot to do between now and then.

In the week she'd been here so far, she'd dived right in, running through all the background material Heather had assembled for her and learning her way around the systems. She'd even sat in on one of Heather's sessions with the telescope so she'd be prepared for when it was her turn.

She hadn't pissed off Heather or killed her roommate or otherwise insulted or injured anyone else in the program. So really, it was all win.

That track record wasn't going to be easy to hold on to, though. She frowned at the dates highlighted in blue on that calendar. Field trips, Dr. Galloway had called them. The whole gang was piling into cars and heading to the beach and the rain forest and even some random little island off the coast for an overnight escapade, and it was fine. Great. She'd always wanted to see the rain forest. But it was also concentrated time in cars and exotic locations with people. And it was time away from work.

Speaking of time away from work…

Jo looked up at the sound of a tentative knock on the door of the office she shared with her advisor. Carol stood there, an uncertain smile on her face. "Hey."

"Hi, Carol," Heather said from behind Jo, and Jo entertained a brief moment of hope that Carol was there to ask Heather a question, but no. Of course not.

"Hey," Carol said again, addressing Jo for sure this time. "I'm heading over to the house. We're all getting together to cook dinner in a bit. You in?"

Something uncomfortable flipped over inside Jo's gut as she pulled the pencil from between her teeth. "I don't know…" She *knew*. Keeping her distance was her best shot at holding on to her streak of goodish behavior. She looked around at all the stuff she'd managed to pile up on her desk already. It was the excuse she always fell back on, but it wasn't like it was a lie or anything. "I have a lot of work to do," she hedged.

"Oh, please." Heather's voice rang out from behind her.

Frowning, Jo looked over at her advisor. "Excuse me?"

Heather had turned to face her computer but was still waving a hand dismissively at them. "You're a week ahead of my schedule for you. Go. Have some fun for goodness' sake."

And that was…really nice to hear actually. This internship was so short, and Jo's expectations for it so ambitious. The whole time, thus far, she'd felt like she was behind.

"You heard the woman," Carol said with a smirk. "Besides, Anna and Adam got someone to give them a ride to the grocery store, and they picked up some stuff specially for you."

"For me?" Now Jo was really confused.

"Um, the whole vegetarian thing?" Right, because Anna had noticed that on the very first day, and a few others had given her sympathetic looks the couple of times she'd been cajoled into joining them for a meal. "We're making stir-fry, and they picked up some tofu or whatever, so you can actually eat real food for once."

Jo's stomach growled at just the thought. She'd been doing okay, sneaking in peanut butter sandwiches between plates of limp vegetables and plain starches, but actual, honest-to-God food sounded amazing. Still, she sucked her lip ring into her mouth with a rough tug. "That sounds great. Just…"

"Just nothing. Come on. Walk back with me now and we can help cook."

Cocking an eyebrow, Jo deadpanned, "Did someone get a fire extinguisher for the place?"

"Whatever. *I* can help cook. *You* can stay out of the way and glower at people. Come on."

Well, when she put it that way.

Giving in, Jo held up her hands, then took a second to save her work and pack up her things. When she was done, she shoved a couple of articles into her bag and slung it over her shoulder.

On multiple levels, it was weird, walking back with Carol. First, Jo was used to walking to and from the lab alone, and second, she rarely made the trek before nightfall. Damn, it was hot during the day. And bright. She directed her gaze upward, missing the darkness and the shining spiral of Scorpius unwinding itself across the sky. And there were other nice views around that time, too.

Several nights now, she'd returned from work to find that guy, Adam, sitting out on the bench between their houses, appreciating the view in a way she wasn't sure anybody else here really did. He usually saw her coming miles away, but every now and then, she managed to sneak up on him. To get a glimpse of him in a tight T-shirt, those big, muscled arms spread out to either side of him, throat exposed and gaze skyward. It made her curse herself again for getting off on the wrong foot with him.

Maybe if she hadn't messed things up so bad, she could have been *getting off* with him instead.

Christ, but she really needed Carol to vacate their room at some point so she could unpack that vibrator from her top drawer. The idle fantasies she'd been indulging in of riding those lean hips into the ground—they weren't smart thoughts, weren't safe thoughts, especially considering this was the guy who'd triggered her into attacking him by sneaking up on her. By trying to help, like she couldn't handle her own stupid bags. The guy who'd gotten here because of his connections and who'd tried to play the whole incestuous system off like it was a good thing.

Still, a guy who spent that much time by himself, with just the stars above for company…he might not have been the worst choice.

Cross that. He *definitely* wouldn't be the worst choice, because the actual worst choice was sitting in the living room, drinking a beer and trying to make the television work.

"Hello, ladies," Jared said with a smirk as he looked up. He did a double take when his gaze landed on Jo, a startled blink that turned into a leer about three seconds later, and she rolled her eyes with a huff.

Managing a bare nod and a wave at Anna and the other girl beside her on the couch, Jo headed to the kitchen to make a drink of her own, only to come face to chest with what might as well have been a freaking brick wall.

A deliciously warm, unfairly good-smelling brick wall.

And it was stupid—fuck, it was so stupid—but instead of stepping aside or slugging him in the face or any of a hundred other normal, rational reactions, she brought her hand up and settled it over the ripples of his abdomen. Heat was just pouring off of him, even through the damp fabric of his shirt, the flesh firm and perfect beneath the cotton.

He looked down at her, eyes shockingly blue. Maybe it wasn't stupid to touch him after all, because he curled his hand around her hip, fingers brushing the skin beside her spine. It sent a shiver to the very center of her, and that wasn't disgust on his face. It wasn't confusion. Damn her if it wasn't a hunger to match her own, and maybe this whole situation between them wasn't as much of a lost cause as she had imagined.

Or maybe it was. In the blink of an eye, he seemed to realize what he was doing, his whole expression blanking. He yanked his hand away and stepped back so fast he half stumbled in his hurry to get the fuck away from her, and yeah. That was a little closer to what she'd been expecting. The impulse to lash out against rejection rose up in her throat, but he let out an awkward, dry chuckle.

"Sorry," he said. "I don't know what I—"

"Yeah." Her palm burned with the memory of his warmth, and the front of her body felt cold for more reasons than one. "Sure."

She felt like such an *idiot*.

Before she could say something she'd regret, she whipped around. The only relief was that Jared and Carol and the rest of them had stayed put in the living room and hadn't followed her. Hadn't had to see that giant pile of awkwardness and weren't looking at the inferno that was her face right now.

She didn't acknowledge them as she stalked past them toward

her room, where she closed the door and put her back to it, burying her face in her hands. Wishing she'd been smart enough to stay in her lab.

* * *

Adam pushed the last bits of his stir-fry around on his plate, scooping it up onto his fork the best he could and shoveling it into his mouth. It was one of the basic meals he'd managed to learn to cook after he'd moved out of the dorms and realized a steady diet of mac and cheese and Burger King wasn't doing him any favors.

Not for the first time, he snuck a glance over at Jo, perched in the corner eating more greedily than he'd seen since they'd arrived. It was compliment enough, even if she hadn't given him a verbal one. Which was fine. It hadn't been much extra work to make up a separate little skillet for the tofu, which hadn't been half bad, if he said so himself. If you, you know, liked tofu. Which he didn't particularly, but whatever. Not up to him to judge. Anyway, it had gotten her over here, and that was a first.

Hell, she'd even said two words to him. Exactly two, and they'd both been effectively a dismissal. He'd been such a lug, putting his hands on her when she'd fallen into him. When she'd touched him and sent a heady jolt of arousal surging up his spine. It'd just felt so *good* to be touched, even if it was only a hand on his stomach as she steadied herself. Even if it wasn't anything like he might have imagined—even if it hadn't been heading where his brain had immediately gone.

A place his mind went entirely too often when he looked at her.

But she was all harsh lines and soft curves and he wondered what that piercing through her lip would feel like against his cock...

He shifted his plate to cover his lap and forced himself to look away. People around the room were finishing up, and there was ice cream in the freezer for dessert. Jared and Kim were flirting like they always were, though there was a level of bickering cropping up in their repartee that was new. He wasn't sure what that said for what was brewing between them behind closed doors.

Carol, who'd already finished, too, rose and started moving around the room, taking plates from anybody who was done. Adam handed his over with a nod of thanks and leaned back in his seat as he reached for his beer. He frowned as he took a sip. Nothing stayed cold for long around here.

On the other couch, across from him, Anna looked at the time and sighed. "Should probably go call my boyfriend."

Of course, that was a cue for half of the people in the room to look at Adam. Right. Because apparently he and Anna were the only ones here who had any significant attachments to people at home. As Anna picked her way over to the door, Jared raised an eyebrow at Adam. "How about you, lover boy? Time for you to go call the girlfriend, too?"

The clattering sound of a fork hitting a plate too hard pulled Adam's gaze to the corner of the room. Jo dropped her head the instant he looked at her, stabbing a piece of tofu with way more aggression than was called for.

Not that Adam could blame her. His own store of hostility welled up as he went back to glaring at Jared. "She's not my girlfriend," he countered, a little more sulkily than he might have liked. But it had been a week now, and all he'd gotten were a couple of erratic texts. Never enough of them in a row for a real conversation, even. They were all apologetic, but actions spoke louder than silent words on silent screens, and it was like Shannon didn't care. Like she didn't miss him.

Sometimes, he wasn't sure he missed her, either. Other times, he felt so damn lonely, he wanted nothing more than to hear that voice. The one that had been a constant in his ear for years, through the good and the bad and the everything in between. Until now.

"I'm sorry." Jared's voice was teasing. "Time to go call Ms. It's Complicated?"

"No." And he shouldn't have added it, but he did. "She probably wouldn't answer, anyway."

He'd been good about not calling her recently, too. He'd given in once on that very first day and again a few days later. And once more over the weekend. But the itch had receded to the back of his mind, mostly. An adequate amount of disappointment could train anyone. Even him.

"Has she ever?" Carol asked, and at least she had the grace to sound sympathetic.

"Not so far." He sucked down the rest of his beer in a few long pulls.

"Then what's so complicated about it?"

He blinked as his gaze darted over to the side, uncertain which surprised him more—the fact that Jo was actually talking or the content of what she'd said. "Excuse me?"

She looked around, taking in the renewed attention being directed her way and visibly stiffening. Her shrug was all casual disaffectedness, but it wasn't particularly convincing. "I don't know, dude. Kinda sounds like she's just not that into you."

She grimaced, maybe at the gratuitous pop culture reference, or maybe at something else. He didn't have a lot of space to concentrate on it, because his heart squeezed at the very idea. "It's—" he started, but his automatic descriptor of "complicated" wasn't going to help him here, now was it? Not when that was what had started the whole conversation. "We…she…" Swallowing, he looked at the empty bottle in his hands, and then at all the people staring at him expectantly. And back to Jo. "We're…on a break. She said she needed some space."

"Ouch," Jared said.

Yeah, pretty much.

Jo's mouth twisted down. "Not sure how that exactly contradicts my theory."

How was he supposed to explain this? Everyone in the program had slowly been trading life stories and histories, but he'd shied away from this very subject time and time again, because it *was* complicated, as cliché as that might sound. "We've been together, sort of, since freshman year. I mean, it's been on again, off again."

There'd been the intense whirlwind his first week of classes, when they'd met in a seminar they'd both needed for their gen-eds, and she'd just sort of carved out this space for herself in his life. She'd been easy to talk to, and a beautiful blonde, and just *different* from anyone he'd ever met. Way different from anyone who'd ever given him the time of day before. Then again, that could've had something to do with the fact that he'd gotten contact lenses and started working out between high school graduation and the start of college.

She'd accepted his closet nerdiness with only a modicum of teasing and introduced him to the girls in the sorority she was pledging, and sure, they'd had different majors and hobbies and schedules. They'd conflicted on those here and there, and she'd thrown her hands up at him a couple of times when he'd insisted he had too much work to do to go along with whatever plans she'd made. But the breaks had been good for them both.

Three years of falling back into each others' arms and beds and then slipping into the same patterns of her getting caught up in her things and him in his. He hadn't even really been surprised this time when she'd said that maybe they should take advantage of the ocean between them for the summer.

He had been disappointed, though.

"But it's really great when it's great," he said, half trying to convince them and half reminding himself. "She's fun, and she makes me do things I never would." He still didn't really care for clubbing, but he'd met so many interesting people because of her, and thumping beats and close dancing usually led to some of their better nights once they made it to his place. "And she listens to me, even when it's mostly boring science stuff. She's faithful." He looked away, out the window, into the distance. "And it's been three years, you know? We both knew we were going to be busy this summer, and the distance is a killer, so she...so we..."

He stopped to listen to himself, and the squeezing in his chest got a whole lot tighter.

"Anyway, it's fine. We've texted back and forth. And I'll see her in a few weeks."

"You will?" Jared asked.

"Yeah, there's this conference in Baltimore I have to go to to present a poster. She's driving down from Philly. We've got it all planned out."

It was an overstatement, but it wasn't too far from the truth. She'd said she'd make it work. He'd budgeted an extra couple of days between the conference and his flight, and everything that was wrong with them—these silences and this distance—they'd figure them out. When they were actually near each other, they always did. They'd manage it this time, too.

"It'll be great," he said. But it sounded weak.

"If you say so." Jo gave another little expression of indifference, this one just as unconvincing as the last.

Only he didn't understand the lines around her mouth this time. It couldn't just be that she was talking in front of the group or garnering unwanted attention. Delicate, shy flower that she was.

"Just...," she started again, hesitating for a second. But then her gaze met his, and there was no less challenge there. "When someone doesn't respond to you, it usually means something. Believe me." She let out a harsh little laugh that made the hairs on the back of his neck stand up and his stomach sink. "I have a lifetime of waiting for somebody to pay attention to me under my belt, and it doesn't matter what you do. If they don't want to, they're not going to." Glancing away, she said, "Better to cut your losses before they really break your heart."

And he... really didn't know what she was talking about, but it got under his skin. "Not how I operate."

"Clearly." She rolled her eyes, and it just *bothered* him that she could be so flippant when this had secretly been eating at him for so long. "Just don't expect sympathy when she disappoints you."

That was it. Something inside him snapped, because for every moment he'd been telling himself it would all be fine, he'd also been thinking that very same thing. This was bound to end badly, and he would deserve whatever he got for leaving himself so open. For clinging to something that was obviously past its prime.

He didn't need to hear it from anyone else.

He was on his feet before he'd fully decided to move, hands clenched into fists at his sides. Jo's eyes widened, but other than that she didn't flinch, and he wanted to do to her what she'd done to him—what she'd been doing since the very first second they'd met. Flipping him and flipping his conception of his relationships and himself. He wanted her to feel what it was like to land that hard on the ground.

Only, from the set of her mouth, he had a feeling she already did.

Still, he couldn't stop himself, needed to get in some kind of last shot. It came out tepid at best, his throat going wobbly at the last second. "Christ, you're just fucking heartless, aren't you?"

That got a reaction out of her, even if she looked more angry than indignant. "Don't you dare tell me a thing about my heart."

"Then don't you tell me anything about mine."

A low whistle sounded out from somewhere in the room. Their surroundings seeped back into his awareness, and his ears rang, his face flashing suddenly hot. For a minute there, it had felt like it was just the two of them. They were still the whole width of the room apart, but it had felt like nothing at all. Like he could have reached out, could have taken hold of her and *shaken* her. Or slammed her up against a wall and kissed her.

Apparently registering the eyes on them, too, she set her empty plate aside and squared her jaw. He half expected her to go storming off the way she was so fond of doing, but then it occurred to him. This was her house. He was the interloper—for all that she seemed the one so intent on trying not to belong.

"Adam?" Carol asked, but he shook his head.

"Excuse me," he said.

He let the door slam shut behind him, striding across the space between the two houses and staring up in frustration at the setting ball of the sun in the sky. He kicked the gravel and tugged at his hair, and none of it did any good. Nothing ever did any good.

From his pocket, his phone gave a little beep, and he pulled it out with a prayer. *Please prove me wrong. Please prove them all wrong.*

It was only his brother, though. Of course it was. He tilted the thing on its side to type a reply, only it slipped from his grip, his hands unsteady, and anyway, the keys were so fucking small. He was always smashing them together and making these unholy amalgamations of words, and why couldn't anyone ever use the stupid thing to actually *talk* anymore?

Miles and miles from home, that was all he wanted. Just a voice in his ear.

His phone seemed to taunt him as he picked it up, and it wasn't the damn thing's fault. He could call anyone he wanted— any of a dozen people who would actually pick up. But not the one person he wanted to.

In a brief second of clarity, he knew it wouldn't change, and torturing himself like this was idiotic. Masochistic.

And that brief second was all it took.

In a burst, he unleashed all the strength he usually kept coiled so tight, and it felt *good* to just let it go.

He came back to himself with that intense kind of instant regret that only followed particularly stupid moves. But there were some things you couldn't take back.

Cursing silently under his breath, he crouched and dropped his face into his hands. The shattered pieces of his phone glittered brightly against the gravel, and he didn't know whether to laugh or to cry. He dropped his ass to the ground and spread his legs out, shaking his head against the combined impulses.

He had insurance on the stupid thing. He'd get a ride into town as soon as he could, and he'd say he dropped it. From the top of the telescope apparently, but still. Just a fall. Not him spending all his useless anger in hurling his best connection to the rest of the world.

Not him leaving himself really and truly alone.

Chapter 5

It was a tribute to just how loudly Adam's mom could scream that he could hear it even over e-mail. He winced as he scanned over the message again, then clicked REPLY with a mental hand held protectively over his balls.

Yes, he should be more careful with his possessions, and yes, he needed to get someone to take him into civilization to get his phone replaced, and yes, it had been four days, but seriously? It wasn't as if there weren't any other ways to get in touch with him, and he was at other people's mercy here without his own ride. He'd already asked Lisa and P.J. and Roberto, so what more could he do?

Except, yeah, maybe remind one of them that they'd said they'd be happy to, any time.

Four days without his phone, and it had been ... nice, actually. The constant itch to check the damn thing had persisted at first, but it kept getting easier and easier to ignore. He didn't have to think about the calls he wasn't getting or the texts that never arrived. He was exchanging actual, honest-to-goodness e-mails for the first time in years, most of them more than two sentences long, and from people he cared about, too. His parents and his brothers and a few of his friends from college. All it had taken was the message from him, letting everyone know he was without a phone for a little bit. All it had taken was him reaching out.

And the people who didn't take advantage of the opportunity? Well, nothing he could do about that. Right?

He worried the inside of his cheek between his teeth and put the thought out of his mind. He finished the reply to his mom, assuring her he wasn't dying of dysentery out in the middle of the jungle or anything, and hit SEND, then minimized the window to get back to his work.

He was just digging into the numbers Lisa had left for him to crunch when the lady herself wandered in, her research partner, Heather, on her heels. Heather, who was also Jo's advisor. Great. After giving them each a quick wave, he observed general office-sharing protocol and buried his gaze in his screen. But before he could get too involved, Heather laughed and said, "At least your student leaves your office from time to time."

His ears perked up, but he tried to ignore it.

"Yours one of the obsessive ones?" Lisa asked.

Jo? Obsessive? Ha.

"She's fine. But it's more work coming up with enough for her to do to keep her happy than I'd been counting on." Heather's voice had a shrug to it. "Anyway, she's got her first observing run tomorrow night. Hopefully she'll get some good stuff."

"Oh, right! I was going to ask you if Adam shouldn't sit in on that with her. The objects you're looking at might overlap with some of the ones we're investigating."

At the sound of his name, Adam put off any pretense at obliviousness. He tugged his headphones off and twisted around in his seat. "I thought I wasn't going to get to use her until next week."

"Well, that's the question, isn't it?" Lisa mused, cocking an eyebrow.

Heather held up one hand. "It's fine by me. It's my research assistant you'll have to talk to about it."

Adam's stomach sank, and he couldn't quite suppress his frown. "Oh."

He'd barely seen Jo since the other night. She hadn't been coming to meals with the rest of them, and he hadn't been sitting out between their houses in the dark, waiting to catch a glimpse of her against the backdrop of the stars. The slow burn of hunger he got thinking about her hadn't faded, but it was all twisted together with what she'd said about him. About him and Shannon. He didn't know which way was up anymore, or how Jo *got* to him so much.

And now he had to ask her for a favor.

"Don't look too excited," Heather said, her tone amused.

Shit. He blanked his expression the best he could. This was personal, not professional, and he wasn't going to let whatever was going on between him and Jo mess anything up. "No. I'll…I'll ask her."

"You can't be too intimidated by people like that. I promise you, her bark is worse than her bite."

"I'm not intimidated." He wasn't. Not exactly. It was more complicated than that, the push-pull of want and anger, and the way she took him apart with her words and forced these awful statements out of him. The way she wormed her way into the thoughts he had when he was alone, in the dark, with the door closed, imagining her on top of him and under him and pressed against him…Heather and Lisa were both looking at him skeptically, and he leveled them with a glare, insisting, "I'm not."

"If you say so," Lisa said with a smirk. "Just ask her before tomorrow."

"Sure." He'd…get right on that.

Swiveling around in his chair again, ignoring the tittering he knew full well was going on behind his back, he focused on his computer screen.

He'd ask Jo. Have a civil, professional conversation with her—one where neither of them aimed for the jugular. One where neither of them ended up, physically or metaphorically, laid out flat on their backs, with their throats exposed.

He ducked his head. He just had to see to every single other item on his to-do list first.

* * *

He checked his e-mail one last time, then closed the window. He'd finished everything he had to for the day, and while there were a couple of items on his list he could get a jump on for tomorrow, even he could admit he was stalling.

Stop being such a fucking coward.

He put the computer to sleep for the night and rolled his chair out from under the desk, standing and stretching his arms overhead. Lisa was long gone for the evening—almost everyone was. If it were anybody but Jo, he'd worry she might've left by this point, too, but there was no way he'd be that lucky.

Turning off the light, he checked his pocket for his keys, ignoring the empty spot where his phone should be, then closed the door and headed down the hall. Scientists were a weird bunch, and even at half past eight, there were a few lights on in offices up and down the corridor. He nodded at anyone who happened to look up as he passed, but no one tried to stop him or draw him into a conversation.

Just outside the door to Jo and Heather's office, he paused. Jo was sitting there, giant headphones over her ears, attention focused intently on the screen in front of her. No sign of Heather, of course, and that was good. He didn't need her listening in or offering commentary the way she had that afternoon.

And...he could always put this off. Could come back tomorrow. He didn't actually have to ask Jo about this until then.

No. Yes. No.

Before he could talk himself out of it, he balled his fingers into his fist and knocked.

Jo startled hard, her gaze jerking up, eyes wide with surprise, and for a second he imagined he saw a softness to her mouth. But if it'd been there at all, it was gone in an instant, replaced with the same hard-set jaw he was so accustomed to by now. The same veiled expression of contempt.

He took a deep breath and managed a smile. "Hi."

"What do you want?"

His smile faltered. Any thoughts of easing her in with small talk vanished, and he crossed his arms over his chest, as if a defensive posture could actually ward off whatever she might throw at him. "You're using the telescope tomorrow night."

"Yep."

"And our advisors work together." He paused, but the jut of her chin said she was waiting for him to tell her something she didn't know. Right. Just get to the point already. "Lisa thinks some of the objects you're looking at might be relevant to what I'm doing, too, and she wants me to sit in."

"Sit in?" She visibly bristled, and aw crap, that was her dander getting up already.

"She didn't really specify what she wanted me to do." He resisted the urge to mop his brow or fidget. "Look, I don't want to get in your way. But this is about work. I'll have some more specifics tomorrow, but this is your experiment. Your show. I'm pretty sure I'd just be an observer, seeing what you're doing and getting a peek at the data as it comes in." He took a deep breath. "If you're okay with it."

That seemed to relax her a little, his granting her the power to turn him down. She gave him a long, appraising look, like she was judging him. And there was always something about the way her eyes lingered when she regarded him like this. Something that fueled his thoughts of her, his sense of heat when his skin felt cold and untouched.

She snapped her gaze to meet his, and he squared his shoulders.

"You come tomorrow night, you're quiet. I'm working and I don't need any bullshit interruptions."

"You'll hardly even know I'm there."

"You don't touch the computer or the sensors."

"Scout's honor."

"Unless I tell you to do something, in which case you do."

"Not a problem."

For what might have been the first time ever, the corner of her mouth twitched up, making the ring through her lip glint and sending an odd little spark up his spine. "Then I'll see you at twenty-two hundred, soldier."

"Yes, ma'am." He grinned at her for real this time, and it felt like ice cracking when she didn't do anything to make him frown.

Better not press his luck.

With a quick nod, he turned and headed off, striding all the way to the corner, well beyond her sight before letting his posture slip. He pushed his hair off his brow and shook his head at himself as he laughed with relief. He was going to get to use the telescope a full week early, and sure it was in a limited capacity, but it was still a good thing. A positive development.

The personal development felt even better, though. He'd said what he needed to say, and when Jo had shoved, he'd stood his ground, but he hadn't pushed back. He'd let her have and keep the upper hand. As a result, she'd given him exactly what he'd asked for. Maybe that should bother the male in him, but it didn't. Not hardly at all.

He pushed through the doors and out into the wet night air. It'd been a while since he'd made the trip to the house alone in the dark or since he'd done so without an anxious itch under his skin.

Because the prickle at his neck and in his abdomen wasn't anxiety. It wasn't that at all.

He swept past the guard station and up the hill, along the gravel path and over to the house. The lights were blazing at the girls' place, while the ones in his were dark, and for a second he wavered, wondering if he should go say hello.

It wasn't a difficult decision to make, in the end.

He let himself in and retreated to his room, closing and locking the door behind himself before flopping down on his bed and closing his eyes. A guy needed to be alone sometimes, and the past few days had been building and building toward this.

Rubbing his palm over the bulge in his shorts, he gave out a low sigh. It had been so difficult to let himself do this lately. He couldn't think of Shannon without getting angry and he didn't want to think about Jo. Had a hard time summoning up any of the other lifeless, expressionless celebrities and fantasies that had gotten him through in lean times before.

But today Jo had smiled at him. Jo had stripped him down with words and demanded his compliance, and then she'd looked at him as if he'd been worth her time.

She'd looked at him with intent. And there had been that one night, when they'd convinced her to come to dinner, when she'd walked right into him and put her hand against his abdomen and stared up at him, and he'd let himself touch her side.

With a barely suppressed groan, he opened his fly and pulled himself out. He was hard and leaking, and the first rough stroke over bare flesh had him pushing up into the circle of his fist. It had been days, days spent adrift and cut off and unsure, and this wasn't going to take much time at all.

Because it could have all gone differently today. He could have gone to Jo, and she could've been difficult, and he could've bitten back. She could've risen to meet him and jabbed her finger at his chest, and he could've grabbed her wrist.

They'd have been so close, the space between them shooting sparks, his body hard and hers bristling. Until the tension finally snapped.

He muffled his own groan, slickness spilling from his tip.

Her mouth would be hot, the piercing an edge against his tongue, and he'd push her against the wall and get just enough of her clothes off. Touch the curves of her breasts and splay his hand across the ink he still hadn't fully glimpsed but that he hoped sprawled the length of her spine.

Sink into her while she wrapped her legs around his hips.

He tugged at his balls with his free hand, arching his neck as he sped his strokes.

Her head would knock back against the wall, her hands scrabbling hard at his shoulders as he fucked into that tight, wet warmth. He'd shut her up with his mouth and with his cock, bring her to the edge over and over until she was begging, saying his name.

Except. Oh, wait, this was even better. He squeezed himself hard around the base, holding off his pleasure.

Because maybe she wouldn't want to be pressed up against a wall. Maybe she'd want to be in control, be on top, and, God, she'd look good over him. Shirt off and tits bouncing. She'd lay him out on the floor of her office and ride him hard and fast.

He'd grasp her around her hips, dig his fingers in until that pale skin bruised. She'd feel so good, and he'd get a thumb on her clit, rub her nice and fast, punishing really, because she'd like that—she'd *love* that. She'd sink her teeth into his throat as she came, and she'd *squeeze* him.

He pumped his fist over himself again, giving in to it this time, imagining her slamming herself down onto him even after she was done, little overwhelmed pants and whines falling from her lips until he thrust up hard and filled her and—

His vision whited out, his whole body bowing with the force of it, toes curling and jaw aching with the effort it took to keep silent in the darkness. Two more slow, careful pumps to milk the rest of it out of him and he let go, still pulsing weakly against his abdomen as he went limp.

He felt wrung out and suddenly exhausted. The stirring under his skin was sated, but there was a new kind of restlessness seeping in.

Because a fantasy of sex was easy enough to conjure, but there was no ending to the story. No way they picked themselves up off the floor or spoke to each other the next day.

Hell, he'd all but been forbidden from speaking to her tomorrow.

He swept his clean hand over his brow and grimaced at the other one with not a little bit of belated disgust. But there was nothing he could do about it now. He wanted her. Obviously, he wanted her.

But there were a lot of things he wanted. And very few of them were things he ever got to keep.

* * *

It was another one of those lessons Jo had learned from her father: never, ever admit you're wrong.

She sucked her bottom lip into her mouth and tongued at the ring there. Darted her gaze from the streams of data coming in from the telescope, toward the sight of Heather and Adam both sitting there beside her.

The sad fact, the one she'd only admit to herself, was that she'd been wrong about a lot of things this summer already. She'd packed the wrong clothes, completely underestimating how oppressively hot it was going to be. She'd assumed the wrong things about who P.J. Galloway was and why she'd assigned her to Heather in the first place. Assumed all the wrong things about what kind of advisor Heather would turn out to be.

And Adam. The big, gorgeous guy who didn't respect her boundaries, and who'd gotten here on account of his professor's connections, and who was uselessly mooning over an ex-girlfriend who clearly didn't care as much about him as he did about her. She'd pegged him for the kind of asshole guys like him usually turned out to be. As an idiot riding other people's coattails. As a cuckolded wimp. And he wasn't any of those things.

Already tonight he'd defied her expectations, keeping quiet when the silence in the observatory was even starting to get to her. Interjecting only to point out an issue with some of the calibrations they'd performed when they'd been getting started. Working steadily on a notebook full of calculations she begrudgingly admitted looked pretty freaking complicated.

Coming to her and asking if he could sit in on her telescope time instead of just running ramshackle over it and barging his way in.

And nobody—absolutely nobody—should look good in a hoodie and running shorts, under awful fluorescent lighting, in the middle of the night. But goddammit all, he did.

Silly her, worrying he'd distract her by trying to make small talk all night. Turned out the biggest distraction was just his stupid, perfect face.

Rolling her eyes at herself, she turned back to her monitor. The next star they wanted to look at was just starting to rise, so she input the new coordinates. Heather pretended not to pay too much attention to what Jo was doing, but she wasn't very good at it. Only after the telescope had swept out to the correct patch of sky did she let out a breath and rise, taking her tablet with her.

"All right, kiddos. Looks like you've got this in hand, so I'm going to take off for a bit." Translation: time for a quick nap on the couch in her office.

It was a heady thing, being trusted to run this baby all by herself. Sure, there were a couple of operators there to call upon if anything really bad happened, and Heather would be right upstairs, but still. Jo was really in charge now.

"Okay."

Heather headed off, leaving Jo and Adam by themselves. Jo tapped her booted foot against the linoleum, her throat suddenly tight. Adam was sitting a respectful three or four feet to the side—close enough to see the monitors but far enough away that he wasn't encroaching on her space or her experiment. It suddenly felt like he was sitting right on top of her, though, her skin buzzing and pulse humming with the promise of proximity. The possibility of contact.

She looked over at him, meeting bright blue eyes, and for the longest moment, their gazes held. Heat bloomed up and down her spine, because there was something about his stare. Something that made her think he was really *seeing* her.

Except then he seemed to remember himself and tore his gaze away, directing it outward, toward the window.

The room suddenly felt even more silent than it had a minute before.

She'd brought a bunch of articles with her, but it was after midnight, and the idea of really concentrating on the text made her temples hurt. She dared another glance over at him, and then another, and she bit her lip. She wasn't going to break. He was the one who was supposed to give in and fill the quiet, not her. That was how it always went. For once, she actually wanted him to, and the fact that he *didn't* made her skin itch.

Who the hell was she kidding?

"What are you working on?" she asked, pushing her papers and any pretense at disinterest away.

He arched a brow. "I'm sorry. I thought I wasn't supposed to be distracting you with small talk?"

Mock-glaring at him, she waved her hand. "It's more of a no speaking unless spoken to kind of thing."

"Oh." His smile got awfully smirky, but there wasn't any malice to his tone. "In that case"—he shrugged, looking up—"it's just some background calculations for my project."

"Yeah?"

He licked his lips, distracting her from his eyes with the soft pout of his mouth. She wondered how it would yield beneath her teeth. How his equations would taste on her tongue.

"Jo?"

She blinked, refocusing. His voice had that quirk to it, like he was saying her name for the second time. Like she was the one who hadn't been paying attention. "Hmm?"

He tapped his pencil against the paper and pushed it closer so she could see. "Did you want me to take you through it?"

"Um. Sure."

He scooted a few inches closer. After a quick glance at the monitor, she did the same.

His voice got softer as he ran through the lines of letters and symbols scrawled out across the page. It wasn't difficult to follow, and half of it she'd seen before, if not quite in the same configuration, but he explained it nicely, answering the couple of questions she interrupted with.

At the end, he frowned. "It's not quite working out right, but I think I'm pretty close."

She traced his calculations back a handful of steps, leaning in even closer. She paused in her scanning and tugged at the corner of the notebook, then without thinking, reached over and grabbed his pencil out of his hand, brushing his skin as she did.

"You dropped this term," she said, circling it, then looking at him.

He'd somehow ended up almost on top of her, their chairs bumping, his knee warm where it pressed to hers. His lashes were impossibly long against the fall of his cheek. He inspected the page, mumbling to himself. When he lifted his gaze again, it was with the most brilliant, beautiful smile on his face.

"How did you catch that?"

"I don't know. Just did."

"Impressive."

The compliment made her warm inside. People didn't say that kind of thing to her very often. Probably because she usually shoved their mistakes in their faces instead of quietly pointing them out. She quirked her shoulder up but didn't move away.

He was so close, and it was the middle of the night, and he'd been *looking* at her. Maybe if she pushed just a little...

His grin faltered as their elbows bumped, and oh yeah. The darkness in his eyes wasn't her imagination.

But neither was the way he sat up straighter a second later. The way he laughed and raked his fingers through his hair and edged his chair a few inches to the side.

Right. Just like that, the intimacy of the space and the math and their lowered voices dissolved, and the softness she'd let out for just a second did, too. She turned to the monitor, but there was nothing new to see. The experiment was chugging right along, the telescope slewing slowly but surely over an unappreciated patch of sky.

"Um...," he started.

She moved the mouse around the screen for lack of anything better to do—for the pure comfort of having something to look at that wasn't him.

And latched on to the first, most hurtful thing she could think of to say. "So. Did Ms. It's Complicated ever call you back?"

He made a low noise in his throat that said she'd hit her mark. But instead of rising to her bait this time, he took a long, slow breath. "No," he gritted out. "Though if she had, I wouldn't know it."

"Oh?" Not that she cared.

"No. I...uh...broke my phone."

He broke his phone. The guy who never stopped looking at it—not at meals and not when she passed his office and couldn't resist peering in. Not during meetings and not at the grocery store, and—

She caught herself before she could turn her disbelieving gaze at him. "You did?"

"Yeah, that night, actually." And did he actually sound sheepish? "I, uh, may have let my temper get the best of me after somebody pointed out some things I wasn't really ready to hear."

What? Wait, did he mean *Jo*?

"And you took me seriously?"

He was absolutely shit at hiding how that wounded him, but he shrugged. "You may have had some good points."

"Good points that you decided to take out on your phone."

"Couldn't exactly take them out on the person who was actually responsible, could I?"

She didn't know if he meant her or the girl at the other end of that silent line. She wasn't sure if she wanted to, either. Careful not to actually press anything, she tapped her finger against the edge of the keyboard. "You going to get the thing fixed?"

"Way beyond that. Gonna have to get a new one." At her low whistle, he fidgeted with his pen. "And yeah. Eventually. Though"—he swallowed wetly, jaw clicking—"it's nice, in its own way. Having it gone."

She understood that. Wow, did she ever.

Nothing like giving up on the person you were never going to get any real approval from to make you feel about a million pounds lighter.

And maybe just a little bit like shit when you realized you were the only one in the relationship to notice.

She kept her gaze pointedly fixed on the data in front of her, trying to soften her tone, even with the tightness in her throat. "You still going to see her when you go to that…conference thing?"

"As far as I know. She said she would, but that was…" Before. He didn't have to say it.

"Well, I hope…" What did she hope? That they'd work everything out and live happily ever after? Hardly.

In fact, the very thought of that bothered her more than it should have. Not just because she wanted to see what was under those running shorts of his. Because she didn't like the idea of him settling for the rest of his life, accepting scraps when he should be getting more. From someone. She didn't know him well, but even she could see he deserved better than that.

"I hope she doesn't disappoint you," she decided on. That was safe.

"Me neither. But I'd only be so surprised."

"That sucks."

"Big time." He sat there without saying anything for a long moment, and she half thought he'd drop it. Let them lapse into the silence that had been working for them so far this evening. Then again, the talking thing hadn't worked that badly, either. He shifted, picking up his pencil and tracing the binding in the margin of his notebook. "Since you bring it up, though, I was wondering."

"Hmm?"

"Who was it?"

Something went cold in her chest. "Who was who?"

"The person. You said someone taught you that it was better to walk away than wait for them to care. Who was it?"

Oh hell. Forget cold—her ribs were suddenly made of ice, and they were squeezing in.

Because where did she start with that one? The father who wanted nothing to do with her, who just wanted his dead wife back? The boys she fucked her way through the minute she was out of his house? The professors who wouldn't give her work when that was all she wanted?

Forget where to start. Where did she end? Where did this go except into the kind of pity party that made her want to scream?

She clenched her jaw and turned her gaze toward the big glass window looking out across the night. "Everyone," she finally settled on. "Everyone."

Chapter 6

It didn't happen often, but there were some things so awesome even Jo couldn't pretend to be unaffected by them. For just a second, she closed her eyes and let the sun soak into her skin. A good solid layer of SPF 100, and she was still probably going to burn, and she didn't care.

She looked up again at the trees surrounding her. Palm trees. Huge and graceful, with broad leaves the size of her whole torso. Everything was so fucking green, but it wasn't even just that. It was the bright red flowers and the golden petals and the shapes of plants that were like nothing she'd ever seen before.

She could die tomorrow, and at least she'd be able to say she saw a real, live, honest-to-God rain forest. She was here, standing in the middle of it, looking out over a pool of water so clear she could see down to the rocks ten feet beneath its surface.

And she was tethered to a bunch of *children*.

Another squeal rang out from the pool behind her, and she gritted her teeth. It wasn't fair. All she wanted was to keep going, keep wandering through this place that made the breath in her lungs feel like it wasn't enough. But no.

Dr. Galloway's warnings rang out in her mind for the thousandth time.

Stick together. No wandering off on your own. Anyone who doesn't check in won't be invited on any future outings.

So here she was. The rest of the group had all stripped down to the bathing suits they'd worn under their clothes to dip under the little waterfall that ran through the rocks. Slipping beneath the surface and popping back up, and laughing, and…

And Jo was standing on the outcrop. By herself.

She kicked at a bit of rock with her boot. She hadn't brought a swimsuit. Hadn't expected perfect, shimmering pools where the sun broke free from the canopy.

Didn't know how to dive in anyway. Especially not with people she'd been holding herself apart from all this time.

She gave in and cast a long, lingering look at them over her shoulder. They weren't paying her any attention—not that she'd expected them to. Jared was chasing the redheaded girl under the waterfall, and Carol was floating on her back. The others were in similar states, and Adam…

Adam was treading water, and *damn*. She'd thought he was a specimen before she'd seen him with his shirt off. The guy was pure muscle, built without being bulky. Defined abdominals and a dusting of hair over pecs that glistened in the sun, and he had *freckles*. She wanted to feel how warm that skin was. Wanted to play the most intricate game of tic-tac-toe. On his shoulders. With her tongue.

And she wanted to stop *doing* this. Standing here, overdressed and overheated and dying to rake her nails across his spine. Quiet and ready to scream and alone.

Fuck it. Just fuck it.

Another pool lay on the opposite side of the outcrop she was standing on. Barely out of sight. She chewed her lip as she stared.

It might be breaking the spirit of the law, but not the letter. She wasn't wandering off by her lonesome.

She simply couldn't stand to be there anymore.

After checking nobody was looking, she ambled down the rock, carefully picking her way to where it dropped off toward the other pool. It was deserted and crystal clear and perfect, and her feet were sweltering in her boots.

Out of sight, she unlaced them one by one. Pulled off socks and the baggy weight of her shorts and her shirt and the tank underneath it. Standing barefoot in her underwear and a sports bra, she tucked her hair behind her ears. She braced herself for the shock of cold and stepped off.

The surface was farther down than she'd thought, the bottom even deeper. Her foot slipped on wet stone, and she scraped her elbow as she slipped under. Cool water closed over her head, and it was like falling and floating and submerging all at once. She kicked hard, pushed her arms, and burst upward into bright air and searing sun, and she'd never felt more alive.

It took all she had not to whoop out loud with the sheer freedom of it. She plugged her nose and dropped back down and laughed beneath the water, sending bubbles rising toward the light.

For the longest time, she just…played. Swam and twirled and held on to the rock with her fingers while she let her legs drift. It was always better like this, with no one to watch. No one to have to pretend for.

Finally, the sounds of laughter on the other side of the barrier shifted, the splashing dying away. She sighed and took one more long dive, then kicked up reluctantly toward the surface. The rest of the gang would probably take their time moving on, but she didn't want them catching her with her pants down. She paddled over to the point where she'd jumped in and looked for a place to grab on and haul herself up.

Only there wasn't one. She looked to both sides and to the outcrop of rock she'd been standing on before, and it was all smooth and slick and angled wrong.

The first little shiver of uncertainty rumbled its way through her, her stomach dipping.

Shit. She knew better than this. Never get yourself into a situation you aren't sure you can get out of.

She closed her eyes and counted to ten, keeping her breathing steady and not thinking about being stranded and left for dead or about having to call for help. She'd be fine. She was a strong climber, and she had always gotten herself out of jams before. This would be *fine*.

Looking up again, she picked her best prospect. Braced her feet against the most solid thing she could find and gripped hard, hauling herself up. She cursed when she slipped, knocking the underside of her chin against the rock. *Fuck*, that hurt. She swiped at the spot and got a thin trickle of red. Nothing major, but it was insult to injury, and her fingers already felt raw from where she'd lost her hold. There was no other way, though, and she tried again, arm muscles straining, only there was nothing to grip onto.

No one to call for help.

Okay. Okay. The panic was closing in on her chest now, but she could do this. She had to. She drifted over to another bit of rock and searched for a place to grab on, but it was all the same. Grasp and haul and slip and fall, and her breathing was too fast now. Oh shit, she was going to die here, in her underwear. She was fucked, and this had been stupid. How could she have been such an idiot?

She didn't hear anyone around. Being by herself didn't feel so great anymore. Nothing did. She shivered despite the sun and clenched her eyes shut tight.

She wasn't going to snivel. Wasn't going to cry. Wasn't going to be the wimp her dad had always accused her of being whenever she showed weakness. But she had to do *something*.

"Hello?" she called, her voice scarcely wavering at all. No answer, and her heart beat harder. "Can anybody hear me?" This was awful. The worst. Her throat caught, jaw shaking, but she said it. She choked out a quiet, pathetic, "Help?"

"Jo?"

In her head, she said every single swear word in the English language as she whirled around. Because of course it was Adam, looking over the lip of the pool. He'd pulled on a shirt, but with the sun behind him, his golden hair looked like a halo, and she couldn't even manage to be mad that he'd found her like this. Helpless and floundering and screwed.

There'd be plenty of time for that later.

For now, all she could do was blink back the tears of relief threatening to form at the corners of her eyes and say, "Hey."

"Hi?" He gestured toward her. "You okay?"

Every instinct screamed at her to tell him yes, of course. It was all totally under control. But the edges of her smile wobbled, and a shudder made its way up her spine. She held herself rigid and swallowed against the lump in her throat. "Yeah. But. Actually. I could use a hand." She bit down hard on the inside of her lip and forced the word out. "Please."

It was the perfect opening for him to be an asshole. Anybody else would have. Hell, the first time they met, he'd tried to swoop in and help her, and she'd put him on his back. He had every right to lord that over her, or to leave her stranded, or to at least make her beg.

But instead he grinned and got down on his stomach on the rock. "Of course."

His arms were long and strong. He braced himself and reached out toward her, broad palm extended and fingers open, and she nodded to herself. She couldn't quite reach from where she was treading water, and her own arms were shaking from all the times she'd tried already, but she had another go in her. Another wild grasp.

She searched out the best bit of purchase she could find, got the pads of her fingers into a sliver of a crevice, and situated her toes against smooth stone. Nothing for it.

She caught his eyes, and he said, "I got you," and that was it.

One floundering lunge, and her palm connected with his. His other hand closed around her wrist, and for a heart-stopping second, she slipped, but he grunted and pulled hard, and she got another toehold under her.

And then her chest was level with the lip. She scrambled with her free hand until she could drag herself the rest of the way up. As soon as she was free, she lurched and twisted and planted her butt on solid ground. Her limbs trembled, and she put her head between her bent knees. "Fuck," she breathed. It was shaky and weak and all she had. "Just...fuck."

"Yeah." He got his legs underneath him and flopped down beside her in a mirror of her pose, shoulder pressed against hers.

And she was almost naked, and he was in nothing but a pair of swim trunks and a damp T-shirt. It was practically a dream come true, but all she could concentrate on was the solidity of him and the dull awareness of the scrapes and bumps and the trembling she couldn't seem to stop.

"You okay?" he asked. He'd shifted, ducking his head so he could sort of see her face.

No. "Yeah." She sucked in a deep breath and straightened up. She wasn't quite ready to stand yet, and his body was so warm. Damn it all. She leaned into him, still shivering, but the tremor cut off when he wrapped an arm around her and tugged her close.

"Shh. You're fine. You're fine."

"Of course I am," she managed between chattering teeth. She didn't move away, though.

He laughed and said, "I know. You always are."

She closed her eyes and leaned even farther into his bulk. He smelled good and felt better, and she could have stayed like that forever. Pressed against him and barely clothed, and it didn't even have to lead anywhere. Not that she would complain if it did. Just the thought made a tickle of heat bloom beneath her skin.

Like he was the sun, and he was piercing deeper than that fire in the sky ever could.

It was stupid—so stupid—but she'd already almost stranded herself in the middle of a rain forest, so how much more stupid could she get? It was relief and comfort and the fact that he'd helped her, without giving her a lick of grief over it. That he'd stayed afterward and wrapped her up like this. She squeezed her eyes shut tight and turned her face into his neck. Opened her mouth against that smooth, salt-and-sun flesh. Not quite a kiss and not quite an invitation, but an intimation. An opening.

One that slammed shut just as quickly as she'd dared to crack it open when someone called his name.

"Adam! Dude, you coming?"

She jerked away, and it didn't hurt when he did the same, all but jumping to his feet and pulling his arm in close to his side, like she hadn't just been nestled there, as if there wasn't any room for her there. Maybe there never had been.

She never really fit into existing places after all. She always had to dig and scrape and build to make her own.

Jared appeared from the path winding through the trees, looking impatient, and then surprised, and then knowing. Jo had never wanted to punch the guy so much. And maybe a rock. And maybe herself.

Never let them see you sweat. Never admit you're wrong or show you have an ounce of shame. She never had before, and damn if she was going to now. Working past the lingering unsteadiness, she rose and looked straight at the asshole before picking her way across the rocks to her discarded clothing. No one spoke, and any chill seeped from her bones, replaced by the heat of the air and the heat of pulling on her shorts and tank like this, while two men watched.

Behind her, Adam cleared his throat. "Um. Yeah. Just...we'd lost Jo, and—"

"Looks like you found her," Jared said with a laugh.

Jo *hated* being laughed at.

Her feet were wet, but she didn't care. She dried them off the best she could on her overshirt, then tugged on her socks and shoved her feet into her boots. By the time she looked back at him, Adam was standing next to Jared and not making eye contact. It made the pit of her stomach roll even worse than it had before.

"Shall we?" Jared asked.

Yeah, they certainly should. With a huff, she made to stalk off toward the path Jared had appeared from, but before she could get very far, a hand closed around her wrist. A familiar hand, broad and strong. One that had rescued her and that was still not letting her fall.

"Hey," Adam said, holding on.

"What—"

He pulled, and she turned around to face him, feeling topsy-turvy. Off balanced and unsettled, her instincts screaming at her that it was time to walk away.

"Hey," he repeated, and he smiled. It was a fragile thing, not his usual self-assured grin. It was more than that. It was the kind of smile she could nearly see to the bottom of, as deep as the sea and as warm as his eyes. "No more wandering off alone. Remember?"

She remembered how it felt, watching them all swim and play and feeling like if she did leave, nobody would notice.

For the first time in a very, very long while, it didn't feel that way. Not anymore.

Not after he came for her and held her when she shook apart. Not when he refused to let her go.

Not when he was holding on still.

* * *

Beer in hand, Adam wound his way from the bar toward the giant table they'd finally gotten set up in a corner of the restaurant. A few of the others had already sat down, and he paused, looking back toward the bar. He thought about it for a moment. It was risky, but...

He nodded at Jared, but instead of taking his usual seat beside him, he headed for the other end of the table. Leaving a seat open between himself and Carol, he pulled out a chair and sank into it. Turning to the door again, he sought out Jo, catching her eye when she paused there. He tipped his head toward the space next to his in invitation.

He really didn't expect her to take him up on it, and when he considered what he was doing, it was kind of a dick move. Jo usually sat as far away from everyone else as she could, and if she couldn't, she ended up next to Carol. In his head, this had been about making her as comfortable as possible, but if she didn't want to sit with him, he hadn't exactly left her with a lot of good options.

Shit. Maybe he should move.

Only...she'd been sticking pretty close to him the last few hours. Ever since he'd stayed behind at the waterfall, after noticing she wasn't with them anymore.

After she'd asked him for help and let him give it to her. Let him hold her, and pressed her mouth against his flesh, and God. He was really fucked now. If Jared hadn't come along, he didn't know what he would have done with that kind of opening, buzzing with adrenaline and pretending he wasn't scared out of his mind, body humming and blood *begging* for it.

He might have taken it. And he didn't know if that was right. Not when he was still all tangled up inside. Not when she went from inviting to distant in the space of a millisecond, at even the slightest hint of hesitation on his part. Not when his goal for the summer had been to avoid any additional complications.

Across the room from him, she paid for her drink and wrapped those pale, hard lips around the tip of her straw. His heart rate picked up just looking at them, and he shifted beneath the cover of the table as she strode their way. Her hips didn't sway—nothing as obvious or seductive as that. Oh no, her gait was as steady as it ever was, only he knew what lay beneath those shapeless clothes now.

Purple panties edged in lace and ink that did indeed flow all the way down her spine to the small of her back, for all that he'd yet to get a good enough glimpse to see what it depicted. Soft, round breasts held tightly to her chest, and a trim waist, and strong, muscular legs that had gone on for miles beneath the water.

And all of them were headed toward him.

It was almost anticlimactic, the way she folded herself into the chair beside him with hardly a glance of acknowledgment, picking up her menu and burying her nose in it. He furrowed his brow and stared at her, waiting for her to say something, to do something.

Except...that was her knee, pressing against his under the table. A shot of electricity danced up his spine, and his throat bobbed. He still didn't know how he felt or what to do, but this was only the latest in a series of advances. Every time he shied from one, she shut him down. Turned cold and hard and mean, and that wasn't her. Not the real her. He was confident of that much now.

Jared called Adam's name, and Adam turned to him, falling into conversation the way he always did. Like everything was normal between them. But where no one could see, he slipped his hand under the table and placed it, carefully but unmistakably, on her knee. He held his breath for what felt like the longest time. Then her hand settled over his with a quick, brief squeeze, and he exhaled in a rush. She wanted this. Wanted *something*.

So he spent the next hour torturing himself and testing his own patience. Tracing patterns on her skin.

* * *

Adam had been riding in P.J.'s SUV all day, so as they emptied out of the restaurant, that was the direction he headed. Only, Jo had ended up in a different car on the way over. She lingered for a moment on the sidewalk, as if uncertain which way to go, and somehow it seemed only natural now to brush his hand against hers and motion for her to come with him.

"There's room," he assured her.

There was. The middle seat in the back had been empty, and it would drive him crazy, but she could squeeze into that space, her whole side pressed up against him.

Carol shrugged, as if granting her permission. "More room for the rest of us in the van if you do."

"Whatever." Jo tugged her hand from his, but she headed toward P.J.'s car.

They clambered in, Jared in the front seat and Kim and Jo and Adam in the back. It was just the way he'd imagined it, Jo's body up against his in the darkness, and he'd been too optimistic, thinking this would only make him crazy. She was all warmth and sharp angles and subtle curves, and he shifted, twisting around so he could drape his arm out over the back of the seat. Letting his hand hang casually, like he didn't know his fingertips were dragging across her shoulder. She smelled like sunscreen and lavender and rum. She'd taste like sin, he thought. Wet and hot, and his patience with his own uncertainty was wearing thin.

Shannon—Shannon didn't call him. Didn't e-mail him or text him or want him, and he was tired of waiting for her to care as much as he did. As much as he used to. He didn't know what Jo wanted him for. Maybe just a night, or a few nights. Maybe just for some comfort and company, but it would be something. He couldn't deny it any longer.

He rubbed a little harder at her shoulder, pressing his thumb into the point of her collarbone. She didn't pull away. This was going to be the longest ride home ever, but as he gave in to it, the anticipation melted into a steady, simmering buzz, one that made him feel loose and heavy in his bones.

One broken only by P.J. speaking his name.

He jerked his head up, pulling his gaze from where it had

drifted—from the gather of Jo's shirt between her breasts. P.J. had an eyebrow cocked as she tried to catch him in the rearview mirror.

"Huh?"

P.J. chuckled, and the knowing cast to it made his neck feel hot. "I said, the stores are probably still open. Do you want to stop and see if you can take care of your phone?"

His...phone. Right. How had he forgotten about his phone?

Without really thinking about it, he drew his arm back, draping it over his lap as he rubbed his other hand over his face. "Um. Yeah. Actually. That would be great." He happened to have the shattered remains of the thing in his backpack anyway. He'd had them there for a week and a half, just in case he ever got around to reminding someone they'd promised to take him, but the moment had never seemed right.

He hadn't been ready to find out what messages he'd missed. Or, more likely, what he hadn't.

"If nobody else minds," he added after a second's thought.

"I've got nowhere else to be," Jared said.

Jo and Kim both made indifferent noises, but Jo had curled into herself while they'd been talking. No more easy, barely conscious press of her knee against his leg. She wasn't looking at him either, and her jaw had gone hard, and oh no. They weren't doing that again.

The car started up, and Adam didn't care if Kim or Jared or anyone could see. Eyes trained forward, breath tight, he reached out in the darkness and took her hand. She went to pull away, but he held on, intertwining their fingers and squeezing her palm, trying to say all the things he couldn't right then. All the things he didn't know how to put into words, about how she was beautiful and tough and *interesting*, and about how he wanted inside her walls. Under her clothes and inside her body and into her trust. Her mind.

But at the moment, his personal life was a mess.

His stomach was a knot as they pulled up in front of a big electronics store. Jo withdrew her hand as they got out, and once they were inside, she gestured toward the rear of the store before heading off.

"I'll find you?" he called after her.

"If I don't find you first."

The others all wandered away, too, leaving Adam to go in search of the cell phone counter. Fortunately, the woman manning it spoke fluent English. She frowned at his declaration that he'd dropped it, but he had insurance on the thing, and with only a little bit of bitchface, she got to work on getting him another one.

In the meantime, he leaned against the glass and gazed around, trying not to think about what might or might not have come in while he'd been phoneless. He *could* have checked online if he'd really wanted to, but he hadn't. There was no more putting it off now.

The lady was just handing him the new phone when Jo picked her way over to him, and the timing seemed a little too convenient. "So?" she asked, disinterested in tone, but the way she gazed off into the distance was pointed.

He braced his elbows against the counter and held the thing out to her with the boot-up screen displayed.

Mirroring his posture, she tapped the blunt, short tips of her nails against the glass. He wanted to reach out and still them. Wanted to pull that lip ring out from between her teeth with his mouth. Instead, he stared at the screen as it finished up its sequence. Searched for signal.

It buzzed in his hands, and he kept it angled so she could see as he scrolled through the list of texts he'd missed. There were a bunch from the first day or two, before everyone had gotten the message that he was e-mail-only for a little while. His brothers and his friends from school.

The last one was from just a couple of days ago, though.

"It's from Shannon."

"Is that her name?"

"Yeah." Had he really not ever told her that? He tapped the message with his thumb.

Got the day off for when you're in Baltimore. See you soon!

The day? He'd booked out the whole weekend just to see her. Delayed his flight and extended the hotel stay. He'd explained all this, sent her an e-mail with the details, and she was...He didn't know what she was doing.

It was like she wasn't listening to him. Like she hadn't been for a while.

But someone else was listening, was hearing this all loud and clear. Jo edged away from him, twisting to put her back to the counter, cracking her knuckles in front of herself and not meeting his eyes.

"That's great. That you'll get to see her. Right?"

A few short weeks ago, he would've said yes. It was fantastic.

But he wasn't so lonely for home anymore. Not so willing to take what he could get—at least not from Shannon.

"I don't know," he said.

Her voice was tight. "When do you leave?"

"Next week."

Finally—*finally*—she looked at him, but her eyes were as guarded as they had been when they'd first started this...whatever it was. "Well, I guess we'll find out then."

Chapter 7

Living in the tropics without goddamn air-conditioning was for masochists.

Christ. Jo mopped her brow as she stormed into her room, tugging at the overshirt she'd just about sweated through on her walk back from the lab and dragging it over her head with a growl.

"Are we mad at the shirt now?"

Somehow managing not to have a coronary or jump five feet in the air, Jo jerked around to find Carol sitting at the head of her bed. Fuck. Jo turned and dropped her gaze, flinging her shirt onto the pile of laundry in the bottom of the closet.

"The shirt's fine. The climate's on notice, though."

"Yeah, it's rough."

Carol was one to talk. She was in another one of her stupid, cute sundresses, her hair tied up and off her neck, the one fan in the room pointed right at her face.

Meanwhile, Jo was in a tank top and baggy shorts, sweating like a pig and feeling *naked*, and—

And Adam was leaving tomorrow. For almost a week. To go

hang out with that bitch who wouldn't even give him a straight answer or make time in her day for him. In *air-conditioning*. And Jo was going to sit here boiling alive and pretending not to care.

Whatever. God knew she had plenty of experience with that at least. Maybe not the boiling part, but the rest of it she'd been practicing her entire damn life.

If she were back in Chicago and feeling like this, she'd spend some quality time with her punching bag, but no. She was stuck here, and Adam's send-off dinner was in an hour. Part of her wanted to say fuck it all and go hide in the lab for the rest of the night. Another part wanted to march over to his room and finally put this *thing* that was brewing between them out in the open. Fight it out or fuck it out.

But all of those options made her feel so cowardly she wanted to scream. She wasn't avoiding her problems, and she wasn't going to let someone turn her into the other woman. No way.

At the sound of movement behind her, Jo sighed and tried to collect herself. She shoved the damp flop of her hair off her forehead, frowning at the way the dye was starting to fade.

Then, out of nowhere, Carol asked, "Is it your arms?"

Jo's skin went cold. "Excuse me?"

"Or your shoulders? That you don't want anyone to see?"

"It's…" What the hell was Jo supposed to say to that? Her insides squirmed, and she was about to tell Carol off. What right did she have to ask? Or to notice, even? So what if Jo always wore long sleeves? There wasn't any law against it or anything. "No, I just…"

She faltered. Just what?

"It's okay," Carol said. "I'm not judging. I just figured, with it this hot, you must have a reason for wanting to dress like that."

"Like what?" A lesbian? A tomboy? She turned to look over

her shoulder at Carol, only to find her standing a couple of feet away, peering into her half of the closet in consideration.

Carol shrugged. "Like someone who likes to wear sleeves."

Hesitating, Jo rubbed at her shoulder.

The thing was, Carol wasn't wrong. Jo's stomach dropped, remembering the time her father had taken her to the university that once. She'd been in ninth grade, and her rebellion of the week had been frilly tank tops and short shorts. She'd walked through the halls, past the other professors' offices, and she'd felt the same way she did now.

Naked. Frivolous. Like she didn't belong.

She'd done a complete one-eighty over the course of the next year. The harder her look, the boxier and more manly, the easier it had been to edge her way into the heavy engineering projects on the Science Olympiad team. The more the guys in the AP Chemistry class had let her into their fold.

She still wasn't afraid of wearing a corset top out to a bar, but never with the people from her department. Never with anyone she'd have to interact with professionally the next day.

"Shoulders," she admitted quietly. That had seemed to be the line.

Carol nodded. She reached into the closet to grab Jo's towel off the hook. Before Jo could ask, she pushed the terry cloth into Jo's hands. "Go. Shower or clean up or whatever. I'll pick out something for you for tonight."

"You don't have to—"

"Of course I don't. But I want to." She cast a quick glance Jo's way. "Girls help other girls out. And I figured with Adam taking off and all...maybe you'd want to look a little extra nice."

Carol had clearly chosen her words carefully. Nothing in it to insinuate that Jo didn't look nice in general—although Jo would be the first to say she didn't. The only implication was the one about her and Adam, and...

And it wasn't as if Jo could really deny it. Not after the way they'd acted on the trip to the rain forest.

She took the towel and swallowed hard. "Thanks."

"No problem."

Grabbing her toiletry case, Jo turned and made her way out of the room and down the hall to the bathroom, which was blessedly empty. She seemed to be on a roll with not being too much of a bitch today, so she called out, "Anybody mind if I get in the shower?"

Nobody spoke up, so Jo stepped inside and locked the door behind her. She stripped, unlacing her boots and piling her clothes atop them before starting the water, keeping it lukewarm. The spray felt good on her overheated skin as she stepped in, the soap that followed even better. Rinsing off, she turned the temperature as cold as it went and braced her hands against the tile as she let it wash over her.

Her nipples hardened, making the barbell running through the left one stand out all the more. She gave it a little tweak between her forefinger and thumb and felt it in her cunt, squeezing her eyes shut and twisting her neck to the side to suck in a greedy lungful of air through her mouth. She dropped her hand away from her flesh. Opened her eyes to cast a glance down her frame.

She'd never really given a good goddamn about what men might think of the things she'd done to her body, the metal and ink she'd put there to make it feel like her own. But it was hard not to wonder how Adam might react. So many of her assumptions about him had been wrong, but he still gave off such a vanilla vibe. If he saw her like this, would he be aroused or repulsed?

She rolled her eyes at herself as she turned off the water. The boy had seen her neck and her face, and he hadn't run yet. The rest of it couldn't come as too much of a surprise.

She really, really hoped he'd be aroused.

The heat in the air crept back in as she dried herself off, humidity making a mist cling to the medicine cabinet mirror. She swiped at the surface until she could see her own reflection. Flushed skin and big, dark eyes and hair dripping into her face.

She dug into her bag for her hair goop and scooped some out with her fingers. She combed it through the wet strands, then pushed the ends behind her ears. Tilting her head to one side and then the other, she looked deeper. Something in her chest thrummed.

There probably wasn't much point to this. She burrowed deeper into her kit all the same, until she got her hands around the little pack she'd buried in there without exactly knowing why. Makeup wasn't part of her usual routine, and all she really knew how to do with it was get ready for a club—or Halloween, not that there was much difference between the two in how she dressed. She could do this, though. Look normal. A little extra nice, just in case.

Wiping the mirror down whenever it got too fogged up for her to see, she dabbed concealer under her eyes and blended in foundation. A tiny bit of eyeliner and lip gloss.

When she stepped back to get the full effect, her shoulders fell. She looked ridiculous. Not strong and powerful the way she did with crimson lips and smoldering eyes. Not *normal* like she did with nothing at all. She felt like a doll. And now Carol was going to play dress-up with her.

What was she *doing*?

Resisting the urge to just wash it all off, she wrapped her towel around her chest and zipped her bag, hauling it along with her as she stormed to her room. If Carol tried to put her in a dress, she'd just say no. Wear the same plain shit she wore every day, and if anybody didn't like it, they could kiss her ass.

At her and Carol's door, Jo stopped. Carol was sitting on her own bed again, her earbuds in, her attention seemingly on whatever she was reading, but her posture was too stiff. She was waiting. Steeling herself for the worst, Jo turned to her own bed, and…

And it really wasn't so bad.

It was her own damn skirt—the only one she'd brought. Knee length and army green with about a million pockets. And laid with it, one of Carol's tops. It was black, thank God, with short sleeves. A little flowy and gauzy, but over one of Jo's typical undershirts, it'd be okay.

"Just a suggestion," Carol said.

Jo's throat didn't quite know how to work. She flexed her jaw. "Thanks," she managed.

"You're welcome. I have some jewelry, too, if you want."

"Nah." She stepped closer to touch the fabric of the shirt. It was soft. "I have my own."

She kept her back to Carol as she dressed, tugging on her underwear before dropping the towel and strapping on one of her few bras that was meant for more than keeping her boobs from bouncing and her piercing from showing. She dressed without thinking too hard about what she was doing, only noticing once she was done that Carol'd left out some sandals, too. They were strappy and black with a barely there heel. Jo stared at them for a long minute.

"You'd be a hell of a lot cooler."

Carol wasn't wrong. Jo stepped into them. They were a little snug, but not too bad. Before turning to face the mirror attached to the back of their door, she opened the bottom drawer of her dresser, shoving aside the rest of the stuff she'd stowed in there until she came up with the silk change purse. She only owned two necklaces, and one of them was a black studded choker. The other, though, was a delicate silver chain with a small oval locket.

Taking care not to twist the links, she extricated it. Brought it up to her throat and fastened the clasp at the nape of her neck. The metal sat cool against the space between her collarbones, and she ran her thumb over the locket's hinge before squeezing it once.

Before she stood and turned around, she pulled in a long, slow breath. Then she opened her eyes and looked.

And there in the mirror was... her. Only a little extra nice. A little more skin.

A few more memories pressed against the center of her ribs.

* * *

Adam gave his things one final check. Five shirts, five pairs of socks and underwear. Five days home in the continental United States, and two of them with Shannon. Maybe.

He'd been looking forward to this the entire time he'd been here, and now that it was time...

He was still looking forward to it. The trip would be a good break, a good chance to find some perspective. He needed to get his head on straight and figure out what was happening with his life.

But no matter how excited about it he was, a nervous itching teased at the back of his mind. He'd finally gotten himself settled in here, and leaving, even if only for a little while, felt like abandoning something unfinished. Like pausing a movie when it was getting to the good part. He wanted to know what happened next.

Pushing his anxieties down, he started piling the stacks of clothes into his duffel bag. It fit with room to spare, and he stood there, considering for a minute. Without really thinking about it, he patted his pocket for his phone.

Before he could pull it out and check the icons for any alerts or missed calls, a knock sounded on his door. He looked up to find Jared leaning against it. He was fiddling with his own phone, tapping something on the screen.

"Yeah?" Adam asked.

Without looking up, Jared gestured toward the other house. "Kim says dinner's almost done."

Adam smirked. The two of them had been disappearing together a lot recently. It didn't surprise him much that she'd been the one to message Jared that it was time to come over. "Is that all she had to say?"

"Shut up." Jared hit another couple of keys, then palmed his phone and tucked it away. "You ready to go or not?"

Casting another glance at the shit he was taking to Baltimore with him, Adam nodded. "Ready as I'll ever be." With a nod, he zipped up his bag.

But instead of moving from the door, Jared grinned. "You didn't forget about protection, did you?"

"Excuse me?"

"Just checking. Because I have extra if you need any."

The back of Adam's neck heated. "Don't worry about me."

"Dude." Jared snorted. "I worry about you all the time."

"Thanks. I think." With that, he shouldered past Jared and out into the hall.

As it happened, he hadn't forgotten about condoms. He'd had the safe-sex talk drilled into his skull about a million times; he basically didn't leave home without one. He sure as hell didn't leave town to see his maybe-girlfriend without a solid half dozen.

Even as he'd been packing them, he'd wondered if it was worth the bother, though. The lack of sex—the lack of *contact*—these past few weeks had been getting to him the way it would any red-blooded male. If he'd still been in the mind-set he'd had when he'd arrived, he probably already would've been imagining the things he and Shannon could do, how good it would be to touch her again, even if it wasn't serious. But he wasn't.

Shannon wasn't the one he thought about any more on those hot, lonely nights when he took himself in hand.

With Jared trailing along behind him, he crossed the path to the other house, where he knocked twice before tugging open the door and striding through. And there, right in front of him, was the girl he did think about. The one he couldn't *stop* thinking about.

"Wow," he said, freezing in his tracks.

Jared narrowly missed slamming into him, but Adam didn't move. He just stood there, soaking it in.

It was definitely Jo all right, all glinting metal and bright blue hair, but she was showing off her arms and her legs, and the lines of characters inked around her ankle. Pale, unpainted toes that never saw the sun.

"Hey." She shifted her weight, leaning back against the arm of the couch.

Adam jerked his gaze up to her face. Even there she looked different somehow. He couldn't quite put his finger on it, but he liked it. A lot.

"See?" Jared said in a mock-whisper, clapping a hand on

Adam's shoulder as he stepped around him. "This is why I worry about you."

"Fuck off." Adam moved to let him pass. It brought him farther into the living room, closer to Jo, and the fire that hadn't lit in his belly thinking about Shannon and him together in a hotel room all weekend ignited. Turned his skin to ash, and he was still feet away, and Jo's posture was tight. Closed.

There was a tilt to her head, though. An invitation, maybe.

He took another step closer and cleared his throat. Shoved his hands into his pockets. "You look, ah, nice. Tonight."

She raised an eyebrow skeptically.

He wanted to shove his foot into his mouth. "I mean, you always look nice, but you look..."

"Extra nice?" she volunteered, a ghost of a smile playing across the corners of her mouth.

"Yeah." He nodded.

Her grin widened. "You don't look too bad yourself."

He didn't look any different from usual, but damn if it wasn't nice to hear.

Behind them, the rest of the gang had gathered in the kitchen, and the sounds of plates and silverware clanging intruded on their bubble of space, but Adam could scarcely hear it.

Her neckline was open, the fabric soft, and that contrast alone was enough to make his breath go tight. Like he was watching himself from a distance, he saw his own hand rise, and then he was touching her skin, her collarbone, grazing a little silver chain that draped along the long, proud column of her neck.

"You don't usually wear jewelry." He let his fingertip trace down toward the pendant hanging from the necklace.

"No." Her inhalation made her chest rise, her voice holding the barest hint of a tremor. "I don't."

Darting his gaze from the fall of silver to the open lights of her eyes, he licked his lips. "It doesn't look like you."

"It was my mother's."

And it felt like it took something from her to say that. She didn't talk much about her life beyond this little island and this slice of time, except when she was using her own history to cut him down. This was different. This was new, and it made him crave so much more.

It made him want everything, and for a second, it felt like all he had to do was ask for it.

Then, just before he reached the metal locket, her hand closed around his, stilling his movements. Her skin was warm, but it sent a chill up his arm as she stopped him.

"Sorry," he said, pulling back. Remembering himself and where and who they were.

"It's okay." She didn't let him go, holding on as their hands fell away. She stroked her thumb across the point of his pulse.

He got the message. Some things he could touch. Others he wasn't allowed to—yet.

"It's pretty," he said, gathering himself. Turning their hands so he could intertwine their fingers.

"Thank you."

Out of nowhere, he blurted, "I'm glad you came." And it sounded stupid. This was her house after all. They had dinner here as a group more often than not. But usually, Jo found reasons to avoid it, to stay at work until the stars had all come out and everyone else had left.

"Well, you're about to go off on your big adventure, right?" She shrugged as if she didn't care, but her eyes were pinched. "Won't have a chance to give you a hard time for almost a week."

"What ever will I do?"

"Whatever you want to." It came out a little too serious. A little too real.

And it wasn't true. If he was going to do whatever he wanted, he'd be swooping in, closing that last bit of distance. Changing this push and pull into the press of bodies and a conversation of tongues and teeth and lips.

Maybe he should. He grasped her hand more tightly.

But before he could make up his mind to take that last step— to try his luck with this girl who seemed so impossible and yet so close—the air was broken by a sound. One even more unlikely than a kiss.

Shannon's ringtone.

Chapter 8

Adam hadn't even meant to do it. One minute he was holding Jo's hand, leaning in to finally touch her, and the next he'd torn himself away. His palm felt cold where his skin had been pressed to hers, but that didn't slow him down. He reached instinctively, immediately for his phone, his heart in his throat from just this one small sign of contact, this connection to home.

And that was all it took.

For a second, Jo's mouth dropped open, her hand still in the air, confusion on her brow. Her gaze darted from Adam's lips to his eyes to his phone. And then in a flash, her defenses snapped into place, every line of her going hard.

Adam was an idiot.

"I'm sorry," he said, silently counting the rings in his head. He needed to pick up, *now*, or he'd lose Shannon.

But turning his back on Jo felt like losing even more.

Jo held her hands up, palms facing out. "No. You should get that." Her voice went pointed. "Might be someone important."

She moved to shove past him, but he caught her. Clasped her wrist. "You're important."

"Sure." A bitter laugh spilled past her lips. "Tell your girlfriend I said hi."

"She's not—"

Shannon wasn't his girlfriend. She hadn't been for a while now, but he'd been clinging to the idea of her as if she were. And nothing about it was fair. Not to anybody.

Disappointment darkened Jo's eyes. She pulled her hand free with force, and Adam let her go. She brushed past him and headed toward the kitchen.

In his palm, his phone buzzed, and he cursed, following Jo with his gaze even as he slid his thumb across the screen to take the call. He brought it up to his ear and froze, swallowing hard, taking in the stares of every single other summer student here. All focused on him.

He was a *bastard*.

Fuck. He'd have to deal with them later. For now, he ducked his head and made for the door. Tried to keep the hope out of his tone as he answered, "Hello?"

"Hey, Adam?"

And it didn't matter that Shannon wasn't his girlfriend anymore. Hearing her voice for the first time in almost a month had a piece of his chest breaking free—a weight he hadn't even recognized suddenly *gone*. With a smile on his face and a lightness behind his ribs, he pushed through the door and out into the open space beyond.

"Hi. Shannon. Yeah, it's me."

* * *

Jo didn't watch Adam as he paced around the little area between the two houses. As he trailed his fingers along the rail of the wooden fence at the back of the lot.

She definitely didn't obsess about what the hell he'd been talking about with that girl that had left him looking so damn relieved.

Fidgeting, she scooped up a forkful of the rice and beans Anna'd cooked tonight. It was good, savory and flavorful and not full of bacon, and she gave Anna an approving nod of thanks. Nobody had had to accommodate Jo's diet, but they'd each made a point of it whenever they decided to step up and make dinner. She just wished she could fully appreciate it.

Then she caught herself staring out the window again, and she forced her gaze away.

What the hell had she been expecting? Just because she'd dressed like a girl for once and let him touch her neck. Let him hold her hand and talked about her *mother* of all the ridiculous things. It didn't mean he owed her anything.

Finally, the door to the house swung open, and Jo trained her gaze on her plate. Across the room from her, Jared hopped off the end of the chair he'd been sharing with Kim, dumping his dish on the coffee table and taking his beer with him as he went to intercept. Jo didn't watch the way he steered Adam toward the kitchen. She didn't keep track of how long they lingered there, just out of sight.

Around her, there was a conversation going on, but she couldn't focus on it. Even if she could, she had nothing to contribute. So she sat there, mechanically eating and swallowing and taking less than measured pulls on her drink.

She was so damn *restless*, this nervous fluttering sort of energy beating around inside her chest, and it didn't make sense.

When Adam and Jared hauled themselves out of the kitchen, Adam had a nice full plate and a drink of his own. Jo held her breath as he made his way into the room they were all gathered in, but instead of coming over to sit by her, Adam let Jared shove him into the seat he'd vacated next to Kim. And what the hell was that supposed to mean? Plunking himself down on the floor, Jared tucked back into his dinner, and Adam finally got to start his. Jo's fork scraped porcelain, and she stopped, crinkling her brow when she found her plate empty.

She chewed the inside of her lip as the agitation inside her simmered and brewed. She should've eaten slower, should've paced herself. Short of fiddling with the clinking ice cubes at the bottom of her glass, what did she have left to do with her hands?

What reason did she have left to be here?

These people didn't know her; they didn't care about her—she'd made sure of that with the way she'd acted. The only person who'd taken the time to push past her defenses, the one guy who'd looked at her as more than a fuck or a bitch or an obstacle in so long...

He was leaving for a week. Going to see a girl he clearly wasn't over.

And all of a sudden, Jo couldn't *breathe*.

"Sorry," she mumbled, pushing off the sofa and letting her plate clatter as she set it down. Half a dozen pairs of eyes turned to her, and the vise around her lungs squeezed tighter. "I need some air."

She didn't look at Adam for real this time as she made her escape. She shoved through the front door of the house and out, not stopping until she hit the fence. Bracing her hands against the wood, she bent at the waist, pulling in air in great heaving gasps and closing her eyes.

Stupid. Dressing like this and pretending to be part of their little club, hanging out and eating dinner like she was one of them. She should be like that weird guy, Tom—should just stay in her room and at the lab. Then she wouldn't have to feel these kinds of things. Wouldn't have to want what she couldn't have, and what she usually went to such lengths to avoid.

She'd just started to get herself put together again when the door to the house swung open. It banged against the frame, and she tightened her grip on the railing. Chances were, it was just Carol or someone coming by to check on her. Jo would tell her she was fine, and Carol would leave, and it would all be okay.

The sounds of footsteps came closer and closer until they were right there. But instead of a quiet voice calling out, a body leaned itself against the railing beside her, settling in as if to stay. She sucked her lip ring between her teeth and opened her eyes. The body wore navy Nikes and tan cargo shorts. And it had really, really muscular calves.

Adam, then. Of course.

Dread and anticipation twisted themselves in her gut, rising and falling and sinking and soaring. But for the longest time, Adam didn't say a word. Jo bit down harder on her lip as she forced herself to look at him—really look at him. Not at his shoes, but at his face. The sharp jut of his jaw as he stared ahead into the trees in front of them. The golden cast of his skin in the fading light.

After a moment, she couldn't look anymore.

With a sigh, she let her lip ring go. "You here to ask me if I'm okay?"

"Would you tell me if you weren't?"

"Nope."

"Well. There's your answer, then."

He said it all so matter-of-factly, like he hadn't been expecting any other response, and a hidden warmth rose behind her ribs at the thought that he knew her so well. But it wasn't enough to burn away the vulnerability, the achy-sticky feeling that had sent her running from the house. It didn't make her any less convinced she was fucking this whole thing up.

"You should go back inside," she said. "Finish your dinner."

"I had enough."

"Right." She huffed. "I've seen you eat."

"I had enough *for now*."

"I'm fine."

"Who said this was about you?" His voice was teasing, the hand he nudged against hers even more so, and she wanted to scream. Here they went again, tiptoeing along this line between acquaintances and lovers, and if they didn't pick a side sometime soon, she was going to lose her goddamn mind.

So because she was an idiot, she inched a little farther, right along the divide. Internally swearing at herself, she slipped her fingers under his, interlacing them against the wood.

"Oh," she said, her throat tight. "Well, if it's not about me, then I guess it's okay."

They stood like that together in silence for a minute, not exactly comfortable but not quite awkward either. His thumb stroked slowly across the back of her palm.

"So what did she have to say?" she asked, still looking away.

"Not much, actually. Just telling me when she'd meet up with me this weekend."

"Oh."

Was it just her, or did he sound sort of disappointed about that? Not that she cared.

Then he leaned in, pressing into the bubble of air that surrounded them. And when he spoke again, it was quiet. Intimate in a way that hardly seemed fair. "We missed the sunset."

They had, but not by much. Brilliant orange and pink and blue still spread out across the horizon, darkness creeping along beside it to fill in the spaces they left behind.

"It's my favorite time of day," he said, softly, like a confession. "The winds always come in. It feels like I can breathe again."

She nodded. "The air gets less heavy."

"And the stars..."

It was the thing that had made her reconsider her first impression of him. The way he'd sat out here at night, gazing upward.

"Scorpius." The constellation's name slipped from her tongue, and in her mind, she traced the shimmering arch of stars, the shining spiral that took up half the nighttime sky.

He grinned, soft and gorgeous, and so damn kissable. "Exactly."

His hand rested warm against hers. It didn't even matter that it was sweltering out, because the heat of his body was more searing, more present, and every place it didn't burn itself into her felt suddenly, impossibly cold.

And fuck this. Just...*fuck* it. You don't ask, you don't get, right?

She barely even had to lean in, they were standing so close. She just pressed up onto her toes, swaying slightly to the side, and he was right there. His mouth warm. His lips soft.

He turned his head away, and everything inside of her flashed to ice.

"I'm sorry—" he started, but she didn't want to hear the rest.

"Forget it." No way was she apologizing. If anything, she wanted to deck him again.

How dare he? All these little signs he'd been throwing out. All these *big* ones. Holding hands and touching knees and talking about the stars weren't things that people did. Not to her.

Except he didn't do them all the time, did he? She laughed darkly to herself as she stepped away. She felt so *stupid*.

The last time he'd come this close, he'd caught her in her underwear, and now here she was, her arms and tits half exposed.

"Jo..."

"I get it." She gestured at herself. "Carol's clothes and every-thing. Easy mistake to make. Thinking I'm a girl or something."

"Jo—"

"I'm just going to go—"

"*Jo.*" He grabbed her wrist with force this time, and it was only a conscious effort that kept her from lashing out—from using fists to try to defend what she couldn't hope to protect. Her heart.

He didn't let go as she tried to squirm free, and she gave up, facing him. Bracing herself. Jesus. She didn't need to hear this shit.

"It's fine," she grumbled.

"It's not."

And there was an edge to his tone. A pleading note that made her stop.

He lifted a hand to touch her face, tilting her chin up. Asking her to look into those warm, blue eyes.

"I can't," he said.

It felt like a blow.

"Fine—"

"I can't, but I *want* to. Christ, Jo. Isn't it obvious?"

She'd thought it was, but then she'd tried to kiss him, and look how well that had gone. "You got a funny way of showing it."

"I've wanted to kiss you since the moment I saw you." His throat bobbed. "Wanted to do a hell of a lot more than that, too." He paused. "But…"

Right. Here it came. "But."

But it'd only be sex.

But I love somebody else.

"But you deserve better than that."

Her breath caught. She let her hand go slack inside his grip.

"Listen," he said, gaze intense, voice fervent. "I like you. So much. I like your fire and how smart you are and all the things I see beneath that—that shell you put up. And I *promise* you"— his fingers tightened against her skin—"I have never, ever had a problem remembering you were a woman."

It set a blaze off in the pit of her abdomen. Between her legs and in the heart of her sex.

"I like you, too." The words came out quiet and weak, and she hated feeling that way. But it was what he had left her with.

"And if we ever kiss—*when*," he revised, "when we kiss, it's going to be when I can give you everything. Because that's what you deserve."

Her stomach twisted. "And you can't give me that right now."

She hadn't forgotten. He had never pretended to be unattached, and she'd kept the reality of it firmly in mind. Right up until now.

She cursed herself inside her head. Just this afternoon, she'd sworn she wouldn't be the other woman, and then he'd touched her and made everything confused. She'd kissed him, knowing exactly what was going on but choosing to ignore it.

Weak. Stupid.

He must have seen her shutting down. "One week, Jo. Not even."

How many times did she have to wait for someone to feel for her what she felt for them?

"You can't exactly promise me anything."

With a weak, lopsided smile, he drew her hand up to his chest. He placed it at the very center of his ribs. "I can promise to get my life straightened out."

That was all she'd wanted a couple of minutes ago. Whichever side of the line they came down on, it'd be better than this. This uncertainty—this balancing act.

"Give me a week," he insisted, pressing her palm to the warm muscle beneath his shirt. "And when I come back to you, I'll give you the answer you deserve. Can you wait one week?"

"A week you're going to spend with her." The silent third in this strange, phantom triangle of theirs.

"Yup. Because she deserves better than this, too. Let me deal with everything, and then I'm going to come back to you."

"With either a no or a yes."

It would be the worst kind of waiting, not even certain what she was waiting for.

"Hey," he said. "What we started here. It isn't over. Please. Don't shut down on me. Just give me the time to do it right."

A part of her, the one that usually won, was screaming at her to walk away. To tell him no. But that was the part of her that always made it so she ended up alone.

"I can't promise you anything, either." But she took a step closer.

"That's not a no."

"It's not," she agreed.

"I'll take it."

He moved so slowly, transcribing his actions so there wasn't any chance she could misinterpret or overreact. Beneath her skin, she was still a roiling mess of conflicting impulses, a wounded thing looking to hurt whatever threatened to leave her bleeding.

An untouched heart, finally getting the chance to beat.

She let him fold her into his arms. Resting her head against his chest, she soaked in the solidity of him and closed her eyes.

What he was asking of her was nothing. It was everything. But as best she could, she'd give it to him.

A week was hardly any time at all.

Chapter 9

Adam's week in Baltimore dragged on *forever*.

It was funny—he'd been looking forward to this for so long. He'd thought the instant he set foot on solid, American soil again it'd be like coming home. The signs weren't all in Spanish, and the buildings were brick and stone. The hotel was a perfect seventy-one degrees. But it didn't matter.

His first few days in Puerto Rico, he'd kept seeing things and wanting to tell someone about them. Shannon, maybe, if he'd thought she would appreciate them. Now he was looking at poster presentations about the Large Hadron Collider and neutrinos, sitting in on lectures about the cosmic microwave background, and he knew exactly who would want to hear about them.

Jo. Jo, who was so damn dedicated to her work.

Jo, who'd looked at him like he was breaking her heart.

Alone in his room, he touched the corner of his lips. She'd pressed her mouth right there, and it had sent a fire roaring up his spine, making his whole body come to life. He'd wanted to reach out and pull her in, or let her back him up against the fence and show him just how hot a night in the tropics could be. He'd wanted her to *touch* him.

Instead, he'd frozen up. He'd said no. Or at least not yet.

And now, a thousand miles away from her, he couldn't stop thinking about that almost-kiss.

While standing beside his poster presentation in the middle of the conference, answering questions about the research he'd done that year. While having a beer with his advisor between sessions.

While waiting for Shannon to arrive—for the two of them to figure out what they meant to each other after all.

He fought to convince himself he'd made the right decision.

And he hoped he hadn't missed his only chance.

* * *

"What are you doing here?"

Setting her things down, Jo blinked blearily at Heather. Out of the corner of her eye, she snuck a glance at the clock. Just after ten a.m., so well past the time Jo usually came in. "Um. Work?" Obviously.

It'd been three days since Adam had taken off; work was pretty much the only thing keeping Jo sane.

But Heather wasn't letting it go. "When did your observation window end again?"

"Four." It'd been almost five by the time she'd collapsed into her bed.

Her second session operating the telescope. Just like the previous time, Heather had stayed for part of it, but instead of retreating to her office once Jo'd had things in hand, she'd packed up her stuff and gone home to bed.

The trust had been staggering, but after a couple of hours, the loneliness had been, too.

Jo had tried so damn hard, but every few minutes, she'd caught herself glancing over at the other seat, some part of her subconsciously expecting Adam to be there. A quiet presence by her side, a warm voice. A gentle brush of fingers against her skin.

She was so *stupid*.

Heather clucked her tongue. "I didn't think I had to tell you this, but it's okay to come in late after that kind of night."

She hadn't been able to sleep, so what would've been the point? With a shrug, she clutched her bucket of coffee to her chest and sank into her chair. Heather shook her head with a sigh. That seemed like as much of a conversation ender as any, so Jo turned to her desk, stifling a yawn and bringing her monitor to life.

By the middle of the afternoon, she could barely keep her eyes open. Fatigue and frustration made her temples pound, and the silence in the office only made it worse. Adam had never really visited her in her office, but apparently, she looked for him everywhere now; apparently she missed him even in the pieces of her life he hadn't occupied.

She hadn't realized how little she spoke to anybody else here until her one point of connection was gone.

Finally, Heather went for a coffee break, and Jo gave up and thunked her head against her desk. She rested there, brow pressed to the cool wood, cursing herself and the shitty situation she'd gotten herself into.

Of course she was still hunched over like that a minute later when someone knocked on the door. She groaned and sat up straight.

From the doorway, Carol flashed her an uncertain smile. "Is this a bad time?"

Was there any such thing as a good time? Jo waved at her to go ahead.

"Roberto agreed to give a few of us a ride to town to grab some groceries. Anything you need us to pick up?" Carol hesitated. "Or do you maybe want to go, too?"

Pushing her hair out of her face, Jo considered it. God knew she wasn't getting anything useful done here, and Heather didn't seem like she would mind. She was running low on snacks.

And it'd be a chance, paltry as it was, to talk to real live people and get out of her own damn head for a while.

She sucked her lip ring between her teeth. "Who's going?"

"Me." Carol ticked the names off on her fingers. "Kim, I think. And if she's going, you know Jared will, too."

Ugh. The two of them were more than she really wanted to deal with. Still...

"Yeah. I could go. If there's room."

Carol's face did a terrible job at hiding her surprise. "Really?"

"Everybody needs food." She shrugged off her annoyance at the question and put her computer to sleep.

When Carol smiled in reply, it looked genuine. "Cool."

Jo left a note for Heather before slinging her bag over her shoulder and following Carol to the parking lot, where the rest of the crew was already assembled. Roberto and Jared and Kim didn't do any better of a job at pretending not to be shocked than Carol had, but Jo ignored them as she got into the van. She left the backseat for the couple and the front seat open for Carol so she could be a normal, friendly person and carry on whatever small talk she wanted to with Roberto. As they lurched forward, she rolled down her window and let the breeze blow through her hair.

Leave it to her to go on a social outing and instinctively find a way to make it as isolating as possible.

The instant they arrived, Jo spilled out onto the pavement and left the others behind as she headed for the store. She cast one glance over her shoulder to find Jared dipping Kim, giving her a big sloppy kiss, and something inside Jo twisted.

She shook it off as the automatic doors parted, cool air beckoning her within. She grabbed a basket and set about wandering the aisles. At the register, the checkout girl took one look at Jo and angled the display her way so Jo could see the total, not bothering to rattle the numbers off. Jo peeled the bills from her money clip and handed them over, nodding and offering a clipped, "*Gracias*," before taking her bags in hand.

She stepped outside to find the van gone.

Her chest went tight, panic and indignation both squeezing her lungs. For a second, they swamped her. Then she took a deep breath and squared her shoulders. Gave herself a good solid mental slap in the face.

It wasn't any big deal. Roberto had probably only agreed to give them a ride because he'd needed to run some errands himself. If she'd stuck around, she would've been privy to the plan. She just needed to sit herself down and wait. They'd come for her. They wouldn't have forgotten her or left her behind.

And yet, as she lowered herself to the curb, she couldn't help it. A tiny part of her was ten years old again, sitting on a stoop outside the school, promising her teacher that her dad would be by to pick her up soon. Lying. Resigning herself to figuring out the bus routes and counting her change in her mind.

The buses didn't run all the way to the observatory. A cab would be expensive, but she had the money. If she was really stranded, she'd be all right.

She was always fine.

"You look like someone kicked your puppy."

Jo startled, whipping around. Kim stood over her, holding a shopping bag of her own, one eyebrow raised. Jo clenched her hands into fists, trying to calm the way her heart was jackhammering around behind her ribs. She knew better than to let go of her surroundings like that—to get so caught up in her own mind that someone could sneak up on her.

She was off her game. Way, way off.

Her fingers shook a little as she combed them through her hair. "Am I supposed to look happy? It's a million degrees out here."

"You could've waited inside." Kim shrugged and plunked down beside her. She nudged Jo with her elbow, and Jo stiffened, quashing the instinct to defend her space, to keep anyone from intruding into it. "Penny for your thoughts?"

Jo shook her head and scooted an inch to the side. "They cost a lot more than that."

Squaring Jo with an appraising look, Kim smirked. "Then let me guess. You were thinking about Adam." She said it with a teasing lilt to her voice, and Jo bristled.

"Hardly." Forget that it'd been one of the first times all day she hadn't been.

"If you say so. Not sure why you're denying it, though."

"Nothing to deny."

"Uh-huh." Kim dragged her purse into her lap and dug around until she came up with her phone and a tube of lip gloss. Watching her reflection in the blank screen, she swiped the color across her lips, then smacked them together. "The program's almost half over. If you two don't stop dancing around each other soon, there's not going to be much point."

And it wasn't as if Jo hadn't known that. The calendar she kept beside her monitor at work made it abundantly clear how quickly the summer was slipping past. She'd kept it in mind every time she thought about her progress on her research. But she hadn't considered it in that context before.

By the time Adam returned, their time together really would be half over. Maybe that was for the best. If he and his girlfriend sorted their shit out, Jo would only have his happiness shoved in her face for another five weeks.

But if they didn't...if he came back and he still wanted her...

She dug her nail into the pad of her finger. Adam himself had said it, and she'd laughed at him when he had. But all the same, Jo found the words slipping out. "It's complicated."

Kim snickered. "It sure as hell doesn't have to be." She capped her lip gloss and dropped it in her purse, teasing at her bangs before stashing her phone. "I mean, we're only here for a little while. Might as well make the most of it, right?"

"Is that what you and Jared are doing?"

Kim grinned. "You'd better believe it. Boy drives me crazy, but he's a monster between the sheets. Or up against the wall, or—"

"I get it," Jo cut her off.

Jo wasn't any stranger to taking a man to bed and getting what she wanted from him. What she usually wanted was an orgasm or two, and once she'd had it, she was good to go. It was the contact and the release she needed to return to her work with a clear head.

Adam, though...He didn't seem like the kind of guy who'd be into that. The way he acted about that girl of his it was evidence enough. He was serious about just about everything, and doubly so about the women in his life. He'd been serious when he'd grabbed Jo by the shoulders and refused to let her walk away. When he'd refused to kiss her.

Until he could give her everything.

"And you're okay with that?" Jo heard herself ask. "Knowing it's only temporary?"

If Adam did come back to her, he'd do it with the same intensity he'd brought to dragging her out of the water and holding her tight, to clasping her hand and to their not-quite-kiss. She'd never wanted more than sex from anyone, but the idea of keeping it casual, keeping it short-term with him made her head hurt.

Kim cast her gaze skyward. "Jared's not the kind of guy you fall in love with. Having a time limit is for the best."

If only things with Adam were so simple.

Before Jo could even begin to figure out the mess of feelings tangled up in her head, the rumble of an engine saved her. Sure enough, it was Roberto and the van. Happy to end the conversation, she rose, taking her packages with her and going for the door. She climbed her way into her solitary seat.

And in the silence and the heat, she waited.

Chapter 10

Adam's hotel room was spotless. He circled it one last time, peeking under the huge, king-sized bed that had seemed like such a good idea when he'd booked it, making sure there weren't any socks or pairs of underwear lurking underneath. His things were all put away in drawers, his suitcase in the closet, his toothbrush and razor and comb lined up in a neat little row beside the sink.

The last session of the conference had ended a couple of hours ago. He'd had a quick dinner with his advisor, then come here to make sure everything was ready. Shannon would be here any minute.

With a restlessness in his hands, he checked his phone, but it was silent.

Lacking anything better to do, he gave himself a once-over in the mirror and winced at his appearance. Not for the last time, he second-guessed his decision to stay in conference attire. Shannon had always liked him dressed up, though, and his khakis were neatly pressed. The blue button-down shirt brought out his eyes, and his tie was the one she'd bought for him last Christmas.

The part in his hair was so maniacally straight, it looked like he'd combed his hair with a ruler.

He looked like an idiot. Stiff and uncomfortable. He felt even worse.

That first week at the observatory, when everyone had gotten together to make dinner at the girls' house, Jo had called him out on everything he was doing wrong with regards to Shannon. She'd told him it never paid off to wait for someone to care about you, and every word of it had hurt. It had hurt because it was true.

What would she think of him now?

"Fuck it," he muttered. He turned on the tap and wet his hands, then raked them through his hair, messing up the style a bit. Making it look more like it did most days on the island. Better.

The tie went next. He opened the top two buttons of his shirt. After a moment's hesitation, he traded out the khakis for the one nice pair of jeans he'd brought.

Much better. Less nervous first date material and more...him.

He coiled up his discarded tie and folded his pants and put them both away. He took another lap of the room and wrung his hands. Maybe he should've stayed in his nerdy professor clothes. Or—it was kind of hot out. Shorts and a T-shirt wouldn't be inappropriate.

He couldn't *take* this anymore.

Shaking his head at himself, he turned on his heel. He patted his pockets for his wallet and phone and headed for the door. Shannon had said she'd just come up to his room, but there wasn't any reason he couldn't head to the lobby to meet her. On the elevator ride down, he tapped out a message letting her know he'd meet her there.

He stepped through the doors, thumb hovering over the button to send as he scanned the space. It was mostly stuffy sciencey types, people lingering even though the conference was over. A few more glamorous people presumably heading out for a night on the town. He scanned red leather couches and the length of the marble floor, the big glass bank of windows, and the revolving door.

Then he stopped. Looked closer.

Her hair was red.

Three years he and Shannon had been friends, or a couple, or something in between. Through all of it, she'd had the same blond fall of hair trailing halfway down her back. He'd loved to run his hands through it, loved the way it glowed in the early morning light. She'd known how much he'd loved it.

The floor beneath him tilted for a second. When it settled, the world looked different.

She'd changed something so basic about herself. She'd *changed*, period. And suddenly, he was pretty sure he had, too.

He was still working to process it when her expression shifted, and she waved, clearly spotting him across the room. He smiled, a wary, fragile thing, as he paused to delete the message he hadn't bothered to send and didn't need to now. And then he moved, closing the distance just as she was doing the same.

With the shock of her hair percolating in the background, he took in the rest of the details of her appearance. Her makeup was light, so that much at least was the same. He recognized the little white shrug she wore across her shoulders, but the sundress underneath it was new. She had a bag slung over her shoulder in addition to her purse, but it wasn't terribly big. She was probably only staying one night, then.

And that was… okay. Really, truly, honestly okay.

They came to a stop with a couple of feet still separating them, like there was some sort of force field holding him back. Before this summer, he wouldn't have hesitated. Her grin was as sheepish as his felt as she tugged at the strap of her bag and shifted her weight.

"Hey," she said.

"Hi. You...I..." Jesus. "It's so good to see you." And with that, he got over himself, stepping forward into her space for that hug. She gave it to him willingly enough, but it was as different as all those unreturned phone calls would have—should have—led him to expect.

He pulled away after just a second, letting her go. His hand caught on her hair.

"I know," she said, reading his mind apparently. "It was a stupid whim, but..."

"It's nice." He wasn't even lying about it. "Different, but... pretty." He regarded her again. "It suits you."

A tension around her eyes seemed to ease. "You think?"

"Yeah. I do." It suited this new version of her that wasn't his, and that probably should've hurt more. But it didn't. It was just a quiet little hint of an ache—a wound that, somehow, while he hadn't been looking, had started to heal.

They gazed at each other for a long moment before he remembered himself. "Here, let me take your bag. We can stash it upstairs, and then..." He had a whole host of potential plans, but none of them felt right. Letting out a long breath, he relaxed his shoulders. "Have you eaten?"

"I'm starving."

She held out her bag, and he accepted it, slinging it over his shoulder as he led the way to the elevator bay. "You in the mood for anything in particular? I went to a good Thai place for lunch the other day. Or there's a sandwich place. Or—"

"Thai sounds good."

They stepped into a waiting elevator. He hit the button for his floor and leaned into the wall as the doors slid closed. She stood opposite him, and he regarded her again, trying to peer deeper.

"What?" she asked.

Right. You could only stare in silence at a girl for so long before it got weird. He shrugged. "You look good."

"So do you." One side of her mouth turned up. "I didn't know you could even get that tan."

"Me neither."

"There's something else about you, too." She regarded him as the floors dinged by. "I can't quite put my finger on it, but…" She trailed off, not finishing the thought, not telling him he'd changed. He didn't need her to. He was pretty sure he knew the feeling.

A louder chime sounded, and the doors opened onto their floor. He got out his keycard as they walked, but at the door, he paused. A tickle of nerves firing off, he turned to her. "Don't read anything into the room, okay?"

"Um…"

He let them in, and he felt her registering that one, big bed.

"Yeah…uh…" He set her bag down on the desk and palmed the back of his neck.

"It's fine."

"If it's not, I can see if they can change it. And anyway, it's so big, it's not like we have to sleep on top of each other." But hidden behind his every word was the fact that the room expected them to sleep together. In the same bed.

Her hand brushed his. "It's fine. Really. Wouldn't be the first time, right?"

"Well, no, but…" It would be the first time since they'd called it quits again. Since they'd spent this summer with so much distance between them, and since they'd come together again as new people.

It wouldn't be the same. And that was okay.

"Come on." She withdrew her hand, and he didn't chase her touch as she retreated. "You promised me noodles."

It was easier, sitting across a table from each other in a restaurant, their knees not touching, their hands restricted safely to their own sides. Between great gulping bites of pad thai, she told him about work and her classes and their friends and all the other hundred little things he'd been wondering about all summer long.

He laughed, shaking his head at the end of one of her stories. "I can't believe you did that."

"What? Why not?" She washed another forkful of her dinner down with a sip of her drink. "The student union was made to be climbed."

"Well, sure, maybe, but—" But she wouldn't have done it, back when he'd first met her. "I just never thought you'd be the one climbing it."

"I guess I can still surprise you."

"Yeah. I guess you can."

She wiped her mouth with a napkin and set her silverware down, pushing her empty plate away from her. She gestured with her head toward the door. "You ready to get out of here?"

"Sure." He motioned for the check and paid it over the sounds of her protests, batting at her hands when she tried to grab for it. "You drove all the way down here."

She rolled her eyes. "And you flew all the way up here! And got a hotel room. You didn't even eat anything."

"I had a drink." He slipped the billfold to the waiter and stood.

She pouted all the way to the door. As they spilled out onto the street, she elbowed him in the side. "I wanted to pay my share."

It probably took him too long to get it. When they went on dates, he insisted on paying. And this wasn't a date. He let his expression soften as he nudged her back. "You can get breakfast."

She gave him an assessing look. "Darn right I can." She glanced down the street, rocking on her heels. "You want to head back, or..." She trailed off, and he considered it.

Going to the hotel meant going to that room. And that bed. His throat went tight. "It's a nice night. We could walk around some first?"

Her sigh of relief matched his own. "Yeah. That sounds nice."

It was habit to extend his arm for her to take. She shook her head at him but slipped her hand into the crook of his elbow all the same.

Baltimore had a pretty terrible reputation, but the area around the conference hotel was nice enough. They ambled along in silence for a block or so, looking at the buildings and the night-life before she asked, "So how about you? How's your summer going?"

He heaved out a breath. "Good." He corrected himself. "Better." Because it had been terrible at first. Lonely. But then he'd worked past it and gotten to know the people around him. Found a way to make it okay.

In fits and starts, he recounted the details he'd been waiting to tell her. His housemates and his advisor and his work. When he got to the list of girls in the program, he hesitated.

And Shannon could tell. She narrowed her eyes at him. "What are you not telling me?"

"Nothing. Something." He chuckled and kicked at a rock. "I don't know."

For a moment, she went silent. "Did you meet someone?"

He'd never imagined he would be confessing this to her. But now, when confronted with it, he couldn't bring himself to evade. "Maybe?"

And she *beamed*. "Oh my God, Adam! Tell me all about her." She squeezed his arm, practically bouncing on her toes.

He tilted his head to the side. "Isn't this weird?"

"Do you want it to be?"

"Not really. Just..." Just, this was the first girl he'd ever been in love with, the first girl he'd had sex with. The girl who, once upon a time, he thought he'd spend his life with. "It seems weird."

"Adam. I'm happy for you."

That twinged a little. He tugged his arm away.

"Adam?" The smile slipped off her face, and she stopped walking.

He sucked in a deep breath. "It's fine. Really. I just..." He hadn't exactly accepted they were over, but he'd been getting closer and closer, and tonight, when he'd seen her hair, he'd very nearly understood it. "I wasn't expecting quite this level of enthusiasm."

"Oh."

"It's..." He trailed off before he could say that it was fine again, because it wasn't. It would be, but for the moment, it had him feeling unsteady. Like a chapter of his life was really, truly ending, and maybe it was for the best. But it didn't make it easy.

"Come on." She put a tentative hand on his arm and led him to a low wall where she tugged him down to sit beside her.

He put his elbows on his knees and closed his eyes. Apparently they were doing this.

"I loved you so much, Shannon. For so long."

Her voice trembled when she said, "I loved you, too."

"It's over, isn't it? For real this time."

At least she didn't pussyfoot around. "I think it is."

"I mean, I knew that. I really did. But somehow it hadn't sunk in."

The warmth of her hand settled on his back, and he let it, accepting the comfort for what it was. "I haven't exactly helped with that, have I?"

A snuffling laugh forced its way through his nose.

"I'm sorry," she said. "I just...we'd been together so long, and I cared—I still care—about you."

"It's okay." He knew how she felt.

"It's such a cliché, but I really do want to be friends."

Her hand had drifted up to his shoulder, and he moved to place his own palm over hers. "I cannot imagine a world where we're not friends."

A couple of months ago, he hadn't been able to imagine a world where they weren't more.

Her voice trembled. "Sometimes, I think, when two people get together when they're as young as we were—when they stay together for so long—you either grow together or you don't, and it's like you don't even notice it happening. I feel like...we don't fit anymore. Not the way we used to."

"We don't," he agreed. He'd known that for ages, but he'd thought it was okay. That if they worked at it, they could push through and find a new way to fit.

So many times they'd broken up only to end up getting together again. But this time...

This time was for real.

He turned to look at her, and her eyes shone, the glassy wetness of them glittering. "I know we always fell back into each other, but it was hard to tell if it was just because we were lonely or if we really wanted that. And it had hit the point where, sure, it was comfortable, but it was also—"

"Suffocating," he finished for her, the word coming to him out of nowhere.

Her smile was wobbly. "Exactly."

He never would have been able to say that before, but this summer without her, when she'd enforced the separation…it had seemed cruel at the time, her refusing to return his calls. But maybe it had been a kindness. Without her voice in his ear, he'd had to branch out. Grow up.

They'd had the chance to finish growing apart.

Sitting up straighter, he reached up to twist his fingers through a crimson curl of her hair. She shook her head and wiped at her face, making his own eyes feel mistier.

"I'm sorry I dragged it out so long," she said.

"You were better than I was." He'd just held on and on and on.

"But I could've been clearer."

"And I could've listened."

She laughed as she dug a tissue from her purse and dabbed at her nose. "It's funny, how it feels like we grew apart. But really, sometimes, I think we're too similar."

She wasn't wrong. Both afraid to upset each other, both trying for so damn long to make something work.

"Maybe." He stood, looking away while she tidied herself up and while he got himself put together, too. When they were both more or less reassembled, he held out his hand. "But that's why we're going to make really, really good friends."

Letting him pull her up, she smiled. "I like the sound of that."

"Me too." He tipped his head toward the next street over. "Come on. This really, really good friend of mine is going through a breakup, and so am I. If that doesn't call for ice cream, I don't know what does."

The gelato shop he'd thought they might end up at was still open, so they wandered in and got a couple of dishes to go. As they hit the street again, she looked at him, twirling her tiny spoon.

"So. Is it any less weird now if I ask you about this girl you met?"

"No." He picked a direction and started walking. "But I'm willing to pretend if you are."

"Then tell me about her."

So he did. Ignoring the awkwardness of it, he tried to encapsulate in words the way Jo had grabbed him and thrown him—literally, in the case of their first meeting. He described her walls and her fire and the visions he had of a vulnerable girl, somewhere just underneath. A vulnerable girl who was still one of the strongest people he'd ever known.

Through it all, Shannon listened, and when his words dried up, she clucked her tongue at him. "You're going to have your hands full with that one."

"That's putting it mildly."

"I think"—she hesitated—"it'll be good for you. You need someone who challenges you."

"You challenged me."

"No, I didn't. Not the way you needed to be."

Maybe she had a point.

Over the course of his rambling, they'd finished their ice cream and wandered back toward the hotel. He took her empty cup and tossed both in the trash. He looked over at the hotel's entrance with a stone in his throat.

Then he swallowed it down.

"Well, here we are," she said.

It was a crazy idea. One he never would have gotten up the guts to say, not to Shannon. Not before. "Do you want to just keep going?"

"What?"

"Let's not go there." Not to that confining room they were supposed to share. "Let's just keep walking."

"All night?"

"Why not?"

A look he couldn't read passed over her face, and he held his breath. But the clouds in her gaze parted, and the smile she flashed him was the freest, realest one he'd seen from her all night. Maybe the best one she'd given him in years. He held out his hand and she took it.

She squeezed his fingers. "All right."

* * *

Adam woke up squinting, blinking hard against the sunlight streaming through the curtains they'd forgotten to close. He was on the floor, still in his clothes, the pillow under his head doing absolutely nothing for the ache in his spine. Groaning quietly to himself, he levered himself up with his arms to sit and glance at the clock. It was barely nine.

He and Shannon had stumbled in at half past five.

It had been good. Weird and different. But good. They'd reminisced about the past three years, and when the sun had risen, they'd returned here, to this room, where he'd insisted she take the bed.

Sitting up straighter, he gazed over at her.

Her crimson locks shone in the morning light, just like her blond hair had, but it didn't stir a pounding in his chest the way it used to. She was beautiful, and dear to him. She was his friend. With any luck, she always would be.

And the girl who got his heart going now was waiting for him. He didn't want to wait anymore.

After the quickest shower known to man, it took him only a few minutes to get his suitcase out and all of his belongings crammed inside. He checked himself for his wallet and his phone, and he was ready to go out the door. Back to another life and another world. To a girl who wouldn't be easy, or comfortable, but who might just fit.

Before he could go, he turned to the woman sleeping in the center of the bed. He scribbled out a note, thanking her, and placed it on her pillow. He left her with one soft kiss against the center of her brow, murmuring, "Love you," beneath his breath.

And then he was off. One chapter of his life well and truly closed.

Another—he hoped—open and ready to begin.

Chapter 11

It's my favorite time of day.

Jo could hear Adam's voice in the back of her mind as she walked. Around her, twilight was settling in, the stars just beginning to come out, and she felt...

Brittle. But okay. Peaceful, in a strange sort of way.

Needing some kind of a distraction from the fact that Adam would be returning the following day, she'd spent the last nine hours in the lab, only leaving when the world beyond the windows of her office had started to dim.

One more night. Tomorrow, he'd be back. And who knew what would happen then.

All week long, she'd been circling, flitting between bitter pessimism and these stupid, ridiculous flares of hope. She'd settled now into something carefully neutral. He'd choose what he chose, and whatever it was, she'd live with it.

Clutching her binder closer to her chest, she directed her gaze up at the sky. A thousand odd miles away, under a slightly different set of stars, Adam was making his decision, or maybe acting on it, even. And she was here, doing exactly what she always did. Working. Surviving. And keeping her expectations low.

Ahead of her, the twin houses they lived in loomed, and she steeled herself. The lights in the girls' house shone brightly, music wafting through the air. The whole crew was probably there, half of them three sheets to the wind. It'd be another late night. She'd put in an appearance, and then she'd excuse herself to her room and try to get some sleep instead of tossing and turning, letting her nerves churn.

Sighing, she dropped her head and sped her pace.

And then a voice called out to her. "I was starting to worry I was going to have to go looking for you."

She stopped cold, peering through the darkness, her gaze homing in on the bench between the houses, the one where Adam liked to sit sometimes, except he wasn't supposed to be here. Not tonight. He was supposed to be in Baltimore with the love of his life. Except—

Except he was here.

Something inside Jo started shaking, but she pushed it down. Adam was here. Even she and her lowered expectations couldn't find a way to twist this into something bad.

At least the night hid the way a smile snuck across her face. It didn't hide the catch to her voice. "I thought you wouldn't be back until tomorrow."

"I caught an early flight."

"And skipped an entire night?"

He rose from the bench, unfurling to his full height, the staggering breadth of his shoulders silhouetted against the light of the house. She stopped a half dozen steps away from him. Her breath fluttered hot inside her lungs.

"And skipped an entire night," he confirmed.

Oh God.

All these worst-case scenarios she'd been spinning out over the past few days—she'd worked so hard to convince herself he'd be spending the entire conference realizing why he didn't want her. She was too jagged, too much to handle. She'd never be able to give him what he wanted.

She hadn't even begun to prepare for the idea that what he wanted might be her.

"And your girlfriend—Shannon—"

"I imagine she's in Philadelphia by now." He took a step closer, until she could see the outlines of his expression in the dim light. His eyes blazed, and there was a nakedness to him. The ways he'd been holding himself back before he'd left were stripped away. "And she's *not* my girlfriend."

Her throat went tight. "No?"

"No."

He reached right through the distance Jo had put between them, demolished it, and shattered the last bit of reserve she'd kept against the storm she'd always known that he would be. Warm and huge, his hand settled on her arm. And then it was drifting up. Higher. To cup her face.

Her body was glass, and beneath his touch, it melted, flowing and liquid and bright hot. Throwing sparks.

"You came back for me."

"Just like I said I would."

"Because you can give me everything now."

The earnestness on his face threatened to break her. "And more."

It was the most terrifying thing she'd ever heard.

Good thing she wasn't a big fan of listening anyway. Before he could get out another word—before she could ask another question she wasn't ready to hear the answer to—she lifted her arm and curled a hand around his neck. His skin burned into her palm, the short hairs at the base of his skull soft and yielding beneath her fingers.

This time when she lifted up onto her tiptoes to press her lips to his, he didn't stop her. She didn't get the barest corner of his mouth. With a sound that set a deeper, hotter fire inside of her alight, he turned into her, pulling her hard against him. Her binder came between them, keeping her from feeling the full expanse of that muscled chest, but it didn't matter. His one hand curved around her cheek, thumb stroking the point of it with a reverence she couldn't think about yet, while his other gripped her hip, possessive in a way that made a lot more sense.

And his mouth—*fuck*, his *mouth*.

She scraped her teeth over the wet flesh of his lip, anticipation and need crashing and combining in her abdomen, twisting together and shooting off sparks. The points of her breasts flashed hot.

And just like that, she couldn't take it anymore.

After all this time, inching closer and closer to each other but never quite getting there, she was ready to wreck him. Couldn't wait to get her hands on every inch of his gorgeous body, wanted to ride him until he screamed. Finally get that fullness and satisfaction to ease the ache that had been building and building. When she was done with him, she'd have him covered in bite marks and scratches and come. And—

Shit. She tore herself away from him, shifting the hand on the back of his neck to his chest to shove at him, stealing an inch of space for herself so she could fucking *think*.

That was the kind of stuff she did with her one-night stands. She picked guys who looked like they were ready for it, and she never made any pretense about what she was after. It never really mattered what they thought of it, anyway, because hell if she ever planned on seeing them again. But Adam was different. That night she'd tried to kiss him, he'd held her off with so much passion in his eyes. Everything about him had said that if they went down this road, he'd be looking for more.

And even if it was just one night—for these next five weeks, they'd be living and eating and sleeping and working within spitting distance of each other. Manning a telescope together, their advisors and all these people here gossiping about them.

She had to stop. Had to slow down.

Except slowing down seemed to be the last thing Adam had in mind.

His gaze was molten in the darkness, his eyes hooded, and he didn't let her get very far. "God, Jo. I want—" He bit off the word, the same way she'd been nipping her own desires in the bud.

It made her breath catch in her throat. "Yeah?"

"I want you. So much." His fingers flexed against her hip, like he wanted to hold her even more tightly but wasn't allowing himself to. "I've been thinking about it. The whole time, ever since I got on that plane to come back here." He shook his head. "Since the first time I saw you. I've tried not to, but I couldn't help it. What I want to do to you—what I want you to do to me..."

There was a hitch in his voice as he said that last part, and a flare of heat licked between Jo's legs. Maybe they were on the same page after all.

"Tell me all about it," she said, tugging him down into a kiss that was even wetter and deeper than the first.

It was a bitch move, because it wasn't as if she gave him a chance to get much more than a word or a grunt out as she sucked on his tongue. With a hand wrapped in the fabric of his T-shirt, she tugged him along, walking backward toward his house. He got with the program fast, quickening their pace as he advanced. When she stumbled over a bit of uneven ground, he knocked her breath from her lungs by catching her. His hands slid from her sides to her hips to her ass, then lower, and she shrieked as he pulled her against him, lifted her up.

And *damn* but she could get into that. With a hop, she let him take her weight. Clutched her binder with one arm and clung to his neck with the other. Folded her legs around his waist to put all of him in contact with all of her, and she ground against him, bracing herself against how sparklingly, impossibly good that felt. He was hard beneath his clothes, and big, too, from the feel of it, and all her plans were back on the table.

"The things I'm going to do to you...," she mumbled, kissing her way to his ear, where she rasped her teeth against the lobe.

He lengthened his strides, a raw noise tearing out of his throat.

Clearly the man wasn't a virgin. But there was something about the way he responded to her, a lack of artifice to the way he pressed into her touch, groaned and panted and made all these perfect little sounds... It made her feel like she was breaking him in. Like she was taking the cover off a cherry ride and finally giving that engine of his a chance to *go*.

In a feat of coordination and strength that was way, way hotter than it had any right to be, he managed to get the front door to the guys' house open without dropping her or hardly even jostling her.

"Jesus fucking—" she started, kicking the door closed behind them.

He cut her off with a stifled laugh and kiss and muttered, "Shh," against her lips. "Tom'll hear."

She didn't really give a shit what his housemate did or didn't hear while they were fucking, but she wasn't the one who had to live with the guy, so she showed a little mercy, working to stay quiet while pushing her hips into his with intent. A perverse pleasure, but a pleasure all the same when she managed to make him whine, and louder than he meant to if his bitten-off curse was any indication.

He hurried them down the hall. The instant he had them in his room, he slammed her up against the door, shifting a hand away from her ass to flick on the light. She blinked hard at the shock of brightness.

The sudden vision of this man, all flushed skin and sinful lips, blond hair and eyes that she suddenly couldn't read.

He tore her binder from her and tossed it on the floor. His forearm slapped against the door beside her head, and she startled. There was a growl to his voice as he said, "You are so... fucking..."

And she couldn't help it. Her mind supplied all the words that should go with that. *Bitchy, difficult, stubborn, such a pain in my...*

"Hot," he finally finished.

Just like that, it wasn't any mystery at all to read his gaze. Their eyes had had time to adjust to the light, but his pupils were still huge, his nostrils flaring, and there wasn't any mistaking the way he pinned her with his hips. That insistent hardness there, pressing exactly where she wanted it to be.

But it wasn't just sex, the way he was looking at her. Sex would have been easy. He had to go ahead and make it tender, too.

"So sexy," he said, his tone warm, fingers gentle as he ran them through the blue and black strands that had fallen into her eyes. "Your hair." His hand drifted down, the broad pad of his thumb sliding across her bottom lip. "Your mouth." He leaned in to kiss her. His teeth tugged at her piercing, and it sent lightning coursing all the way to her clit. "And this." Stroking the tendrils of ink that crept above the neckline of her shirt, he kissed her deeper. "Teasing me all this time."

Maybe it was a fetish. Maybe this clean-cut, all-American guy had a thing for a girl with a little bite.

But it didn't feel like that. Not then.

The reverence in his touch brushed against something she kept locked too deeply away, and she squirmed against the way it threatened to break free. She hitched herself up higher against his hips and looked him straight in the eye. Made her tone drip sex when that was only the beginning of it.

"Maybe it's about time it finally stopped teasing you, then, huh?"

He paused for a second, and she held her breath. But then he grinned. Warm and open as he let her deflect. "Yeah. Yeah, that sounds so good."

With a little grunt, he heaved her back off the door again, supporting her weight as he turned and stumbled the half dozen feet or so to the bed. He dropped her onto it before climbing up himself, settling his knees to either side of her thighs, bracing himself on his arms so he hovered above her. Christ, his eyes were blue, his mouth red and bitten. It'd look amazing between her legs, his chin slick with her.

Who was she kidding?

It'd look amazing just about anywhere.

Still smiling, he dipped to kiss her, drifting a hand down the length of her torso. When his palm curved around her breast, she closed her eyes, feeling her nipples constrict. Feeling the way he paused at what he found there.

"No way." He said it under his breath, but there wasn't any

missing it. Her lips curled up despite herself. If he liked the ink and the hoop through her lip, he was going to lose his shit over this.

"Way," she countered.

Taking it for the permission it was, he scrambled to shove her shirt up. She helped him get it off, raising her arms, pulling her overshirt and tank top away as one. He leaned in to press his mouth to the center of her ribs, wet, sucking kisses that had an urgency to them, just like the nudges of his dick against her hip. When he peeled the edge of her bra down and got up close and personal with the barbell through her nipple, he groaned aloud.

"You like?" she guessed, running her fingers through his hair as he stared.

He buried his face against her chest. "Fuck. If I'd known this was under here, too..."

She laughed. When had sex ever been this fun? When had a partner taken this kind of *joy* in looking? Touching? Discovering?

When had she ever let them?

Lifting his gaze, he circled the hardened peak of her tit with his finger. "Can I?"

She gestured helplessly, because seriously? Was this guy for real? "Be my guest."

He made another little noise that threatened to turn her inside out and cupped her flesh, shifting to get his mouth on her, and *Jesus*. She let her head fall as heat zipped down her spine, another rough surge of wetness making her ready to move this all along already. She didn't want to rush him or anything, but she was dying here.

Without dislodging his mouth or interrupting that thing he was doing with his tongue, she shifted to prop herself up on one elbow, reaching behind herself to undo the clasp of her bra.

She flopped back down and pulled the straps off her arms, and he seemed to like that even better, helping to tug the thing off before sucking her piercing between his lips again.

She'd always been a fan of equality, though, both between the sexes and between her breasts. Her nipple was getting over-sensitive, so she redirected him to her other one. He went at it with nearly the same enthusiasm, if perhaps a bit less curiosity. Arching into the warmth of those probing lips, she ran her hands down the length of his spine until she could get at the hem of his top. With what seemed like real reluctance, he separated himself from her flesh long enough to let her get his shirt over his head. But when he made to dip toward her tits once more, she rolled her eyes and stopped him, pressing a palm to his chest.

His big, broad, rippling chest.

"Uh-uh," she tutted. "No fair. My turn. I wanna see."

It shouldn't have been possible for him to smirk and seem shy all at the same time, but Adam managed it. Like he knew exactly how good he looked—and he damn well should, considering how hard he must have worked for it—but like he was self-conscious about it anyway.

She hummed, running her hands over his pectorals, tracing the lines of tight abdominals with her fingers. "Yeah."

"Yeah?"

"You pass inspection." She gave his side a teasing slap and pulled him down toward her mouth. As he kissed her, nice and wet with tongue, he cupped her curves, tweaking the barbell he seemed to like so much between his forefinger and his thumb. She laughed. "That is really doing it for you, isn't it?"

"You have no idea."

Actually, she had some, because she'd developed a brand-new kink in the time since he'd pulled off his shirt. As they kissed and kissed, she ran her palms over miles of perfect skin. Smooth muscles and shoulders, damp with sweat. A smattering of hair between his nipples and trailing down toward the good stuff.

She cupped his ass and pulled him against her, and he got over his preoccupation with her boobs faster than she'd thought he would, releasing her nipple to slam his palm into the mattress. Steadying himself as he ground his hips into hers.

"Oh," he groaned into her mouth. He trailed a hand down her side, slipping fingertips into the waistband of her shorts. Finally. "Can I?"

"Carte blanche," she assured him. "If there's something I don't like, I promise you'll know about it."

He snickered as he opened the button and pulled her zipper down. "Really? Considering how we met, I find that kind of hard to believe."

"Sarcasm? Now?"

"What better time?"

And then she wasn't laughing anymore as he dipped his fingers into her underwear.

Roommate or no, she had managed to squirrel away the occasional pocket of time to take care of herself, but it wasn't nearly enough. Her body felt like it was on a knife's edge from the first blunt nudge of his fingertips against her clit. Just that glancing touch was so slippery and slick, and she was gasping for it.

"That's right," he said, soft and low against her throat. His other hand plucked at her piercing, turning her into a shivering mess in the sultry air. "Though you might have to give me some directions here."

"Want me to draw you a map?"

He chuckled, leaning in closer, and the rush of breath across the row of studs through her ear had another burst of electricity winding her tighter. "Think I know the general lay of the land." He proved it, too, rubbing with just the right amount of pressure, wringing another cry out of her—too loud, but she couldn't help it. "But feel free to point out any specifics."

He shifted, changing the angle of his wrist so he could get a finger up inside, and *oh*, her own furtive efforts to take the edge off had never been this good. His thumb stroked her clit, and she sucked in a breath.

"Harder. Rub—"

Fuck, the boy took direction well.

"Yes," she moaned. She clutched one hand in his hair, had the other on his arm, begging him, pleading with him through her touch to stay right there, just there… "Adam—"

Her voice broke off in a rasping curse as her body snapped, pleasure flowing through her in waves, an echoing void like delirium blanking her vision to everything. He nursed her through it, keeping close as she came back to earth. Shifting over to kiss her mouth, nice and soft and wet and slow.

"Jesus," she panted, trying to catch her breath, releasing her hold on him to let her hands flop beside her head on the pillow. "*Damn* I needed that."

* * *

Adam chuckled, nosing at her cheek and pressing gentle kisses to the spot beneath her ear. He was pretty sure he'd needed that, too. Sure, he was still hard enough to pound nails, and he hoped like hell there was going to be a second act. But it'd been so long since he'd had this. Not just sex, but a chance to be close to someone, to touch and be touched. He'd missed it.

That he was getting to do this with Jo only made it better.

God. That first day of the program, he'd tried to describe what it had been like to meet her. His fascination had been clear from the beginning, and Jared had seen it on his face. He'd asked Adam if she was cute, and Adam had frowned, told him she was more hot than pretty.

How had he been so wrong?

Lying here beside him, naked to the waist and with her shorts undone, she was *beautiful*. Her body was lean and wiry and yet still soft in all the right places. Strong. Small firm breasts that fit perfectly in the palm of his hand, and the metal. The ink.

It made him a little dizzy, looking at it all, made his cock throb. When he'd first seen the barbell through her nipple, he'd been ready to lose it against her thigh. He loved the bite of her lip ring against his tongue. He hadn't had a chance yet to get a good look at her back, but he was going to, goddammit. The marks on her neck didn't connect to anything on her front—all that flesh was clean and smooth. He could just imagine the tattoo that must run the length of her spine, though...

But it wasn't even just that. Jo was always so careful, so coiled. She hid herself away. He didn't have any illusions that she was showing him everything now, but there was an openness to her he'd never seen before. It felt like he was getting closer. Like the secret core of her lay but a few layers deeper. And he'd peel them all away. Coax her apart with his lips and hands, if she'd let him.

Slipping his fingers free from the soft, wet warmth inside her, he grinned. "Glad I could be of service."

"No, seriously." Her eyes were glazed in a way that filled him with pride. "You don't understand. I have a *roommate*. Do you know how hard it is to get a minute to yourself when you have to share a room with someone?"

Actually, he did. His first two years of college, he'd taken an awful lot of long showers.

Then he stopped. Thought about what she'd really said and had to stifle a groan against her cheek. The vision of her touching herself, forcing herself to climax did it for him the same way her piercings did. She wouldn't be easy on herself, either, would she? Wouldn't take the time to enjoy it.

And then she made it even *worse*. "I mean it. My vibrator is so lonely. It's crying in my underwear drawer right now."

"Fuck." It was almost a whimper.

She hesitated for a second. When she spoke again, it was with a flirty edge to her tone. "That really gets you going, huh?"

"You have no idea." And this was stupid, but... "Don't suppose you'd let me see that sometime, would you? You, uh, using that?"

She laughed, a free, wild sound. "Crap. You're a dirty fucker underneath it all, aren't you?"

"What can I say?" he panted. "I like what I like." And he was learning all kinds of things about what that was right now.

Needing a second to recover from the image of her working a toy between her legs, he rolled over onto his back, the heated skin of his spine hitting a stretch of mercifully cool sheets. She came right along with him and fit herself to his side. And screw getting a minute to put himself together. It probably shouldn't have surprised him, but she dove in without any preamble. Reached over to wrap her hand around his cock through his clothes, and he shuddered all over. The sudden, unexpected touch punched a sound of need out of his lungs.

"And what would you *like* me to do with this?" she asked, giving him a rough stroke.

"Anything you want to." And he meant it, by God. She could

just jerk him off, and he'd be happy. And if she wanted to give him more than that—wanted to let him feel her mouth or take him inside—it would be gravy.

He may have only slept with one woman before, but they'd been together long enough to have experimented some. Still, they'd settled into patterns over time. Missionary had been a favorite. He'd always had idle fantasies of a woman who would want to push the boundaries a little more, though. Someone who'd push *him* around. Show him what two bodies could do.

"Well, let's see what we're working with." She smirked as she climbed on top of him, straddling his thighs. She worked his belt open and then his fly, and he was only too happy to help push the fabric down his hips. Grabbing the waistband of his boxer briefs, she tugged them out of the way. The air hit him, and he bit his tongue as she took him in hand. Warm slender fingers and brush of thumb over the slit. God, it had been so long since anyone had touched him like this. Looked at him like this. "Oh," she said. "This is very nice."

"Glad you like." It came out shivery and strained.

"Very much so." Starting up a slow rhythm, she leaned over to nip at his bottom lip, and he arched up into it, the kiss and the heat of her hand. "Just might have to take it for a ride."

"Oh fuck, yes."

That sounded *so* much better than a hand job.

Shifting her balance, she worked his clothes farther down his body. When she hit the middle of his thighs, she rose up onto her knees and sat back. He didn't waste any time getting the rest of the way undressed, kicking off his sneakers and peeling his socks away as he rid himself of his underwear and shorts.

It took her a little longer. Her boots were blue today, nearly a match for the shock of dye in her hair, and unlacing them seemed to be a bitch. He moved to help, but she batted at him, undoing the knots with deft fingers. She finally got them gone and shoved her bottoms down, and then she was naked. Gorgeous. And urging him down, climbing on top of him. His slick tip nudged her thigh, and he choked on her name, wanting in, in, in right now.

"One second," she muttered.

And oh thank fuck she was a smart one. Somehow, she'd ended up with a condom in her hand. As she tore the wrapper off and tossed it aside, he gave it a look. It wasn't one of his.

"Shut up, I keep one on me, okay?"

"So much more than okay." Kind of a turn-on actually.

But not as much of one as her grabbing at him and rolling the latex on, lifting the length of him and lining him up.

"Holy *shit*." His whole spine arched as she sank down onto him. She was searing hot inside, smooth and tight around him, and he grabbed at her hips, blindly holding on to her while he fought for some kind of control over himself.

Hell if she was having any of that, though.

"Thought you said I could do whatever I wanted with it." She braced herself over him, hands on his shoulders and spine wickedly arched as she started to move, sending tremors through every inch of his nerves.

"Not complaining," he gritted out. There wasn't any keeping her still, just the torturous pleasure of the way she gripped him. He slid his hands up and down her sides, cupped her ass and felt it bounce as she picked up the pace, taking him, riding him. "Oh, Christ."

She had the balls to smile, wicked and sharp, and then she was leaning in, kissing his mouth. "Feels even better than I thought," she said. "Nice and full."

"You feel *amazing*." The smooth skin beneath his palms, the brush of her breasts as the tips of them scraped his chest, the way the piercing dragged. And being inside her like this, having her over and surrounding him...

For a moment that seemed to stretch on and on, everything else faded away. It was just her and him and the connection between their bodies. The fire of their initial confrontations, the heat of her spark, and how it had flowed into careful touches. Cracks in her exterior. And then this. Now.

In this room, on this island, with this girl.

He closed his eyes and held on.

Time sped up again a second later when she bit her way down the column of his throat. The sucking pressure of her mouth had a familiar warmth gathering in his gut. She was going to leave marks.

"Lower." He threaded his fingers through her hair, and she made a sound of displeasure but allowed herself to be moved. The next bite was beneath his collarbone, and the next on his biceps, and he fucking loved it. Bending his knees, he got his feet on the mattress, finding some leverage to shift his hips into hers, and she groaned, low and throaty, just like she had before she'd fallen apart the first time.

He'd already been about to do it, but she grabbed his wrist and dragged his hand to the place where they were joined. It wasn't easy with the way she was moving on him, but he curled his hand into the crease of her thigh, got his thumb up into all that soft-ness. The edge of his thumb slid along the length of his own cock before he found her clit, and she made this beautiful sound.

"Can you come again?" he asked, because he didn't have a whole lot left in him, not the way she was taking him apart, but he'd hold out if it meant he got to feel her.

"Guess we're about to find out." She dropped down onto her

forearm as she rode him with prejudice, slipping one hand to tug at her own breast.

He joined her, twisting the barbell through her nipple at the same time he rubbed her harder with his thumb.

"Oh—" She clenched up around him, her mouth dropping open, and if she'd been gorgeous in orgasm before, it was nothing compared to this. Her skin was slick with sweat, a hot flush covering her chest, and she groaned like she was *dying*.

And he couldn't take it anymore.

He left his one hand between her legs and slapped the other to her thigh, keeping her steady as he thrust up into her. Pounded into that tight, wet heat, let himself really *feel* it...

His eyes snapped shut and he threw his head back as the pleasure overtook him. He emptied himself into her in a rush, turning inside out with the sheer expansiveness of it, the connection.

The inevitability. For all that they'd spent so long working up to it.

It felt, somehow, that they'd always been meant to end up here.

Chapter 12

Jo's whole body thrummed with satisfaction as she gave in to the shakiness in her arms and legs, letting herself collapse onto Adam's bulk. They were sweaty and disgusting, but he smelled good and felt better, and when she clenched around him, wringing out the last licks of pleasure, he twitched inside her in the best way.

He let out a soft, embarrassed laugh and wrapped his arms around her, and that was...different. He didn't slap her ass or thank her for the fuck and show her the door. Instead, he held her like she was precious, like he had no real intention of moving anytime soon. It made something uncomfortable and warm unfurl in her gut.

She refused to think too much about it, lying there on top of him, working to catch her breath. Finally, though, the swelter got to be too much. Fucking in the tropics was going to be such a pain in the ass. "God, you're like a furnace," she muttered as she peeled her chest from his.

He was a good, responsible sex partner, easing his hand between them to hold on to the condom as he slipped free.

Collapsing to the side, she got out of his way as he rose to deal with the cleanup. She craned her neck to watch him stumble across the room.

Hot damn but the boy had a fantastic ass. He'd looked good from the front, but the bare expanse of flesh he showed her when he turned was another entire level of hotness.

"You don't have any tattoos." She said it without really thinking, letting her gaze sweep over miles of virgin skin.

"Nope." He made a soft sound, then drew a couple of tissues from a box.

"You ever thought about it?"

"Not really."

"You sure seem to like them, though."

He dropped the trash into a wastebasket in the corner of the room before facing her again. And maybe she'd been wrong. The front of him looked damn good from this angle, too.

Grinning, he gave her a none-too-subtle once-over. "I like looking at them. Doesn't mean I like needles."

"Wimp."

"Whatever."

He stood there gazing at her for a moment too long. A flicker of self-consciousness broke through her haze as she remembered herself. Sure, he'd held her with an unusual amount of tenderness, but this was typically the part of the evening where she picked up her clothes and beat a dignified retreat.

Except before she could act on the impulse, his smile deepened. He crossed back over to the bed and climbed onto it, lying on his side, curled around her. His fingertips grazed her neck where her tattoo spilled over. "I like looking at them a lot," he said, intensity shading his tone.

Too much intensity. She glanced down, away from his eyes.

"Yeah, I could kinda tell." It was supposed to be a joke. He'd been so obviously turned on by all the things she'd done to her body. But it came out weak.

"Hey."

She stilled, expecting him to say something else. A second passed and then another. But instead of speaking, he tucked two fingers under her chin and tipped her head up.

When his lips met hers, it was soft. Gentle. She let him deepen it, but the pace stayed slow. The warm brushes of his mouth were building toward something, though—something that wasn't sex. Overwhelmed, she slumped against the pillow and closed her eyes.

He gave her a second to get herself together. The bed jostled as he half sat up, grabbing the thin cover of the sheet and dragging it over their lower halves. She accepted it, tucking the fabric under her arms so her tits weren't hanging out before opening her eyes.

Even partially covered, he was gorgeous, his warm skin a contrast to the white of the sheet. He lay on his side, propped up on his elbow, his other hand resting in the scant inches of space between them. Expression soft, he gazed at her, not seeming to expect anything. But something about him said he'd accept whatever she decided to volunteer.

"Hi," she said. She wasn't embarrassed, not exactly, but this wasn't usually a part of sex for her. She didn't know how it was supposed to go.

Reaching across her body, he swept her hair from her eyes. His fingertips lingered on the edge of her face for a moment. Just when it threatened to become uncomfortable, he dropped his hand, moving it to rest on her stomach instead.

He nudged her ankle with his. "So how was your week?"

"Really?" The word was out of her mouth before she could stop it, a barked-out half-laugh of a question. All that intimacy and kissing and orgasming, and now he wanted to have a normal conversation? Like this?

Forget that they'd scarcely had a normal conversation in all the time they'd known each other, not without other people pushing them along. They'd had weird, brief moments of over-sharing, and arguments, but not small talk.

His eyebrows rose to match hers. "Why not?"

"It's just…" After a moment, she settled on, "Weird."

"Not really. We haven't seen each other in a few days. It's pretty typical for people to want to catch up after that."

"Is it pretty typical for them to tear each other's clothes off first?"

"*Typical* is a strong word." Consciously or not, he stroked his thumb just under the curve of her breast through the sheet. "In my limited experience, though, people are usually even more interested in how each other are doing if clothes-ripping-off is also a thing they like to do."

She shook her head. "Your limited experience is really different from mine."

Sadness darkened his eyes, but in the end all he said was, "Humor me."

"Okay." She drew out the end of the word. "Um, my week was pretty boring. I worked a lot."

"Shocking."

"No, like, a *lot* a lot." She twisted a few strands of her hair between her forefinger and her thumb. "Unhealthy a lot."

She really didn't want to have to fill in the blanks. The work had been work, because that was what she did. But the unhealthy part of it had all been his fault.

He seemed to hear enough of what she didn't say, because his expression softened, a soft smile curling his lips. "Okay. More work than normal, even for you. Check. Get anything cool done?"

"Yeah, actually." And she was preparing to self-censor, except she didn't have to with him, did she? Letting herself relax, she recapped some of the progress she'd made with her project, told him about her observing run. As she did, she shifted to rest her hand atop his on her belly. "It wasn't as much fun, though. Baby-sitting the telescope alone."

And hadn't that been a surprise? After all those team projects where she'd fought for the right to work by herself. Now, all of a sudden, she was eager for a partner?

Adam nodded, tapping a finger against her abdomen. "I've got another session scheduled with it this week. You wanna come and keep me company?"

"I guess. If I've got time." Inside, her heart leapt at the chance.

"Cool."

She hesitated before she spoke again. She didn't have a whole lot else to say about herself, and all week long she'd been wanting to know... had been dying to hear about...

In the end, she decided to ease into it. "How about you? How was your week?"

He gave her a laugh that was almost too easy, too casual. "Not that different from yours, actually. You know how conferences are."

Oh. So he was going to dance around the subject, too.

She let him, for a little bit. His descriptions of the lectures he'd attended were interesting enough, and there were a couple of papers she'd have to look up when she got into the office tomorrow to learn more. But that wasn't what she'd been asking.

When he started to wind down, she walked her fingertips up his wrist, watching her own movements instead of his eyes. "And after the conference?"

"Oh. Right." The motion of his throat, bobbing as he swallowed, drew her gaze. "Shannon came."

Jo had kind of figured as much, and really, it wasn't as if she didn't already know at least part of the outcome. Adam was here with her, after all, naked and postcoital. But uneasiness still plagued her, making her ribs tight. "How did that go?"

"Really well, actually." His voice went fond and just a little bit wry, and it made her chest squeeze harder. "We had a good time. Went out to dinner, had ice cream, walked around the city."

The affection in his tone was what did it. Jo wasn't going to overreact, wasn't going to screw this whole thing up. But this was important. "Did you fuck her?"

His gaze snapped to hers, creases forming between his eyes, and it was like he hadn't even considered the question, much less that she would actually want to know the answer. "What? No."

"It's a valid question."

"Of course it is. But…but how could you…" He visibly took measures to calm himself, breathing out through his nose and closing his eyes for a second before sitting up and turning so he faced her. "Believe me," he said, looking down at her with fire in his gaze, "we would not be lying here like this if I had."

"Well, how was I supposed to know that?" For all she knew, they could have decided to break it off after getting it on, or figured they'd have one more go at each other before they parted ways.

Or their breakup could have been a whole lot less final than he'd implied.

She squirmed. She didn't like him having the vantage point

over her that he did. Keeping the sheet wrapped around herself, she scooted up the bed, coming to sit with her shoulders braced against the headboard. She crossed her arms over her chest and stared at her feet.

"Jo." He paused for a beat, waiting before repeating her name. "Jo."

Ugh, he was doing that thing again where he wanted her to look at him before he told her something. Begrudgingly, she lifted her gaze.

It was such a subtle change. Talking about Shannon, he'd had this warmth to him, this soft affection, but it had been directed at nothing. He'd been looking off into some middle distance. Now all of that was trained on her, layered with that same intensity from before that had made her want to pull away.

She wasn't sure if it was really all that different at all.

"Look," he said. "You know me and Shannon were together for a really long time."

"Uh-huh."

"You know how important she was to me. Is. She'll always be someone I care about." He put his hand on her leg, pulling her focus and keeping it on him when she wanted to look past him. "But we're friends. Just friends now. I think we have been for a while."

He hadn't acted like it, those first few weeks they'd been here. "What changed?"

"I don't know. Me. Her. Everything. We had a good long talk about it, while she was there. About how people can come into each other's lives at these points when they're exactly what you need. But then as you grow, maybe things don't fit so well anymore." He shrugged. "Sometimes you hang on too long."

It struck Jo all at once. When Kim had been talking to her about making the most of a summer fling, Jo had doubted her.

Nothing about Adam had said *short-term*. He'd basically already told her that he would throw himself into it and give her everything. And when it was over, when it came time to part ways...

He'd hold on too long.

It was what he did. He loved with the safety off, while Jo scarcely knew how to love at all. Yet she was going to have to be the one to keep whatever this thing between them turned out to be in check. Really, if she wanted to save them both a lot of heartache, if she wanted to keep him from wasting months trying to make this work, she should cut it off now.

But she looked at him, gazing back at her with those guileless eyes. She took in the dirty blond of his hair and the warmth of his cheeks, the cut of his jaw and his *shoulders*. His chest. There were still so many things she wanted to do with him.

"Yeah," she said, vaguely helpless to it. "I see how that could happen."

She did see it, and she knew the smart course of action. But the smart course *sucked*. There wasn't any point giving it any real consideration. And anyway, she was smart enough that maybe she could walk the stupid path and not get burned.

Resolve and hope lit in her chest. She could keep both eyes open. She could curb his expectations. When their time was up, she'd let him down gently. And in the meantime, for just a little while, she could have this.

Smiling, oblivious to her decision, he leaned in closer. He took her hand in his. "Long story short, we talked things out. We decided we were better off as friends. And as soon as I could, I caught a flight back here, so I could see *you*." With that, he squeezed her palm. He nudged her nose with his own in a gesture that was far too sweet, then caught her lips in a kiss.

It was almost as good as their first kiss—maybe better because she had some clue about what was going on between them now. She parted her mouth and let his tongue inside. Idle sparks of arousal darted from her breasts to between her legs, and if the drape of the sheet was anything to go by, she wasn't the only one who was ready for another go.

It would be so easy, too. If she just put her hand on his chest, or hell, right on his cock. Kissed him a little deeper or climbed up on his lap, they could be off and running for a second round in no time. After, they could end up the same way they had at the end of their first, holding each other through the afterglow.

She could fall asleep, right here in his bed.

Temptation clawed at her. She'd never really done that before, not on purpose, and he was so warm and held her so nicely.

But they had to pace themselves. It was her job to keep this thing in check.

Groaning out her reluctance, she tore herself away from him. "I should go."

"You should stay." He pursued her as she tried to retreat, kissing her and pressing her into the headboard.

"I should *go*," she repeated. She shoved at his chest.

He heard her this time. The disappointment on his face killed her, but as he retreated, giving her room to breathe, she took it.

And then fucked everything up, leaning back in to kiss him.

No. No, no, no, no, no. Releasing another noise of frustration, she put a finger over his lips and pushed him away with it. "Okay. Just so we're clear, I want nothing more than to have you fuck me into this mattress right now."

She preferred being on top, having control. But seriously, at some point, that was *happening*.

He visibly twitched beneath the cover of the sheet. Against her finger he got out, "Then why—"

"But it's getting late. And I really shouldn't stay here."

His forehead crinkled. "Why not?"

She scrambled, trying to think of something. Sadly, all she was left with was the truth. Well, a version of it. She dropped her hand from his mouth and slipped past him to start gathering her clothes. "Listen, I know we jumped into bed together pretty fast." She stopped him before he could question that. "And it was awesome. No regrets. But"—she drew in a deep breath—"I don't want to rush things."

I don't want you to do anything you *might regret.*

And besides… "I know we're not going to keep this a secret or anything." Apparently, everyone knew, just from their flirting. "But Carol will know if I stay out all night, and I don't want to deal with Jared making comments in the morning. I don't want to be…" It was part of why she'd always selected her conquests from anonymous clubs. "I don't want to be the girl who sleeps with the guy." She wasn't saying this right. "I need people to respect me."

His eyes were sad, but he didn't put up any further protest. Except… "Are you saying you'll never want to sleep over here?"

Shit. That sounded terrible.

But when he brought up the other aspect of staying the night—the part about how she would be *sleeping* with him, it made a vulnerable little piece inside of her tremor. It made another piece of her glow.

Fighting both reactions, she took a deep breath. She found her underwear and shorts and drew them on before climbing onto the bed to press an insistent kiss against his lips. "Not never. Just not all the time. And not tonight."

"Okay." He didn't sound entirely happy about it, but he didn't sound like he wanted to argue anymore, either. He let her go, and she slipped away to claim her bra from the floor.

She was pulling her shirt over her head when he piped up. "I never did get a chance to really look at your tattoo."

He hadn't been lying about really, really liking her piercings and ink, huh? "Maybe next time."

Then he was rising off the bed in all his naked glory, stalking over to her.

"What—" she started.

"Definitely next time." With that, he grasped her face between his hands and hauled her into a kiss so deep and dirty it stole her breath.

When he let her go, she felt a little dazed. But he didn't press. He went to his dresser and pulled a fresh pair of underwear from a drawer and stepped into them. For a second, all she could do was stare.

"Next time," she agreed faintly.

"Okay, then." When she stood there, staring at him dumbly, he rolled his eyes. "I'm using willpower here to not act like a caveman and drag you back to bed. But if you're going to go, you should probably do it now."

Right. She got her socks and boots on and found her binder under his shirt. More or less put together again, she straightened up and cast one last glance at him. Gorgeous, barefoot, shirtless him.

He wasn't the only one using a hell of a lot of willpower now.

Without another word, she turned to the door. In a few quick strides, she was through it and down the hall and spilling out into the warm night air. She pressed her spine to the door as she pulled it closed behind her.

This was the right decision. No matter how much it felt wrong.

Chapter 13

Y ou kids got everything you need?" Lisa stretched her arms up overhead, pushing back from the bank of monitors.

Adam cast a quick glance at Jo for confirmation, then smiled and nodded at Lisa as she stood. "Pretty sure we're good."

More than good. Great. Once his advisor headed home, it'd be just him and Jo here, manning a bazillion-dollar telescope until three in the morning. Sure, there'd be a tech in the other room, but they'd be more or less alone.

A night with nothing to occupy him except science and a beautiful girl. His girl. He wasn't sure he could ask for anything more.

Gathering her papers, Lisa ran through his plan for the rest of the night's data gathering with him, and Adam gave her as much of his attention as he could. Finally, she slung her bag over her shoulder, said her goodbyes, and headed for the exit. Adam watched her as she went, until finally she turned the corner and he heaved a sigh of relief.

"I thought she'd never leave," he groaned.

Closing the gap he'd been so careful to maintain these past

few hours—these past few days, except in the privacy of his room—he hooked an ankle under one of the legs of Jo's chair and yanked her toward him.

"What the—" she started, but then she was right there, warm and tucked up against him, the seats of their chairs jammed together.

God, he'd been waiting so long to *touch*.

In the weeks before they'd gotten together, he'd built up the idea of being with her so much; deep down, he'd half worried that finally sleeping with her would take the sheen off, but it had done precisely the opposite. They'd met up twice more in the handful of days since he'd returned from his conference, and each time only made him hungrier. Right now, he was starving.

He leaned in to nose behind her ear, and she gave a little shiver, tipping her neck to the side to give him access, even as she pushed him away.

"Not here," she insisted.

"But we're all alone."

"Miguel's up in the booth."

"Half asleep and watching telenovelas on the TV in there. You know he never bothers us after midnight."

"B-but—" she stuttered as he brushed his lips over her pulse. "Your experiment." She reached past him toward the data scrolling in.

"The cluster we're looking at doesn't set for an hour."

"But don't you want to see what you're collecting?"

"I'd rather see *you*." Naked. Three times now they'd taken some or all of their clothes off, and he still hadn't managed to get a really good look at her back. The tattoo was of an animal, he was pretty sure, and it spanned the length of her spine, rippling waves of black ink curling out across her ribs. A tail or a tip of a wing climbing up onto her neck.

He wanted to lick it.

"You can see me anytime," she argued.

He wished that were true.

He wanted to press, wanted to talk her into going out on the deck with him, or off to one of the restroom stalls. But she was squirming for real now, the playfulness giving way to actual annoyance.

He sighed. "Fine, if you really insist on me doing my job—"

"I do."

"Instead of taking you apart with my tongue." He drew back and raised his brow. It was another thing he hadn't gotten a chance to do that he was dying to.

For a second her resolve faltered, her gaze flickering to his mouth. But then she took a deep breath and gave him a look that could peel paint off a wall. "Adam."

The curl of disappointment was only a little one. He'd known who he was getting into bed with when they'd started this.

"Fine, fine." He could admit when he was beaten. Mostly. He dropped his hand from her waist, but when she made to roll to her side of the desk, he locked his ankle behind the wheel of her chair, holding her there.

"What—"

"One kiss." He held up his hands and showed her his cheek.

"You have got to be kidding me." But she didn't grumble too much before leaning in.

At the last second, he turned his head, darting in to cup her jaw and hold her there as he pressed his lips to hers. He swept his tongue over the loop of metal and then past it and into her mouth.

And it was the last thing he'd been expecting, but she opened to his kiss. Let him deepen it and keep her close. Her fingers dug into his arm, her teeth scraping just right against his tongue, and for a minute, he could honestly believe she wanted this as much as he did.

But he wasn't going to push.

With more than a little reluctance, he pulled away, pressing one last kiss to her lips before releasing his foot. She stayed there, gazing at him with bitten lips and dark eyes for the span of a breath. Then she seemed to remember herself. Easing off slowly, she steered her chair to where it belonged. She picked up her pencil and turned the page of her notebook, and just like that, she was back to work.

Which was probably what he should be doing, too.

Returning to the monitor in front of him, he clicked over to the graph the computer was building from the readings streaming in. He bounced his knee up and down, fighting to stay focused as he reviewed the numbers. But it was a losing battle.

The thing was, the actual work of an astronomer wasn't all it was cracked up to be. It was waiting for objects in the sky to rise and set, and analyzing data, and sitting around for hours on end. More often than not, it was about plodding and patience. Nights like this, it was just plain *boring*. While the woman beside him was anything but.

She was a puzzle and a mystery and just about the sexiest thing he'd ever seen. Already, just looking at her or thinking about her had his chest pounding too hard. He wanted to figure her out, to literally and figuratively strip her bare.

He wanted to *know* her. And if she wasn't going to sleep with him during his shift, the least she could do was talk to him.

Giving up, he let his gaze drift to the side. Jo was bent to her notes, the metallic glint of her lip ring sharp against her teeth, the long, pale column of her neck exposed. The skin looked beautiful and naked where it disappeared beneath her shirt, the side she'd turned to him devoid of ink or ornamentation.

He paused. That first time she'd tried to kiss him, the night before he'd left to finish things with Shannon, Jo had been wearing a necklace. Before she'd made her move, he'd fixated on that bit of delicateness draped across her collarbone. He'd lifted his hand to touch it, had traced the silver chain to just beneath the hollow of her throat, and she'd told him...

"What?"

Adam blinked, and he was back in the present, in the observatory in the middle of the night, miles of inches between his body and hers. She was looking at him, one eyebrow cocked, a half-grin stealing across her face like she'd caught him doing something particularly lecherous, and like she didn't mind.

His gaze dropped instinctively to her breasts, but only for a moment. Because he'd said these words before. "You don't usually wear jewelry."

"Excuse you?" She touched the studs in her ear and the hoop through her lip. "These aren't enough for you?" She glanced around before lowering her hand to graze her nipple. "*This* isn't enough?"

Heat flooded him. "Believe me. They're more than enough. It's just..." Rolling his chair closer, he circled her wrist and moved her arm to the side. He settled his fingertips at the dip where her shoulder met her neck, trailing them down to where the pendant would have hung. "The other night. You wore a necklace. I haven't seen you wear it since."

Her smile bled from her lips, and shutters seemed to fall, one by one, across her eyes. She pushed his hand away. "No. I haven't." She said it like a challenge, only he didn't know to what.

"Why? It was..." He trailed off before settling on, "Pretty."

She flinched. "Guess I just don't feel like looking pretty very often."

"That's not what I meant."

"Then what did you?"

And that was the question, wasn't it? He tried to put it into words, licking his lips and closing his hand around nothing. The little bit of decoration had been striking, for sure, a contrast to the utility of how she usually dressed. It had drawn his attention to the fragile parts of herself she rarely showed.

The ones she never spoke about. Except that once.

Swallowing, he lifted his gaze to meet hers. "You told me it was your mom's."

And he watched all the color drain from her face.

* * *

Shit. Jo really had said that, hadn't she? Adam had looked at her that way he tended to, with that weird mix of reverence and lust, and he'd asked her about the necklace, and she'd just given it up.

Inside her chest, her heart started racing, adrenaline flooding her veins. And she knew that fight or flight was a reflex, was a choice people made based on instinct, but it had never struck her as much of a choice at all.

She fought. And if you fought hard enough, if you fought people before they even imagined they should make the first strike, they tended to run. It saved you the effort of having to fly yourself. It saved you ever having to fight or fly from them again, because they knew. They understood what they were dealing with.

But Adam was sitting there, his knees almost touching hers,

his gaze expectant. The skin of her throat burned from his touch, and her lips were kiss-bitten and damp.

The very first thing she'd ever done was attack him. And yet here he still was, pushing her. He hadn't run.

And for the first time in her life, she didn't want to fight him off.

She closed her eyes and took a deep, shuddering breath. Setting her pencil down, she braced her elbows on the desk and dropped her head into her hands. "Yeah. It was."

A tentative hand settled on her shoulder. She stiffened beneath the weight but didn't shake him off. "Are you okay?"

Was she ever okay? "I'm fine."

"You don't seem fine."

He was the one who'd had to go and ask her revealing questions. Then he wanted to give her a hard time when she reacted badly? Bullshit. "What do you want to know?"

"You don't have to tell me anything."

She lifted her head to glance at him through narrowed eyes. "You asked me about my mother for a reason."

"I asked you about your necklace."

Right. "As a way of asking me about my mom."

Something complicated happened in the vicinity of his mouth, not quite a frown and not exactly a smile. It was too open, too revealing. Too kind. "Actually, I was just trying to make conversation. And looking at your neck. Because it's sexy as hell." One corner of his lips crept up. "But if you want to tell me about your mother...I'd like to listen."

Oh, hell. He was trying to *get to know her*, wasn't he? She stifled an ugly laugh by covering her face again with her hands. That shit was for couples—real couples, ones who didn't have five-week expiration dates. Ones who had time to hug and kiss and cluck at each other over the slow revelation of their pasts and then move on from them.

They didn't have that kind of time. And deep down, she was pretty sure he didn't really want to know.

She sighed, concocting in her head how best to deflect and change the subject, when the pressure of his hand on her shoulder lightened, easing to a gentle stroking of his thumb.

"Only if you want to," he said, quieter now.

She paused, the patience in his voice halting her. The air itself seemed to shiver as he slid his palm down her arm, letting her go. Letting *it* go, without pressing or asking too much of her.

And it was like a puzzle piece suddenly turning in her mind, a link that hadn't been there just a second before clicking jarringly, unexpectedly into place.

Maybe their expiration date didn't have to be a constraint. Maybe it was a kind of freedom unto itself.

She didn't have to tell him everything—no way in hell she ever would. But there were pieces she could let him know, parts of herself she could give away without toppling the careful, precarious tower she'd built. Because when this was over, when they left this island, he could take those pieces with him. She wouldn't have to live with the version of herself he ended up with. It could be just for now.

For this handful of weeks they had, she didn't have to carry it all alone.

She grabbed at him, curling a hand around his wrist before he could retreat any farther. She held him there. He went still.

"Jo?"

"She died. When I was really young." When she was negative seven minutes old, if you trusted the birth and death certificates. "I don't remember her at all."

"Oh God."

"It's fine. It's just…" What?

Just the precipitating incident that had led to the rest of her life.

"It doesn't have to be fine." He turned his wrist inside her grip, getting his hand around hers, making it so she was the one being held on to. Maybe so they were holding each other. "I'm sorry. I had no idea. I wouldn't have brought it up if—"

"No, really." She lifted her head and turned so she was facing him, because… because it was fine. She wasn't lying. She felt okay. Way more okay than she'd ever thought she would when she'd imagined someone prying this from her.

She managed a half-smile as she gazed at him, and the tension in his shoulders deflated by a fraction. Grasping her hand, he brought it up to his mouth and kissed the knuckles. "I am so sorry."

"Nothing to apologize for."

One side of his brow quirked up. "That's a phrase people say when they're expressing their condolences. You know that, right?"

"Of course." The words came out a little shakier than she wanted them to.

Lowering their hands, he cradled her palm in both of his, there in the space between their knees. Rubbed his thumbs across her knuckles.

And she could almost taste the decision he was making about whether or not to press—about how many assumptions he should make.

Finally, he settled on, "That must have been so hard for you."

A raw ghost of a laugh bit at her throat. He had no clue.

After another long moment, he asked, voice careful and calm, "So how did you grow up, then?"

She could've kissed him. The phrasing was so neutral. No implicit questions about a father or a family, no expectations about a kind of life he must've thought she should've led.

She restrained herself. Kissing would be easy; kissing would be fun. It'd just be a distraction.

Shrugging, she unfurled her hand, stroking her fingertips over the exposed lines along the insides of his wrists. "It was just me and my dad." Ripples of low, subverted anger crushed against her ribs, but she kept it in. Kept it just to the facts. "He was…not around a lot, honestly. When he did show up, it was mostly to tell me I was doing something wrong. He's a scientist, too. A professor." And they both knew plenty about what that kind of life was like. "It was a lot of nannies and day care. But none of them stuck around for very long."

His thumbs dug into her skin even harder, but it wasn't like being constrained. It was…grounding. Nice.

"That sounds lonely." Nothing about his tone said he was surprised.

It opened up a tattered place in her heart, one she'd always curled around, teeth bared, biting and ready to defend. She'd never imagined it was anything but obvious. She was such a cliché. Daddy issues and mommy issues, and all of them meshing into the savage scar that was her way of holding the rest of the world at bay.

Right up until now. Until this man—this boy, the one who was so intent on holding on—gently teased her edges apart.

It hurt, trying to keep them closed. All the same, she took a deep breath and stilled her hand inside of his.

He didn't need to know the sad, bitter details. He'd never look at her quite the same if he did. Even her summary statements, the conclusions she'd come to after years and years of living with it all, gave away too much.

But he could have them.

"I think he was really angry is all," she said.

With that, she tried to pull her hand back, but he closed around her, declining to let her go. "About your mom?"

"About everything." His career that was never good enough, and his child who would never be the one he wanted. The life he'd lost on a delivery room floor. "But yeah. I guess..." She worked her jaw and throat, willing the words to come. Because this had been the hardest conclusion of them all to draw. "He must have loved her a lot."

She wasn't sure if she believed it, because it was hard to imagine him loving anybody. But it had sounded good. It had fit the models of families and marriages she'd seen portrayed in movies and on TV. The bereaved widower, silently drowning in his pain while he let everything around him go to hell.

And so she'd told it to herself. That story.

That once upon a time, the hard, cold man she'd shared a house with had been capable of a love so fierce it had destroyed him.

And so what if he hadn't had any of it left for her?

Her eyes burned as she stared down. They were painfully dry, and thank fuck for that much, at least. She didn't need to be putting on some kind of hysterics, and she hadn't cried in such a long, long time. She wasn't sure she still knew how.

"Well," Adam started, consolation pouring from the softness in his tone.

But she didn't want to be consoled. Not with platitudes, not with anyone trying to make the best of the shitty story she'd just served up the barest scraps of. As a child, in her bed alone, she might have been comforted by the idea that her father had once loved the woman she shared half of her genes with. But it didn't change... It didn't stop...

"He always wanted a son." Her throat croaked, because this part *hurt*. "So badly." There wasn't anything to brim over, no dam to break or tears to shed, but her vision swam all the same. "And all he got was me."

The silence of the room echoed in her head. The ventilation system whirred, and computers hummed, and far off in the distance, the nighttime chorus of frogs and other wildlife sang their song. But here in this space, where this man held her hand, everything was eerily, impossibly still.

And then Adam stood. He pushed his chair out and ascended, all the power in those muscles of his making itself known in one graceful movement that left her reeling. She tipped her head up to look at him towering over her, and for a second, an eerie chord of uncertainty twisted in her gut.

But he tugged at her hand, his gaze intense. Not menacing, though, just focused entirely and fully on her. Maybe that was scarier than anything.

"What?" she said as he pulled her from her chair.

"Come on."

"Where are we going?" She hung back as he turned to go, pointing at the monitor. "Your experiment—"

"Still has thirty-two minutes to go."

But seriously, what the hell? Her mind skipped through the evening, and he wasn't...he didn't mean—

She halted him with a firm jerk on his arm. In a hiss, she breathed out, "I am not going to go fuck you in the bathroom."

That stopped him all right. He twisted around to look at her with something like horror on his face, and what *was* that? What did any of this mean?

"Jesus Christ, Jo." He scrubbed his free hand over his face. "Look." He stepped in closer to her, and it was too intimate, too near for this sterile space. "We have time. Just. Please. Come get some air with me, okay? Just air. I promise."

She glanced at the monitors like they could save her. But then she stopped herself. This was Adam.

What exactly did she think she needed saving from?

Trepidation making her skin feel too small, she followed him, not to the rear of the observation area that led toward the offices, but forward. He nodded at the booth where, crap, she hoped Miguel hadn't been watching that entire ridiculous display, and called, "Back in a minute." And then he was pushing through the door onto the deck that looked out over the telescope.

In the distance, far up above, the dome that housed all of the optics and electronics was lit up against the blackness of the sky, silently slewing through the night. And behind it lay the stars.

So many stars.

"Come here."

Adam led her into the shadows, away from the light of the door. She wanted to make another crack about not intending to screw him out here either, but he stopped her with a look. With a hand on her arm.

Putting his back to the wall, he drew her in close to him, her spine to his chest. His arms came up around her, his chin resting on top of her head. It almost made her feel claustrophobic, being tucked in against him like this, surrounded by him and his scent and his warmth.

But it didn't.

"Adam—"

"Just let me hold you. For a minute."

The question came out before she could second-guess it. "Why?"

A low tremor went through him, and he squeezed her tighter.

She closed her eyes. She was missing something here—she was always missing things, and *fuck*. What would it be like to be a real girl? One who understood this kind of stuff?

But then he spoke, voice as raw as her lungs felt. "If you don't know why a person who—a person who cares about you would want to hold you after you said those things..."

She wanted to fill in the blanks. *Then there's no point having this conversation. Then there's no hope for you at all.*

"Then I'm even sorrier," he said. "I'm sorry you had to grow up like that. That you didn't get to know your mom. I'm sorry your dad...I'm sorry he couldn't see how amazing you are. Exactly the way you are."

Opening her eyes, she stared up into a brilliant sky, full of science and distance and things too big for her to understand. And for a moment—one incredible moment—her chest cracked open, and she felt like she was just like those stars.

Infinite, and worth looking at and trying to comprehend.

"I'm sorry," he said again.

"Shh." She turned into him, burying her face against the warm solidity of his frame. And she did exactly what he'd asked of her—the only thing he'd asked of her since she'd begun to speak. She let him hold her.

She'd given him such a tiny glimpse into her history, and he offered her all of this.

What would it be like if she ever told him everything?

Chapter 14

Occasionally, even Jo could appreciate the irony in her behavior.

She eased the front door of the girls' house shut, taking care it didn't make a sound before she stole across the lawn. Adam's light was on, just like he had promised it would be, and flutters went off inside her chest.

Ridiculous. She shook her head at herself and quickened her pace.

Ever since she'd opened up to him the other day, there'd been this restlessness to her limbs, this itch just under her skin. Sharing even as much as she had had left her feeling exposed. Naked.

And here she was. Planning to gain the upper hand again by...well...getting naked. Literally, this time.

She snuck into the guys' house and crept through the deserted living room, past the sliver of light peeking out from under Jared's door. Pausing there for a second, she listened for voices, and maybe that was him and Kim? Either way, it was muffled enough. She kept on going, down to the end of the hall. Adam was expecting her, so she didn't knock.

She found him sitting on his bed in nothing but a pair of

shorts, the muscled flesh of his chest and abdomen gleaming in the low light of his bedside lamp. He looked up from the book in his lap as she closed the door behind her, and his eyes went dark.

In a flash, he set aside the book and clambered off the mattress. Warm hands landed to either side of her face, and his mouth was all eagerness against hers. Something inside her went soft and easy at the heat of his kiss. A girl could get used to a welcome like this—especially the growing ridge of him in his shorts, pressing against her belly and making tingles shoot straight up her spine. Sparking off a low throb of want in her cunt.

She bit down hard on his lip and ate his groan.

Except she *couldn't* get used to this kind of welcome.

If she did, it'd hurt way too much when it was gone.

When she pulled away, he let her go, but not far. His eyes were huge, his pupils blown, and the wet, red fullness of his mouth just made her want to kiss it again and again.

"Hey, there," he mumbled, palms still cupping her face.

"Hey yourself."

"Was starting to wonder if you'd stand me up."

"Never." The word just slipped out, but she didn't even have time to regret it. His answering smile was too gorgeous and too wide.

He slid his hands down her neck, skated them over her arms and to the curves at her sides before resting them firmly on her hips. Sucking his bottom lip between his teeth, he made a soft little hint of a growl. "I've been waiting to get my hands on you all day."

Longer than that, if his antics during their observation run had been any indication. Her mouth went dry. She liked that he didn't try to hide how much he wanted her, how delighted he was by every inch of skin and every touch she gave him.

Heart beating harder, she put her palm to his chest and pushed him a little farther away. Damn, she hoped she was reading this right. She hoped he'd be dying for the touches she *didn't* give him, too.

Releasing his lip, he honest-to-God pouted at her, but he let himself be moved.

"I brought you something," she said as she retreated to his bed. Avoiding his gaze, she dragged her bag into her lap.

"Oh?"

She undid the zipper and pushed her binder out of the way. Her fingertips connected with the velvet pouch she'd smuggled out of her underwear drawer while Carol had been in the bathroom. She took a deep breath and pulled it out. She shook the best little buddy money could buy into her palm and finally looked up. Arched a brow.

"I seem to remember somebody expressing some interest in this."

Jesus, it was hot the way his throat bobbed, the hard line of him swelling beneath his shorts. "Is that what I think it is?"

She pressed the button on the base, and the vibrator hummed to life. Eyes widening, he licked his lips.

She barely recognized his voice, it dipped so deep. "You gonna show me how to use that on you?"

She shook her head, and his eyes actually went wider. "I'm gonna let you watch me use it on myself."

"Fuck." He bit off the word, head falling forward, and he rubbed the heel of his hand over himself. "Jo—"

"Strip."

He didn't hesitate. The button on his shorts popped beneath his fingers, and then he was shoving both them and his underwear down. His cock pulsed, the tip shining, the thick flesh hard enough it looked like it had to hurt, and her clit gave a needy twitch.

All her plans, the things she'd been daydreaming about all goddam day, threatened to waver, because she wanted that in her. Now.

Then again, what kind of plans would they be if they couldn't be adjusted on the fly?

"Don't," she said, when he made to wrap a hand around himself. "I'm going to want that later."

He moaned aloud, fingers curling into fists at his sides. "You're killing me here."

And it was a rush, his letting her take the lead like this. The restlessness that had been plaguing her faded away. She might not be good at feelings, but sex... sex she understood.

"Come on." She motioned with her head toward the spot on the bed beside her.

As she wriggled out of her own clothes, he came to join her, lying down on his side, propped up on one elbow. Vibrator in hand, she lay down, too, flat on her back. Absently, she tugged at the barbell through her nipple and sighed.

Adam cleared his throat. "Is that how you usually start?"

"When I'm by myself?"

His voice was thick. "Yeah."

"Depends." She shrugged, trying to act unaffected, but it was a losing proposition. It had been a couple of days, and all her plotting had gotten her motor running well ahead of time, and now this man was here, all smooth muscle and hot skin.

Really, really hot skin. Sweat prickled at her brow and at the small of her back. He was just pouring off heat against her side, and the fan in the window didn't seem to be doing anything at all.

And then he lifted a hand. Broad fingertips traced the centerline of her body, through the valley between her breasts and lower. At her navel, he turned around, though, and it didn't matter that it was sweltering in here. She shivered into the touch.

"How do you get started, then?"

She plucked harder at her tit, twisting the metal and the flesh and letting out a breath. "Breasts are good. If I need to get myself warmed up. Other times I just go straight for..."

Trailing off, she drifted her hand lower, and her eyes fluttered shut. Fuck, she was soaked. The first glancing touch of her fingertip over her clit had her arching up.

Hot lips pressed to her shoulder, and he swore beneath his breath. "That's even hotter than I thought it would be."

And the man was a genius, because she barely had to twist to the side before his hand was cupping her, the warm flesh of his palm a perfect pressure against her nipple. She dipped a finger inside, spreading her wetness around before going back to her clit. All gentle, circling strokes at first. And then firmer ones.

Adam groaned. "When do you turn it on?"

"Soon." This felt too good right now, this steady rise, this low, rolling pleasure as she got herself primed.

She forced her eyes open, and he was close. Gaze raking over her body, up and down, from his own hand on her breast to hers between her legs.

And she wanted his voice.

"How about you?"

"Me?"

Vibrator still clenched in her fist, she reached over to the side and glanced the backs of her knuckles over the long line of him. The hot, silky flesh. It bobbed toward her, and he let out a shaky breath.

Pushing her hand away, he kissed his way up her neck, to the tender spot beneath her ear where he sucked.

"Well, typically," he said, voice wet, "I find some time to myself. I get myself naked. Maybe slick."

"Oh?"

He swallowed, and the sound went straight to her clit. "Wrap my hand around myself." Then his breath hitched. "Think of you." Oh fuck. She wasn't ready for this, wasn't ready at all, but he was still talking. "Think of you on me or under me. Up against a wall." He sucked on the shell of her ear. "Or sometimes just like this. Touching yourself, and I touch myself, and…"

"And?"

"It gets me so hot. So ready to come."

He wasn't the only one.

Switching the vibrator to her other hand, she pressed the sweet little point of it to her clit and flicked it on.

Her whole body jolted with the first humming rush as it started to buzz. Adam stifled a noise against her throat, and his hand tightened hard on her tit.

"Oh, hell, Jo, that's beautiful. Better than I imagined. You look—"

She shook her head, cutting him off. Darting her free hand up, she grasped the back of his neck and hauled him in, and *fuck*.

She'd never had a problem taking care of her own needs before, but he was here and he felt so good, hot lips and hotter tongue, and she got lost in it, thighs shaking, body straining.

Empty.

She tugged on his hair, and he pulled back from her mouth. "You have about thirty seconds to get in me or I swear—"

He barely even needed ten.

In a flash, he was up and kneeling between her spread thighs, reaching into the drawer of his bedside table for a condom and rolling it on, and then he was there, all that thick, hard flesh filling her up, exactly how she'd needed. She raked her fingernails down his chest, and he fell over her, mouth open, eyes shut tight.

"Fuck, Jo, fuck, you feel—"

"You feel better, I promise." She reeled him back in to kiss those soft, red lips. Bit down his throat and wrapped her legs around his hips. "Come on."

His hips stuttered against hers, but then he was pulling back. The first, fast drive forward hit this tender place inside her. She dug her fingers into the meat of his ass and shifted the toy to a higher setting.

"Yes, that's it," she babbled, "right there."

Getting his arms underneath him, he braced himself and pounded in even deeper.

And fuck him. She'd always been happy enough with just her vibrator before, but this was so much *better*. This was kissing and teeth and her mouth on his chest, the thick rod of his cock fucking her open and the sound of his breath, all those beautiful, pitchy noises he made as he hurtled toward his peak.

"Jo, I'm—"

That was all it took. Orgasm exploded out from her clit and from the depths of her all the way down to her toes. His mouth was on hers, swallowing her moans as he carried her through it, long thrusts that hit her in the best of places, right up until the fog in her mind started to clear, and then he buried his face in the pillow. Another couple of strokes and his whole body tensed.

And she pulsed around him as he groaned her name, pleasure making her stupid, making her crazy. Even crazier than she'd felt before.

Because this was too good. This was amazing.

How had she ever gotten by without it before?

* * *

"Jesus *Christ*," Jo moaned as he flopped to the side. She flicked the vibrator off and let her hand fall to the sheets.

Adam nodded dumbly, staring up at the ceiling. His whole body felt like jelly, his skin slick with sweat. There might be bruises on his hips and ass from how hard she'd dug her fingers in, and there were *definitely* claw marks.

It was awesome.

"Is it actually a million degrees in here? I don't *think* we're in the center of a star, but—"

"I don't know." Adam laughed. Something felt like it had come unstuck in his chest. "I sure as hell saw stars."

She swatted vaguely at his chest. "Not the same thing."

"Oh." Some coherency had returned to his brain, and his gross motor skills seemed to be coming back online. He lurched up and swung one leg over the side of the bed to deal with the condom. Once that was taken care of, he turned to Jo.

She was lying there on her back, naked and fucking gorgeous, hair damp with sweat, breasts glistening. His gaze trailed down—

"Nope. No. Do not get any ideas." She held out a hand in protest, arresting his admiration. She dragged the sheet up to cover all the good bits.

He leaned over her, letting his lips hover just above hers. "I have lots of ideas." Hooking a finger into the top of the sheet, he peered beneath. "Many of them good." Before she could yell at him to stop it, he gave her a quick peck against the corner of her mouth. "Such as going and getting us both about a gallon of ice water."

She actually moaned at that, and it made a bunch of other ideas fight for precedence. She wound her fingers in his hair and dragged him down for a wetter, more open kiss. Then she summarily shoved him away. "I knew I was fucking you for a reason."

Something twisted in his chest, hearing her refer to it so flippantly.

Sure, most of their meetings were after dark. Sure, she still hadn't spent the night. But you didn't tell a guy about your dead mom—didn't let him hold you afterward when it was just fucking.

They might not have a huge amount of time, but Adam was patient. Sooner or later, he was going to get her to see that.

Mock-grumbling, he said, "And I thought it was just because of these." He patted his biceps before peeling his skin from hers and hauling himself from the bed. He dragged on a pair of basketball shorts and turned toward the door. "Back in a sec."

As an afterthought, he strode to the window and grabbed the fan he'd had running on high all night and angled it directly at the bed. The stream of air flowed right over Jo, blowing her hair to the side and rustling the sheets. She melted into the mattress, letting out a throaty moan that had him ready to forget his trip to the kitchen in favor of trying to convince her to stay for round two.

He checked himself. Water. Right.

No matter how much it killed him, he left her there in his bed. Closing the door behind him just in case, he padded out into the house. With every step, his mind drifted further off into what he wanted to do to her next. How he wanted to have her, how he wanted to take her apart. They had all night; they practically had the house to themselves. He could...

He made it almost to the kitchen before he realized his mistake.

The light over the stove was on. And there were people talking. Hushed and laughing and maybe a little bit slurred.

"Shh, shh," a male voice hissed, "no, be quiet. Maybe he's just going to the bathroom—"

He rounded the corner, his stomach sinking. And there were Jared and Kim and a deck of cards. And what used to be a bottle of rum.

Oh, hell.

"Too late," Kim mumbled, her hand over her mouth, her gaze on Adam.

Jared snuck an exaggerated, faux-stealthy peek over his shoulder and whispered, "Oh, shit." Then they let out another round of giggles, and Jared turned around for real, his expression sloppy and his arms wide. Speaking louder now, he addressed Adam as if noticing him for the first time. As if they hadn't just been talking about him. "Adam! We didn't know you were up!"

Like hell they hadn't. He and Jo hadn't exactly been quiet. But it was after one in the morning, and on a Thursday night, and he and Jo had been the only ones pulling graveyard shifts with the telescope. Nobody else was supposed to be awake. His heart thundered in his chest. What if they'd heard? What if—

His stream of thought stopped itself in its tracks as he really took them in.

He furrowed his brow, quirking his head to the side. "Are you guys wearing…swimsuits?"

Kim struck a pose. "We're going to the beach on Saturday!"

Yes, yes, they were. Well, the group was going. Adam was going. And he really needed to ask Jo if she was, too.

Still…"But you're wearing your swimsuits now."

"And you are, too," Jared said.

"These are my running shorts." Adam glanced down at himself, ready to point out just how different his bottoms were from swim trunks. Only his gaze caught on his own chest. And his words stuck in his throat.

He hadn't been wrong about Jo, back when he'd fantasized that she might be a biter. They'd been good and kept most of their marks to places that would be covered by their shirts, but he wasn't wearing one right now.

A misplaced surge of arousal moved through him. He wanted to press his fingers to the line of purpling bruises she'd made with her mouth. There wasn't any mistaking what they were.

He swallowed hard. Maybe Jared and Kim were drunk enough they wouldn't notice. If they did, maybe they'd forget.

Then, from down the hall, he heard a door open.

"What's taking you so long?" Jo whisper-yelled into the night.

Adam dug his thumb into his eye, pulling it away just in time to catch her coming down the hall. Wrapped in a sheet.

It all happened in slow motion. He needed to stop her, tell her to stay put, but even that would be evidence she was here. She came into view, and everything went silent.

He knew her well enough now. The tick in her jaw and the way her fingers tightened in the fabric. He steeled himself for the worst.

But she didn't freak out. She looked at him with an expression he couldn't decipher, and then at their two friends slumped over the table. "You both look ridiculous," she said, neutral as anything.

She crossed the room to the cabinet to pull down two glasses, then got them filled without dropping the sheet. As they all gawked, she handed one of the glasses to Adam and then marched down the hall toward his room.

Adam locked gazes with Jared and Kim in turn. Without another word, he turned on his heel, following after Jo, his heart in his throat.

Sure enough, back in his room, she'd flung the sheet off and was stepping into her underwear.

He held up his hands in front of him. "I swear, I had no idea they were up."

"Their light was on when I came in. I should have remembered." She let out a dry echo of a laugh and a bitten-off, "Stupid."

She hadn't so much as paused in her efforts to get redressed, and something in his chest went cold.

He reached out and grabbed her shirt off the floor as she dragged on her shorts. When she recognized he had her top, she moved for it, but he held it out of reach. Because he was an asshole with a death wish. "Jo. I'm sorry."

She rocked on her heels, deflating. Then sagged to sit on the edge of the bed, dragging her hand through her hair and pushing it off her face. Her voice didn't sound so guarded this time, so jagged. "I know. It's fine."

He…didn't know what to do with that. Because she didn't sound like she was lying. "It is?"

"Honestly?" She looked up at him, dropping her hand and bracing her elbows on her knees. "Kim guessed we were fucking even back before we were."

Oh. *Oh.*

He stood there speechless for a second. Kim had known. Had everyone known?

Something inside him twisted. Then why had Jo been so opposed to the idea of staying here with him?

She held out her hand for her shirt, and this time he forked it over. He didn't know what to do with his hands. With his whole body.

"Christ," Jo said, shaking her head. "Come here."

Dumbly, he joined her on the bed.

She covered his hand with hers and repeated, "Seriously, it's fine."

"I thought you didn't want anyone to know."

"I said we'd never be able to keep it a secret. I just didn't want to be treated like everyone knew. Like I was...that girl."

"Oh." He'd understood that, he really had. But all that secrecy hadn't exactly been real, had it? Now their relationship—arrangement, whatever it was—was even more out in the open than it had been. And her response to that had been to put on her clothes. Intertwining their fingers, he gazed down at where his thumb stroked over her knuckles and tried not to let his disappointment show. "You're still not staying over, though, are you? Even now that they really know."

"Adam..."

It was his turn to say, "It's fine. I was just wondering. That's all."

After a moment, she touched his face. "You're a terrible liar." She said it fondly, like it was something she recognized about him and didn't mind.

"Don't have a lot of practice, I suppose."

She leaned in and pressed a kiss to his cheek, just a hair from the corner of his mouth. "Another night."

"Sure."

With that, she pulled away and got her shirt on. Rose to grab her socks and boots, too.

When she was dressed to go, he nodded at the door. "They're still out there, you know?"

"Yeah. I know." She laughed. The sound made the tension

shiver in the air, parting just a little. "What the hell were they wearing anyway?"

"Swimsuits. They were, uh, getting ready for the beach trip this weekend. I think." He considered for a second, then shrugged. "That or just being drunk. It was kind of hard to tell."

"Yeah..." She glanced down, trailing off.

"Are you going?" They were heading to the southern coast of the island, just an hour and a half or so by car. It wouldn't keep her from the lab for too long.

And he wanted to see her. Out in the sand and sun, swimming in the ocean. He wanted to kiss the salt from her skin.

In front of everyone.

She frowned, and his shoulders sank. "I don't know. I don't have a swimsuit. And all that sun." She made a face. "I'll burn."

He latched on to that not-quite-no. "I have an extra pair of trunks. Tie the drawstring tight and I bet they'd fit you."

"Only half the issue."

"I've seen you go swimming in a sports bra before."

She gave a little shiver. Because, right, she hadn't meant for him to see that. She hadn't meant for him to pull her out of the water she'd gotten herself into. "I'd still burn."

"I'll loan you sunscreen. Rub it on your back for you and everything." He was pressing. He'd always said he wouldn't press with her.

Still, he found himself rising to his feet. With every step he took toward her, she took a half step away until she was flush against the door and staring up at him. She didn't look cornered, though.

He grazed his finger down her cheek, his voice going husky as he stood before her. "Come to the beach. With me." And this was the real killer. "Let me kiss you in the ocean." *In front of our friends.*

They already knew. Everyone knew.

He wanted them to know.

"Maybe?"

"Maybe you'll come, or maybe you'll let me kiss you?"

"Which do you care about more?"

He didn't know. Closing the last of the distance between them, he bent down, got in her space. Let his forehead brush hers, his lips hovering close enough to feel her breath. With one hand on the door and one at her side, he asked, "Will you?"

She closed her eyes. But when she opened them again, she said, "Okay."

Chapter 15

Well. The one thing Jo could say about Adam's spare set of swimming trunks was that they probably looked worse on him than they did on her.

They were bright red, and they came to just below the knee on her, so they must have been unflatteringly short on him. And she knew his waist was trim—she'd had her hands around it as she pushed him into a mattress before. But she didn't realize it was this trim.

She tugged at the draw cord all the same. She'd tied it plenty tight and didn't really think the things were going anywhere. But she couldn't help worrying. She couldn't stop worrying about a lot of things.

She shouldn't have come.

The soles of her boots dug into her thighs as she tucked them underneath herself, trying to find a comfortable way to sit on the sand. Even under the shade of the umbrella one of their escorts had had the foresight to bring, it was scorching hot. Stifling enough she almost wanted to take off her shirt.

But Adam had talked her into the whole sports bra and swimming trunks thing. And she looked ridiculous.

Face burning from more than just the heat, she cast her gaze out across the glittering white expanse of beach before her. A couple of the other girls had lingered away from the water as well, but they were wearing bikinis and luxuriating in the sun. Out in the water, looking deliciously cool and comfortable, Adam and Jared were horsing around, tossing a beach ball back and forth. Pretty much everyone else was out there, too.

Letting go of the drawstring of her trunks, she fiddled with the zipper of her bag. Adam hadn't said anything about her bringing a book with her; he'd even stayed quiet about her sneaking in her binder, too. But even she knew it was crazy to spend a day at the beach like that. It was simple instinct, though. How many lunches had she spent with her nose buried in a set of calculations? Pretending she wasn't watching everybody else letting go and having fun?

"You know, 'sand between your toes' is an expression for a reason."

Jo let go of her bag and jerked her head up. Heather of all people plunked herself down beside her, and Jo sucked in a breath. Sure, some people socialized with their advisors, but Jo wasn't some people. Hadn't she proven that yet enough?

It was just her luck that Heather *and* Lisa had volunteered to be chauffeurs/chaperones for this particular field trip. Roberto had the day off, and Dr. Galloway was busy getting things ready for some hotshot visiting scientists. And so both her and Adam's bosses had decided to tag along.

She hadn't even been able to let herself sit next to Adam in the van. Not with the two of them looking.

"Sounds overrated to me," Jo said, before casting her gaze out across the water.

Heather bumped her shoulder against Jo's, and Jo just about went out of her skin. The touch was so casual, like it was nothing to press past the bubble of space she projected out around herself, and something inside Jo felt like it was crumbling. "Don't knock it until you've tried it."

Jo crossed her arms over her chest.

A moment of silence passed before Heather asked, "Have you ever been in the ocean before?"

Jo shook her head. When would she have had the chance? She'd grown up landlocked, had ended up going to college in Chicago. It wasn't as if there'd been a lot of family vacations when she was a kid.

Quieter this time, Heather said, "Then maybe you should give it a shot."

"I don't know…"

"Why did you decide to come today?"

Wasn't that the question of the hour? Despite her reservations, their outing to the rain forest had been more than worth it. Maybe she'd hoped this would be the same.

Maybe she hadn't been able to resist the heat in Adam's gaze as he'd pressed her up against the door and asked her.

He looked so good, out there amid the waves. The bronzed musculature of his chest glowed in the sun, the darkened mop of his hair slicked back against his skull.

"Peer pressure," she settled on. "Mostly."

Heather hummed. "Yeah. If he'd asked me to go somewhere, I don't know if I could have resisted, either."

Forget the heat. Forget everything else. The pit of Jo's stomach flashed with ice. She turned, following Heather's gaze, and sure enough, she was staring at Adam. Her mouth twisted with a knowing smile.

Shit. Jo blinked hard and flexed her jaw. "Does everyone know?"

"Nah. A few suspect, maybe. But you've been playing it pretty cool. Him, on the other hand?"

"Oh."

Heather's voice went soft and warm. "If you could see the way he looks at you..."

Only Jo had. She'd caught him more than once. He'd been completely unguarded about it, gazing at her with a deepness to his eyes.

"Plus," Heather added, "he's started to come over here about a dozen times, only he keeps stopping himself."

Right. He'd been trying to abide by her wishes. Sure, Kim had always known, and she and Jared had gotten more than enough confirmation a couple of nights ago. But their advisors. The scientists they work with...

"We were trying to be discreet."

"Oh, please. Picking out which summer interns are hooking up is a national pastime around here. It's the most fun we get all year."

Off in the distance, Adam's head swiveled around, and it was just like Heather had described. His gaze sought her out. It wasn't easy to see from where she sat, but Jo knew his expressions well enough by now.

Nudging her with her elbow again, Heather said, "Do what you want, Jo. But if I were you, I would be taking as much advantage of that as I could. There's more to life than just work." With that, she stood, dusting the sand off her legs as she went to rejoin the rest of the grown-ups beneath another umbrella a respectable distance away.

Alone again, Jo tried to force her breathing deeper. But it wasn't any use. Around her, the world was twisting on its axis.

She'd come to this island dressed in anger, convinced she was being passed over for a choice assignment on account of her gender. She'd taken a guy who was only trying to help—one she'd since learned could be so tender—and she'd literally thrown him on account of some misguided fear, some reflex.

She'd been letting that same fear guide her ever since.

Had she ever *not* been operating on fear?

The spots in her vision faded, resolving the space around her into hues that seemed even more vivid than they had just a moment before. Bright white sand and the red of her borrowed shorts. Ocean blue and Adam blond. Adam eyes and Adam flesh. And beyond him, a sky that stretched out into infinity, an atmosphere of limitless colors, illuminated by a single star.

It was literally night and day versus the last time she'd stared up at the heavens in wonder. Wrapped in Adam's arms, still shaking from the revelations she'd made to him about her mother, she'd cast her gaze skyward. For the first time, she'd allowed the possibility she might deserve more.

And here she was, eyes blinded by brilliance instead of darkness, considering almost the exact same thing.

More was out there, swimming freely in the water. More had sunlight dancing off his shoulders. More kept looking her way and waiting for her to join him. All she had to do was stop being afraid to.

For one long, aching moment, she rested her forehead on her knees.

Then with trembling fingers, she reached out and unlaced her boots. When her bare feet touched the sand, she let out a single, cut-off fragment of a laugh. Heather had been right enough. The sand squished between her toes, cool beneath the umbrella's shade and searing hot beyond it.

She'd scarcely gotten to her feet, scarcely begun to lift the hem of her shirt before Adam was jogging up the beach toward her. And it wasn't even fair. He looked like something out of a movie, or from television, and here she was. Looking like this.

"Hey." He came to a stop before her, grinning widely. Water droplets slid in rivulets down his chest. "Are you coming in?"

"Thinking about it." She was thinking about a lot of things. Casting her gaze aside, she fingered the edge of her shirt again. Quietly, she asked, "You sure I won't look ridiculous?"

"You'll look perfect." He put a hand on her shoulder, ducking to put them eye to eye. "You'll look like you."

Fuck her if he didn't sound as if he actually believed that.

She wanted to laugh, just as much as she wanted to shove her boots on and go hide in the van for the rest of the day. Unwilling to actually do either, she brushed her hair off her face and shook her head.

"Here," he said, crouching to reach for his pack, which he'd left in a pile with the rest of them. "I promised I'd sunscreen your back."

It was a relief, not having him looking right at her as she stripped. He probably knew that. Still, she hesitated. "You're supposed to put it on at least fifteen minutes before you go out there, you know."

"Then we'll dawdle here for as long as you think we have to."

He rummaged through his bag for what seemed like an awfully long time, and she stood there, dumbstruck, until she remembered what she was supposed to be doing.

And it wasn't any big deal. Adam had seen her naked plenty of times at this point. She was wearing shorts that covered her to her knee, and her sports bra was almost a tank top. It was just her shoulders and a little bit of midriff. And cleavage and arms and…

Fuck it. She closed her eyes and tugged her shirt over her

head. Her heart stuttered, and she held her breath. But when she looked again, nothing had changed. The world had kept on spinning. Their advisors still sat a stone's throw away, talking amongst themselves, while the rest of their friends played in the waves or lounged in the sun. No one looked their way.

No one cared. And it was the biggest, most impossible *relief.*

* * *

Jo was strangely still beneath Adam's hands as he massaged the sunscreen into the skin of her arms. She was even paler than he was, and she probably would burn if they didn't follow the instructions to the letter. Protectiveness surged inside him, telling him to take care of her however he could. But there was also an instinct to get her down the beach and into the water right now.

She felt so *good*, and she'd look even better out there in the surf, salty and wet, black and blue hair shining bright in the midday sun. The bra she was wearing would keep her covered, but once it got wet, he bet he'd be able to make out her piercing through the fabric. The shapeless, too-long trunks hanging off her hips would cling to her skin.

Kind of like his own shorts were clinging to him, and he really needed to start thinking about other things before he gave the game away but good.

Who could blame him, though, getting a little excited while rubbing her down like this? Maybe her kludged-together suit wasn't as revealing as what some of the other girls were wearing, but he hadn't been lying. It was the kind of swimming getup she looked like she belonged in. And that was more than enough of a turn-on for him.

Slathering his hands again, he coated her shoulders before

shifting to stand behind her. And he had to stop—for a second he had to squeeze his eyes shut tight, smoothing the cream into her neck entirely too thoroughly to buy himself some time.

When he'd gotten himself under control again, he opened his eyes and swallowed a groan.

The bra blocked the upper half of her tattoo, but this was still the best look he'd gotten of it. The lines of ink twisted and curled around the top of her spine, tendrils of it spilling out toward her arms. He'd been right about it being an animal of some sort, maybe a dragon or a lion, legs with talons or paws standing strong beneath the line of her bra.

"Adam?"

He bit the inside of his lip and forced his hands to move again, slipping his fingertips just under the elastic around her shoulder blades.

"Is everything okay?" she asked.

He made a pained noise, and she started to turn around. He dropped his hands, grasped her waist, the skin slick with sweat and lotion. And he was trying so hard to be good.

Pressing his brow to the top of her head, he exhaled long and slow. "I am having a very, very difficult time not throwing you over my shoulder and finding a dark corner somewhere to take this"—he snapped her bra strap—"off of you."

"Oh."

"Your tattoo looks so gorgeous. You look so goddamn sexy. I know you're trying to keep this quiet." He drew in another, sharper breath. "But I cannot explain to you how much restraint is involved in keeping this PG right now."

She went very still, just the expansion and contraction of her ribs beneath his fingertips even betraying that she was alive. A low, deep fear rose inside of him.

Maybe this was Shannon all over again. A girl who didn't want as much from him as he wanted from her. Maybe this was him, building something up inside his mind.

Cursing himself, he squared his jaw and took a step back. With mechanical motions, he finished rubbing the last of the sunblock into the flesh at the dip of her spine, then made to pull away entirely.

Except she caught him. Closing her hand around his wrists, she held him where he was, and his heart lurched. Ever so slowly, she turned around to face him.

And maybe this wasn't what he'd thought it was at all. Maybe it was *better*.

Her eyes were darkened with a wanting he could recognize well enough by now, but her mouth had that stubborn set to it. Like she was about to tell him off for waiting to be loved, like she was about to tell *everyone* off for having gotten to this island based on their connections. Like she was about to kiss him.

He held his breath. But then she was reaching up, settling her forearms on his shoulders to clasp her hands behind his neck. He gripped her by the hips, trying like hell not to get the wrong idea. She eased up onto her tiptoes.

Leaning in close to his ear, she whispered, "There's a pier, maybe a quarter of a mile down the shore."

"Excuse me?"

"Looked like a dark corner to me." She inched back so he could see her face, one of her eyebrows wickedly arched.

"Oh." Just like that, his breath returned to him.

"For later. Just so you know."

He could so get behind that idea.

Just like he could get behind the way she was closing in, the way her lips approached his, and her eyes closed.

And yet he made her close the gap, standing motionless but for the press of his thumbs into her hip bones. She was the one with all the reservations, all the restrictions. If she wanted this, she'd have to take it. And then he'd give her everything he had in return.

She kissed him, gentle and slow and in the broad light of day, and it was his heart restarting, blood pulsing fast into every one of his cells. His hesitation fell away, and he hauled her in, lifting her and spinning her and claiming her mouth exactly how he'd been longing to since the very first day. She tasted hot and filthy, like sex and want and something so much more—something better because she'd offered it to him. Here. Where he'd thought he'd never have it.

And he was so damn glad. So happy.

She broke the kiss after a few long, heart-pounding moments, but he kept her, safe in his arms and flush against his chest. With a growl in his throat, he nipped at her jaw and then her ear, just to hear her laugh and feel her squirm.

"You sure you want to hold on to that whole dark corner idea for later?" he asked.

Swatting at his head, she hugged him back, those lean, strong arms of hers wrapping around his shoulders as if she didn't want to let go, either. She did, though, and a whole lot sooner than he'd have liked her to. "Put me down, you lug."

"You sure?"

"Yeah." The words came out a shade too serious, too soft.

He let her go, setting her on her feet on the sand. Grasping his hand, she gazed up at him, eyes just as tender as her voice had been.

"Take me into the ocean with you?"

She said it like she wasn't sure if he'd say yes.

He squeezed her palm. "Happily."

With her hand secure in his, he led them down the beach. The scorching sand beneath their toes pulled a squeak out of her, and he grinned, tugging her along faster until they hit an all-out sprint. At the shoreline, cool dampness eased the burn. "You ready?" he asked, facing the surf.

Nodding, she took the first step. He watched her as she slipped her feet into the ocean, an unusual tentativeness guiding her movement. But her eyes were bright, her smile unguarded in a way it rarely was. Until the water lapped at her knees and they hit the jagged patch of rocks and shells. She winced, her steps faltering.

"It's just a few feet of this." He pointed to where the rest of the gang played in the waves. "Just a little farther and it all goes smooth again."

"If I get stung by a jellyfish or step on a sea urchin…"

"I'll carry you to shore."

Grumbling, she said, "And this is why I never go barefoot anywhere."

As promised, the way eased quickly enough. "There. Better?"

"Something just touched my leg."

"Probably seaweed. You're fine."

"Are you sure?"

"Absolutely."

He stopped them there, still a little ways off from everyone else. The water came up past his waist, the low rocking of the waves sliding in toward shore making them sway.

He turned to her. Rested his free hand at her hip and ducked to put them face-to-face. "Are you okay?"

"Fine."

"Fine-fine, or fake fine?"

She narrowed her eyes at him, and that right there made him feel a little better. He looked her up and down. Then with his arm, he jostled her. "Loosen up a bit."

She snickered. "Not exactly my strong point."

Arching a brow suggestively, he grinned. "I've seen you loosen up plenty."

She huffed. "Very specific circumstance."

"Well, pretend it's the circumstance right now." He put his palm on her hip. "Let the waves move you."

She scowled, but her posture softened. Transcribing his every movement, he drew her in closer until her breasts brushed his chest. Their legs tangled beneath the water.

Heat pooled low in his gut.

"See?" he asked, mouth close to hers. "Isn't that better?"

"I suppose…" She pushed off the bottom, rising with the swelling of the tide. Her thigh slid against him, slipping between his knees.

His hindbrain had him reacting. He curled his arms around her. She was so warm, so soft in his arms, there in the sun and the calm cool of the ocean. He trailed his lips along her cheek, giving her plenty of room to stop him. She didn't.

The kiss tasted of summer and salt, and he glided his hands up and down the bare expanses of her back and shoulders as he licked into her mouth. She wrapped her legs around his waist, and he scraped his teeth against her lip.

They were getting carried away, and fast.

His voice came out gravelly as he forced himself to break the kiss. "I thought you wanted to spend some time in the water?"

"I do." Her hips ground into his, and he hissed at the relief—pleasure and torment all at once—before grasping her more tightly. Stilling her.

"I really don't think you want me to take you up on that."

As if to underscore his point, laughter from just behind them interrupted the quiet bubble they'd dropped themselves into. She glanced over his shoulder and sighed. "You're probably right."

He twisted to follow her gaze. Kim sat atop Jared's shoulders, hands clasped with Carol's, who was riding Anna. Struggling, Carol shrieked. Their kicking churned the water.

Jared noticed Adam and Jo, nodding at them cockily from between Kim's thighs. "You guys want winner?" he called.

For fuck's sake.

Adam nudged at Jo, prompting her to unwind herself from around him. Getting himself some breathing room. Looking to her, he asked, "What do you say?"

"What the hell are they doing?" Jo's forehead was all scrunched, her mouth confused.

Oh, this was going to be fun. "What? You've never been in a chicken fight before?"

"A *what* fight?"

That decided that. "Come on." He took her hand again and led her into deeper waters.

They'd nearly reached the rest of them when, with a squeal, Carol toppled over, falling from Anna's shoulders. She came up spitting seconds later while Kim raised her hands in the air in triumph. Jared squeezed her thighs, beaming up at her before turning to Jo and Adam.

"You guys up for this?" Jared asked.

"Hell, yeah, we are." Adam grabbed Jo, unsurprised when she flinched.

"Um, *no.*"

"It'll be fine." He lowered himself so his shoulders sank beneath the surface of the water. "Just climb on board. It's easy."

"You have got to be kidding me." She came up behind him despite her protests.

He took it as the closest to permission he was going to get. "Hop up." Hooking one hand under her leg, he gave her a boost, while with the other he plugged his nose and dropped down.

He held his breath as he got her situated. She clawed at his hair, clambering and sliding slick skin over skin as she fought her way onto his shoulders. When he rose above the surface again, it was to a chorus of noises he had never heard from her before.

"What do I *do*?" It was nearly a wail.

He sluiced the water from his face, shoving his wet hair back before grabbing her legs and holding them to his chest. "Just lean forward. You're fine. You got this."

"I don't know—"

"I do."

He didn't care if they won or lost. She was here with him, on the most beautiful sort of day, in front of their friends. A couple.

A team.

Before Jo could protest any further, he located Kim and Jared in the water. "Okay, no big. You just lock hands with Kim and try to shove her off."

"But—"

"No one gets hurt. Jared's got her and I've got you. Whoever falls just ends up wetter."

"You sure?"

"Positive."

He stood a couple of feet from Jared.

"Oh, man, you're going down," Jared says.

Maybe. But either way, Adam was pretty sure he won.

Still looking hesitant as hell, Jo took Kim's hands. Jared counted off. As soon as he got to three, all hell broke loose, water everywhere. Jo may have been out of her element, but the girl was a fighter, both on land and at sea.

And she was gorgeous. Wet and half naked and sitting astride him, her thighs closed tight around his ears. Bare arms glistening, teeth bared.

Just as soon as it had begun, it was over. Jo gave a particularly savage twist, and Kim screamed before toppling, taking Jared with her. Adam whooped, gazing up at Jo, whose smile lit the whole damn world.

Instead of issuing any additional challenges, Jo released her grip on him, widening her legs to slip down his body. He swiveled with her fall, coming to meet her face-to-face and nose to nose. Lip to lip.

And suddenly they were right back there, curled around each other, the simmering heat of holding her and touching her like this bringing desire screaming to life.

"Good job," he said, tugging her close.

"I had a good partner."

With that, she threaded a hand through his hair and tugged him down and kissed him. He was done worrying about the world around them or about who might see or what they might think. He'd *been* done with that, and she was clearly right there with him now. Around them, whistling and catcalls erupted, but he didn't care.

She jerked away, eyes hooded, fingernails digging into his scalp. "Want to go find that dark corner somewhere?"

They'd been building up to it all day. And yet, as he gripped her ass and wound her leg around his hips, all he could say was, "I thought you'd never ask."

Chapter 16

Jo was scarcely listening as Adam made their excuses. All she could hear was the buzzing in her ears, the rush of blood through her veins overriding the hum of the surf. The sounds of the people around her faded into white noise.

She'd just...Fuck, what had she done? She'd kissed this man, this boy who stripped her of so many of her defenses, in front of her boss and her colleagues and the world. She'd let him lead her out beyond her comfort zone in every possible sense of the words.

She'd put her feet in the ocean. And she hadn't even come close to drifting away.

Now, with the memory of his head between her legs, his shoulders strong and firm beneath her thighs, she took his hand. Leaving yet more chatter behind them, they traversed the tricky layer of shells beaten into the sand, emerging out to a point where they were scarcely wading. The tide pulled at the sand beneath her toes with every lap of the waves. And yet she remained on solid ground.

Only after they'd gotten a decent ways off did she find her voice again, the noises of the world filtering back in.

"What did you even say to them?"

He cast her an uncertain look but didn't question her. Maybe he was just as far gone as she was. Driven by lust, if not by the tangled exhilaration of letting go. Of not keeping her distance anymore.

"Just that we were going to walk along the beach a little. Maybe see if we can find something to eat."

It was a flimsy excuse at best. There were carts all over the place peddling empanadillas and ice cream. They really didn't need to go very far to find one of them.

She felt a little light-headed as she asked, "Do you even have your wallet?"

"No. But they don't need to know that."

She considered that for a second, alarm bells sounding. "Wait. Do you have *anything*?"

She'd told him that very first night she always kept a condom on her, but without her pack or her boots or real pants—

His voice took a low tone that told her he knew exactly what she was asking him. "I promise. I have everything we need."

A heady tension thrummed through her, and she shifted closer, letting him slip his arm around her. The hot, wet press of his skin made her heart go into overdrive, tingles flowing inward from every place they touched.

The beach hadn't exactly been crowded even over on the prime real estate they'd staked out for their umbrellas and blankets. As they neared the pier, the shore got rockier, the waves choppier. The place more deserted.

Perfect.

She cast a glance over her shoulder as they fell beneath the shadow of the structure. The rest of their group was far enough off that she couldn't tell if they were looking or not, but even if they were, she doubted they could see. None of the strangers on the beach paid them any mind.

And it was a good thing, too. They'd barely passed the first pylon before Adam was tugging her along behind it, slamming her back against the wood.

"Don't you want—" She gestured farther into the cover the pier provided.

"You. I just want you." With that, he captured her lips and stole her breath.

She'd thought their kisses out in the water had been building toward something, but she'd had no idea they were building toward *this*. Those embraces had been all slow sensuality and the warmth of contact, out where anyone could see.

They were still only barely hidden, but these were kisses of a different kind, harsh and impatient. He must've been keyed up as hell for the dam to break so spectacularly, now they were alone.

It didn't take her long to catch up.

His hands seemed to be everywhere, tugging at the sodden fabric of her top, kneading her breasts through the cotton and plucking at her nipple ring, coaxing the peaks into stiff, aching points. She groaned aloud as he hoisted her up. He pinned her with his hips and kissed his way down her throat, probably leaving marks. All she could do was wrap her legs around his hips and hold on.

"Jesus." She got her hands into his hair and thumped her head against the wooden post behind her.

"You have no idea." His teeth bit into her collarbone. "Seeing you out there, getting to kiss you in front of everyone. Showing you off."

It was male pride at its worst, and damn, fuck, she loved it in a way she'd never thought she ever would.

She closed her eyes. "Yeah, because I'm such a prize."

"You are." His fingers fumbled with the drawstring of her trunks, the ridiculous, shapeless things she'd worn because she was too stubborn to let her colleagues see her bikini line.

"I look like a lesbian." She raked her nails across the nape of his neck as he snuck a hand between them, a sudden pressure exactly where she needed it, almost too intense. She sucked in a gasp before biting out, "Not that there's anything wrong with that."

He lifted his head, gaze fierce. "You look so fucking sexy I wanted to take you on the beach and in the water. In front of all our friends."

She hadn't doubted his sincerity before. But the way he said it now, his voice rasping, hands clutching, the evidence of just how hard he was for her pressed against the hollow of her hip…

Something that had been coiled so tightly inside of her unfurled. Blossoming.

How long had she said she didn't care what anybody thought of her? It hadn't been a lie, but the acceptance in his voice cracked her open. Made that lack of caring into something new.

Made her free.

With a sharp tug at his hair, she hauled him up to her. His mouth was hotter than the day or the air or even the sun, his tongue a soft, slick caress between her lips, probing inside the way she wanted *him* inside. With his hand in her trunks, he slipped his fingers up and down her slit, nudging at her clit only to slide back to her opening, blunt pressure there to spread her wetness around.

"God, stop teasing me."

"It's called foreplay."

"Overrated." It was such a lie, but she didn't care. "Come on."

She bit her way to his ear. "Don't you want to fuck me?" She looked around them at the ocean just past their feet. Listened to the sounds of people walking above them on the pier. "Here? Where anyone could see?"

He made a noise that sounded like it'd been punched out of his chest. He tapped her thigh in warning so she could get her feet underneath her before he set her down. Then it was a mad scramble, her getting the trunks the rest of the way unfastened and shoved off her hips. For the first time, she regretted not wearing a normal bathing suit, the skimpy kinds of bottoms a girl could push to the side.

Adam took a more optimistic view. "Not that I don't love your boots…" He'd fished a condom from wherever it'd been hidden in his suit and tore it open with his teeth. "But damn it's nice not having to stop to get you out of them."

"Don't get used to it."

The trunks landed on the sand with a damp splat, and that was all the time she got before he had her up against the beam again. He pulled himself out of his own suit, giving his length a couple of rough, quick strokes before rolling the condom on.

And then he was lifting her, pressing her spine to the wood. She wrapped her arms around his neck and hooked her ankles at his ass. With one hand, he held her up, while with the other he guided himself, putting the head of his cock right against her cunt, gliding it through her liquid. Still being so goddamn careful.

She kicked him, trying to force him to move.

His gaze met hers and he asked, "You sure?"

"I swear to God—"

Whatever threat she'd been about to pull out died in her lungs as he finally, finally thrust forward. Her eyes rolled back in her head at the sudden stretch. The rough pleasure of being filled the way she needed to.

He buried his forehead against her shoulder, his big body tremoring. She was just this side of wet enough and open enough, but that made it all the better. The rough, tight fit that felt like it had brought him to his knees. Stroking her hands up and down his spine, she murmured encouragement against his ear. Little filthy things about how good he felt inside her, how strong his hands were on her flesh as he held her up, supported her. Fucked her. "Come on, baby," she breathed. "Doesn't it feel nice?"

He gave another shiver before lifting his head. The dampness on his skin was his sweat and the sea, and his eyes burned. "You feel incredible."

He drew back only to slide right in again, the whole movement easier this time, slicker, and she moaned. A half dozen or so strokes, and a slight shift of his hips shot sparks up and down her spine, grinding his pubic bone against her clit.

She arched forward to meet his thrust, chasing that pleasure, raking her nails over his flesh. "Fuck. Do that again."

"This?" He pressed into her harder, and the sparks turned into flames.

"Yeah, God." She squeezed the nape of his neck, rocking into the shallow movements of his body into hers, riding the tide as they sped and lengthened. She tightened her thighs around his waist. "Come *on*," she urged. No foreplay, and she was already spinning out of control; she just needed a little more, a little harder. She whined and tugged at his hair.

He made a grunting sound that went straight to her clit. The hand that wasn't on her ass slammed into the wood above her head. He shifted his stance.

And with that, he started to fuck her in earnest.

It was exactly what she had been waiting for. Sure, she liked to be the one on top in general, but his strength intoxicated her, and she'd already given up so much. What was a little more? She was at his mercy like this, pinned by his hips and held in place. Taken.

Safe.

He dropped his head, pressing his brow to hers. He was watching every movement, every expression that flickered across her face, and she let him have them all.

He lowered his arm to brush her jaw. "Come on, beautiful."

And it was too intimate, too much for any situation, much less for having sex up against a wall. But it was that echoing *beautiful* in the hot ocean air, the quiet, claiming kiss he laid upon her mouth while his thrusts met just the perfect place inside her—

Her vision whited out when she came, and he followed right after, spilling out a groan that was only her name.

Through it all, through the shudders of pleasure and the sudden slackness that came after climax, he never relaxed his grip. He took her weight and held her up.

And what was more, she let him.

* * *

Absently running his fingers through Jo's hair, Adam stared out the window of the van at the dim silhouettes of palm trees passing by. He was surrounded by faint strains of music and hushed laughter, all muted by the rushing of cool, wet air flowing in through the open windows. Above the tree line, the stars were just beginning to rise.

It had been a good day. Maybe one of the best.

He glanced down at Jo. The edges of her face were cast in the glow from her book light, and sure, maybe she was spending the trip with her nose buried in her work, but she was choosing to do it with her shoulder tucked under his arm, her whole side pressed against him.

It was a stark contrast to the distance she'd kept from him earlier in the day, refusing to even sit near him with their advisors watching on. He didn't know what had changed her mind. Only that Heather had sat down beside her on the beach, and after that, she'd stood with this intentness to her gaze. She'd let him kiss her in front of everyone, had practically asked him to take her down the beach and then to *take* her. His sex life in the past had been fulfilling enough, but he'd never been so overcome like that, so wanton.

God. His heart squeezed, just thinking about the way they'd connected there beneath the pier. She'd been so gorgeous and unselfconscious, wet suit stuck to her breasts, her arms and legs wrapped around him, consuming him as he'd lost his mind, staring into her eyes and pressing into her, deep inside where she was warm and perfect and accepting. Holding on to him exactly the way he wanted to be held, making him feel strong and wanted and … well.

She might not love him yet. She might not ever. But he wasn't going to kid himself about the warm rush he felt every time he looked at her, the cracking feeling in his ribs with every step she made to meet him in the middle. Every additional inch she let him in.

And she'd let him get so far today. Not just the kissing and the hand-holding and the sex. Even after they'd reassembled themselves, she'd stayed more or less by his side the rest of the afternoon. At dinner, she'd gone so far as to laugh a little, talking to their friends. With her cheeks flushed from the sun and the better part of a margarita, she'd looked so *open*. Still fierce as anything, but looser somehow. Less hidden within a suit of armor and more letting people see behind the plates.

If the smirk Jared had shot him as they'd piled into the van was anything to go by, Adam wasn't the only one seeing the change. Wasn't the only one who thought it was a good thing.

He glanced back down at her, expecting to see that little wrinkle in her brow she got when she was particularly absorbed. But instead... His breath caught in his throat. Her head, which had already been resting against his arm for the better part of the ride, had lolled to the side. Her mouth was slack, her eyes closed.

It was the first time he'd ever seen her asleep.

The warmth behind his ribs grew and grew.

Taking care not to jostle her, he reached over and shut off her reading light. He wrapped his arms around her more securely.

He wasn't inclined to count his chickens, but he resolved it there and then. Tonight would be the night he'd get her to stay with him. Clearly, the cat was out of the bag. There was no more reason to hide. She'd sleep in his bed, maybe after another slower, quieter round, and in the morning he'd kiss her awake. Bring her coffee and make her breakfast and simply... care for her.

Love her.

It ached, just thinking the words. But if he wasn't fooling himself about the other things, there wasn't any point denying this one. It was stupid, probably the most idiotic thing he'd ever done. At the end of the summer, it was going to hurt like nothing else.

Unless he could convince her to love him back. To keep this fire they'd kindled alive, this summer spark that could grow into a warmth that could last them all winter long. Even apart.

The whole rest of the drive, Jo slept peacefully against his side. It wasn't until the van came to a stop outside their houses and the lights came on that she stirred. She jerked away from his shoulder, twitching a hand up to swipe at the corner of her mouth and then at her eyes. As everyone else started to clamber out, she looked around, confused. "Are we here already?"

Her eyes were wide, her mouth sleep-soft, and her voice hoarse. And it struck him square in the chest. This is what she would look and sound like, every morning, waking up in his bed.

And in that moment, he loved her so fiercely it burned.

"Yeah," he said. His voice hitched on the word, and she looked at him strangely. A lick of panic curled inside him. What if she saw? She wasn't ready yet, and she'd...

She'd end it, wouldn't she? If she knew?

"Oh." She glanced away, toward the front of the van, as if he hadn't said anything at all. She'd missed the feelings he had written all over him. It was a relief, and at the same time, it almost made him feel worse. Raking her fingers through her hair, she called out, "Are you taking the van back to the observatory?"

In the driver's seat, Heather tipped her head to look at them in the rearview mirror. "Yeah. Why?"

"Can you drop me off there?" Jo asked.

Heather scrunched up her brow. "Now?" Adam was thinking the same thing.

Jo nodded. "I just need to check some things real quick."

Shrugging, Heather said, "Sure, I guess."

"Awesome." Jo turned to Adam and shifted as if to move out of his way so he could get out.

Nope. No chance. He had less than zero interest in stopping at the office now, at eight o'clock on a Saturday night after a day at the beach, but if he let Jo go, his chances of coaxing her to his room declined exponentially. He cleared his throat. "I'll go with you."

Heather's mouth twisted up into a too-knowing smile, but Adam wasn't focused on that. Jo turned to him. "Really?"

"Sure." He didn't have to explain what he'd be doing there. Chances were he'd mostly be following her around, trying to keep her from staying too late. "Why not?"

"I can only think of about a million reasons."

So could he. He kept them to himself.

Once everyone else had cleared out, more than a couple of them shaking their heads at him, he and Jo hopped up to sit closer to the front for the quick drive to the observatory. Heather and Lisa were nice enough to drop them in front of the office building instead of making them hike in from the back lot where the van usually got parked.

"Have fun," Lisa told them as they got out.

Heather winked. "But not too much fun."

"Ha-ha," Jo said, desert dry, and Adam marveled again that she was having such an easy time joking about it now.

He kept his peace, walking alongside her halfway down the empty hall. Until finally he couldn't contain it anymore. "What happened?"

"Hmm?"

"You were so worried about everybody finding out, or thinking less of you. Then today, you suddenly decide you don't care?"

"Why? Do you care?"

Of course he cared, only not in the way she was implying. "I told you. I've been wanting to show you off since day one."

She rolled her eyes at that but didn't actively call bullshit.

And maybe he was pressing. He grabbed her arm, stopping her before they could go any farther. Pulling her around until she was facing him. "Seriously, though. What changed?"

She hesitated, her gaze going to the side before returning to him. Even then, it focused somewhere to the right of his ear. "I don't know. I just..." She shrugged, no affectation to it at all. Her defenses were so low he could hardly see how they were continuing to fall, but they were. For him. Standing straighter, she looked him in the eye. "I didn't want to be afraid anymore."

His beautiful, brave girl.

He leaned in, cupping a hand around her cheek. Laughing. "I've never met anybody less afraid than you."

He wanted to prove to her just how courageous, how amazing he thought she was, but before he could take that last step forward to catch her lips with his, a voice sounded out from the other end of the hall.

"Ms. Kramer! There you are."

They turned as one to find P.J. peeking out of the doorway that led toward the telescope control room. Her expression was oddly expectant. Like she'd been waiting for Jo to drop by.

Jo curled her hand around Adam's and drew it down, away from her face without letting it go. "Dr. Galloway?"

"Oh, and you've brought Mr. McCay with you. Lovely. Come along. We're in here." P.J. waved them to follow her. Adam looked to Jo questioningly, but she seemed as mystified as he was. P.J. held the door to the control room open for them, saying, "I wasn't sure if you'd get my message, but we were able to squeeze in some observation time, and I was sure you'd want to see—"

P.J. cut off as Jo froze. Her palm went clammy in Adam's, and when he turned, it was to find her suddenly, shockingly pale.

"Jo?"

Jo's throat worked convulsively before she choked out, "What's he doing here?"

Adam frowned, following her gaze to the bank of monitors. To the same chairs where he and Jo had sat together just a handful of nights before. A woman Adam had never met sat scrolling through the data, while to the side, near the racks of servers, stood a man. He was a little shorter than Adam, dressed in a black collared shirt and khakis, his hair going gray at the temples.

At the sound of their voices, he looked over his shoulder at them, eyes sharp and dark. His chin lifted, his shoulders drawing back. He was staring right at Jo.

P.J. faltered, and a sinking feeling crept into Adam's gut.

"Jo?" he repeated. "What's going on?"

"The hell if I know."

The man at the other end of the room took a single step forward. "Josephine." He looked her up and down. "What on earth are you wearing?"

Jo flinched, and Adam did, too. Gripping her tighter, Adam asked, "Jo? Who is that?"

She pulled her hand from his.

Voice wavering, speaking only loud enough for Adam to hear, she said, "My dad."

Oh, of course, her—

"Wait, what?" For a second, all Adam could do was stand there, gawking between the two of them, absorbing all the things he'd missed the first time around. The shape of the man's nose and the set of his eyes. The way he carried himself.

A low, sudden burst of rage rolled through him.

In this very room, Jo had told him about this man. Adam didn't pretend to know the half of it, but he knew that this was the guy who'd made Jo feel like crap about herself for most of her life. The guy who'd made her feel like she wasn't enough.

It took everything he had in him not to walk right up to him and punch him in the face.

But while he'd been wrapping his head around it all, Jo had taken a step away. And then another. She turned on her heels. Adam made to reach for her and pull her back, calling her name, but she shrugged him off and shouldered her way through the door.

It felt like he'd been slapped.

By the time he came to his senses, the door was slamming closed.

And Jo was gone.

Chapter 17

Jo stormed down the hallway, scarcely seeing where she was going and not even giving a flying fuck.

It wasn't *fair*.

Here. Her father was *here*. Just when Jo had finally managed to make these huge strides in her life, the very day she'd opened up and let her goddamned guard down. Let herself stand in the ocean half naked, let her boyfriend kiss her in the surf—even fallen asleep on his shoulder. Just when she'd allowed herself to actually have fun for once, surrounded by these people who had become her friends.

He had to show up here. Now. When for one fraction of a second she'd managed to be *happy*.

The unfairness made her want to scream and stamp her feet like a fucking five-year-old.

And oh God. The things Dr. Galloway had been saying as she'd beckoned Jo to join her. They hadn't made any sense at the time, but they came together now, forming an ugly picture she could hardly stand to look at without spitting bile.

She'd assumed Jo *knew* he was here. Of course.

Jo turned the corner, out of sight, and put her back against the wall, rubbing the heels of her hands into her eyes until it hurt, until she saw stars, and she could claw them right out. A barking mockery of a laugh burned her throat, choking her like smoke. Like the ashes of the last twenty-one years. Because any normal father would tell his kid he was coming a few thousand miles to end up at the same tiny point on the map where he *knew* she was going to be.

She'd told him. In an e-mail, the same way she communicated anything in the rare instances she had to. She'd gotten a terse acknowledgment, so he'd seen it all right. And shit. Fuck. She skated her hands to her hair and tugged, hard, yanked until her eyes watered, but her stupid brain still wouldn't shut up.

She'd done everything she was supposed to. Followed him into the sciences and kicked *ass* at it, even if she was a girl and it was so goddamn hard. She hadn't meant to, but she'd even picked astronomy, because she loved it, because it made sense to her. Not even out of any idiotic desire to prove something to him or to herself.

And yet. Deep beneath it all, beneath the tattoos and piercings and bitch boots and everything else that told people to stay the hell away from her, she'd hoped. Hadn't she?

Still hoped, somewhere in the softest, most useless part of herself, that he'd…what? Be *proud*?

She'd been so *stupid*.

Dr. Galloway had said it herself. Her dad was here to do some observations. Not for her. Never, ever for her.

And yet she still managed to be surprised.

He'd insisted on calling her by her full name. Worse, the only thing he'd had to say to her beyond that was to ask her about her clothes. She tore her hands from her face and glanced down at herself, and hell, of course he had. She was grimy and covered in salt, her hair a wreck, and she wanted to tear these awful trunks off her body. She'd walk the whole way home buttfuck naked for all she cared. Because that would be better, wouldn't it? At least that would make it clear exactly what she was.

Back the way she'd come, a door opened, the sound of it followed by the rapid thuds of footfalls against linoleum tile. She calculated in her head. Probably Adam, but it could be her dad, and her heart rate soared. Neither option was good. Lord knew what she'd say to her father, and if it was Adam...

No way could she handle that. She was falling to pieces here, and he'd want to, what? *Hold her?* No. Absolutely not. He already knew too much, and if he saw her like this...Just the idea of it had her muscles going taut. Not that it mattered. She was shaking. She'd been such a fool to let him see as much as he had already.

She had to move.

Peeling herself off the wall, she started putting distance between herself and whoever it was. She'd turned the wrong way in her rush to leave, toward her office instead of the exit, but that was fine. Maybe Adam or her dad would go the opposite direction. She'd sneak out the other door and circle around, get to her room—

Where she'd have to hide this all inside again. Because she had a roommate. A roommate who was nice and normal, and Carol didn't deserve...*this*. No more than Adam did. No more than *Jo* did.

She didn't deserve to have the root of all her fears show up here, in this place where she'd decided she was safe for once.

The walls around her blurred, but she didn't stop. The hallway disappeared beneath the soles of her boots, and she wasn't hearing much, but if there was anyone behind her, they weren't close, or they weren't making a lot of noise. Hell, maybe they'd given up. That would be for the best, even if it ached.

She somehow made it almost all the way to the observatory gates before the sound of someone running behind her broke past the buzzing in her head. Fuck. It had to be Adam then. Her father would never go to such lengths.

Steeling herself, curling her hands into fists, she rounded on him. She didn't want him here, and she was good at driving people off. It was what she did. What she'd always done, even when she hadn't meant to...

But he'd stopped. A good half dozen paces behind her, and he had his hands held up in front of himself like she was the cops or something. Trying to show he wasn't armed.

As if she couldn't have figured that out for herself. The expression on his face...Fuck, unarmed, he might as well have been naked. Everything about him was soft and accommodating, and...

And what would it be like to go ahead and fall into that? He'd wrap her up tight and safe, encourage her fucking breakdown even. She was sure of it. She could let herself go in his arms, shatter apart.

But how would she ever hold herself together again if she did?

She shook herself and stiffened her spine. "Don't," she warned.

He raised his hands even higher. "I just wanted to make sure you were all right."

"Do I look all right to you?"

"No." He edged forward, driving her farther back. "Running out of a room like that actually gives the opposite impression, you know."

Awesome. She shifted her gaze skyward, but it only made the

stinging in her eyes burn hotter. She dug her nails into her palms as hard as she could, maybe hard enough to bleed, because there's no way in hell she was crying.

"Go away," she managed.

"No."

"Seriously, just *go*—"

"No."

She threw her hands out to the sides. "What the hell do you mean 'no'? A girl tells you to leave her alone, you do it, okay?"

"Not my girl. Not when she's hurting."

"Fuck you." His girl, her ass. "Just because we fucked a few times—"

"Don't." He shook his head, and he was maddeningly calm. It made her even crazier. How *dare* he? How could he try to turn this into…into…"You're upset, and you're saying things you don't mean."

"Don't tell me what I'm feeling. Don't tell me what I think." She jabbed her fingers at her own chest. "Don't pretend just because we…whatever…" He didn't want her to call it fucking, fine, she wouldn't. "It doesn't give you any right."

But he turned soft eyes at her. "Jo. Please."

"You want to say no? Well, I can do it, too. No. I don't have to." Have to what? Pour her fucking heart out to him? Let him in on her whole pathetic story? Didn't he already have enough of it?

He'd already dug so goddamn deep, getting her to talk about her mother, getting into her pants, getting her to kiss him in public.

"Look," she said, "maybe this has all been a mistake, so just… just, go back to the lab or to your house or whatever." She swept her arm out toward the road ahead of them. "I'll give you a head start and we can pretend none of this ever happened, and you don't have to feel obligated to give a shit."

"Is that what you think this is?" And how dare he look so...
so...*wounded*? "An obligation?"

What else would it be?

What else was she supposed to say?

Oh, hell. Her eyes threatened to brim over, and she couldn't do
this. She felt so weak, like such a girl. Such a sad little cliché. She had
to get rid of him, and fast, before she became even worse than that.

Her throat wobbled, and she turned around and closed her
eyes. She couldn't look at him for another minute. "Go. Just go."

For a long moment, she thought he actually might listen, and
a whole new well of emptiness opened itself up inside her heart.
Him turning away from her—it was her fault. She'd done what
she'd always done, pushing and pushing, and she shouldn't be
surprised it had finally worked.

She'd known she couldn't keep this for long.

And then his voice rang out against the night. "Jo." It came
out soft. Pleading, and that made the hole inside her ripple,
threatening collapse. Why did he have to sound so kind?

But of course it had to get worse.

"Please, Jo. Please don't shut me out."

Her entire chest cavity squeezed, a river of pain she didn't
begin to know how to cope with. She'd always been so good at
pushing it down, ignoring it, but this display of fucking tenderness. It broke her.

Something inside her snapped.

She whipped around, the loss and hurt coalescing into one
last flare of flame. Consuming heat, and anger, and there he was.
Open and vulnerable and all the things she couldn't afford to be.

She surged. The rage carried her, and she was right up in his
face, ready to bite, ready to spit, and she drew her arm back to let
it go, to throw her fist into his awful, perfect, understanding face.

Except he caught it. Unflinching, he grasped her knuckles in his big palm and held her hand there.

"No," he said.

"Fuck you. Fuck you and just…just—" She flung out again, but he grasped her other wrist, too.

And he gazed down at her, expression unchanged, jaw firm. "You can say whatever terrible things you want. Hurt me as much as you feel like, but not like this. You want to let off some aggression, we can do that. But you don't want to do this."

She struggled against his hold, squirming and writhing and working to get a hand, a fist, an elbow out. She'd kick him in the balls or step on his feet or—

But his grip was solid. He turned her around and fit her spine to his chest, wrapped her arms around herself and held them there, her hands pinned, and she couldn't breathe. She couldn't see and couldn't hear, and he was *restraining* her, and how could he?

How could he still be here?

"Shh," he said, but it wasn't condescending. It wasn't cruel.

She didn't have any idea what to do with it.

And it was a different kind of snapping. A wholly new sort of a disconnect in her misfiring, awful brain.

He was here. The boy who'd earned her respect, and whose respect she was pretty sure she'd gotten right back. The strong, beautiful man who took her apart and who allowed her to pin him to his bed.

He'd given her every inch of leeway, right up until now. When she was throwing everything she had into pushing him away, because people always went away. They found out who she was, or in her father's case, they knew from the start. And they left.

But Adam was right here, putting his foot down in the face of her bullshit and refusing to let her self-destruct.

And all the fight went out of her at once.

He caught her before she could sag too far, the iron bars of his arms going cradling instead of confining. As the first hiccup of breath forced its way past her throat, he was shifting her, getting her turned around, and the next thing she knew, they were on the ground. Right there by the side of the road. He set her in his lap, her face pressed to his neck, and he was surrounding her, supporting her. Keeping her, even after all the ugliness she'd unleashed.

"It's okay. It's all right." He petted her hair and kissed her brow, and *oh*.

There were the tears she'd been keeping in for all these years. Apparently, she'd been storing them up, because they flowed out of her like rain, sobs bubbling up with a kind of violence she hadn't been prepared for.

She fisted her hand in his shirt, clinging on and crying against his chest. "I'm sorry." She mumbled it, repeating it while he gentled her.

Wordlessly, he shifted his grip, holding her closer. "Shh."

"I just—"

"I know."

She lifted her head, and she was covered in tears and probably worse, but it couldn't have been as bad as what she'd already shown him. "You didn't need to see that."

His smile was tiny and sad. All tenderness, he brushed the damp strands of her hair from her face. "I want to see whatever you're willing to show me."

"I tried to hit you."

The corner of his mouth quirked up higher, a ghost of a grin she could almost believe. "Not very hard."

He wasn't exactly wrong about that, but still. She knew

enough about what she was doing when it came to fighting; she could have done some damage if she'd really wanted to. He rubbed her spine, and unsure of what else to do, she gave in to it, dropping her head to rest against his chest again. The tears kept coming, but they were quieter now. The kind that she could breathe through. She took a few slow, shaking breaths.

When she opened her mouth again, the words tumbled out. "He didn't even tell me he was coming."

Adam's hands only stuttered a little, a there and gone again flicker of hesitation before he returned to stroking across her shoulder blades. It loosed another shiver from her frame.

"Two years it's been since I've seen him. Then he comes here, and he knew I'd be here. And he what? Surprises me?" She sniffled, dragging a hand under her nose. "If Dr. Galloway hadn't interfered, maybe he could have avoided me entirely."

"Maybe..." Adam trailed off. Because yeah. There weren't really any good ways to spin this.

"And then the first thing he says is some shitty comment about what I'm wearing."

Adam pressed his lips against her temple hard, his grip on her tightening. "Can I tell you a secret?"

She snorted half a laugh. "Sure. Why not?"

"I've never wanted to punch a person in the face as much as I did when he said that."

And it was so strange—sure, he'd showed his strength a dozen times today, holding her up against a post with the force of his hips. Grabbing her fist before she could land a blow.

But the idea that he would have turned that power on someone else, taken the offensive—that he would've been willing to do it for her. The shattered edges inside her seemed to smooth over. Just a little.

"Really?" she asked.

"Say the word. I'll go back and do it now."

She shook her head, and her heart squeezed. As satisfying as that might be to see, "back" was the last place on earth she wanted to go.

Confession bloomed like blood from a wound. "I don't know how I'm going to face him again." She flattened her hand against his chest. "Everything had been going so well and—" And now it was all ruined.

"That doesn't have to change."

"Of course it does. He's here, and I turn into a different person around him."

She'd felt so open these past few days. This afternoon. Just thinking about trying to work around her father at the lab, worrying about running into him in the hall or the cafeteria or anywhere. It was a set of broad oak doors, slamming shut.

"Then I won't let you."

"Ha." That was too much to hope for, wasn't it?

"Come on. Saying no worked out okay today, didn't it?"

Not at first it hadn't. But eventually…

At her quiet, he pressed more kisses to her hairline. "You don't have to do anything you don't want to do, or be anybody you don't want to be."

"Hey. I really *wanted* to shove you away earlier."

"No," he said against her skin. "You didn't."

She didn't have a reply for that.

So badly, she wanted to believe him. But what were a few words from a guy she'd only barely started seeing? What were a few weeks against the years and years of her life?

Everything, a quiet voice inside her said. But a louder, more familiar one insisted, *Nothing*.

Chapter 18

Okay. This was *not* how Adam had pictured spending his evening.

And yet, as he rocked Jo in his arms, there beneath the open sky, he couldn't bring himself to regret it. He wished he could've saved her the pain that'd had her sobbing, but...

She'd shown him something new tonight. Let him in.

Eventually. God. This could've gone so much worse. When he'd first tracked her down, she'd scared the shit out of him. There were a lot of things he was willing to endure for someone he cared about, but she'd been skirting a line. One he hadn't been entirely sure they could recover from. *He'd* been skirting another one.

If he'd pushed her too far, insisting on following her...if she'd actually gone through with fighting him...or if he'd hurt her, trying to defend himself...

But no. He'd made the right call. She'd been scared and hurt and lashing out, and once she'd seen there wasn't any point to it, that he wasn't the enemy...

She'd fallen apart. How long had that been coming? She

curled up against him, trembling and showing a depth of vulnerability he'd always known lurked somewhere under there, and it had broken his heart.

He had to force his hands to be gentle as he cupped her head and kept her close. Considering what she'd told him about her family, she wouldn't have had any reason to expect someone to do this for her. To hold her while she cried. To comfort her with their touch.

It made the same anger that had almost overtaken him at the observatory rear up and growl. She deserved better than she'd gotten.

And she was going to get it. The fire inside him resolved into decision. He was going to take care of her. He was going to give her all the love and affection she'd been missing out on.

He didn't know how long they sat there, but eventually her breathing seemed to settle back down, and she started fidgeting inside his arms. He patted her shoulder and loosened his grip, half bracing himself just in case. She'd let him awfully far behind her walls. He'd only be so surprised if she responded by building them up again, thicker and taller than ever before.

She took the slack he'd given her to sit up straighter, sliding off his lap to land beside him on the ground.

"Sorry," she said, and he was prepared to tell her not to be. But she turned to look at him, her expression sheepish. "I could've picked a more comfortable place for my little meltdown."

He rolled his eyes, striving for normalcy when all he wanted was to reel her back in. "Yeah. Plan ahead next time, would you?"

"Hopefully there won't be a next time."

He nudged his knee against hers. "But if there is. You know I'm here for you, right?"

This was it. The moment of truth.

And instead of pushing him away, she leaned into him. "Yeah. You've proven that much tonight."

He let out his breath, flooded with relief. "Come on." He stood up and held out his hand. "Let's get you home."

Placing her palm in his, she allowed him to help her up. They took a second to right themselves. When they were as put together as they were going to get, he stooped to grab their bags, then put his arm around her for the rest of the walk.

When the houses came into sight, she slowed their pace. "By getting me home, did you mean...?"

He tightened his arm around her waist. Preparing himself for a no, he said, "Come back to mine? Only if you want to. But if you do, I'd..." He'd love it was what he'd do. "I'd like that. I don't really want to let go of you yet."

As accustomed to it as she might be, he didn't want her to be alone.

She nodded, though her posture was stiff. "I'm not promising you anything."

Seriously? Voice firm, he said, "I'm definitely not expecting it."

With that, he headed them down the path to the guys' house. Mercifully, the windows were all dark. The rest of the crowd must be hanging out at the girls' place again. Thank God. Neither he nor Jo was really in a position to be putting up a cheerful front right now.

Sure enough, the place seemed deserted, save for a light on under Tom's closed door. But he almost never stuck his head out there. No chance he'd be bothering them.

Plunking their bags down in the entryway, he looked to Jo. It felt so normal to have her in his space now, and yet at the same time that normality itself was strange. He scratched his salt-stiff hair and glanced around. "Do you want something to eat? Maybe a drink?" He gestured at the television in the living room. "We can just...hang out. See if there are any movies on."

She scowled, looking down. "I feel disgusting, actually."

Okay. That was an objective he could deal with. "Shower," he agreed.

He led her toward the bathroom, ushering her inside. But then he hesitated. Hovering in the doorway, he swallowed and gestured at the space within. "Do you want? I mean, I could really use one, too. I can wait and take my turn, but—" Fuck it, after everything they'd been through today, the least he could do was put what he wanted into words. "We could share. I'd like to, if you don't mind."

She shook her head, and his heart fell, but then she sighed and beckoned him in. "Insert joke about saving water here."

His throat went dry. "You sure?"

"Get in here already."

Taking her at her word, he stepped inside, closing the door and locking it behind him. She stooped over to get the water heating up, then without ceremony started to strip.

With her back to him.

The doorknob in his hand and the floor beneath his feet were his only touchstones to the world as she shimmied her way out of her bra, baring the long expanse of her spine. There was no rush of desire to keep him from looking his fill, no wicked smile as she pinned him to a bed or sucked him in or started to ride him.

Just her, inked and damaged and beautiful and taking her clothes off in front of him.

He reached out his hand but stopped before he could touch.

The tattoo stretched across her shoulder blades was an animal all right, but not one of the ones he'd originally suspected. The tiger prowled across the landscape of her flesh, coiled strength and sinewy muscles that followed the curves of her spine and ribs. It rippled with strength and grace and implicit threat, its teeth and claws all hidden but *there*. Ready to be bared at any instant.

It was dangerous and beautiful. Just like her.

"Well? You planning on getting naked at some point, too?"

While he'd been gawking, she'd managed to get her boots and bottoms off. Fully nude, she gazed over her shoulder at him, one eyebrow raised, like she was trying to be teasing. Only she wasn't quite managing it. She shifted her weight between her feet, look-ing...self-conscious? It seemed impossible after the brazenness with which she usually took off her clothes in front of him. Then again, in all the time they'd been together, she had yet to let him see her like this.

Releasing his death grip on the doorknob, he took one careful step toward her and another. With his already extended hand, he worked to bridge the gap, her tension like a force field between them. But he pushed through it.

The first brush of his fingertips over her skin made her shud-der, a tingle of electricity rushing down his arm. She was warm to the touch, the inked lines on her skin lightly raised. He traced the tiger's flank, the fine detail that made up its fur. Dropping her head forward, she leaned into him.

"Right," she said, voice strained. "Almost forgot you had a body mod kink."

"I have a Jo kink." With the utmost reverence, he stroked his thumb down the side of the tiger's face. "This is gorgeous."

Some of the stiffness seeped out of her shoulders. "I knew you'd like it, but—" She stopped, and he had to still his tongue against the impulse to fill the silence with more praise. "It's per-sonal, you know?" He hummed, waiting a couple of beats before she volunteered, "My mother was born in the year of the tiger. My dad, too, but it was for her. Originally."

"Originally?"

She shrugged. "Can't really ignore the fact that they were born in the same year. I could have done something that was unique to her, you know? But instead I went with this. Subconsciousness, what?"

He paused the motions of his fingers across her skin.

Her voice dipped lower. "I guess maybe I was hoping he'd like it, too."

Adam almost didn't want to ask. "Did he ever see it?"

"Eventually. The last time I wore a bathing suit."

Oh. "And what did he say?"

In a rushing whoosh of an exhalation, she answered, "Nothing."

With that, she climbed into the shower and pulled the curtain partway closed, leaving him out there alone, still clothed and staring after her.

Well. He wasn't waiting around for a written invitation.

He got undressed and stepped inside. In what little time he'd wasted, she'd gotten her head under the spray, and she stood there, facing him, her eyes closed, wet hair plastered to her head. She'd crossed her arms over her chest, making a shelf beneath her breasts where water pooled. Rivulets ran their way across her skin, tracing the slopes and valleys of her curves, and his breath got caught inside his chest. His body responded the way it always did, but he bit the inside of his cheek, trying to ignore it.

Her eyes fluttered open, and she sluiced the water off her face as she stepped to the side, offering him a chance under the spray. He shook his head. He'd get his crack at it eventually. For now, he had something else in mind.

"Turn around?" It came out more a question than a directive, his tongue thicker around the request than he had planned.

To his surprise, she did as he'd asked, though she did give him a little lip, so he didn't have to wonder if she was really in there or not. "Need some more time to ogle my tattoo?"

"Side benefit." He bent to grab his shampoo, then paused. There wasn't any telling what was whose, but the bathroom at the girls' house was stocked with all kinds of things. All he had was basic drugstore stuff. "Do you need to use something special for your hair? Because of the dye?"

She peeked over her shoulder at him, her gaze registering the bottle in his hand. She turned back around and shrugged. "It'll make it fade faster, but whatever. I need to redo it soon anyway."

Taking her at her word, he popped the cap and squirted some into his palm before setting the bottle down. He raised his hands, letting them hover above her crown. "Can I?"

"Knock yourself out," she said, flippant as anything, but with a shiver running down her spine the instant his fingertips connected with her flesh.

He spread the lather through her hair with gentle strokes and soft kneading of her scalp, taking care not to let it run down into her eyes. Taking his time. When he was done, he pulled away. "Okay."

He used the time she spent rinsing the shampoo out to rub his bar of soap between his hands. She twisted to face him and took one look at him before narrowing her eyes. "Just because I agreed to shower with you doesn't mean I suddenly became incapable of washing myself."

Of course she would interpret this like that. He kept his expression open, hiding how sad that made him. "Humor me?"

She rolled her eyes but dropped her arms to her sides.

All his efforts to keep his arousal at bay went to hell as he ran slick fingers over her skin. The grit of sand and sweat and the dried tears of the ocean melted beneath the water and the lather and his oh so careful touch. When he got to her waist, he braced himself for the joke he knew was coming as he dropped to kneel before her.

With a shaky laugh, she tangled her fingers in his hair. "Always wanted to get a man on his knees for me. Not exactly how I pictured it, though."

"Disappointed?" He kept his gaze on the way the bubbles clung to her thighs as he lathered them up.

"No."

Silence hung in the air as he finished, the space around them shrinking. The intimacy of this small act making him feel like he could stay right here. Forever.

When he nudged her hip, she turned around, and he did the backs of her legs, working not to linger too long on the curves of her ass. He moved to stand to get her shoulders, to clean the skin of her tattoo, but she stopped him, reaching to get a hand around his wrist.

"Wait."

The bathtub floor beneath his knees wasn't getting any softer, but she'd trusted him enough so far. The least he could do was return the favor. Resisting the urge to get up, he watched her as she sluiced the suds from her thighs. Then she turned to him and said, "Close your eyes."

Warm water rained down on his face, wetting his hair. Her fingers moved through the strands, and his throat bobbed. He knew what she was doing.

Finding his voice, he said, "I haven't forgotten how to wash myself either, you know."

"Humor me."

She reached over him for his shampoo.

And it was strange. In a sense, she'd been taking care of him all along, leading the way through most of their sexual encounters. But the gentle touch of her hands on the nape of his neck, sweeping up behind his ears and massaging at his scalp...it was different.

When she was done, she moved as if to shift away, but he curled his hands around her hips. For a second, he rested his brow against the softness of her belly. And he breathed.

Finally, she rubbed her knuckles beneath his jaw. "The water's going to get cold."

It never got *cold*, per se—not in this climate—but it was as good a segue as any. Keeping one hand at her side, he lifted his head and rose to his feet. He caught her face in his hand, holding her still so he could brush his lips against hers. "Thank you," he said.

Her only response was another kiss.

They moved around each other in silence for the last few minutes of their shower. He got to wash her back after all, and she snuck in strategic touches as he soaped himself up. By the time they were done, the water had cooled all right, and after a nod of approval from her, he turned it off.

Without the shower raining down on them, the room went eerily quiet. He only had the one towel in here, so they took turns with it, neither one getting really dry, but the steamy air was suddenly oppressively wet, the dampness clinging to their bodies. They might not have had much luck with a dozen towels, if they'd had them, much less two.

She stared down the door as he finished swabbing off. "So. Are we running for it, or...?"

Oh. Right. They hadn't stopped to grab spare clothing, either. He turned to her and stretched the towel out, waiting until she sighed and stepped into it before wrapping it around her breasts, under her arms. She took the edges and tucked them in before tilting her head at him.

They weren't going to run into anybody, so it didn't matter. Still, he scooped up their discarded clothes and held them in front of himself before gesturing for her to go ahead.

Sure enough, the coast was clear as they retreated to his room. While he tugged on a pair of boxers, she went to the window to turn on the fan, then flopped down on his bed, legs and arms spread out to either side.

And...

It didn't seem too much to presume, but he still didn't want to reach too far.

"Are you staying, then?"

She lifted her head. "Do you mind?"

"No." The crack of light spreading its way through his ribs put pains to the understatement. Did he *mind*? He shook his head. "No, not at all."

Chapter 19

Jo gazed up at the ceiling for a long moment. She didn't actually think it was about to cave in on her, didn't think the walls were going to close in or that the world was set to shake apart. But it seemed smart to keep an eye out, just in case.

It wasn't all that big of a deal, was it? Sleeping over in a guy's room? People did it all the time. So what if it happened that *she'd* never done it on purpose before? No BFD.

She took a deep breath. It was just that she was tired, wrung out, and she didn't feel like getting up or dealing with all the people at her house. Adam's bed was comfortable.

And when Adam put his arms around her... it was like all the jagged pieces grinding around inside her, always spinning, always hurting—their edges dulled. Things went this tiny bit quieter in her head. And she didn't want to let go of it quite yet.

It didn't have to *mean* anything.

Except Adam was standing on the other side of the room, trying and epically failing to hide the fact that his eyes were lit up like fucking Christmas. That probably did mean something. She'd worry about that some other time.

Finally, once the silence between them had officially dragged on for way too long, Adam cleared his throat. "Do you want to, like, borrow some clothes or something?"

Probably not a bad idea. "Sure."

The sound of drawers opening and shutting filled the space, followed by soft footfalls. The mattress dipped beneath her as he sat on the edge of the bed. He offered her a balled up T-shirt and a pair of boxers. "Sorry. They'll probably be really big on you."

"Whatever." She shifted her gaze to meet his. "Wore your trunks all day, didn't I?"

"Yeah." He held the boxers up. "But these don't have a drawstring."

She accepted them and set them down beside her. "They'll be fine. Thanks."

"You're welcome." He dipped to press a soft, brief kiss on her lips before sitting up again. Leaning back against the headboard, he nudged her with his knee until she shifted over enough for him to stretch out his legs. "You want me to look away or something while you put them on?"

"Please. I think that ship has sailed, don't you?"

"Maybe." His smile went warm and soft, and it set off an answering glow behind her breastbone. He resettled his legs so his foot rested against her thigh, a single point of casual contact that was anything but. "Just don't want you to think you're obligated to show me your breasts because I've seen them before."

"Chivalrous."

She fingered the edge of the towel where it lay stretched across her chest. The fabric was damp, which should've been kind of gross, but the air was warm enough she didn't mind. Plus, the towel smelled like Adam. Hell, after using his soap and his shampoo, *she* smelled like Adam. That probably shouldn't have been as okay with her as it was. After a moment's hesitation, she dropped her hand to the side and stayed like she was.

"So," Adam said. "Did you want to…talk? Or anything?"

"About what?"

"Oh, I don't know." He moved to run his fingers through the wet strands of her hair. "Maybe any of the hundred unusual things that have happened today."

He didn't specify further, though she didn't have any doubt what he was angling for. After the tantrum she'd thrown, he had every right to demand an explanation. Only he wasn't demanding anything, just giving her an opening in case she wanted to talk. Chances were, she could start in on chicken fights or public indecency and he'd roll with it.

And that was what made her tongue and chest both loosen up. Not quite all the way, but enough.

"I don't know." She inched her hand a little farther up the bed until her knuckles grazed the hem of his boxers. The solid, lightly haired skin underneath. "Not a whole lot left you haven't heard already."

She'd told him more than she'd ever told anyone else.

"Tell me again, then. If you want to."

Where to even start? A darkness rumbled inside of her. The beginning was probably the most logical. Her throat tried to constrict against the words, but she pushed through it, an old pain mixing with the story she always told herself.

But when the confession came out, it was flat. Lifeless. "I killed my mother."

His fingertips didn't even pause against her scalp. "No, you didn't."

"How do you know?"

"I just do."

Bastard. "Fine." She turned her head to the side, looking at his leg because it was easier than looking at anything else. " 'Complications due to childbirth.' Or at least that's what my dad told me."

"I'm so sorry, Jo."

She shrugged. What was she supposed to say? "I try to be cool about it. Rationalize it. But I don't know if my dad never got over her, or if he was just always that way. If I was just—" She cut herself off, because it was bullshit. Self-indulgent ridiculous bullshit, but she was so worn out, it was hard to censor.

If I was just that disappointing.

She picked back up again once the lump had passed from her throat. "He wasn't around much, and when he was, he didn't want a whole lot to do with me. I spent all this time trying to do things to get his attention. I got the nannies to dress me up pretty before he came home, but he'd be late or he wouldn't notice." She'd seen the pictures, and she'd been fucking adorable. How the hell could he not have noticed? "Then when I was seven, I got it into my head... You see, he always said he'd wanted a son." When Adam's whole body went tense beside her, she clarified. "He never said he didn't want a daughter. And maybe it was just that 'a man is the king of his castle' crap that guys from that generation like to say. But he talked about a son like..." Like it would have made him happy.

She frowned, tracing a series of birthmarks across his thigh. "And he had these graduate students. He'd have them over for parties he threw at the house a couple of times a year. The nanny tried to keep me away, but I always found a way to sneak down, because he was *different* with them, you know? All those guys. He'd laugh. Pat them on the back." All the things he never did around her. "I decided maybe if I were a boy... maybe everything would be better somehow."

"That's a terrible thing for a kid to have to decide."

"You're telling me." The worst of it was, it had almost worked. Sort of. Cutting her hair off had gotten some attention, and her math and science tests ended up on the fridge the way her drawings never had. But at its heart, she'd still been the same lonely girl, rattling around an empty house. Wishing her dad would give her a hug for once. She swiped her wrist across her eyes, but they were dry. Apparently there weren't going to be any more hysterics tonight. Thank God. "It actually helped a little, but not enough." Underneath it all, she'd still been the thing he'd never wanted.

The child who had killed his wife. The error of genetics that had robbed him of a son.

"I took it so far, too," she said. Past junior high, going into high school and beyond, and it had been good, hadn't it? Her short hair and her ugly boots and the clothes that covered all her curves. They'd kept people exactly where she'd wanted them.

Because after growing up alone, she hadn't known how to be anything else.

To make matters worse, she'd been good at it, too. Being the bitch, the tomboy, the one that nobody could ever get close to. Science had started as a desperate ploy for her father's attention, but her first trip to an observatory with a program after school and she'd fallen in love. With the stars. The sky. This vast universe where she could just be.

A quiet place in the night that was just for her.

Adam trailed his fingers down her cheek, caressing the edge of her jaw. "Did you ever talk about it with him?"

She couldn't help it. She laughed out loud.

Frowning at her, he gave her leg a nudging kick. "I'm being serious."

"So am I." She caught his hand in hers and interwove their

fingers. "I barely managed to get a 'How was your day?' out of him most of the time. You really think we were ever going to have that kind of conversation?"

"I don't think he's ever going to start it. But maybe you could. It might…make you feel better about things, you know?"

Now he was being obtuse. "I doubt it."

"I don't know." The lines around his mouth had gone strangely somber. "I mean, I don't want to overstep or anything here. But earlier…" Right. When she'd completely freaked out on him. "It seemed like maybe you'd been bottling some stuff up. If that's how you deal with things, okay. But it doesn't seem healthy." Determination flooded his eyes. "It doesn't seem like it's been making you happy."

Happy. Until this week, here with Adam, she hadn't even known it was something she could aspire to.

This week when she'd made herself open. Let him peel down her barricades, inch by painful inch.

He must have seen her resolve faltering. He sat up straighter and pulled at her hand until she sat up, too. She folded her legs underneath her, trying not to flash him too much when the edge of the towel rode up her thigh.

"Come on," he said. "Try it. Pretend I'm your dad."

"Oh God, no." She shook her head. "Role-playing is a hard limit for me. I mean, maybe if one of us is a naughty schoolgirl or something, but—"

"I'm not joking around."

She dropped his hand. "Neither am I." Her voice went small, and she hated it. "I can't."

"You can. Please?" His gaze had an earnestness to it that had her resistance yearning to melt, only—

The very idea that this was a conversation she could have, one that she *should*. It was hot and uncomfortable inside her throat and behind her eyes.

He put his hand on her bare shoulder, warm and broad. "Just try it. Here, I'll start you out. 'Dad, I feel like...'"

"Fucking hell." She wanted to cover her face. "We're both almost naked and you want me to call you Dad?"

"Jo..."

It was the same way he'd said her name out on that street. The same way he'd said it the night at the observatory when she'd told him about her mom.

It wasn't sexy. It was real.

"Try. 'Dad, I'"—he hesitated, but then went ahead—"'I wish you would've...'"

And wasn't that cutting a little too close to the bone?

For a second, she closed her eyes. What if her father really were here? What if she could tell him, ask him, anything she wanted to?

She took a deep breath. She couldn't look at Adam, so she focused on a point to the right of him. A smudge on the plaster of the wall.

Dad, why didn't you love me?

Dad, why did you leave me all alone?

Dad, I...

Her chest felt like it was cracking open. "Dad, why were you so disappointed in me?"

Adam's palm on her shoulder went heavier, his grip tighter. He dipped his head, putting his eyes right in her field of vision, fierce and beautiful and real.

"I wasn't. I never, ever, ever was." With that, their role-playing session was apparently over, thank God. He drew her up in a crushing hug, and she let him, curling herself into his strength and his heat. Trying to pretend she wasn't shaking. Rocking her back and forth, he murmured in her ear, "And if he doesn't tell you that, you just point me at him."

She laughed, a sad, low sound that was more choked than it had any right to be. Wrapping her arms around him, she buried her face against the solidity of his shoulder, hanging on. "Please tell me I can stop calling you 'Dad' now."

"God, yes."

"Phew."

"You were so brave, baby. So brave."

Hardly. But it felt so nice to hear.

His hands traveled up her spine, one coming to settle at the nape of her neck, and he dug his thumb into the muscle there. "You're so tense," he said.

"Imagine that." Her eyes stung, and the wrung-out, exhausted feeling from before had magnified a hundredfold. "Almost as if talking about all that shit stresses me out."

"Almost as if," he echoed. Releasing her, he shifted to the edge of the bed and gestured at the empty expanse of mattress. "Lie down. Let me take care of you."

Whatever resistance she would've normally had to that sort of thing was officially on vacation. She flopped forward, landing on her stomach. Moaning, she petted the surface underneath her. "Mmm, bed. You're my best friend."

"I know where I rank in this situation."

"Shh, I'm trying to have a conversation with your bed."

"Well, don't let me get in the way."

"I won't—" she started to say, but the words cut off when he put his hands on her shoulders. The warm pressure, gently kneading at the precise place where so much of her tension always lived had her eyes squeezing shut, a noise escaping her that she'd never admit to later.

"Is this okay?"

"I think I can manage to put up with it." She was such a liar. It felt so good.

And it was uncomfortable, too. Clearly he meant for her to lie there and let him give her a massage or a backrub or whatever he wanted to call it, but that was weird, wasn't it? Her skin prickled with self-consciousness, a guilty selfishness at accepting that kind of gift.

"Shh. Just relax."

"I'm trying."

He leaned in closer so his breath was in her ear. "That's the problem."

The mattress rocked as he moved. Heat to either side of her made her breath suck in as he straddled her thighs. His hard-on wasn't touching her, but she didn't doubt it was there. The guy got aroused at the drop of a hat, but somehow this wasn't about that. His hands drifted lower on her shoulders, one of his thumbs finding a knot, and he shifted to dig his knuckles in. The deeper pressure was too tender, too hot—

Until it released.

"Holy shit," she groaned.

"I'll take it that was nice?"

"So nice." A part of her was melting, but another part felt all the more aware of the one-sidedness of this act. "Want me to do you, after?"

"If you're still capable of it by the time I'm finished with you, I won't have done my job correctly."

Another little stab of guilt ran through her. "But—"

"Shh." He dipped to kiss the nape of her neck. "Enjoy this. Okay?"

His reassurances didn't change the squirminess inside her, the sense of being looked at and on display. Of taking something she wasn't sure she could return. But he went about this with such an easiness, touching and caressing with sure hands.

Gradually, her muscles loosened, and she sank deeper and deeper into the mattress. Some of his quiet confidence seeped into her bones.

"That's right," he said, soft and low.

By the time her shoulders had officially been reduced to jelly, she was almost calm. When he tucked a finger into her towel in question, she lifted up.

He peeled the fabric from her slowly, exposing her flesh to the breeze coming in from the fan. She was damp with perspiration and the water that had clung to them after their shower. He pulled the towel out from under her and then guided her down to lie flush against the mattress again. Naked. His bare thighs brushing the outsides of hers, the whole long line of his torso a radiant heat from above.

"Adam—" His name spilled out from between her lips. She didn't want him to stop, didn't want anything but for this to go on and on, her flesh faintly giving off sparks as a new sort of anticipation banked and built. A low arousal settled warm and patient in her abdomen.

"Shh."

He shifted, hands making their way down her sides. He kissed her sacrum and gripped her hips and then—*Oh*. A cool rush as he blew a low stream of breath across her spine. Her skin prickled, gooseflesh coming up, but then he was soothing it, massaging her with heated palms.

He worked the whole length of her back over and over before edging even lower. Thumbs dug into her thighs and teased the insides of her knees. Her calves rippled with the best kind of achiness as he rubbed them. One at a time, he took her feet into his hands. And that was really weird, except when he ground a knuckle into the arch, she just about came off the bed.

"Too much?" he asked.

"No." Fuck, no. "It's fine."

And she was so glad she was on her stomach like this—that he had no way to see her face.

Because it was more than fine, more than not too much.

It was perfect. Too perfect, and her heart panged.

She didn't know if she would ever, ever get enough.

Suddenly, she felt every inch of her nakedness all over again, and Adam was too far away. She stretched her arm out toward him, trying to tell him without words that she needed him closer, hot and real and pressed against her.

"What?" he asked.

"Just...come here."

He rose up easily enough, climbing higher on the bed, but of course the asshole had to do it all sweet and fond, laying a line of kisses up the backs of her legs and along her spine. He kept that careful space between their bodies, too, and she wanted it gone, wanted to be blanketed by him, protected from all the things today that had left her shaking. From her own mind. From herself.

She lifted up onto one elbow, craning her neck and reaching to get a hand on his skin. She couldn't look into his eyes, but she could drag him in—in and in until their lips met. Opening for him, she held him against her and licked into his mouth, suddenly desperate.

She didn't want to think anymore, didn't want to be taken care of. She wanted to lose herself.

"Jo." He broke away enough for air. He sounded dazed but still too cautious. "Are you okay?"

"I'm fine, I just—" What? Everything inside her felt like it was cracking apart. Deep in her gut, it hurt. *I just felt really vulnerable. I needed you close.* She swallowed and gripped him tighter. "I want you."

"I want you, too," he said, and how did he make it sound so simple? Admitting that? "But—"

"No buts." She pulled him to her mouth and kissed him with another level of need, hot and dirty. Fumbling, she took him by the hand and led him to her breast, the one with the piercing through it, and that never failed to get him going.

Sure enough, a filthy noise fell out of him as he rubbed the metal between his finger and his thumb. Her nipple perked up, going hard and swollen as lines of heat shot straight to her clit.

"Isn't that good?" She ground her hips into the mattress, squeezing her thighs together. "It feels so good when you touch me like that."

He cut off a curse, sagging lower against her until *finally* his cock dragged against her ass. He moved into the contact, flesh bobbing through the thin layer of fabric still separating them, and his throat worked like he had things to say but had lost the words. "But I was going to…"

Right. Take care of her. Treat her right. She shook her head and kept him close. "You're taking such good care of me now."

And that seemed to do the trick. He melted into her at last, letting her bear some of his weight. She wedged her legs apart until he fell into the space between them, and fuck, maybe someday they'd do this bare. Someday when they'd done the whole going and getting tested thing, and she'd had her implant checked out.

She pulled away and buried her face against her own arm. Shit. *Shit.* They were never going to get that someday. No way in hell they were begging a ride to a fucking clinic, or waiting around for results from someone who might not speak English.

They had a few more weeks. That was it.

And it made her feel empty in a way she'd never imagined it would.

Adam pulled back, sounding startled as he shifted his hand from her tit to her side. "Are you okay?"

"Yeah." She would be, goddammit all. "Get a condom?"

"Already? Don't you want me to..."

She shook her head, collapsing down onto the bed and slipping her fingers between her legs. Momentary jag of sadness or no, she'd just been rubbed and stroked and petted for longer than she would normally be able to stand. She was ready.

"Just want you in me," she said, and her voice faltered. She squeezed her eyes closed, going for broke. "Want you close."

He hovered for a long second, and she was going to lose her mind if he put her off or tried to make them talk some more. They'd already talked; they'd talked until she was hoarse.

She forced herself to look at him. Gritted out the word, "Please."

A shudder went through him, and he kissed the tip of her shoulder, a closed-mouth press of lips that felt like a balm. "Okay. Okay."

Running his palm down her flank, he pushed off and opened the drawer of his nightstand. While he got himself ready, she turned her face into the bedding and played with her clit. When he came back to the bed, he was gloriously naked, all hot, smooth flesh sliding against hers.

"Like this?" he asked.

"Yeah." She wouldn't be able to look at him, but the urge to be surrounded by him hadn't faded at all.

"Okay." Kneeling between her legs, he nudged her hand out of the way and replaced it with his own. He'd gotten so good at working her body in the time they'd been together, but it all felt like a tease.

With a little growl of frustration, she bucked her hips, only to be pinned down. A hot palm at the base of her spine. More of his weight bore into her, and she was ready to throw him off, to climb on top and take what she wanted the way she always did, only…

Only…

So many times already tonight, Adam had asked her to let go. To let him care for her, to let him… She blinked hard against the warmth surging through her. There were other words for what he was doing here, the way he was treating her, and she wasn't prepared to hear or think or say any of them. But she could accept him.

She could give him the chance to offer her this moment. This safety.

Shutting her eyes, she buried her face against the mattress and breathed out long and slow. His fingers slipped through her lips and over her clit, then dipped down to press inside, and she groaned his name.

His erection throbbed against the back of her leg, hard and hot even through the layer of latex. "That's it, baby. Just let me—"

Something inside her went suddenly, achingly soft. A warmth blooming through her cunt and in her heart, and maybe they were both the same.

Maybe they were both about making room for him. Letting him in.

Then the warmth was a heat, was a fire just waiting to ignite, and she shook her head. Reached out a hand behind her until she connected with his skin. "No, not without…I need…"

His fingers drew away, leaving her empty and alone and hanging over the edge until his hips settled between her thighs. Until the blunt head of him slid wetly across slick flesh.

And she didn't beg. She didn't plead. But she shut her eyes.

"Adam..."

He sucked in a breath, bracing himself with both arms over her, and she thought, *Finally*.

Then he sank into her, so slowly she could've cried.

She kicked out hard, foot connecting with the mattress. Fuck, she was so full, and it felt so good—the way his weight pressed her down and held her. The soft kiss of his lips against her shoulder and her neck, and she whined.

There was something untethered in her, something frantic, but he had her. He wouldn't let her float away.

He murmured her name against her temple, and it was a word and a prayer. She turned into it, and he dipped down to meet her lips, driving even deeper and forcing choked groans out of them both. His mouth was hot, the angle all wrong, but she didn't care. It was just the rasp of his teeth over her lip and the softness of his tongue. They were one circuit, every part of him touching every part of her, electricity zipping up and down her spine. *Life*.

And then he started to move.

Her eyes flew open as he thrust back in hard. She'd been so close before he'd even gotten inside, overwhelmed by his touch and his kindness, and now he was hitting this tender hollow deep inside, winding her higher. She pushed into his thrusts, but his weight pressed her back down, and she gave in to it. She *took* it.

Sneaking his hand beneath her body, he got his fingers on her clit again. The quick circling strokes shot lightning through her, and orgasm was right there; she could *taste* it—

But it wasn't until his own unsteady breathing went shallow, the strain making his kisses harder, that the pleasure gathered into a storm. For what felt like an infinite moment, they hovered there on the edge together, and she wanted it to come crashing down, and she never, ever wanted it to end.

He bit down on her lip and choked on her name, hips stuttering against hers. One more rough rub against her clit—

The feeling exploded out of her, too much and not nearly enough as it dragged her under. Blackness washed out her vision as wave after wave of it overtook her. Adam took a final, punishing thrust forward and stilled, mouth hot and open against her cheek, and the low pulsing of his body in hers wrung another surge of pleasure from her that blanked her thoughts all over again.

When she came back to herself, he lay half slumped over her, heavy torso barely supported by the shivering columns of his arms. She clenched around him, and it still felt good. But he twitched, a pained sound slipping past his throat before he withdrew. She gave a little whimper at the emptiness.

How was it possible she still wanted more?

"Yeah?" he asked as he climbed off of her, and there was intent there, for all that he was shaking. An offer. Blessed air swept in to fill the sweaty gap between their bodies, but it didn't help to clear her head.

"Don't think I can move," she said. It wasn't quite an answer, but it was somehow, too. Yeah, she could go again—she kind of *wanted* to go again—but she didn't have the strength left. He'd pulled it all out of her. Left her feeling weak and shimmering and *amazing*.

She wasn't sure she'd ever felt so good.

With a low, rumbly laugh, he put a hand on her hip and rolled her over. The new stretch of mattress was deliciously cool against her burning skin. She blinked her eyes open to find him kneeling beside her, all the dips and rises of his musculature gleaming, damp strands of hair framing his face.

Ridden hard and put away wet. She probably looked even worse.

And then he eased her legs apart and moved to lie between them. Her sex gave a hot pulse, but she stopped him—fumbled a hand toward his shoulder when he spread her lips and stroked his thumb across her clit.

"You don't have to." It would've been more convincing if she didn't groan out loud at the heat of two fingers pressing inside.

He smirked, lopsided and beautiful. "Believe me. I've been dying to do this for a very, very long time."

Then he was sliding down the bed, and all the breath left her lungs.

She'd partied with some cunning linguists in her time, but it wasn't usually a part of her sex life. It felt too intimate, and besides, she probably tasted like latex, and with one orgasm down, this second one wasn't going to come quickly.

Except the first hot swipe of his tongue had her hands going to his head. With the second she closed her eyes. His mouth was warm and wet, and apparently the guy could still surprise her. He knew what he was doing, coaxing the barely simmering embers of her last climax right back up into a pressing need, something too big to fit within her.

She arched her spine and surrendered. He licked and sucked and filled her with hot fingers, and something inside her threatened to shatter. Curling his hand up, he hit this perfect place inside, and his tongue sped, flicking over her harder and harder, and she couldn't hold herself against it...couldn't hold back—

When she broke again, this time, tears trickled from her eyes. But they were good tears. Amazing tears.

He climbed back up her body, worry written all over his face. She pulled him into her and kissed her desire from his lips.

She was still herself. But somehow, in that instant, everything was different.

And she wished—God, she wished—that she could keep it.

Chapter 20

It was probably creepy, how long Jo lay there, watching Adam sleep. Pale, early morning light spilled in from the window, falling across his bare, wide shoulders. His hair was a mess, his lips parted, and she was pretty sure the hint of a shadow under his mouth was the beginning of a puddle of drool, but she didn't care.

She'd slept here, beside him, and the earth hadn't shaken to pieces. Only her perception of it. And now it was a brand-new day, and she couldn't go back. She didn't want to.

Okay, fine, maybe she wanted to go back *to sleep*, but that wasn't happening, either. There was too much going through her mind. Adam and work and...

Her dad. One way or another, she would have to deal with that situation today. Passive-aggressively ignoring and/or avoiding him held some appeal, but as she stared at the fall of Adam's eyelashes across his cheek, she kept coming around to everything he'd said the previous night.

And it made her want to laugh. She'd given up on the whole optimism thing a long, long time ago. She'd given up on her father. But the way Adam had spoken, the way he'd treated her...maybe she'd given up on love a little too soon.

Finally, even she had to admit she'd flown straight past creepy and was rounding the corner of obsessive. She should go. Should sneak out and steal some clothes and head to her house to start her day. Except...

Except Adam had been so eager for her to stay. If he woke to an empty bed, he'd be okay about it, but he wouldn't be happy.

When had making Adam happy become something that warmed her heart like this?

Nervous, she reached her hand out and stroked her knuckles down his cheek. "Adam?"

He sighed and smiled and nuzzled deeper into his pillow.

She tried again. "Adam?"

This time, his eyes fluttered open, soft and hazy, and the glow in her chest grew and grew.

"Hey there, handsome," she said.

"You stayed." He made it sound like it was the best thing in the world.

"Yup." Leaning in, she brushed a kiss against his brow.

And he might have seemed lazy and half awake, but the guy was strong. His hand snapped out, and he held her in place, dragging her down toward his mouth.

She squirmed. "I haven't brushed my teeth yet."

"Neither have I."

And then he was kissing her, and yeah, it was a little gross, but it was also sleep-warm and soft, his lips parting slowly and his tongue licking into her mouth. He tugged her body against him, into the cradle of his naked side, and suddenly she kind of got it. Why people liked to spend the night together. Why waking up with the person you were fucking was something to be prized.

His grip slackened, that bleary smile overtaking his mouth again. "Do you have to go?"

Thank God he brought it up. Her will to leave had started to evaporate with the first blush of their kiss, but her antsiness hadn't. "I probably should."

"Okay. Thanks for waking me."

So she'd chosen correctly after all. She would've decked a guy if he'd made her get up just to say goodbye. But she wasn't Adam, and Adam was glad.

She was kind of glad, too.

She pressed another kiss against his lips. "I'll see you at work?"

"Yup. Eventually."

With that, she rose and found the T-shirt he'd loaned her the night before. Boxers alone weren't going to cut it, so she grabbed a pair of his basketball shorts off the chair in the corner and tugged them on. She shoved her bare feet into her boots and laced them enough that they wouldn't fall off.

Yeah. There wasn't any question about what she'd been up to last night.

Before she left, she cast one last glance at the bed. Adam's eyes had half closed, but the soft curve to his mouth told her he was still watching her. He cast a sleepy wave in her direction, and her face nearly cracked with the force of her smile.

It was early enough that she didn't run into anyone, either in the guys' house or in hers. She tiptoed past Carol's unconscious form to the closet, where she grabbed some actual clothes. Normally, she'd be as bad as the rest of them, sleeping in, but not today.

The entire walk to the observatory, she kept her gaze on the horizon. The sky seemed a brighter blue than usual, the greenery more vibrant, and the air smelled like it was teeming with life.

Her muscles felt sore in the best possible way. She just felt *good*. Satisfied.

Right up until she got to the cafeteria, where her feet stopped cold inside her boots.

Shit-fucking camel balls.

As far back as Jo could remember, her father had always been a morning person. Up at the crack of dawn and on his way to the lab. So it shouldn't have been a surprise to see him at one of the little tables outside, neatly dressed and reading something on his tablet. She'd *known* she'd have to deal with him, that she was bound to run into him at some point.

She'd just really, really hoped she'd at least get to have a cup of coffee first.

Her heart throbbed inside her chest. Maybe she still could. If she kept her head down and didn't talk too much, she could probably buy her breakfast and sneak off without his even noticing her. After all, it wasn't like he'd ever noticed her before.

And just like that, she was seven years old again, standing at the entrance to his kitchen. Hair in pigtails with her knee socks and her pleated, plaid skirt. Waiting for him to tell her she looked pretty or that he'd liked the pictures her nanny had promised she'd leave out for him to see when he came home. Or anything.

Anything at all.

She took a step back, and then another, cursing at herself. The same rush of anxiety that'd had her running and flailing out with words and fists came over her again. She'd sworn she'd never be that little girl again. She'd never wait for anyone to love her.

She didn't *have to* wait for anyone to love her.

Because somebody already did.

Closing her eyes, she took a deep breath.

Adam hadn't said the words aloud, but the words were

unnecessary. All the signs she'd always looked for from her father—the care and patience and attention—Adam showed to her in spades.

Jo wasn't that desperate, sad, lonely kid anymore. She was a grown woman. A smart one, an accomplished one. She was a scientist and an A student and she was capable of being cared for.

She deserved it.

And she wasn't hovering in this doorway for a second more.

Sure enough, her dad didn't look up at all as she made her way toward the service line. She got her coffee and picked out a mediocre muffin and paid for them both, then turned toward the tables.

Did you ever talk about it with him? That's what Adam had asked her last night, and she had laughed. It'd seemed so impossible, so absurd.

Her heart in her throat, she crossed the distance to his table. With the last few steps, her gait faltered, but she lifted her chin and threw her shoulders back. She slipped into the chair across from him and felt like her lungs were squeezing her.

Her father's gaze darted up, a casual glance before he buried it again in the text splayed out across his tablet. But before Jo could curse herself or rise or say something stupid, he raised his head in a near-comical double take that he barely managed to recover from. "Josephine."

She bristled, but no. She was here to be a reasonable person, or as close to one as she got. "I prefer Jo."

"It's not what your mother named you."

Yeah, because that wasn't a fucking cheap shot. "No. It's not."

The past was a thing that happened. You could be hemmed in by it forever. Or you could redefine yourself, choose over and over and over again to be someone better. Someone new.

He gave a suppressed little snort and turned the screen of his tablet off, then leaned back in his chair and grasped his mug. "You're looking better than you did last night."

She was feeling better, too. Still, the way his eyes took her in said he didn't think her appearance was all that much improved.

She made a conscious effort of shrugging. "We'd been at the beach all day and hadn't had a chance to get cleaned up."

"The beach?"

She'd ask if that was really so hard to believe if she weren't entirely aware that it was. "It was nice."

"Good."

Neither of them spoke for a long moment. It would've been so easy to just let it go at that. To tell him to have a nice rest of his trip and head to work. The worst of the awkwardness would be over, on the off chance they did have to see each other again.

She'd be able to say she hadn't run.

Except that wasn't what she was here for.

She sucked her lip ring between her teeth and worried it with her tongue. Then she lifted her gaze from the table, and for the first time in she didn't even know how long, she looked her father straight in the eye. "What are you doing here?"

She wanted to punch herself for the way her voice wavered at the end, but damn it all, she should be able to show some emotion here. It didn't have to be a sign of weakness that his answer mattered.

His mouth darted down toward a frown. "We observe here regularly. It's got the best sensors for the objects we're studying. You know that."

And she did. Of course she did. But… "That's it?"

"What else would there be?"

"Oh, I don't know." A low ball of fire sparked in her lungs, a tightness she'd been trying for so long to deny. A single ember flew loose and fought its way into her throat. "Maybe something about your freaking daughter being here."

"Josephine—"

"You couldn't have told me? Sent an e-mail, or hell, had one of your lab monkeys send one? Anything?"

"I didn't think..." He had the balls to look genuinely confused.

In a flash, the flames licked upward and spread. "You didn't think. Of course you didn't *think*. What kind of dad would possibly even dream of thinking about their only damn kid and how she might feel if her father just showed up at her job out of the blue. Not because he"—shit, she was actually going to say this out loud—"wanted to see her or anything. But because he had regularly scheduled *work* to do."

"That's not fair."

"None of this is fair!" How many times had she screamed that into her pillow at night. *It isn't fair, it isn't fair, it isn't* fair. Even last night, it'd been one of the first thoughts to come to mind. "It isn't fair that you blindsided me like that or that the first goddamn thing you said to me in person after two *years* is that you didn't like what I was wearing. You haven't even asked me how I am—" She cut herself off, an ugly choked sound that tasted like bile in her mouth. Because that was what burned the most.

He stared at her as if he'd never seen her before, and maybe, in a lot of ways, he hadn't. "You haven't exactly invited a conversation."

Somewhere in the distance, a seven-year-old's heart shattered and broke. "Why should I have to?"

She'd gone through so many different rationales over the course of her life. She'd explained it to herself that he was sad and in mourning, or that he was angry, or that he just didn't care.

That she was unlovable, and her best defense was to never give anyone the chance to not love her again.

But maybe it'd never occurred to him.

Maybe he'd never realized he *should* care. Maybe it'd never been her at all.

Her ribs were the circle carved into the ground, the line of scorched earth, laid waste to keep the flames at bay, and inside, she was a conflagration. She rose, scarcely able to breathe for the smoke in her lungs.

"I'm sorry," she said, because she was. Sorry she'd ever imagined this could be worth her time. "I can't do this."

Except...

Did you ever talk about it with him?

Instead of storming off like she wanted to, she rounded on him. "I'm sorry your wife died, and I'm sorry you didn't get to have the son you always wanted. But I'm not sorry I didn't 'invite a conversation.' That was your job, twenty-one years ago, and you sucked at it. I don't care why. I don't even want to know. I just. I tried so hard to make you happy, and it was all a waste, wasn't it? Because you were never going to be." She drew in a ragged, burning breath. "You were never going to be proud of me."

She picked up her coffee with shaking hands. "So I'm done. I'm going to live my life, and it's *amazing*. I'm doing so damn well, Dad. I may have gone into science to impress you, but I love it, and I kick ass at it. I have top grades, and the best summer job in the world, and I'm going to go to a better grad school than you did. I have a...a fantastic boyfriend. And I'm just...I'm going to be fine. I'm going to be great. All on my own."

But not alone. Not anymore.

Adam had been right after all. She'd been holding on to that hurt for so long. She filled her lungs with air, and it was cool water, dousing the flames. All that was left inside of her was ash, but that was fine. Ash was the soil from which new things grew.

She was really going to be okay.

As satisfied as she was ever going to be, she turned around. Her father's gaze bore into her, but she kept on walking, her head held high.

"Josephine...*Jo*."

She wasn't going to stop, but the nickname caught her by surprise. She paused, heart pounding, still facing away. Closing her eyes, she waited. Listening. He had until the count of ten and then she was walking, moving on with her day and her life and—

"I know you're great. I know you're...*incredible*."

It was the last thing in the world she'd ever expected to hear, much less in that tone of voice. Screaming at herself in her head, telling herself not to invite this kind of trouble, she looked backward over her shoulder.

She blinked and blinked again, because instead of the powerful, unapproachable lord of the manor who'd presided over her home, there sat an old man. Not ancient, but tired, his spine bent, hair graying.

He caught her gaze and seemed to realize his chance. "Will you sit down again? Please?" He glanced toward the serving area. It was still mostly empty, but a couple of people had started trickling in.

Maybe it was cowardice, helping him avoid making a scene—or any more of one, in any case. But she had to work here a few more weeks, too. Feet leaden, she crossed the distance to him and perched on the edge of her seat, ready to go if he said one more wrong thing.

He hesitated for a moment, thumb moving against the rim of his mug. "You're right. You have no reason to be sorry." Well, at least he was off to a good start. "I was a miserable excuse for a father while you were growing up, and I never figured out a way to fix it. You don't want to hear my excuses, so I won't give them to you. But believe me. I know."

She sat there, speechless.

So he continued on. "The summer after your freshman year of college, you made it very clear you had no intention of coming home again."

She had. The instant the dorms had opened up, she'd been out the door. She hadn't waited for a ride to the airport. And she hadn't left a damn thing behind.

"You had every right not to want a relationship. I've done my best to respect your wishes."

What? "You—" she sputtered, unsure where to even begin.

"But I've watched you. I've followed your career. Pulled whatever strings I could for you."

He'd— Oh, fuck.

Her cheeks flushed hot while the rest of her went ice cold. "You what?"

After she'd told all the other interns that she'd gotten here on her own merits. After she'd judged them all for needing connections. She'd worried herself sick about being Dr. Kramer's daughter, but when no one had called her out on it, she'd thought she'd avoided the association. That she'd forged her own path, never asking for a favor, never dropping a name. Sure, she'd known all along that her father had some pull here, but she couldn't have dreamed—

He'd never stuck up for her before.

He held up a hand, like he could hear her protest. "You never needed it. You were always a top applicant, but I made whatever calls I could."

"How did you even know I applied here?"

His smile was small and sad. "Where else would my daughter want to go? You never did set your sights low, Jo." He struggled visibly with the name. "It's part of why I'm so proud of you."

It was like the floor falling out from underneath her.

Finally, she managed to choke out, "This doesn't change everything."

"I didn't imagine it would." His hands flexed around his coffee mug.

The same way her fingers wrapped so tightly around her own.

"But," he said, "if you were willing, maybe we could finish having coffee together. Talk. A little."

He didn't even deserve that much. But being angry was exhausting, and the freedom she'd felt walking away from him hadn't been about the walking away. It'd been about letting go.

Despite every instinct telling her she should, she didn't get up. She raised her coffee to her lips. And took a sip.

* * *

Adam dozed for another hour or so after Jo snuck out. By the time his alarm went off, he was basically awake, but he lay there a little longer anyway.

How was it possible to feel so drained and so energized at the same time? Jo had worn him out last night, emotionally and physically. He'd given her everything he could, and he'd received more than enough in return. She'd been so pliant beneath him, that spark that had always drawn him in still there, but a layer of her armor stripped away. She'd shown him who she was beneath it all and fallen asleep in his arms. The well of love inside him ran almost too deep.

How was he supposed to go back if she decided to raise her walls again?

He wanted her any way he could have her, but Jo herself had warned him never to wait for someone to feel about him how he felt about them. His first few weeks here, missing Shannon had proven her words a hundredfold. He couldn't go through that again, holding out for scraps.

He rubbed the sleep from his eyes, then threw the covers off and sat up. Lounging around here worrying about what happened now wasn't going to help him any. He'd get up and get moving, and Jo would do whatever and *be* whomever she wanted to be today. And he'd be patient—with her father still here, she was going through so much. But after that...

God, he hoped she wouldn't shut him out.

He skipped his run and scarfed down a bucketful of cold cereal for breakfast as opposed to braving the cafeteria. By the time he left, Tom was already gone, and Jared's door was closed, Kim's bathing suit hung up to dry in the shower leaving him with a pretty good lead as to what was going on there. So he made the trek up to the observatory alone.

And he really was planning to head straight to his office. But when he went to turn down the hallway that would take him there, a nagging voice in his head had him turning around. It wouldn't be overkill to swing by Jo's office and say hi. Hell, it wouldn't even be all that far outside the norm. Most mornings, his visits weren't about checking in on her, though. She didn't usually have a reason to accuse him of coddling her or acting like she was fragile.

Well, he wouldn't act like that now, no matter how shattered she had seemed the night before.

Decided, he picked a direction and quickened his pace.

Only to find her office door closed.

That was weird. He knocked regardless, but there wasn't any answer. Across the hall, one of the other staff scientists tapped away at his computer. Adam considered asking him if Jo had been in today, but the guy looked pretty engrossed. And besides, after he'd made out with Jo on the beach yesterday, there'd be more than enough fodder for the rumor mill without him giving them any more.

He retreated to his own office, which was empty, too. He let himself in and set his bag down beside his desk. A sticky note from Lisa said that she and Heather were working in the library for the morning, so at least that explained Jo and Heather's space being completely deserted. Maybe Jo was with them? He shook his head. Something still seemed off.

Not a whole hell of a lot he could do about it. He fired up his computer and sat down. In another hour, he'd go get a soda and skulk around some more, see if Jo was in, or maybe think up a question to go ask Lisa.

In the meantime, he settled in to try and get some work done. Except he couldn't focus. Protectiveness flared inside him. What if Jo'd run into her dad again? Her reaction last night had been bad, but if she felt cornered, it might be even worse.

She could be somewhere alone right now. Hurting.

He smacked his fist against the desk and spun around in his chair.

Only to find Jo in the doorway, staring at him. Eyes glistening. Oh, hell.

He rose in a single motion and crossed the room, hands going to her arms, her face, her side. "Are you okay? What happened?"

But she just shook her head. Slipping past him, she stepped inside, then motioned for him to shut the door. It closed with a click, leaving the two of them there in that space.

"Jo…"

She gazed at him, an expression he'd never seen before on her face, one he didn't know how to read.

His heart stuttered in his chest, his mind skipping straight to the worst possibilities. Something *had* happened. Something bad, and it was all his fault. She'd made herself vulnerable for him last night, and he'd taken advantage. Maybe literally. They'd both been so lost in each other, and making love to her had felt so right. Only, what if it hadn't felt right to her?

But then she smiled, and it was a hole punched clear through his chest, but in a good way. The best way. It was the most open smile, the most beautiful one, pure Jo but *different*.

Free.

He sucked in a breath, daring to hope. "Jo?"

"You were right," she said, and then she was launching herself at him.

He caught her without a second thought, thrown back against the wall beneath the weight of her body and the weight of his feelings. Pure relief rushed over him like a wave as she wrapped her arms around his neck and hauled herself up. He bent at the knees and lifted her to put them face-to-face.

Dizzy, he asked, "I was?"

"I talked to him. I told him everything. *Everything*," she repeated.

"About—"

"How…" Her smile faltered, but for being smaller, it somehow got brighter. More real. "How I was sorry he'd never gotten to have the son he always wanted. Told him I knew I was a disappointment to him," and didn't that just gut Adam, that she could say that so blithely? "But that I was fine with it. I was done trying to please him or even care about what he thinks."

Adam didn't know what to say, so he clutched her closer and held on.

Something in her eyes went soft. "And he apologized."

"Holy shit."

"I know, right?" Stray drops of moisture beaded in her eyes but didn't fall. Her lips curved up so hard it was like her face was about to crack. "Adam. He said he was proud of me."

His own mouth drew into a grin. "I knew he would. Fucking hell, Jo, I'm so happy for you."

She let go with one hand to brush the inside of her wrist across her eyes. "And we, like, talked. Nothing's really fixed, you know, but it was just...good. Really good."

"What did I tell you?"

"You were right," she said. "About everything."

With that, she latched back on and used her leverage to pull herself closer. She kissed him full on the mouth, a hard clack of teeth and the bite of her lip ring, and it was the best, most awful kiss he'd ever had.

She buried her face against his shoulder and squeezed him tight. "Thank you."

He held her against him, reeling. It struck him like a blow—a vague, shapeless hint of a hope that somehow, maybe, despite all the obstacles, despite the way that time was running out on them... *maybe*...

Everything might work out all right.

Chapter 21

The day Jo's father left, they had coffee again. She brought her data, and he brought his. She found two mistakes in a paper he was drafting, and he found none.

It might've been the best conversation they'd ever had.

At the end of it, he stood up and held out his hand. She took it, shook it twice. But when she went to pull away, he held on.

"This Christmas," he said, looking past her. "The house is always open."

She swallowed hard. "Are you cooking?"

"Dear Lord, no."

She laughed, uncomfortable and uncertain. "I'll think about it."

"It's all I can ask."

With that, he let go of her hand. She stood there, watching as he walked away.

"You okay?" asked a voice from behind her.

She peeked over her shoulder, knowing full well who she would find. Once Adam was close enough, she leaned into him, letting her head fall back against his chest. "Yeah. I think I am."

Wrapping his arms around her, Adam kissed her temple. "Good."

He came up behind her again that night, while she was washing up for bed.

"What are you looking at?" he asked.

Jo leaned in closer to the mirror and ran her fingers through the streaks of fading blue. "It's about time to redo it."

Bright colors like hers always washed out faster than normal ones. Such a pain in the ass. She'd been neglecting it for a while now, but it was starting to look sort of sad.

"Do you have the stuff to touch it up?"

"I do." She pulled the strands straight, then let them go.

"But?" he asked.

"I don't know." She shrugged. "I think I might be ready for a change."

The package she ordered arrived a few days later, and she gave thanks to the modern miracle of Internet shopping and free shipping. She felt like kind of a dick, asking the five other girls she lived with if she could have the bathroom for a while. Barricading herself inside, she prepped the way she always did, greasing up her hairline and snapping the bottoms of a pair of gloves as she pulled them on.

Before she could get very far, a knock came on the door. She grimaced. "Yeah?"

"I'm sorry, but can I sneak in?"

Yeah, sharing a single bathroom with that many women was an experience. She tugged off one of the gloves, turning it inside out in the hopes of being able to reuse it when she was done. She opened the door to find Carol standing outside.

"Sorry," Carol said.

"No big."

She stood outside with dye half applied to her hair while Carol did whatever she needed to. When Carol emerged, she gave Jo a considering look.

"Do you want any help with that?"

"I can do it myself."

"I know you can." Carol rolled her eyes. "But it can be annoying trying to make sure you've gotten everything if you can't see. I don't mind."

Jo hesitated. A handful of weeks ago, she would've thrown Carol out without a second thought. But things were different now. Bracing herself, as if the offer were really a trick, she pulled out a fresh glove and handed it over. "If you really want to."

Carol had Jo sit on the closed toilet seat and stood over her, working the pigment into her hair. As she did, she asked, "Is this stuff permanent?"

"Semi. Washes out in maybe a month or so?" Trying something new—especially on top of the other chemicals left over from her last color—Jo hadn't wanted to take the risk.

"Do you think we could do a streak in mine?"

Jo managed not to jerk her head up. "You? Really?"

"I think it might look cool."

With Carol's fair hair, it would probably take. "Sure. I guess."

Carol finished up Jo's hair, and Jo tugged on the ever-attractive shower cap. Together, they picked out a lock of pale, blond hair. Jo scooped out some dye and hovered, her fingers just above the strand. "You absolutely certain about this?"

Carol took a deep breath and nodded decisively. "Yes."

It didn't take long to get the color worked in. Jo sectioned it off and secured it in plastic wrap, then hopped up to sit on the counter. "Now we wait."

In the thirty minutes or so they had to kill, the better part of the household wandered by and ended up lingering around to chat. And it was…weird. Sitting in a bathroom in a shower cap, talking about nebulae and star clusters. An uncomfortable bubble of feeling rose up in her chest.

This was the astronomer-friendly version of girl time. Of friendship.

And she was a part of it.

Kim was the one to ask, "How much longer?"

Jo checked the clock on her phone. "About negative five minutes."

"Oh shit." Carol's hands flew up to her head. "Is my hair going to burn off?"

"Hardly. This stuff is tame, don't worry."

They took turns rinsing it out. Someone produced a hair dryer—because blowing hot air at your head when it was a million degrees out was an awesome idea—and Jo almost balked. But it would be the fastest way to see how the color had come out…

Kim stole the dryer about three seconds into her attempt with it. "Hey!" Jo grabbed to take it back.

"Trust me. Let the professionals handle this."

Jo grimaced, but she could admit when she was out of her depth. Kim did her work, and when she was done, Jo turned around to look.

"Oh, wow." She reached up to touch the strands. The faded blue with the pink dye over it had come out a vivid purple.

"What do you think?" Carol asked, shouting over the sound of the blower as she worked on her own damp mess.

It was her best happy accident yet. "It's perfect."

When Adam came over later, he stopped dead in his tracks at the sight of her. She crossed her arms in front of herself, holding her breath.

Not that she cared. A dude's opinion was irrelevant. Even this dude's.

But she wanted him to like it.

After a heart-stopping moment, he smiled. "I love it."

Only, the way he was looking at her, the softness in his eyes...

It sounded like he was talking about more than her hair.

She forced a smile and uncrossed her arms, moving in close. Before he could say anything else, she kissed him.

She had a new look, and she was trying out a new attitude. But some things hadn't changed. They were still here to work, and in a few short weeks, they'd be going back to their lives.

And she had no idea what hers would look like, after.

Chapter 22

The final weekend of the program found Adam on a ferry, surging across the water, Jo in his arms as they gazed out over the railing. It was their first and only overnight trip.

She turned her head, raising her voice to be heard over the wind. "What's so special about this place we're going to?"

"This place we're going to" was Vieques Island. And the attraction they were traveling all that way to see was called "the bio bay." He settled his hands on her hips and spoke into her ear. "It's full of little creatures called dinoflagellates, and every time they move or get disturbed, they glow." He kissed her neck. "If you'd been listening, you would've known that."

She shrugged. "I was busy."

They all had been. Their final presentations were coming up, and everyone was scrambling to get them done. And then once they were over…

He swallowed hard, dropping his head so he could rest his brow against her hair. In a handful of days, they'd all get onto different planes. She'd be in a different state, a different time zone, even. No more late nights staying up talking, no more sleeping curled around her. No more cutting gazes or sharp remarks. And no more kisses. Before long, he'd be back in Philly, settling into his apartment with the guys, checking his phone for missed calls or messages or anything. Again.

They hadn't talked about it yet, but they had to. Tonight. They'd get checked into their hotel and tour around the little tourist trap. Go out on the bio bay and maybe have some drinks with the gang, and after... He'd take her out on the beach. Get her to tell him what she thought happened next. Try to convince her she wanted what he did.

More.

The wind picked up, and Jo patted his wrist before wriggling out of his arms. She retreated over to where some of the others were sitting, and that right there made his heart swell. She wasn't an open book by any means, but he wasn't the only one she'd stopped pushing away. She patted Carol's leg to get her to take it off the seat, then sat down right beside her. Sure, she pulled out a book as soon as she did, but at least she was being a crazy workaholic with other people instead of by herself. Adam would take progress where he could get it.

He was just about to go join her when Jared stood up and made his way over to Adam. "Hey, man."

"Hey." Adam gave him the dudebro handshake that was expected of him and leaned his hip against the railing.

"Did you talk to Jo about her and Kim rooming together?"

"Yeah. She said it shouldn't be a problem."

Tom had elected to stay behind at Arecibo, so Adam and Jared were the only guys on the trip. They roomed together, and Kim and Jo bunked up. It worked out perfectly for them to switch.

"Awesome."

Convenient, definitely. And then it struck him—he and Jared had more than just their rooming preferences in common right now. He leaned his head to the side and lowered his voice. "Have you guys talked yet? About the whole going home thing?"

"What, me and Kim?"

"Yeah." He shrugged. "I mean, you seem kind of serious."

He'd been prepared for a lot of reactions. Jared smacking his shoulder and laughing in his face wasn't one of them. "Dude. No. Are you shitting me?"

Adam's brow scrunched up. "She sleeps over all the time."

"Because we do it *all the time*. That's it, though. We decided that before we started this."

"Oh." Adam's chest went tight.

"That's why summer flings are so great. You get it on and you get out. No worrying about commitments or feelings." Then he paused, as if hearing what he'd said. "Wait. Are you...you and crazy girl aren't—"

"Don't call her that." Adam was pretty sure Jared didn't mean anything by it. But it grated all the same.

"Okay, okay." Jared held his hands up. "But for real, though. You aren't going to try the long-distance thing, are you?"

"I want to. We're..." There wasn't any denying it. After everything they'd been through, all the work it had taken to get to where they were. "It's kind of serious."

"Dude. Dude, no." Jared looked like Adam was physically paining him.

Clearly, this had been a mistake. "Never mind." He moved to walk away, only to have Jared grab him by the arm.

"It's suicide. You realize that, right? It never works out, and in the meantime you're, what, celibate? Not worth it."

It made Adam's shoulders draw up. If anything in the world was worth it, Jo was. *They* were. He shrugged Jared off. "Thanks for the advice."

He made his way over to the section of seats with the rest of them and took the empty one across from Jo. She looked up from her work just long enough to smile at him, and any doubts he might have had faded away.

Worth. It.

The ferry docked not too much longer. With P.J. leading the charge, they filed off the boat and into a couple of taxis that took them to one of the less awesome hotels he'd ever seen, but for the price they were paying, he couldn't exactly object. They put their stuff down in their assigned rooms—they'd figure out the switching part later.

"Anybody want to go exploring?" one of the girls called from down the hall.

Adam stepped out to peek his head into Jo's room. "You want to go?"

"Nah." Jo waved him off. "But you should if you want."

Adam reminded himself that Jo was intent on getting a paper out of this summer's work. He shouldn't give her any shit about it. With a kiss to her temple, he headed off to join the others who were heading out.

In the end, the town was as much of a tourist trap as Adam had figured it would be. Lots of little bars and grills, populated by burned-out surfers. Shoes were a rarity, and shirts almost as much so. Everything was island themed, which made sense, but it all looked sort of cheap.

Beyond the rows of restaurants, clean, white beach loomed, and Adam's spirits rose. Ocean water and sand had treated him well the last time. He motioned to head that way, and the others followed along. But then he stopped when a woman at a shack of a roadside stand called out to them.

Normally, it wouldn't have caught his interest. But the lady was peddling jewelry, and not complete and total crap at that. His gaze caught on a necklace. A black leather cord, strung with metal and wooden beads, and hanging from the center of it, a wooden pendant.

Okay, so it was kind of crap. But not entirely. And most importantly of all, burned or etched into the wood was the image of Scorpius, the constellation he and Jo had spent so much time staring up at.

"How much?" he asked, reaching for his wallet.

He didn't even bother to haggle. It was inexpensive enough, and once he'd seen it, he had to have it. The only jewelry he'd ever seen Jo wear had been for her mother, and she put that on rarely enough. He doubted she'd get much use of this, either, but she'd have it. Have something to remember him by. He tucked the little bundle in his pocket.

"Come on," Carol called. They were all waiting for him.

He smiled and jogged to join them.

* * *

Okay, it wasn't as if Jo hadn't been paying *any* attention when P.J. had been talking up their final field trip. She'd caught that it was going to be cool and sciencey, that it would cost eighty bucks, and that Adam wanted to go.

She hadn't needed to know a whole lot more.

That said, she didn't have the best of ideas about what she was in for as she rode along in an old, decommissioned school bus toward the mythical bay they were visiting. Up at the front of the bus, a woman gave them some background on the biology behind how the place supposedly glowed, and Jo half paid attention while sneaking glances at Adam in profile beside her. It was just after nightfall, his face mostly in shadow, but the rough shape of his nose and the jut of his chin, the cut of his jaw all stood out against the darkness beyond.

He'd been quiet tonight. Not in a bad way, she didn't think, but a coiled up sort of tension made his shoulders rise and his spine stiffen. The guy had something on his mind.

She had a really bad feeling it was her.

With a sinking feeling in her abdomen, she dropped her gaze.

She'd known from the start that Adam wasn't the sort of guy you had a quick little summer fling with and then walked away from. The perfect, gorgeous idiot fell in love with his whole damn heart and he held on past the point of reason, past the point of sanity. She knew. She'd watched him do it with Shannon. Hell, he'd said it himself. He'd been clinging to some idea of her long past the point where it made any kind of sense. Fuck if he wasn't going to do it with Jo, too.

She couldn't let him. She was such a mess. Her entire life, she'd been holding herself together with fear and anger and resentment, and ever since he'd stripped her of them, peeling them away piece by piece, she'd been holding herself together with his arms. It couldn't last. Sure, she was a good lay, but when they were half a country apart, she wouldn't even be able to give him that. She wasn't here to be saved or to be idealized. She had to figure herself out, see what strings could tie her insides in when she was on her own.

And while she was off doing that, he'd go on and find the perfect, sane girl who'd give him everything he really needed. He deserved that. Not the memory of some pierced-up chick who once upon a time he'd helped a lot.

So why did just the idea of it have to *hurt* so much?

Before she could dwell on it any more, the bus pulled off the main road, rocking as it hit the unpaved path. Adam squeezed her hand, and the gesture only made it worse. After a few more minutes, they finally came to a stop, and the lights came on, making her wince. Groans came out from around her, so apparently she hadn't been the only one getting her night vision on.

They filed off the bus and followed their tour leader toward a boat docked at a tiny pier. She accepted her life jacket and climbed aboard, still unable to see what all the fuss was about.

Once everyone was settled in, the boat slipped out into the bay, unusually quiet but for the rushing of water. The lights at the dock receded into the distance.

And then she glanced behind her.

"Adam. Look."

Behind them, the boat's wake shimmered with a living, breathing, cascading blue. She looked over the side, and it was everywhere. The boat met liquid and light erupted.

Adam nudged her shoulder and pointed into the distance at trails of brilliance dashing beneath the surface. "Fish."

And suddenly, she got it. Why they'd come all this way, why they'd had to come at night. Their guide was giving them yet more information about the billions of tiny creatures in the water, responding to motion by emitting light, but Jo was only half listening even now. All she could do was watch.

In the very center of the bay, their pilot cut the engines off. "If anybody wants to, now's your chance to jump in."

Jo was the first in line. A quick check of her life vest from their guide, a nod of approval, and then she was jumping. Falling. Plunging.

Into a universe of stars.

Everything was silence, weightless floating and pinpricks of light dissolving into churning swaths of ethereal glow. Each movement of her hand and twitch of her foot. A flash of inspiration, and she twirled, sending brightness spiraling out and swallowing her whole.

She came up when she needed to breathe, breaking surface into cool night air. "Oh my God."

Adam came up splashing beside her, and she turned to him.

"Oh my *God*," she repeated.

His smile was lit by the wash of blue coming up from the water. Tiny trails of luminescence flowed down his hair and across the planes of his chest.

"It's all stars," she said, breathless.

"Millions and millions of stars." He lifted his hand out of the water, and the cosmos poured from his palm.

Because he got it. He understood.

She launched herself at him, and he caught her, their legs tangling, every kick sending blooming clouds of light sweeping out beneath the surface. He trailed his fingers down her cheek. "You're glowing."

"So are you." Just the faintest traces of it when they were still, so she wouldn't be still. She kissed him hard, licking wonder from his lips and running her hands through his hair. Setting off showers of phosphorescent sparks. She broke the kiss off all at once. "I'm going under again."

In the end, they dove together, hands entwined, and she opened her eyes underwater to watch the way he moved. The trails of light bloomed out between them.

As soon as they surfaced, she wanted to drop down again. To look at the world from a silent depth. But he pulled her into his arms and kicked his legs higher. She floated supported by him. And she looked up.

The air left her lungs in a rush.

With his mouth against her ear, his breath a warm wash, he said, "I thought the stars at Arecibo were the most beautiful I'd ever seen."

But these were better. Here on this tiny island, twenty minutes' ride from the closest town. Floating on a moonless night.

And all at once, it was like his touch was the only thing grounding her. The only thing keeping her from spinning off into some infinity where the sky and the water met, and everything was stars.

Her voice caught, and nothing came out.

"I'm so glad I got to see this here." He kissed her neck. "With you."

Just like that, the vastness of it all came crashing down. The boat lurched into focus, the murmurs of amazement from all the others seeping in. She shivered in his arms. "Me too," she managed, because she was. It would be something to hold on to. Later.

She was still out there, still swimming on a glowing sea.

But already, it felt like a memory.

* * *

The three biggest things Adam wanted after they got back to the hotel were a shower, a burger, and at least an hour alone with Jo, preferably in that order. Apparently, he wasn't the only one who was starving, though, because as soon as they were off the bus, Jared was leading the way to the bar next door.

Adam looked to Jo. "Food?"

"All the food," she agreed, following the herd. Their hands stretched out between them when he hung back. She glanced over her shoulder at him, brow quizzical.

He tugged her toward him. "You okay?"

It'd been dark enough in the bus that he couldn't exactly say she'd been avoiding his gaze, but she definitely hadn't been entirely with him. She'd been so joyful while she'd been swimming, lit up like the waters they'd floated on. But sitting in the boat after, listening to the tour guide map out constellations they both knew by heart, she'd withdrawn in a way that hadn't sat right with him. Still didn't.

"Fine," she said.

Yeah, right. "We can go somewhere else." He swept his hand toward the row of hotels and restaurants lining the strip. "Just the two of us, if you want."

She shook her head. "Let's stick with everybody else."

"You sure?"

"Yeah. Of course I am." She leaned in and planted a quick kiss to his lips. Stepping away, she met his gaze. "I promise. Everything's okay."

He still didn't believe it, but how much of a hypocrite would he be to call her on it? He wasn't "fine" either, but at least he knew what was bothering him. And not knowing what was going on in her head was half of his problem.

"Okay." He squeezed her hand, and this time when she went to join their group, he took the lead. The things they had to say to each other could wait, at least long enough to get some grub.

In back of the bar, the gang had managed to shove a few tables together, and they were squeezed in around them, two seats left conveniently free for Adam and Jo to slip into. He draped his arm over the back of Jo's chair and grabbed a menu to share. While they looked it over, a waitress in cutoffs and a bikini top came by to take their orders.

Jared called for a round of shots, and Adam gave him a look.

"It's our last time out," Jared said. "Live a little."

Jo seemed game enough. "I'm in."

They put in the rest of their orders. A couple of minutes later, eight tiny glasses appeared, all full of amber liquid. Adam took a whiff of his and sucked in a whistle. They weren't messing around. He lifted it up, and the others did the same. Carol asked, "So what are we drinking to?"

Everyone looked around. When no one spoke, Adam raised his shot higher. His throat bobbed. "To the best summer ever."

It was a cheesy, easy thing to say. The kind of sappy crap that came with their time running out.

But fuck him if there, in that moment, it didn't feel true.

They all met in the middle to clink their glasses. He tipped the liquor to his mouth and gulped it down, then shook his head against the burn.

Quiet descended over the table like a realization. This was really it. Their last hurrah.

Adam's stomach sank.

"Kind of hard to believe, huh?" Carol said. "Feels like we just got here, and in a few days we'll all be home."

"For certain definitions of it." Jo rolled her empty glass between her fingers, and Adam rubbed her shoulder.

A few of the others chimed in with where they were heading next, how they were spending the remaining week or two before the semester began.

Jared set his shot glass down with a *thunk*. "Well, I don't know about you guys, but I can't fucking wait."

"Excuse you?" It made something hot like betrayal rise up in Adam's throat at the idea that anyone could be eager to go.

"I'm sorry. It's been a good time and all. Maybe not the 'best summer ever,'"—he made little finger quotes—"but sure, good.

But I *want* to go home. I'm gonna get there and drive my car anywhere I want and eat like a million cheeseburgers and hit on waitresses who understand what I'm saying because they speak freaking English. Then I'm gonna crank my AC until I blow a fuse. Home is awesome, and I can't wait to go back."

"I'll miss you, too, asshole," Kim said, jabbing him with her elbow. Her tone was mostly playful. Mostly.

"Of course I'll miss you guys," Jared said it to the table as a whole. "But don't you miss your friends back home?"

"Sure," Adam started. "But…" His words trailed off. Because Adam did miss his parents and his brothers and everyone. But not as much as he was going to miss…

Jo stared at the center of the table like she could burn a hole in the wood with her eyes.

Adam's hunger disappeared, his interest in anything except that time alone with her vanishing. He put his hand over hers, wanting to say something. Drag her away somewhere.

Then Kim said, "Well, you won't have to miss me for long. When I come visit you—"

And Jared laughed. Right out loud. In her *face*.

Jesus Christ.

"What the hell is so funny?"

Jared didn't seem to understand what he'd just stepped in. "You're not coming to visit me." He said it like it was a fact, something he'd already decided.

"Like hell I'm not."

Finally, Jared sat up a little straighter. "Babe. We said from the beginning."

"I know what the hell we said. But that was before… before…," Kim sputtered. Her face went pale.

"Babe? Kim?"

Kim tossed her napkin down and stalked out of the restaurant.

The table went silent again for all of half a second. Adam could have smacked himself. Or better yet, Jared. "Go after her, you idiot."

"But my burger's still coming."

"I'll go." Jo of all people stood up.

Adam tried not to look too surprised. "Jo?"

She touched his shoulder. "Have them pack my stuff if I'm not back, okay?"

He wanted to question her again. But instead he nodded. "Okay."

*　*　*

What the hell was Jo's life?

She'd come to this island a veritable fortress of solitude, and now here she was, walking away from her overly concerned boyfriend to chase after a girl who, improbably enough, had actually become her friend. Not that it was entirely altruistic. Jared and Kim and Adam and she were the only ones who'd paired off this summer. They were the only ones really going through this kind of thing right now. The chance to talk about it with someone who understood... Well, that was why normal people had friends, wasn't it?

By the time Jo chased her down, Kim had crossed the street. She was bent half over, her arms braced on the railing looking out over the beach below. Jo slowed. "Hey."

Kim flinched, glancing over at her. "I'm fine."

"Yeah. That's what I say when I stalk away from all of my friends, too."

Kim snorted at that, facing the water again. Jo didn't offer anything else. She crossed to stand beside her, turning to lean her ass against the railing. A couple of quiet moments passed.

It was weird to see Kim like this. Jo and Adam's relationship had been fraught with all this turmoil, while things between Jared and Kim had seemed so much simpler, at least from the outside.

"That time at the grocery store." Jo paused, staring across the street at the restaurant where everybody else was probably sitting around talking about them. "You made it sound like it was casual."

Kim chuckled sourly. "It was. We said it at the outset. We were just two people having a good time, no strings." She finally looked over at Jo again. "He was such a dick when I met him, you know?"

"He still kind of is."

"Yeah, but you don't *know* him. There's a lot more underneath. God." She pushed her hair back from her face. "It was one of the best parts. He was a jerk, so staying casual was easy. No way I could get invested. Stupid me."

Sounded nice. From their very first not-quite-kiss, Jo and Adam had been in way too deep. "What changed?"

"Everything. He's just—he's not like that when it's the two of us. Not anymore."

Jo chewed on her lip ring for a minute. "You really think you could make it work? After we leave?"

"Hell if I know. But the idea of not at least trying…"

"But if you try and it all falls apart…" Because this was the thing that had been killing her. "Wouldn't it be better, in a way? Ending it before it goes to shit?"

Having something to hang on to. One good thing, one good memory. Didn't Jo deserve that?

"But can you imagine it?" Kim raised her gaze toward the sky. "Never talking to him again? Not even a chance of getting to kiss him again?"

No. Jo couldn't.

Kim smiled sadly. "Me neither."

"So what are you going to do?"

"Yell at him, mostly. He'll either come to see it my way or he won't."

"And if he doesn't?"

"Then I guess it'll have ended and gone to shit, too."

Jo's heart squeezed.

Across the street, a figure emerged from the restaurant. Jo squinted, but there wasn't all that much question as to who it was; she'd recognize those shoulders anywhere. She waved at Adam, and he headed over, a plastic bag in his hand.

"You have no idea how you look at him, do you?"

Jo jerked her head to Kim. "I—What?"

But Kim just patted her shoulder. "Good luck."

"Do I need it?"

"Tonight? I'm pretty sure we both do." Kim turned to Adam as he approached. "Is the asshole still in there?"

"Yup."

"Well, here goes nothing." She smiled at Jo. "Thanks, by the way. For coming after me."

"No problem." Jo had a feeling she was the one who should be thanking her.

With that, Kim took off, leaving Jo and Adam alone. "She okay?" he asked.

"She will be."

Leaning against the railing beside her, he held up the bag. "I had them box up both our stuff."

"You didn't have to."

"I know, but..." His mouth did something complicated. "I was kind of ready to be away from them all."

And a part of her wanted to run. She'd been avoiding this conversation more or less since they'd started whatever it was they were doing together. Avoiding thinking about it and avoiding giving Adam opportunities to bring it up. But they were running out of time, and Kim had all but started it for them anyway.

There really wasn't any more holding back.

"Okay," she said.

When he held out his hand, she took it. And with a sinking feeling, she let him lead the way.

Chapter 23

They ate their dinners on a bench by the side of the road, knees touching. Barely speaking. It all tasted like ash to Jo. When they were done, Adam balled up their trash and threw it away.

They had to be careful, finding their way down to the beach in the darkness, but Adam's footing was sure, and with him guiding them along, Jo could trust in where she was placing her steps, too. They left their shoes behind and walked barefoot onto the sand. Any fears she would've had about cutting her toes died unspoken.

It wasn't until they hit the water's edge that Adam cleared his throat. "We should probably talk." His face lit by the palest sliver of moon, he gave her a sad half-smile. "Before one of us ends up screaming at the other or stalking out of a restaurant."

It forced a weird rumble of laughter out of her. "Like that would even hit the top ten for scenes we've made this summer."

"You're not wrong." His chuckle echoed hers. "I don't know, though. If we really worked at it, we could definitely crack top fifteen."

"If we worked at it."

He led them in a path parallel to the shore, the tide just licking at their heels, the wet sand firm beneath their steps. "We have had a time of it, haven't we?"

And hell, this already sounded like goodbye. It made something skittery and painful twist inside her chest. But she'd always known this was how this would have to go.

At her silence, he tightened his grip on her hand. "This time next week, I'll be at my parents' place in Florida. Hang out there for a little while, then head up to Philly before the semester starts."

"And I'll be in my apartment in Chicago." The "alone" didn't really need to be said.

Before him, she'd always been alone.

"Philadelphia and Chicago are really far away from each other."

"Yeah." The twisting feeling deepened, sharp enough to steal her breath. "They are."

"Jo." He said her name like he meant it, like it was the most important syllable in the universe, and shit, fuck, she couldn't *do* this.

"Don't."

He stopped, and she turned, put her back to him. Pulled her hand free from his to cover her face, as if that could hide her. As if that could make any of this go away.

His palms settled on her shoulders. They should've been reassuring, but they felt like even more weight driving her down into the sand. "Jo." He drew closer to her, his chest a broad expanse of heat against her spine, and they were alone on this deserted beach at night, but it was as if the walls were closing in. He sucked in a breath that sounded like it choked him as much as hers did to her. "Please."

"I can't." She shook her head. It was too much. To have had this and to have to give it up.

"Please. This summer is almost over, and…God, when I came here, I never expected to find someone like you. I wasn't looking for it. Didn't want it, even."

Then maybe that would make it easier for him to let her go.

"But there you were," he said, and nothing in his tone said he was anywhere close to letting go. "Angry and full of spit and fire, and I wanted you. More than I'd ever wanted anyone. And that was before I got to know you. You didn't take any bullshit. You told me the truth to my face, and it was like you opened my eyes. You *changed* me."

Except she hadn't. He was still the same strong, amazing, giving person he'd been before he'd turned her whole life upside down.

"Not as much as you changed me," she said.

"I'm not ready for it to end."

And then there they were. The words she'd known would ruin everything.

She dropped her hands from her face, her mouth crumpling. When her voice came to her, it was scarcely a breath. Scarcely anything. "But it has to."

The world around them seemed to go very, very still.

Then he was turning her, whirling her around to face him, and his face—those eyes. They radiated a hurt that reached straight into her chest.

And yet beneath that, beneath that glaze of pain, there was a fierceness. "If you don't want more from me, just say the word." He paused, giving her the time to tell him she didn't want to spend the next few days, weeks, hell, the rest of her life with him.

There were a lot of things she could do. Lying to him right now, though? That wasn't one of them.

Except honesty was cruel, because the hope that sparked in his gaze at her silence was even worse.

"Jo." The fingers around her arms dug in. "We can do this. I'll do anything, I swear…"

Of course.

Of course that was what he would say.

All the parts of her that had unfurled this summer began to slowly, achingly close. "I know." A shudder coursed through her, and she shook herself free of his grip. Took a single, terrible step back. "And that's the problem."

"What—" He looked like she'd slapped him.

"You think I don't remember what you were like? When we first got here? How many times did you check your phone a day?"

"How does that—"

"I *know* you." Goddammit, it'd only been a few short weeks, but she did. "I saw you. With Shannon, you kept that alive for how long? You thought you were head over heels for her, and you held on to it. Way past the point where you should've. You said it yourself."

"That was different."

"How?" The word came out too loud, and her voice cracked, her eyes going hot.

And she'd cried in front of Adam once before. She'd cried for her father and for the childhood she hadn't quite gotten to have because of him. No way she would hold it in now.

But no matter how badly her eyes burned, the tears didn't come. Her voice didn't shake as she wrapped her arms around herself and gazed up at him. "When you came back from seeing her, you said you'd realized you'd been wrong all along. You were settling. And I'm not going to let you settle for me."

He worked his jaw, but no words came out.

"You would've done anything for her, too," she said. "Don't you see? You keep these things going for too long, and I can't." The pressure crushed in on her, grinding through her ribs. "I can't have you do that to me."

How much time could they waste like that? Her clinging to the only person who'd ever clawed his way past her defenses and him staying out of some sense of obligation. Because it was comfortable.

He'd accepted scraps of affection from his last girlfriend. What if scraps were all Jo had to offer him?

What if one day he realized he could've had a meal?

In the reflections of the moonlight off the water, Adam's eyes gleamed, his skin pale. "Jo. Is there anything I could say to convince you? It's not like that. Not this time, with you."

And this was the sad truth. "I don't think there is."

Maybe, if they'd had more time. But not going off to different states, different parts of the country like this. They'd see each other a couple of times a year if they were lucky. Once they graduated, they might be able to figure something out, but that was a long, long ways away.

Except then his shoulders squared. "I don't accept that."

"Well, you don't exactly have a choice about it."

"I'll convince you. Somehow. I just...I..."

Oh no. She could hear it on his tongue.

She put her hand over his lips. "Don't say it."

Didn't he see? It would only make this worse.

Catching her wrist, he tugged her fingers from his mouth and clutched them tightly between his palms. "But it's true."

"It doesn't matter."

"It's the *only* thing that matters."

It wasn't. It couldn't be. Not if the last twenty-one years of her life had been worth a damn.

As if registering the panic in her eyes, he loosened his hold, but he didn't let go. "I...let me say this. I..." His posture deflated by a fraction, and he chose his words with what looked like care. Softened them. "I care about you. So much. I know the idea of being apart for a year is scary. I don't have time to prove myself to you. But haven't I earned something from you?"

After everything he'd done, he'd earned the world. But... "That's not what this is about."

"We can apply to the same graduate schools. If we were going to the same place, would you be willing to try?"

In another world, another life.

Then again, if there'd been a chance of something permanent from the beginning, would she even have risked a kiss?

"Did we ever have a chance?" he asked.

She looked down at their joined hands. "I don't know."

"Can you give me something? Anything?"

"I don't know what you want me to say."

He ducked his head, evening out their heights. Crooked a finger under her chin to raise her gaze. "Do we need to role-play this out?"

She couldn't help but laugh. "Oh God no."

"Come on. I'll help you start. Just repeat after me."

She blinked the dampness from her eyes and waited. His smile cracked, and her throat went tight, her vision mistier.

"Adam," he said, then lifted his brows in expectation.

"Adam."

"I care about you."

Fuck. The words clawed like fire from her lungs. "I…I care about you." It was the understatement of the century, and forcing even that much out felt like she'd taken her skin off, and he could see straight inside. "More than I can tell you right now."

The brittle edge to his smile melted away. "And maybe someday, if the stars align…"

This was serious, but a twisted huff of a laugh escaped her mouth. "We're astronomers. We can't say that shit."

"Humor me." He lifted one hand to touch her cheek. "It's a metaphor."

"I was never good at English class."

"I know. That's why I'm feeding you your lines."

Her lip wobbled, and her throat bobbed. She squeezed the palm still gripping hers. "Maybe someday, if the stars align…" And then she went off script. "But right now, they're not."

"Right now, they're not," he repeated after her.

And then it was out there, in the universe and surrounding them. He pulled her into him, and she went as easy as could be, pressing her face to his chest and letting his arms surround her.

"Did we just break up?" she asked, suddenly cold.

"I don't know. Did we?"

She lifted her head enough to look at him. "I don't want to break up."

"Then we didn't." It came out in a breath and sounded like relief.

"But we agreed we will? When this is over?"

When he nodded, she dropped her face into the warmth of his embrace. They stayed like that for what felt like hours. Water lapped at their feet, and around them the world turned. The constellations kept mapping out their constant sweeps across the sky.

He squeezed her tight and let her go, taking her hand. "Well, I say we make the most of what time we have left."

* * *

They walked the beach until their feet grew tired, and then they lay down in the sand. With her head pillowed on his shoulder, she stared upward. The sky was dark and clear, the Milky Way a shimmering band shining down on them.

"I got you a present," he said, his voice quiet in the night. He reached into his pocket. When he pulled it out, his hand was curled around something.

She frowned, but he pressed whatever it was into her palm. She lifted up a string of beads. In the darkness, it was hard to make out the carving in the center of it. But then she ran her thumb over the spiral of stars she knew by heart.

"Scorpius?"

His shrug jostled her. "Something for you to remember"—he hesitated, licking his lips—"the summer by."

Something to remember him by.

"I love it." It was the closest she could come to saying what she meant. She rolled over to lie on her stomach, bracing herself on her elbows. "I love it."

"You can't even see it."

"Doesn't matter." She sat up the rest of the way, putting her back to him. "Put it on me?"

With steady hands and with a silence that bore down on them, he took the necklace from her and strung it across her collarbones. He fastened the clasp at the nape of her neck. Touching the pendant, she rubbed the polished wood between her forefinger and thumb.

She turned to him and kissed him, still holding on to this memento, this trinket.

As if there were any chance that she could ever forget.

* * *

It was late by the time they got back. The bar was closed, and the hallways were all empty. Exhausted from everything, Jo wanted nothing more than to wash off the sand and salt from her skin and fall into bed beside this man she'd already said goodbye to. To sleep safe inside his arms.

They turned down the corridor toward the block of rooms where they were staying.

And sitting on the floor in front of Jo's door was Kim. She was curled up in a ball, arms wrapped around her knees and face buried against them. Jo and Adam stopped short there in the middle of the hall.

Kim looked up, and her cheeks were red, her eyes wet. "I can go sleep on the floor in one of the other rooms if you want." She pointed across the way at the room she and Jared had been planning to share. "But I can't stay in there."

Adam's arm tightened around Jo's waist. She glanced up at him.

And it wasn't fair. After a night like tonight, she should get that small amount of comfort, that chance to be held while she slept, because she wouldn't get to have it many more times. But it looked like Kim had had an even worse night than she had.

Releasing Jo, Adam stepped away.

"No," Jo said, though it killed her. "It's fine. Right?"

Adam echoed her. "Right."

The expression on Kim's face radiated gratitude. "Thank you." She let herself into the empty room, while Jo turned to Adam.

Cupping her face softly, Adam pressed his lips to hers. As he pulled away, he trailed his fingers down her throat until they lingered on her necklace. "I'll see you in the morning."

"Yeah."

Then they'd pack up, and then they'd leave. They'd finish the work they'd come to this island to do.

And it was decided. When it was over, she'd let him go.

Chapter 24

The ferry ride back to the mainland was subdued, half of them hung over, Kim and Jared not speaking to each other. Adam unsure of what to even begin to say now that Jo had made her choice. The worst of it was that he could hardly blame her, considering how he'd acted those first few weeks. Considering all the lessons life had taught her long before they'd even met.

Home at the observatory, they spent their last few days packing up and finishing their work. When it came time for them to make their final presentations, Adam and Jo combined their two reports into one. It only made sense, given how related their topics were, and yet still. Staring at her in the light of the projector's beam, he couldn't help remembering the bristly girl who'd nearly refused to let him sit in on her telescope time at all. Now here she was, sharing the spotlight with him as they announced their results.

His smile *ached*, he was so damn proud.

That final night, after everything was settled, their offices shut down and their suitcases zipped, Adam sought her out. While the rest of the group tried valiantly to use up their remaining stores of alcohol, the two of them locked gazes, and he held out his hand. And she came.

He hadn't told her his plan for the evening, but when he started down the road toward the observatory grounds, she followed without a word. Once they were through the gate, instead of heading to the main building, he took a left at the fork.

Jo tilted her head to the side. "Are you taking me where I think you are?"

"Are there really all that many options at this point?"

The only place this particular path went was the lookout point at the top of the hill. Past the visitor's center, past all the displays meant for tourists. By itself, the place wasn't all that remarkable, but...

"Wow." Jo paused, catching her breath. From the edge of the lookout, near the railing, the whole of the campus was spread out before them. The offices and the cafeteria, the control room and the deck beyond it where he'd held her the night she'd first let him glimpse her past.

And farther in the distance, the telescope.

The dome suspended above the reflector dish was always lit up at night, viewable from just about anywhere, but from up here it seemed closer, the deep darkness of the valley below it starker.

Jo crossed forward to place her hands on the banister. "I knew it was beautiful at night, but..."

"I've never actually been up here after dark before. Always meant to come check it out. Figured this was our last chance." It hurt to say, but there wasn't any point denying it anymore.

Bracing himself, he came to stand behind her, cupping her bare arms with his palms. Ducking his head, he placed a kiss at the top of her spine, right below the clasp of the necklace he had bought her. The one he had yet to see her take off.

"Good choice," she said, and she shivered.

"Jo—" His voice caught. He'd just said it himself. This was their last chance. His last chance, and he wasn't going to waste it. If only he knew what to say, what to do...

"Shh." She turned in his arms, one hand coming up between them, gentle fingers settling over his lips. Her eyes met his, and all the fight went out of him at once.

There was nothing left *to* say. Nothing left to do.

Except savor this.

Closing the distance was giving up and giving in. Her mouth tasted of warmth and rum and sex and love, and he could drown in it. He kissed her and kissed her, with the telescope in view, the night sky and the stars hanging over him like a future that had finally come for them.

When she slipped a hand under the hem of his shirt, the desperate ache within him surged.

He broke away from her long enough to retrieve the blanket he'd smuggled along for the hike. He spread it out across the ground right beside the railing. Right above the edge of the precipice. She didn't ask him if he'd planned this or make any sort of implication. Just dropped to sit in the center of it, arms open.

He peeled off her clothes a piece at a time, pressing his lips to every inch of skin he exposed. He couldn't think about it as the last time—not if he wanted to stay sane. The last time he touched her piercing, felt her warmth, kissed the point of her ankle or the crest of her hip. But the temptation was there. The last, the last, the last... The corners of his eyes went damp as he took her in.

Before he could get lost in it, she urged him over onto his back.

She stripped him with as much care as he'd taken baring her, and his heart echoed around inside his chest. She wasn't indifferent to him. She wasn't cruel.

So if she felt half of what he felt for her, how could she *do* this?

How could she still not trust him? How could she still not trust herself?

Choking down the rush of feeling that threatened to spring forth, he put his hands and lips to every piece of her he could. Loving. Memorizing.

When he was naked, flat on his back beneath the stars, she straddled his lap. Rolled protection onto him, and then in a single stroke, consumed him. He grasped for her, searching blindly for her skin in the inferno of her body, the heat of her touch. He pulled her close, and they gazed into each other's eyes, kisses that weren't kisses. Shared breaths.

She moved on him, and he held her tight. He bit his lip to contain the storm inside of him, the crash of climax and the words she'd asked him not to speak. Keeping him deep, she ground down hard, hips to hips.

"Adam—"

He kissed her for real this time, took her bottom lip between his. Orgasm rolled through her like a wave, warm pulsations that pulled him under with her, and he wanted to stop time, to freeze it. Wanted this to never, ever end.

He closed his eyes, lost to the power of his release.

After, she slumped over him. With everything he had, he held on.

* * *

The van pulled into the driveway at quarter to eight the next morning. Adam sat beside Jo at the curb, her suitcases stacked at their feet. Her flight was one of the first to leave. Adam had tried to worm his way onto that early shuttle ride out to San Juan just so he could spend the extra hour by her side, but between people and baggage, there wasn't room.

Roberto got out of the van, giving Jo a wry look as he approached. The first time Adam had ever seen her, it had been right here, wrestling with her luggage after giving poor Roberto hell. She grinned at him sheepishly and allowed him to take one of her suitcases. Adam grabbed the other one and carted it to the van's rear doors.

As they loaded up her things, the others started wandering out. There hadn't been any concrete plans to meet and say good-bye, but apparently everybody'd had the same idea. They stood around in a silent circle as more suitcases got crammed in. Once everything had made it on board, Roberto climbed into the driver's seat, leaving the nine of them staring at each other.

"So," Adam said, looking around. "I guess this is it." His heart pounded inside his chest.

"Guess so," echoed Carol.

For a long moment, everyone was frozen.

Finally, Jared rolled his eyes. "Come on. We gonna hug this out or what?"

Adam huffed out a sigh of laughter. It was the exact sort of bullshit comment they needed. Intentionally facing away from Jo, he moved around the circle. A manly bro-hug for Jared and an awkward handshake for Tom. Polite hugs with most of the rest of the girls.

And then there was no more stalling. Nothing left to do but the one thing he desperately wanted not to.

The rest of their party receded into the background as Jo stepped into his space. "So."

"So."

She twisted her knuckles in front of her, teeth teasing at the ring of metal through her lip. She looked miserable, as bad as he felt. God, he wished things were different.

But they weren't. And it was time.

He lifted a hand to curl his fingers around her neck and forced a lopsided smile. "No regrets?"

"Only one," she said, and he believed—he had to believe—she meant the same thing he did.

He regretted they hadn't gotten more.

He pulled her in closer and swallowed, blinking off the misting in his eyes. "I'm going to miss you so hard."

Leaning up onto her tiptoes, she sealed their lips together. He kissed her back, as deeply as he dared.

And then she tore herself away. "Goodbye," she said.

She was the last one into the van, and the engine fired up as soon as the door latched shut behind her. Adam stood there on the curb. He waved as they pulled onto the road. "Goodbye."

And his heart quietly broke in two.

Chapter 25

Two years now, Jo had lived in her apartment alone. Hell, the vast majority of her life she'd spent pretty much all by herself in her father's house.

Now she'd been back for scarcely a week, and she was ready to go out of her mind.

She tossed her magazine to the ground and dropped her head into her hands. So much of this summer she'd longed for one goddamn minute of silence. Now she had days of it, stretched out on end, and it was the last thing on earth she wanted.

She missed the crowd of people at that awful cafeteria. They might not have all liked her at first—maybe not ever—but they'd always welcomed her and let her sit with them. She missed the smiles of the observatory staff. She missed having someone on the couch in the living room at nearly any hour of the day. Hell, she missed Carol in the bed on the other side of the room. She missed noise and activity and things to do.

She missed Adam. But at least that particular ache she'd seen coming.

Growling beneath her breath, she scrubbed at her eyes. She'd given him so much grief about not being able to let go, and yet here she was, no better than he had been. Sitting up straighter, she lowered her hands to her lap, then cursed aloud. Unconsciously, her gaze had flickered straight to the darkened alert light on her phone. Just like his had every three freaking seconds those first weeks they'd spent at the observatory.

Shit. She was *worse* than him.

At least he'd had some hope that his girlfriend might get in touch with him. Nearly a week, and she'd gotten the odd text from Carol and Kim, but from Adam, there had been only silence. And it was her own damn fault. She'd been the one to end it. Worse, that last night, when he'd looked like he wanted to try and talk it out again, she'd shut him down, and so they'd never had the conversation about staying in touch. About ever hearing a thing from each other at all.

Well, fuck this. Pocketing her phone, she hauled herself off the couch. Beyond her window, darkness had fallen. It was only a Wednesday night, but in a city like Chicago that didn't matter. By the time she was ready and could get downtown, things would just be getting fired up.

She crossed her shoebox of an apartment and threw her closet doors open. Her club clothes were in the back. She grabbed out an old standard that had worked well enough the last time she'd gotten an itch. Before Adam and before everything else this summer had changed.

It'd be great. Precisely the thing she needed to move past this. She'd drink and dance and find somebody to take home. It'd be just like it had always been, a release and an escape and—

Empty.

She stopped, her hands at the nape of her neck, set to unclasp the necklace Adam had given her. The one she hadn't taken off except to shower. Her fingers fumbled, again and again, and she closed her eyes, breath stuttering. The room around her swam.

By the time it righted itself, she'd fallen to sit in a heap beside her bed, her spine propped up against the frame. Her dress lay beside her, and she pressed a palm to the center of her chest, right above her breasts. Stroked her thumb across the stars Adam had given her and shuddered.

She didn't want to do this. At all.

But she had to do something.

* * *

The next morning, she suited up in the closest thing to fitness clothes she had and dug up a ratty old pair of sneakers she'd never gotten around to throwing away. She thought of Adam, slipping into the house after a morning lap of the telescope dish, covered in sweat, skin gleaming, smile exhausted and energized and gorgeous.

Running. It seemed worth a shot.

* * *

Running sucked.

Which left her with only one thing. Heaving for breath, chest and legs aching, she collapsed onto her couch.

One thing she was willing to consider, in any case.

* * *

With one hand on the door, Jo braced herself. This wasn't settling for less, and it wasn't kowtowing to the patriarchy. It wasn't anything she'd always assumed it would be. She wasn't lowering herself. Hell, for all she knew, she was about to get laughed in the face.

She put that thought straight out of her mind. She might deserve it, but she had to go into this hoping for the best. After all, you don't ask, you don't get. She nodded to herself one final time, then pushed through the door.

The soles of her boots made dim thudding noises on the tile of the hallway. More than one face looked up from a computer or a lab bench as she passed, curious expressions peering out at her through open doors, and for a moment, the déjà vu of it shivered through her spine. The last time she'd gone out on a limb like this, beating down Dr. Galloway's door, it had bitten her on her ass.

Finally, she arrived at the office she'd been looking for. Rehearsing the words she'd been psyching herself up to say all morning, she raised her hand and knocked.

Ever so slowly, the chair behind the desk swiveled around. The woman who faced Jo was in her late forties, her short, dark hair going gray, the lines around her eyes and mouth just beginning to stand out. She raised one eyebrow.

Jo straightened her posture and lifted her chin. "Dr. Jung. I'm—"

"Jo Kramer. Yes." Dr. Jung nodded. "How can I help you?"

Well, that was either a really good sign or a really bad one, that her reputation preceded her. "I know it's an awkward time." A week and a half before the start of the semester. A week and a half early. Or maybe, three years too late.

"Not at all. Have a seat."

Following direction, Jo took the chair beside Professor Jung's desk and folded herself into it.

Three years ago, Jo had gone to the head of the department and requested a research position, only to have the smug bastard roll his eyes. He'd had no interest in an overly ambitious freshman who would probably end up switching to the humanities anyway. *Maybe Jung'll be able to find something for you to do,* he'd told her, already turning away.

He'd looked at her like she was a maggot, or worse, like what she was. A girl. Rather than go crawling to the lone woman in the department, Jo'd gone looking elsewhere. She'd focused on her coursework and left her research goals for summer programs. She didn't need any second-rate castoffs. She didn't need *anyone.*

She'd made a mistake.

This time, instead of going in guns blazing, pretending she knew everything and deserved whatever she demanded, she forced herself to be calm. It didn't come easy, and she almost laughed, envisioning Adam in front of her, asking if she wanted to role-play this out.

He would've helped her so much, if he'd been there.

But he'd already helped her—already changed her enough. She could do this herself now. She took a deep breath and asked, "I was wondering if you had any work an undergrad might be able to help out with."

And Dr. Jung smiled.

Two hours later, Jo left her office with her arms full of background reading. They'd talked about Jo's experience from this past summer and the summers before it. Her interests and her history. Her ambitions to go to graduate school next year. About why she hadn't come to Dr. Jung as a freshman. Jo had answered her honestly and noncombatively.

At the end of it, Dr. Jung had offered her a project of her own. Heading to the "L," Jo felt like she had her feet under her for the first time since the van had driven her away. Away from Adam and her friends and the first place where she'd ever really belonged.

But maybe, just maybe, she could find a place here.

She kept that thought right up until the moment she strode through her apartment door. She closed it behind her and set her collection of articles and books and papers down, and—

And the same four walls that had been haunting her for the past week still surrounded her. Still threatened to close in. And it wasn't fair. She'd made a positive change in her life, goddammit all. Maybe even made a real connection with another human being.

She wasn't still supposed to feel like this. Alone.

Sinking to her haunches against the wall, she tipped her head back and gazed at the ceiling. Her ribs squeezed in and her throat thickened. Because who the hell did she think she was kidding? She knew exactly what she wanted to do.

But it was a disaster waiting to happen. The worst idea in the world.

Reaching her hand into her pocket, she closed her fingers around her phone. She tugged it out and stared at the alert light that had yet to blink, the message that hadn't ever come through.

She'd always thought, eventually, Adam would be the one who'd want to talk to her.

She turned on the screen and pulled up his contact. And stared.

* * *

"Hey. Bro."

Adam darted his gaze away from the screen, mashing buttons

on the controller as he did. No way that zombie was taking him out because he wasn't paying attention. Not this time. "Yeah?"

"Mom's heading to the store. Wants to know if you need anything."

"Think we're out of chips." Okay, he *knew* they were out of chips. He'd finished them off himself at one in the morning the night before.

"That it?"

"That's all I can think of." On the screen, his character's hatchet swung wildly, and he groaned as the bad guy snuck in a good hit.

His brother said something else, but it probably wasn't important, considering he only said it once. By the time Adam thought to look up again, he was gone.

Huh. Maybe he was a little overinvolved.

Spending the last week at his parents' house had been just the break he'd needed. He was getting a little too old for this shit, but there was nothing like plopping down on your mom's couch and eating all her food and playing video games all day. He was surrounded by people who loved him unconditionally and unreservedly. There wasn't any tiptoeing around anybody's emotions or constantly having to hold back what he was feeling. Everybody talked about normal stuff like TV shows and politics, not scientific journal articles. He didn't have to work or arrange meals or anything.

It was...

Actually starting to get kind of boring.

But that was okay. He'd be heading up to Philly soon to start the semester. It'd be good to see his friends again. He had an ass kicker of a course load ahead of him, one that would keep him plenty busy and distracted. Plus he had to take the GREs and start figuring out where he was applying for grad school next year. He'd hoped maybe he'd be figuring that out with Jo, but... he'd decide on a list of schools on his own. It'd be fun. Exciting.

He covered the twinge the thought evoked with a particularly vicious sideswipe of his ax, and zombie gore splattered the screen in a satisfying arc. "Yeah. Take that." He braced his elbows on his knees, sending his character full-tilt toward the end of the corridor and the big boss fight and—

Where it sat on the coffee table, his phone buzzed. Through sheer force of will, he ignored it, attention firmly on the screen. Just because he'd let himself get maudlin there for half a second between kills didn't mean he had to turn back into the sap Jo had basically accused him of being. She hadn't been in touch with him, not even once since they'd left the tropics. He could still hear the pity in her voice. He held on too long. He settled. Accepted scraps of affection.

Well, he'd shown her. This whole week, he'd scarcely looked at his silent phone. He hadn't sent her any pathetic texts or left any embarrassing messages. It'd killed him, but he'd respected her wishes. To the best of his ability, he'd moved on. Taken up more healthy pursuits than moping.

Like playing video games for fifteen hours straight. In his boxers.

He furrowed his brow in confusion when his phone kept buzzing. Not a text then—this was an actual call. Which was weird. Despite his misgivings, he tore his gaze from the TV to steal a quick peek at the vibrating screen.

Jo. Holy shit, it was Jo.

He stabbed at the button to pause the game, then muttered, "Fuck it," when it didn't work. Tossing the controller aside, he dove for his phone, managing to pick it up before it stopped ringing, sliding his thumb across the screen to take the call. Around him, his character made a horrible noise as he got torn in half by a zombie horde. Tucking his phone between his shoulder and his cheek, Adam plucked the remote off the ground and turned the TV off. Everything went blessedly silent.

Except the breath in his ear. The voice. "Adam?"

"Jo." His whole body seemed to sag in relief. "Hi."

"Hey." She sounded like she was smiling, and God, he missed her. All that stuff about moving on had been a joke. Deflating, he flopped against the couch and slung his arm across his eyes.

"How are you?"

"Okay. I guess." The tension in her voice made him pause.

"Just okay?"

"I don't know." She hesitated, and it had him sitting up straighter. What if something was wrong, or she was in trouble? Chicago was a hell of a long ways away, but he could be on a plane or in his car in an hour if she needed him. If she wanted him. "I guess I just…" When she trailed off again, he held his breath. "I missed you."

Jesus. Those were the best words he'd heard in…maybe ever. He curled in closer around his phone. His voice went soft and raw. "I miss you, too."

On the other end of the line she laughed, but it was grating. Harsh. "Guess I got used to having someone around to talk to."

His chest panged. "Just someone?"

He'd have liked to think he'd been a little bit more than that.

But instead of rising to the bait or giving him shit, she sounded smaller. "This is hard for me, okay?"

And that didn't make him feel like crap. "I know, baby. I know."

One quick beat of silence, and then, "Baby?"

She would call him out on that. He shrugged.

"I'm trying it out."

"Oh." She didn't tell him not to call her that. Even if they weren't... what they'd been to each other. Not anymore.

He let out a long, slow breath. "Tell me what's going on."

And then, to his surprise, she did. Like she'd been bursting with it, she let the story of her last week pour out. Everything she'd done and everywhere she'd been. The words sped up as she went, like she was remembering how to use her voice again, and God, had she talked to anyone since she'd gotten home?

When she got to the part about going clubbing, his heart sank. Sure, they'd agreed to move on, but he hadn't been ready for that. If he wanted to hear any more from her, though, he had to be cool about it. He couldn't freak out.

"Except I couldn't," she said.

And the heavy waters that had closed over his heart parted. "You—"

"The idea of picking up someone else. It just... I couldn't."

Oh. *Oh.* "Jo..."

"What are we doing?"

Hell if he knew. "Right now?" He closed his eyes and tried so damn hard not to fuck this up. "Being friends?"

Another huff of pained laughter came through the speaker. "Being friends sucks."

"It's better than some of the alternatives."

"And a hell of a lot worse than some of the others."

"Tell me about it."

It was what she'd chosen, though. Not that he was enough of a dick to remind her of that.

For a long moment, they were quiet. When they spoke again,

it was quieter. She told him about her new research project and how she'd handled it. "That's great," he said.

She hummed. "And what about you?"

It was sad, the prospect of telling her he'd spent the whole week in his underwear killing bad guys on a screen. But as he shrugged and started to relate it anyway, she encouraged him. Asked him questions, getting him to ramble about his family and his parents' house and this swamp of a town where they lived.

"I can't believe we never talked about any of this. Before," he said.

"Guess we were busy with other things. But I was always interested, you know."

He hadn't doubted it. Still, it was nice to have her ask these questions. Show an interest in his life.

Being just friends sucked, but maybe...

Maybe it was a gateway to being a hell of a lot more than they had been before.

Chapter 26

"What's got you smiling so much?"

Adam looked up from his phone, squinting against the sunlight at the face in silhouette above him. His grin shifted, becoming less the soft, private one he reserved for conversations with Jo and more the public one that everybody else got to see. Including his ex-girlfriend.

Funny how much could change in a couple of months.

"Nothing much," he lied. Looking down again, he finished typing out his reply and blanked the screen of his phone before tucking it in his pocket.

Dropping her bag, Shannon plunked herself beside him. He was camped out on a bench, killing time until his next class and soaking up the sunshine while it lasted. The sky shone a crisp, clear blue, the leaves barely starting to hint at changing colors. Autumn would be descending for real, soon. He shook his head at himself. At the time, he'd never thought he'd miss Puerto Rico's heat, and now here he was, longing for it. Among other things.

Shannon nudged his foot with hers. "Was wondering when I'd run into you."

He'd only been back for a week and a half, and most of that had been spent settling into his apartment and getting ready for classes to start. Still, any normal semester, he would've seen her by now. He hadn't exactly been avoiding her, but he hadn't been seeking her out, either. Not the way he would've in the past.

He shrugged. "Been busy, I guess."

"Busy with that girl you're texting?"

He stretched his legs out in front of him and rested his arms on the back of the bench. "Who says it's a girl?"

"Please."

"What?"

"I know that look." She stopped, and there was a sudden heaviness to the air.

She knew that look because he used to wear it around her. Because of her.

He cleared his throat. "Maybe it's a girl," he conceded.

The girl.

He'd thought that was true over the summer, when Jo had woken his body and heart, but now he was even more sure. Ever since she'd made that first overture and picked up the phone, they'd fallen into a routine of exchanging messages a few times a day and talking every couple of nights. They caught up on all the stuff they hadn't gotten around to learning about each other in their time together. Sometimes they just *talked*. Normal stuff about their days and her research and his apartment mates. Stuff about life. Nothing felt real anymore until he'd viewed it through the lens of her perception, the sharp filter of her wit.

Shannon's mouth went soft around the edges. "The same girl from this summer?"

"Lucky guess."

"Luck didn't have anything to do with it."

Adam raised his brows at that. "Excuse you?"

With a sad smile, she said, "You don't exactly give up easy, you know."

Right. Of course he didn't.

He shook his head and shifted his gaze, a low grunt of a laugh scorching his throat. "So I hear."

"Sounds like there's a story there."

"Not a very happy one."

"Tell it to me anyway?"

For a long minute, Adam stared off into the distance, across the quad.

Then he turned to Shannon. He shrugged, sadness like a weight on his shoulders. "I fell for her. We only had this handful of weeks, and I knew that, right? Stupid." He bit off the word. He brought his hand to his face and worried the edge of his thumbnail with his teeth. "She was just…"

Amazing. As brilliant as the stars they studied, only—

Only she'd been a comet. Flaring into his life one minute and gone the next, never to return. Not in his lifetime.

He shook his head. "This is weird, right?"

"No weirder than it was this summer."

Well, she had a point there. Only… "It gets weirder." He dropped his gaze and his hand, leaning forward to brace his elbows on his spread knees. Jiggling his foot up and down. "Because she…she saw how things were. When you and I were drifting apart." He glanced to Shannon and then back to the ground. "And she saw the same damn thing you did. I don't let go. She said I—" This might be cruel. But Shannon had asked. "I was settling. With you. Waiting for you to call instead of moving on. Worst part is, she wasn't wrong."

He had to give Shannon some credit. She didn't interrupt to apologize or make this about her. Because it wasn't.

Sighing, he let his shoulders fall. "At the end of the summer, I told her I wanted more. She said she didn't."

"She's an idiot."

"Says the last girl who broke my heart."

She cast her gaze skyward. "I didn't break your heart. Not the way this girl did." Her smile went strained. "I didn't have as much of it to break."

"Shannon—"

She waved him off. This still wasn't about them. "Is that really what she told you? That she didn't want more?"

"Not in so many words. It's all circumstances, you know? We even said, maybe someday, if the stars aligned, you know?" He made vague hand gestures toward the sky before giving up. "But long distance sucks, and she just…" He worked his jaw fruitlessly. "She didn't trust me."

"Not to *cheat*?"

"What? No." The closest he'd ever come to giving in to that temptation had been with Jo herself, and if he'd been able to resist her, he could resist anything.

"Okay. Because that's totally not you."

"It's not."

She'd known him better than that.

He took a deep breath, and said, "She didn't trust me not to do the same thing to her I did to you." His throat ached. "Hanging on too long. Settling."

"And so now you're settling again?"

He twitched his head up, twisting his neck to the side. "Wait. What?"

"You just said. She's afraid you're going to settle for her. But instead you're sitting here, alone, looking at your phone like it's the most precious thing in the world, settling for *not* her."

"I—" Whatever protest he'd been about to make died in his lungs.

Jo wasn't feeding him scraps of affection to string him along. If anything, she was withholding them to keep him at bay.

Never, not once, had she said she didn't want him. Only that she thought she couldn't keep him.

"Oh my God." He scrubbed the heels of his hands into his eyes. Sitting up straighter, he dragged his palms down his face. "Oh shit."

He'd let her push him away. Let them become just friends, not even daring to fight for fear of losing what little he had.

He was settling.

"Lightbulb," Shannon said, opening her hand above his head, fingers starbursting out.

He batted at her, moving to perch at the edge of the bench. "What am I going to do?"

"I don't know." With a knowing, fond expression, she darted in past his defenses and ruffled his hair. When he gave her an unimpressed look, she drew away. Slinging her bag over her shoulder, she stood. "But I'm guessing you'll figure it out."

* * *

Three days. There was no reason to panic, because it had only been three days.

Jo's stomach turned over all the same. She flipped her phone so it sat facedown on her desk. The lack of a blinking light was too much of a distraction. Too much of a reminder.

Sure, she'd gone more than a week without talking to Adam right after they'd left Arecibo. But since then, the calls and texts had come more and more regularly. They'd been the best parts of her day. Perfect breaks from classes and studying and research.

And now she hadn't heard a thing from him in three days. She rolled her eyes at herself, then kept her gaze trained skyward against the pressure behind her eyes. Okay, fine, after the second voice mail she'd left and the third unanswered text, he'd fired off a quick message letting her know he was fine, just busy, and he'd be in touch soon.

Busy. She'd heard that before.

It wasn't even fair. She might be sitting here alone with nothing but her books and her laptop to keep her company, but he wasn't like her. He'd proved that often enough. He had his family, his friends. Shannon. He went to parties and left his goddamn room sometimes.

Even if it wasn't his ex. A guy like him, single on a college campus? They'd eat him alive, and fuck knew he hadn't waited long between things falling apart with Shannon and jumping into bed with Jo. That he *hadn't* hooked up with anyone until now was the miracle.

The worst part of it all was that this was what she'd wanted. Him moving on was a best-case scenario, and she'd be fine. She was always fine.

Who the hell was she kidding?

She took the time to mark her book before slamming it closed and shoving it aside. Adam had waltzed into her life and gentled her open. He'd been the best damn lay she'd ever had and the best friend—

And she'd pushed him away. Why? So she didn't have to watch when he eventually walked off?

All her reasons came rushing back. She'd been protecting him, from himself and from her. Letting him tie himself to her was cruel, when she knew how he was. How faithful and constant and…

She shoved a hand into her hair and tugged hard.

Fuck. Was that really the worst she could come up with?

She was a coward. The worst kind. And now she was alone. Maybe he'd be nice enough to let their…whatever this was fade off quietly. Maybe he'd call at some point to tell her he'd moved on.

Crazy thoughts flooded her mind. Leaving voice mails, trying to keep him in her atmosphere, hadn't worked. She shook with harsh laughter at the idea of showing up at his apartment. Did they even make boom boxes for idiotic jilted lovers to hold over their heads anymore? She could wave her goddamn Bluetooth speaker at him. Something.

She was losing him.

She'd already given him away.

Pushing back from her desk, she rose to stare at this tiny apartment she'd locked herself away in. All this time, it'd been her refuge, the place she'd escaped to. Now it felt like a prison.

She had to get out of there. Maybe she wasn't driving to Philadelphia tonight to make a fool of herself. It was a Saturday night, but she sure as hell wasn't trying the whole losing herself at a club thing. But she couldn't stay here, brain circling and circling, returning again and again to the same point. She'd fucked up. Made a terrible mistake.

Her gaze caught on the sneakers she'd tossed near the door in disgust a few days prior. She'd tried running a handful of times now, and it hadn't gotten any better. Credit where credit was due, though. It left her wrung out and sick to her stomach with shaking muscles, but it blanked her thoughts, at least for a little while.

Pulling up an angry playlist, she tucked a pair of earbuds in. With her keys clenched firmly in her hand, the jagged edges sticking out between her fingers in case anyone decided to fuck with her, she made her way downstairs. She did a couple of perfunctory stretches in the entryway of her building.

The cool, early autumn air enveloped her as she spilled out onto the sidewalk, scanning it for anyone coming her way. Cranking up the volume on her music, she set an easy warm-up pace toward the corner.

She made it barely a dozen strides before, out of nowhere, a hand closed around her arm.

And it was instinct. Jesus Christ, but it still was. She kicked her leg out to get into a solid crouch, had her weight just right to lay the guy out on his ass, only...

Only fighting her way out of every situation wasn't her only option. Not anymore.

Not yielding an inch, she tore her earbuds from her ear. The roar of thrumming bass subsided into a tinny echo as the speakers fell, letting the rest of the world seep in around her again. The voice.

"Goddammit, Jo, I am *not* letting you do this to me again."

Her heart stopped.

It was impossible. There was no way.

She shook free, pulse thundering to life again as she tried to get her head around the concept. The hands on her retreated, but she didn't let her guard down. Twisting away, she got a foot of space between herself and the person who'd taken her by surprise.

And she might as well have been the one who'd gotten flipped. The one flat on her back and gasping for air.

He'd taken her by surprise all right. Here and now, and at every single turn. With his kindness. His attention and his patience, and the fact that he wouldn't let her push him away. Even when she thought she'd managed it for good.

Because there, hands up in front of him, looking like the best thing she'd seen in her entire life, was Adam.

Chapter 27

You're here." Jo stuttered the words out on an exhalation, the pavement or her legs or possibly both going out from under her. She staggered backward until the brick wall of her apartment building came forward to meet her. Slumping against it, she stared at him.

"Jo—" Adam held out a hand, but then paused, not making contact.

It wasn't quite disappointment coursing through her at the distance lingering between them. How could she possibly be disappointed? "You're *here*," she repeated, like she needed to say it out loud to have any chance of believing it.

He dropped his hand and lifted his chin, looking for all the world like he was gearing up for a fight, and that made her pause. "I am," he said. "And I know—you probably weren't expecting this. Hell, you probably didn't even want it. But—"

Forget gearing up for a fight. He was ready to make a speech. And Jo wanted to hear it, whatever it was he'd come all this way to say, but right there, in that moment, it didn't matter.

He was here. After all the times she'd felt alone and abandoned and like it would be absolute idiocy to ever depend on anybody else. She hadn't asked, even though she'd wanted him, *needed* him, to come. The man she'd been so worried would hold on too long to something that wasn't there, compromising and accepting less.

He was here for her.

So she cut him off before he could get another word out, before he could even try to convince her. She said the only thing in her brain at that moment. The only thing that mattered.

"I love you."

Her own voice echoed in her head, the words she'd never imagined she'd ever say. It felt like the world should be spinning even harder on its axis with the weight of them. But the wall behind her didn't give. If anything, the ground solidified, and her heart lit up, up, up.

Adam stopped in his tracks. He opened his mouth and closed it again, confusion warring with a desperate flicker of hope in his chest. "Excuse me?"

"I—" Her own mouth ached with the force of her smile. "I love you."

Still frozen in his spot, he gawked at her, but the lines were seeping away, the worry going with them. How could she have left him so uncertain? Given him so much room to doubt?

"I love you," she repeated one last time, because apparently she was brain damaged and only had two phrases left in her vocabulary, but that was fine. She didn't need any more.

Except when he still didn't move, and she didn't move, she found a third phrase. "Fuck this," she mumbled, and she launched herself at him.

He caught her as if it were nothing at all, winding his arms around her as she looped hers around his neck, lifting her and holding her tight against the plane of his chest. They lingered, noses brushing. He beamed. "Hi," he said.

"Hi."

He surged upward and she crashed into him, and then it was just the heat of his kiss breaking the cool night air, the wet slide of his tongue and the nipping of teeth, flesh catching on the metal of her lip ring, and it was so good she could barely breathe. Her spine hit brick, and he pressed her up against it as she hooked her legs around his waist. Panting into each other's mouths, they kissed and kissed, and forget running. This was the rush she'd been looking for, the racing pulse and energy, every atom in her body coming alive.

He laughed, bringing a hand up to touch her face, scarcely parting from her lips as he spoke. "I had a whole speech planned, you know."

"I want to hear it." She ground against his hips and found him hard. "Later."

"Later," he agreed.

Time went hazy as she lost herself in the warmth of him. She wanted to touch every part of him and have him touch every part of her. It hadn't even been a month, but she was suddenly starving for it. Not for sex, but for him.

But sex was totally where she was going to start.

Except, out of nowhere, someone called, "Get a room."

Adam jerked away, face flushing tomato red. Jo laughed, letting her head thunk against the wall. Jesus. For a minute there, she'd completely forgotten where they were.

"This isn't funny," Adam murmured. He leaned forward again to rest his brow against her shoulder. "I was about to ravage you in public."

"And I was about to let you."

Lifting his head, he fixed her with that gaze of his. "I never thought I'd get to touch you again."

Something inside her went terribly soft. "Well, you do." She placed one gentle kiss against his lips, then tilted her head toward the building behind them. "But maybe you should do it somewhere else."

Glancing up, Adam asked, "This your building?"

"Yup."

"Can I come inside?" And he probably didn't mean it as seductively as it sounded, but she didn't care. A shiver wracked through her.

"Absolutely."

They untangled themselves, getting another comment from some asshole pedestrian as Adam set her down. On shaky legs, Jo led him to the door and up the stairs. They made it into her apartment without any additional public indecency. She closed and locked the door behind them and stayed there, facing away from him, closing her eyes and breathing.

Heat soaked into her back as he came to hover over her, static flowing with the closeness of him. She ached for contact to discharge the spark. So softly, his fingertip traced the curve of her spine.

"We are going to talk this time." His voice was rough like sex, and her skin felt too tight, her abdomen molten.

She nodded.

"We're going to have a reasoned, intelligent, extended conversation about what we both want from each other and how we're going to make it happen."

"Uh-huh."

"I'm not going to let you shut me down or tell me what you think I want."

"Totally fair."

His tone deepened. "But if you'll let me…" He wavered, swallowing audibly. "I've spent the last few weeks not kissing you. I have so much I have to make up for."

"Oh thank God."

Turning, she dragged him down until their mouths met again, and it was like coming home and being safe and having her sex drive jump-started right into high gear at the same time.

"I missed you," he gasped out between kisses. "I missed you so much." His hands were all over her, broad palms skating up and down her sides and curving around her breasts. One rose to span the width of her ribs. When his fingertips stroked the beads of her necklace, he made a choked sound. "You're still wearing it."

"I never take it off."

He pulled his lips from hers, crushing her to him. It was a bone-crunching hug that wasn't about sex at all, and the trembling need inside of her shifted, becoming something new.

It might've been the best damn thing she'd ever felt.

She stayed there for a long minute, arms wrapped around him just as tightly as his were around her, the side of her face mashed hard against his chest. Finally, she sighed out a humming breath. "Come on."

She walked them backward, across the tiny room that just an hour ago had felt like a cage and was now a haven, a place where she could be herself and where she could be with him. When they reached her bed, he sat down on the edge of it, tugging her along with him. She climbed to rest astride his thighs, knees digging into the mattress on either side of his hips.

Hand over her heart, he asked, "Say it again?"

She didn't have to ask him what he meant. Her lower lip wobbled. "I love you."

His eyes drifted closed, his grin beatific, like he'd been waiting to hear that for the longest time. And who knew? With all his silences there at the end, maybe he had. When his eyes opened again, his lips parted, too. "I love you. Every piece of you."

All her torn-up edges seemed to knit. Not closed, perhaps, but no longer gaping. She was held together by his presence. His acceptance of who she was.

The meeting of their mouths was softer this time, slower. He skimmed his palm down the center of her chest, tracing the edge of her breast before cupping its curve, sending showers of sparks off in her flesh. His thumb tweaked the metal running through it, and he moaned.

"Did you miss that, too?" She placed her hand over his, firming his grip.

"Would it be crass if I said yes?"

"Not even a little."

Because really, what more could she want? A man she could kiss and talk to and laugh with and fuck. One who loved her like this.

And fuck her, but his body didn't hurt his case one bit. She ground down on him with a groan. "I have *definitely* missed this."

He was hard beneath her, the thick ridge of his cock hitting her exactly where she needed it—except not, because she needed him in her, hot and wide and filling her up.

"That reasoned discussion we're going to have," she panted, interrupting herself to scrape her teeth over his lip, "we're not just putting it off to kiss, right?"

Because all these weeks without his mouth on her, without the promise of ever sliding her lips over his again, they'd been torture. But so was this emptiness, this screaming need under her skin reminding her just how long it had been since she'd been touched. Since he'd made her come.

He slipped his hands under her shirt and bucked his hips. "There are a lot of different kinds of kissing," he conceded.

"How about the type where you're inside me?"

He moaned against her mouth. "Best fucking kind."

And then his hot palms were less holding her than gripping her, and she was airborne, shrieking in delight as he manhandled her onto her back in the center of the bed. Settling over her, he pushed the fabric of her top higher, kissing across her cheek to her jaw and down the column of her throat. She spread her legs and pulled him down, and when he pressed his hips to hers, she outright whined.

Shaking her head, she plucked at his shirt. She wanted so many things—wanted his cock and his mouth and the smooth flesh of his chest, muscled and warm—and she wanted it all right now.

And it hit her as he sucked at the skin beneath her collar.

She could have it. All of it. This wasn't just a fuck and it wasn't just a handful of weeks. Whatever way she didn't get to have him tonight she could try tomorrow. She loved him and he loved her, and somehow—somehow they'd make it work.

She got to keep him.

A laugh bubbled past her lips. Adam lifted his head, turning questioning eyes on her. "Are you okay?"

"So okay."

So deliriously, impossibly happy.

She pulled his mouth back up to hers, tasting his tongue and reveling in the sting of his teeth against her lip ring. Between kisses, they managed to get their tops off. She cursed at her sports bra and smiled at the dull thuds his shoes made as he kicked them to the floor. Their stupid grins kept getting in the way, but neither of them could seem to bring themselves to stop. When he ran his fingertips under the hem of her shorts, thumbs slotting into the hollows of her hips, she lifted up.

Naked, she spread her legs. Watched his eyes go dark and wide as he stared at her.

Then he was pushing the rest of his clothes off his hips, taking a single, slow stroke of his own curled palm around his length before resting his hand on her thigh.

When he dropped onto his elbows before her, she clenched her eyes shut tight. Threaded her fingers through his hair and held on against the breath of air he blew over slick flesh. But she still hadn't been ready—hadn't been prepared. His tongue was as hot and clever as it had been when he'd done this before, his lips as sweet when he pursed them around her clit, but the pleasure hit her harder, making a warmth gather deep.

Because it wasn't just the sex, for all that the sex was a *relief*. It was being so close to a person again. To this man.

A bare few minutes of his mouth on her had the pressure in her belly coiling, the heat rising to the point where she drew her thighs up, tensed every muscle. Scratched at his scalp and sucked in a breath—

Only to have him draw away.

Her eyes snapped open, her grip going iron in his hair, but he shook free of it, dragging a wrist over the wetness smeared across his lips. He climbed her body like a man possessed and claimed her mouth. The hot line of his cock bobbed against her skin, the tip slick, and she pulsed helplessly around nothing, bucking upward with her hips.

"I want—" He panted, palm curling around her thigh.

"Fuck yes."

She threw him off her long enough to get an arm flung out to the side. She pulled open a drawer and fumbled for a condom, but when she went to get on top of him the way she'd tried not to dream of doing for weeks now, he shook his head and got a hand around her wrist. Tugged her down to lie beside him until their fronts were flush, the hard points of her breasts pressed just right against the plane of his chest. He put his hand to her side as he licked his lips, darting his gaze between her mouth and her eyes.

"Like this?" he asked.

Together. Face-to-face and on even ground.

Throat dry, she nodded and leaned in.

They lay there side by side, kissing as he got the condom on. Without breaking from her mouth, he pulled her in, hitching her thigh over hips, and oh hell yes. She reached down between them to curl their hands together around his cock.

Together, they dragged the head of him over her slit, across her clit, and back down, and the moment seemed to last forever, all shared breaths and intimacy. Anticipation and love.

Then finally, she tilted her hips forward. Stared straight into his eyes as she let go. Skimmed her hand up his chest to rest it warm over his heart.

And he pressed forward.

"Jo," he groaned as he slid home. Eyes drifting shut, he gripped her hard by the hip, and she tightened her leg where it draped over his waist. He looked to her again, and her lungs stuttered, an unbearable ache behind her ribs.

Because he'd been open for her before. He guarded nothing, where she guarded everything, but in that moment it felt like there were no walls. Nothing between them.

Gaze glowing and warm, he lifted the corner of his mouth. He touched her face and cupped her cheek.

"I never thought I'd get to have this again," he said, and it made her eyes sting.

"Neither did I."

"But we do. We get to—"

They got to share this. Maybe for the rest of their lives.

The words seemed to get stuck in his throat, but she heard them anyway. Bridging the bare gap between them, she captured the soft warmth of his lips. She shifted her hips.

And it was the slowest, softest fuck of her life. Probably because it was so much more. For the longest time, they rocked as one. He stayed buried deep inside her, and she'd never felt so full. So complete.

But eventually, the low heat that built with every hint of pressure against her clit overwhelmed her.

"Adam…"

He nodded, skating his hand down the length of her spine. "I've got you."

Gripping her hip, he slipped a thumb between them, a single point of strength to grind against as he lengthened his strokes. Driving into her, he hit that perfect place inside and rubbed at her clit. She whined, straining.

"Yeah, baby?" He thrust in harder. "Can you come for me? Like this?"

As if she could stop herself.

As if she ever could have stopped herself for falling for this man.

When it finally hit her, she strained to keep her gaze on him, to not look away for one instant, one second. Blackness blurred the edges of her vision as she shattered. Against his lips, with all the breath that she had left, she said, "I love you."

Following her over, he gripped her tight. "I love you."

And she believed him.

* * *

So. That had gone about a billion times better than Adam had dared to hope it would.

He and Jo lay curled up together in the center of her bed, on their sides and facing each other, the sheet pulled up to just beneath their arms. Their legs and hands tangled in the space between them, and he had never felt so secure, so in love with another person in his life. He was here, and this was real. Everything around him bloomed in brilliant color.

Stroking her knuckle with his thumb, he stared at her. She'd bleached and redyed her hair to the roots since the last time he'd seen her, the once-blue strands past purple now and simmering into a deep magenta, warm and beautiful and just like her.

"Would you ever have said anything?" he asked, speaking into the quiet space they'd created around themselves.

"Probably." A wry smile stole across her lips. "Earlier today I was half convinced I should drive out and set up shop outside your place."

"I would've loved that."

"I think I would've. Eventually." She squeezed his hand. "I hope I would've. But I was scared."

"Of me?"

Her smile wavered. "Of how much it would hurt if you said no."

"You couldn't honestly believe I would."

She shrugged, and the protectiveness that'd flared up inside him that summer rose anew. Of course she could believe that of him, and worse. Her whole life, she'd practically been trained to.

Well, he'd just have to spend the rest of his life showing her she didn't have to.

Lifting her gaze, she asked, "What flipped the switch for you?"

He chose his words carefully. "It was talking to Shannon, actually."

She didn't flinch. Just ghosted her fingertips against his.

His chest filled with air a little more easily.

The things Shannon had said had resonated so deeply within him. It had him tied up in knots for days. The whole time, he'd been itching to get in his car and drive, but he'd had responsibilities. He'd finished out his classes and stayed in Friday night getting all of his work done for the weekend. Then this morning, he'd gotten up and gone. Twelve hours straight across half of the Northeast and the Midwest to arrive here, at her address. To see her form retreating down the road, and it had been too much, literally watching her run from him.

So he'd stopped her, and nearly gotten decked for his efforts. Right until she'd realized who he was, and all the walls he'd been ready to set up siege against had crumbled before him.

And she'd said the words he'd been waiting for, the ones he'd come here specifically to ask her for.

He licked his lips. "I realized—she helped me realize—you were afraid I settle too easily, but that was exactly what I was doing with you. Settling for less than what I want."

"And what is it that you want?"

His throat burned. "Everything."

She swallowed, her gaze flickering between his hand and his eyes. "It's funny. My dad had this thing he used to say when I was a kid. 'You don't ask, you don't get.'"

"Oh?"

"He was an asshole about a lot of things, but he wasn't wrong about that." She tiptoed her fingers higher up his wrist toward his forearm. "I'm glad you're asking."

"Does it mean I'm going to get?"

Looking at him straight on now, she said, "Everything that's in my power to give you." Her smile flickered. "It isn't going to be easy, though. Twelve hours isn't exactly commutable."

Nothing with Jo had ever been easy. Then again, maybe that was why it was…"Worth it." He clasped her hand in his again, holding on. "Besides, it's not forever."

"It's not." She considered for a second. "Just a year. So next fall…"

"We apply to the same places and hope for the best. There are plenty of grad schools, and it's not like either of us is bound by geography." He'd prefer someplace closer to his family, but he'd already spent three years the whole height of the country away from them. He'd go where he needed to. If Jo went with him, he'd go anywhere.

She wrinkled her nose. "Playing devil's advocate, though, you really think it's a good idea, planning our grad school experience around this?" With her free hand, she gestured between the two of them.

He'd given this a lot of thought, actually, while he'd been driving. He hadn't been kidding when he'd told her he'd prepared a speech.

Rising up onto his elbow, he grasped her hand more firmly.

"Listen, I know it wasn't a perfect metaphor, but what we said right before we left. Maybe, someday, if the stars align…" Just thinking about it made his chest go tight. "Here's the thing. The stars…We study this stuff. We can predict where every visible point in the sky is going to be ten, twenty, one hundred years from now. We know the statistics and the odds. Next fall"—he paused, taking a deep breath—"we *make* them align."

Sure, there'd be some waiting involved, but it wouldn't be hopeless or idle. It would be with the two of them in their own separate cities, on opposite ends of the same wire, putting things in motion.

Her body curled toward him, and her eyes shone. "You really think we can make it work."

"I know we can."

Because she wasn't a comet, and he wasn't some idle stargazer, watching her burn past from the ground.

She was a star. Maybe they both were. A binary system, two points of light circling around each other and spiraling closer. Drawn in by gravity, fueled by a fire as old as the universe itself.

And he was never letting her out of his orbit again.

Epilogue

One year later…

If everyone would please take their seats?"

Jo's heart did a weird, fluttery thing in her chest. She glanced around the room, and it barely took any work. Adam wasn't exactly hard to miss, standing a full head above most of the rest of the crowd, but even if he hadn't been, her gaze just seemed to go to him.

And his to her.

Craning his neck, he caught her eye and smiled. Jo excused herself from the rest of the group she'd been talking to and made her way over to him.

As she approached, Adam held out his hand, and she slipped hers into it. "You ready for this?" she asked.

"Born ready."

They found a couple of empty seats near the middle of the room. It took a few minutes, but everyone else settled down soon enough.

Adam leaned over and whispered in her ear, "You want to put any money on this?"

She rolled her eyes at him, but it was all bravado. Nerves had her jostling her knee up and down, tapping the heel of her boot in staccato against the ground.

The year she and Adam had spent apart had been one of the best and worst of her life. She'd missed him constantly, but there'd still been that connection. Text messages and phone calls and the occasional visit. Over winter break, she'd spent one awkward day at her father's house and then headed down to Florida for a full week with Adam and his family, and it was the least alone she'd felt in her life.

When the time came, they'd coordinated their top picks for graduate programs. Adam hadn't gotten into her top choice, but they'd both been accepted at her second.

"I don't want to hold you back," he'd said, his voice guarded over the phone.

And it had taken her a minute. A long, anguished minute. But her priorities weren't the same as they'd been before. "You're not."

He never did. He held her up. Supported her and everything she chose to be.

So they'd packed up their individual apartments and moved into a tiny one-bedroom place ten minutes from campus, and things were great. So great she never could've imagined being so happy.

But she couldn't pretend she didn't have a hell of a lot riding on this announcement.

While this had been her second-choice school, it'd been one of her first choices for advisors. This past month, all the first-year students had interviewed with various faculty to find the one whose lab group they'd join, the one they'd spend the next four to five years working in close proximity with. It wasn't make or break, but if she ended up with Maria...Dr. Maria Evans...

Well. Then she wouldn't be giving up anything. She'd have her boyfriend and her career and a top-notch professor to help her shape her dissertation. It'd be perfect.

In a calming gesture, Adam placed his hand on her knee. The weight and warmth of his touch eased her nerves and her restless fidgeting. She forced out a slow, deep breath.

Releasing her knee, Adam clasped their palms together. Then he trailed higher, letting his fingertips drift over the new ink on the inside of her wrist. It matched the tattoo he'd gotten on his shoulder, the one she loved to trace while they lay together in bed at night.

Just a dozen points of deep black sewn into their skin, connected by the faintest of lines. A map of the Scorpius constellation.

Their shared confirmation that their stars had aligned.

And just like that, she didn't have to work nearly as hard to keep her breathing easy and slow.

As the room quieted down, the head of the department took the podium, welcoming them and congratulating them on surviving their first month as PhD candidates. "And now. The moment you've all been waiting for."

Jo *hated* this overly dramatic bullshit. Why couldn't they just e-mail out their matches like normal human beings?

She sat there on the edge of her seat, listening and applauding politely as pairs of students and mentors were called up.

"Adam McCay?"

Jo's heart thundered as Adam released her hand and stood.

The chair of the department smiled. "You'll be working with Sally Durand."

One of his top selections. Jo warmed with relief, while at the same time tensing, because...

"And Jo Kramer?"

Oh hell. As Adam sat back down, Jo rose. She couldn't breathe. This could be it.

"Your advisor is Sally's collaborator, Maria Evans."

She made eye contact with the woman across the room. Maria grinned and mouthed, "Congrats."

The next student's name was called, but Jo barely heard anything else that was going on. She sank into her chair like all of her strings had been cut. Beside her, Adam beamed, eyes sparkling.

"You got what you wanted."

"I did." It seemed almost too good to believe.

He nudged her, leaning in close. "Though, you know, this means we'll be working together pretty closely. You think you can handle it?"

She could handle anything.

Not caring who saw, she ducked her head and pressed a kiss to the ink on his shoulder through his shirt, shuddering as his thumb stroked the stars on her wrist.

"Bring it on."

Please turn the page for a preview of Jeanette Grey's next
emotional, heart-pounding, and sexy romance

SEVEN NIGHTS TO
SURRENDER

Available November 2015

It was ridiculous, how pretty words sounded on Kate's tongue. Right up until the moment she opened her mouth and spoke them aloud.

Worrying the strap of her bag between her forefinger and thumb, she gazed straight ahead at the woman behind the register, repeating the phrase over and over in her head. *Un café au lait, s'il vous plaît.* Coffee with milk, please. No problem. She had this. The person ahead of her in line stepped forward, and Kate nodded to herself, standing up taller. When her turn finally came, she grinned with her most confident smile.

And just about had the wind knocked out of her when someone slammed into her side.

Swearing out loud as she was spun around, she put her arm out to catch herself. A pimply teenager was mumbling what sounded like elaborate apologies, but with her evaporating tenth-grade knowledge of French, he could have been telling *her* off for running into *him*, for all she knew. She was going to choose to believe it was the apologizing thing.

Embarrassed, she waved the kid away, gesturing as best she

could to show that she was fine. As he gave one last attempt at mollifying her, she glanced around. A shockingly attractive guy with dark hair and the kind of jaw that drove women to paint stood behind her, perusing a French-language newspaper with apparent disinterest and a furrow of impatience on his brow. The rest of the people in line wore similar expressions.

She turned from the kid, giving him her best New Yorker cold shoulder. The lady at the register, at least, didn't seem to be in any big rush. Kate managed a quick "Désolé"—*sorry*—as she moved forward to rest her hands on the counter. She could do this. She smiled again, focusing to try to summon the words she'd practiced to her lips. "Un café au lait, s'il vous plaît."

Nope, not nearly as pretty as it had sounded in her head, but as she held her breath, the woman nodded and keyed her order in, calling it out to the girl manning the espresso machine. Then, completely in French, the woman announced Kate's total.

Yes. It was all she could do not to fist-pump the air. She'd been exploring Paris now for two days, and no matter how hard she rehearsed what she was going to say, waiters and waitresses and shopkeepers invariably sniffed her out as an American the instant she opened her mouth. Every one of them had shifted into English to reply.

This woman was probably humoring her, but Kate seized her opportunity, turning the gears in her brain with all her might. She counted in her head the way her high school teacher had taught her to until she'd translated every digit. Three eighty-five. Triumph surged through her as she reached for her purse at her hip.

Only to come up with empty air.

Oh no. With a sense of impending dread, she scrabbled at her shoulder, and her waist, but no. Her bag was gone.

She groaned aloud. How many people had cautioned her about exactly this kind of thing? Paris was full of pickpockets. That was what her mother and Aaron and even the guy at the travel store had told her. An angry laugh bubbled up at the back of her throat, an echo of her father's voice in her mind, yelling at her to be more careful, for God's sake. Pay some damn attention. Crap. It was just... She swore she'd had her purse a second ago. Right before that kid had slammed into her...

Her skin went cold. Of course. The kid who'd slammed into her.

Tears prickled at her eyes. She had no idea how to say all of that in French. Her plans for a quiet afternoon spent sketching in a café evaporated as she patted herself down yet again in the vain hope that somehow, magically, her things would have reappeared.

The thing was, "watch out for pickpockets" wasn't the only advice she'd gotten before she'd left. Everyone she'd told had thought her grand idea of a trip to Paris to find herself and get inspired was insane. It was her first trip abroad, and it was eating up pretty much all of her savings. Worse, she'd insisted on making the journey alone, because how was a girl supposed to reconnect with her own muse unless she spent some good quality time with it? Free from distractions and outside influences. Surrounded by art and history and a beautiful language she barely spoke. It had seemed like a good idea. Like the perfect chance to make some really big decisions.

But maybe they'd all been right.

Not wanting to reveal the security wallet she had strapped around her waist beneath her shirt, she wrote off all her plans for the day. She'd just head back to the hostel. She still had her passport and most of her money. She'd regroup, and she'd be fine.

"Mademoiselle?"

Her vision was blurry as she jerked her gaze up. And up. The gorgeous man—the one with the dark, tousled hair and the glass-cutting jaw from before—was standing right beside her, warm hand gently brushing her elbow. A frisson of electricity hummed through her skin. Had he really been this tall before? Had his shoulders been that broad? It was just a plain black button-down, but her gaze got stuck on the drape of his shirt across his chest, hinting at miles of muscle underneath.

His brow furrowed, two soft lines appearing between brilliant blue eyes.

She shook off her daze and cleared her throat. "Pardon?" she asked, lilting her voice up at the end in her best—still terrible—attempt at a French accent.

He smiled, and her vision almost whited out. In perfect English, with maybe just a hint of New York coloring the edges, he asked, "Are you okay?"

All those times she'd been annoyed when someone spoke English to her. At that moment, she could have kissed him, right on those full, smooth lips. Her face went warmer at the thought. "No. I—" She patted her side again uselessly. "I think that guy ran off with my wallet."

His expression darkened, but he didn't step away or chastise her for being so careless. "I'm sorry."

The woman at the register spoke up, her accent muddy. "You still would like your coffee?"

Kate began to decline, but the man placed a ten-euro note on the counter. In a flurry of French too fast for her to understand, he replied to the woman, who took his money and pressed a half dozen keys. She dropped a couple of coins into his palm, then looked around them toward the next customer in line.

"Um…," Kate started.

Shifting his hand from her elbow to the small of her back, the man guided Kate toward the end of the counter and out of the way. It was too intimate a touch. She should have drawn away, but before she could convince herself to, he dropped his arm, turning to face her. Leaving a cold spot where his palm had been.

She worked her jaw a couple of times. "Did you just pay for my coffee?" She might be terrible at French, but she was passable at context clues.

Grinning crookedly, he looked down at her. "You're welcome."

"You really didn't need to."

"Au contraire." His brow arched. "Believe me, when you're having a terrible day, the absolute last thing you should be doing is *not* having coffee."

Well, he did have a point there. "I still have some money. I can pay you back."

"No need."

"No, really." Her earlier reservations gone, she reached for the hem of her shirt to tug it upward, but his hands caught hers before she could get at her money belt.

His eyes were darker now, his fingertips warm. "As much as I hate to stop a beautiful woman from taking off her clothes. It's not necessary."

Was he implying…? No, he couldn't be. She couldn't halt the indignation rising in her throat, though, as she brushed aside his hands and wrestled the hem of her top down. "Stripping is *not* how I was going to pay you."

"Pity. Probably for the best," he added conspiratorially. "The police are much more lenient about that kind of thing here than they are in the States, but still. Risky move."

Two ceramic mugs clinked as they hit the counter, and the barista said something too quickly for Kate to catch.

"Merci," the man said, tucking his paper under his arm and reaching for the cups.

For some reason, Kate had to put in one more little protest before she moved to grab for the one that looked like hers. "You really didn't have to."

"Of course I didn't." Biceps flexing, he pulled both cups in closer to his chest, keeping them out of her reach as she extended her hand. "But it sure did make it easier for me to ask if I could buy you a cup of coffee, didn't it?"

For a second, she boggled.

"Come on, then," he said, heading toward an empty table by the window.

This really, really wasn't what she'd had planned for the day. But as he sat down, his face was cast in profile against the light streaming in from outside. If she hadn't lost her bag, she'd have been tempted to take her sketchbook out right then and there, just to try to map the angles of his cheeks.

As she stood there staring, all her mother's warnings came back to her in a rush. This guy was too smooth. Too practiced and too handsome, and the whole situation had *Bad Idea* written all over it. After the disaster that had been her last attempt at dating, she should know.

But the fact was, she really wanted that cup of coffee. And maybe the chance to make a few more mental studies of his jaw. It wouldn't even be that hard. All she had to do was walk over there and sit down across from him. Except…

Except she didn't *do* this sort of thing.

Which might be exactly why she should.

Fretting, she twisted her fingers in the fabric of her skirt. Then she took a single step forward. She was on vacation, dammit all, and this guy was offering. After everything, she deserved a minute to let go. To maybe actually enjoy herself for once.

Honestly. How much harm could a little conversation with a stranger really do?

* * *

Rylan Bellamy had a short, well-tested list of rules for picking up a tourist.

Number one, be trustworthy. Nonthreatening. Tourists were constantly expecting to be taken advantage of.

Number two, be clear about your intentions. No time to mess around when they could fuck off to another country at the drop of a hat.

Number three, make sure they always know they have a choice.

Lifting his cappuccino to his lips, he gazed out the window of the café. It hadn't exactly been the plan to buy the girl in front of him in line a cup of coffee or to pick her up. It definitely hadn't been the plan to get so engrossed in the business section of Le Monde that he'd managed to completely miss her getting pickpocketed right in front of him. But the whole thing had presented him with quite the set of opportunities.

Trustworthy? Stepping in when she looked about ready to lose it seemed like a good start there. Interceding on her behalf in both English and French were bonuses, too. Paying for her coffee had been a natural after that.

Clear about his intentions? He was still working on that, but he'd been tactile enough. Had gotten into her space and brushed his hands over her skin. Such soft skin, too. Pretty, delicate little hands, stained with ink on the tips.

Just like her pretty, pale face was stained with those big, dark eyes. Those rose-colored lips.

He shifted in his seat, resisting looking over at her for another minute. The third part about making sure this was all her choice was necessary but frustrating. If she didn't come over here of her own free will, she'd never come to his apartment, either, or to his bed. He'd laid down his gauntlet. She could pick it up right now, or she could walk away.

Damn, he hoped she didn't walk away. Giving himself to the count of thirty to keep on playing it cool, he set his cup back down on its saucer. Part of him worried she'd already made a break for it, but no. There was something about her gaze. Hot and penetrating, and he could feel it zoning in on him through the space.

He rather liked that, when he thought about it. Being looked at was nice. As was being appreciated. Sized up. It'd make it all the sweeter once she came to her decision, presuming she chose him.

Bingo.

Things were noisy in the café, but enough of his senses were trained on her that he could make out the sounds of her approach. He paused his counting at thirteen and glanced over at her.

If there'd been any doubts that she was a tourist, they cleared away as he took her in more thoroughly. She wore a pair of purple Converse that all but screamed American, and a dark skirt that went to her knees. A plain gray T-shirt and a little canvas jacket. No scarves or belts or any of the other hundred accessories that were so popular among the Parisian ladies this year. Her auburn hair was swept into a twist.

Pretty. American. Repressed. But very, very pretty.

"Your coffee's getting cold," he said as he pushed it across the table toward her and kicked her chair out.

A hundred retorts danced across her lips, but somehow her silence—and her wickedly crooked eyebrow, her considering gaze—said more. She sat down, legs crossed primly, her whole body perched at the very edge of her seat, like she was ready to fly at any moment.

He didn't usually go in for skittish birds. They were too much work, considering how briefly they landed in his nest. He'd already started with this one, though, and there was something about her mouth he liked. Something about her whole aura of innocence and bravery. It was worth the price of a cup of coffee at the very least.

She curled a finger around the handle of her cup and tapped at it with her thumb. Wariness came off her in waves.

"I didn't lace it with anything," he assured her.

"I know. I've been watching you the whole time."

He'd been entirely aware of that, thank you very much. He appreciated the honesty, regardless. "Then what's your hesitation? It's already bought and paid for. If you don't drink it, it's going to go to waste."

She seemed to turn that over in her mind for a moment before reaching for the sugar and adding a more than healthy amount. She gave it a quick stir, then picked it up and took a sip.

"Good?" he asked. He couldn't help the suggestive way his voice dipped. "Sweet enough?"

"Yes." She set the cup down. "Thank you."

"You're welcome."

She closed her mouth and gripped her mug tighter. Reminding himself to be patient, he sat back in his chair and rested his elbow on the arm. He looked her up and down.

Ugh. Forget patience. If he didn't say something soon, they could be sitting here all day. Going with what he knew about her, he gestured in her general vicinity, trying to evoke her total lack of a wallet. "You could report the theft, you know."

Shaking her head, she drummed her finger against the ceramic. "Not worth it. I wasn't a complete idiot. Only had thirty or forty euros in there. And the police won't do much about art supplies and books."

"No, probably not."

The art supplies part fit the profile. Matched the pigment on her hands and the intensity of her eyes.

He let a beat pass, but when she didn't volunteer anything else, he shifted into a more probing stance. Clearly, he'd have to do the conversational heavy lifting here.

Not that he minded. He'd been cooling his heels here in Paris for a year, and he missed speaking English. His French was excellent, but there was something about the language you grew up with. The one you'd left behind. The way it curled around your tongue felt like home.

Home. A sick, bitter pang ran through him at the thought.

He cleared his throat and refocused on his smolder. Eyes on the prize. "So, you're an artist, then?"

"I guess so."

"You guess?"

"I just graduated, actually."

"Congratulations."

She made a little scoffing sound. "Now I just have to figure out what comes next."

Ah. He knew that element of running off to Europe. Intimately. He knew how pointless it all was.

Still. He could spot a cliché when he saw one. "Here to find yourself, then?"

"Something like that." A little bit of her reserve chipped

away. She darted her gaze up to meet his, and there was something anxious there. Something waiting for approval. "Probably silly, huh?"

"It's a romantic notion." And he'd never been much of a romantic himself. "If it worked, everybody would just run off to Prague and avoid a lifetime of therapy, right? And where would all the headshrinkers be, then?"

She rolled her eyes. "Not everyone can afford a trip to Europe."

Her dismissal wasn't entirely lighthearted. Part of his father's old training kicked in, zeroing in on the tightness around her eyes. This trip was an indulgence for her. Chances were, she'd been saving up for it for years.

Probably best not to mention his own resources, then. Mentally, he shifted their rendezvous from his place to hers. Things would be safer that way.

"True enough," he conceded. "Therapy's not cheap, either, though, and this is a lot more fun."

That finally won him a smile. "I wouldn't know. But I'm guessing so."

"Trust me, it is." He picked up his cappuccino and took another sip. "So, what's the agenda, then? Where have you been so far? What are your must-sees?"

"I only got here a couple days ago. Yesterday, I went out to Monet's gardens."

"Lovely." Lovelier still was the way her whole face softened, just mentioning them.

"I mostly walked around, this morning. Then I was going to sit here and draw for a bit."

Asking if he could see her work sometime would be good in terms of making his intentions clear. It was also unbearably trite. He gave a wry smile. "A quintessential Parisian experience."

"And then...I don't know. The Louvre and the Musée d'Orsay, of course." The corner of her mouth twitched downward. "Everything else I had listed in my guidebook."

Ah. "Which I'm imagining just got stolen?"

"Good guess."

Eyeing her up the entire time, he finished the rest of his drink. She still had a little left of hers, but they were closing in on decision time. He didn't have anything else going on today—he never really had anything going on, not since his life had fallen apart. But was he willing to sink an entire afternoon here, offering to show her around?

He tried to be analytical about it. Her body language was still less than open, for all that she'd loosened up a bit. Given her age, probably not a virgin, but he'd bet a lot of money that she wasn't too far off. Not his usual fare. He preferred girls who knew what they were doing—more importantly, ones who knew what he was doing. What he was looking for.

This girl...It was going to take some work to get in there. If it paid off, he had a feeling it'd be worth it, though. When she smiled, her prettiness transcended into beauty.

There was something else there, too. She was romantic and hopeful, and between the story of her lost sketchbook and her delusions about Paris having the power to change her life, she had to be a creative type. Out of nowhere, he wanted to know what kinds of things she made, and what she looked like when she drew.

He kept coming back to her eyes. They hadn't stopped moving the entire time they'd been sitting there, like she was taking absolutely everything in. The sights beyond the window, the faces of the people in the café. Him. It was intriguing. She was intriguing, and in a way no other woman had been in so long.

And the idea of going back to the apartment alone made him want to scream.

Decision made, he pushed his chair out and clapped his hands together. "Well, what are we waiting for then?"

"Excuse me?"

"Travel guides are bullshit anyway. Especially when you've got something better." He rose to his feet and extended his hand.

Her expression dripped skepticism. "And what's that?"

He shot her his best, most seductive grin. "Me."

Kate stayed firmly planted in her seat as he offered to help her up. Trying her best to appear unaffected, she arched one eyebrow. "Does this usually work for you?"

The guy didn't pull his hand back or in any other way appear to alter his strategy, and Kate had to give him points for that. "Yes, actually."

"Interesting."

The sad truth was, his offer was beyond tempting. The attention was nice, especially after her self-esteem had been beaten down the way it had in the past year. Hell, in the past twenty-two. It wouldn't hurt to have someone who spoke fluent French showing her around, either. That he was as attractive as he was just made the deal sweeter.

"Not working so well on you, then?" he asked as she considered him.

"Not so far."

His smile only widened. "Good. I like a girl who's hard to crack." Standing up straighter, he held his palms out at his sides. "Come on, what have you got to lose?"

"I'd say my wallet, but that's already gone."

"See? Low stakes. Listen, you don't trust me." That was an understatement. Was there a man left on earth that she did? "I don't blame you. Devilishly handsome man wanders into a café and buys you a drink without asking? Offers to show you around town? Very suspicious."

"Very."

"So let's make this safe. You said you wanted to see the Louvre? Let's go to the Louvre. I'll show you all my favorites, and then if I haven't murdered you by suppertime, you let me take you someplace special. Someplace no guidebook in the world would ever recommend."

She was really running out of reasons to say no. It was a good plan, this one. They'd be in a public place. She'd have time to feel him out a little more. And if he wasn't too much of a psycho, well, everyone had to eat, didn't they?

Still, she kept up her air of skepticism. She rather liked all his efforts to convince her. "I don't even know your name."

The way his dimples shone when he lifted up one corner of his mouth was completely unfair. Extending his hand again, he offered, "Rylan. Pleased to make your acquaintance."

Rylan. That was unusual. She liked it.

"Kate," she volunteered in return, and with no more real excuse not to, she accepted the handshake, slipping her palm into his. Warm fingers curled around hers, his thumb stroking the side of her hand, and oh. The rake. He bent forward as he tugged on her hand, twisting ever so slightly so he could press his lips to the back of her palm.

"Charmed."

"I'll bet you are." But her pulse was racing faster, and the kiss felt like it seared all the way to her spine.

This man was dangerous.

He straightened up but he didn't let go. Sweeping his other arm toward the door, he asked, "So?"

She hummed to herself as she gazed up at him, as if there was any question of what she was going to do. His blue eyes sparkled, like he already knew her answer, too.

"Well." She rose from her seat, feeling taller than usual. More powerful. Maybe it was all the flattery of a guy like this hitting on her. Maybe it was the headiness of making this kind of a decision. Either way, it made her straighten her shoulders and insert a little sway into her hips.

"Well?"

"Lead on," she said.

He didn't let go of her hand. "That's what I was hoping you'd say." With a squeeze of her fingers, he took a step toward the door. "Let's go look at some art."

External pressures aside, she had come to Paris to be inspired by beauty. She could find it on the walls of a famous museum. And she could find it in the lines of this man's shoulders and throat. The latter might not have been what she'd had in mind when she'd set out, but what was a little bit of a diversion?

You couldn't find yourself without taking a couple of side trips, after all.

* * *

The girl—Kate—wiggled her hand free as they approached the front of the café. Disappointing, but not really a problem. Rylan reached forward to get the door for her and shepherded her through it with a gentle touch at the small of her back. Following her out onto the sidewalk, he gestured down the street. "It's only a little ways. You up for walking?"

"Sure."

Good. Paris came alive this time of year, with the trees and flowers in full bloom, the sky a brilliant blue. Even the traffic seemed less suffocating now that summer was on the horizon. The influx of tourists made the walkways more congested, but at least the travelers occasionally smiled.

As he led them off in the direction of the museum, she fell into step at his side. He pressed his luck whenever the crush of pedestrians got thick, keeping her close with a hand on her hip, letting his fingertips linger. She fit so well against him, every brush of their bodies sending zips of awareness through him. Making him want to tug her closer in a way he hadn't entirely anticipated.

The whole thing seemed to amuse her, but her efforts to act like she wasn't affected were undercut by the flush on her cheeks. The way she allowed him to keep her near.

Until they paused to wait for a light to change, and she pulled away, turning so she was facing him. "So. Rylan."

A rush of warmth licked up his spine. His name sounded so good rolling off her tongue. Far better than Theodore Rylan Bellamy III ever had. He'd rid himself of the rest of his father's burdens only recently, but he'd shed the man's name years ago. And yet it still made him smile whenever someone accepted the middle name he'd taken as his own. Didn't question it the way his family always had.

Ignoring the ruffle of irritation that thought shot through him, he met her gaze and matched her tone. "Kate."

She looked him up and down. "What's your deal?"

Right. Because this wasn't all just flirtatious touches. He'd asked her to a museum for God's sake, not back to his bed. She wanted conversation. To get to know him.

Just the idea of it made him feel hollow.

He put his hands in his pockets and shifted his weight, glancing between her eyes and the traffic going by. "Not much to tell." Liar. "Jaded expat skulking around Paris for a while. Ruthlessly showing lonely tourists around the city in exchange for the pleasure of their company."

"What makes you think I'm lonely?"

Shrugging, he put his hand to the base of her spine again as the light switched to green, feeling the warmth of her through her jacket as they crossed the street. "You have that look."

"For all you know, I could be here with a whole troop of friends, or my family. My"—her breath caught—"boyfriend."

And there was a story there, a faint, raw note. Temptation gnawed at him to press, to dig to the bottom of it.

But if he went digging into her pain, that gave her the right to do the same.

He hesitated for a moment, then went for casual. "Ah. But then you'd be with one of them, and instead you're here with me."

She didn't contest the point, moving to put a few inches between them as they stepped up onto the opposite curb. Changing tacks, she asked, "How long have you been—what was it? Skulking around Paris?"

"About a year. I wander elsewhere from time to time when I get too bored, but a man can do a lot worse than Paris."

"And what do you do?"

Nothing. Not anymore. "I pick up odd jobs from time to time," he hedged. The things he had to do to get at his money felt like a job, sometimes. "But I don't have a lot of expenses. Buying intriguing women coffee doesn't put too much of a dent in the wallet."

"Hmm." One corner of her mouth tilted downward.

"You don't like that answer?"

"I'm sure there's more to it than that."

Perceptive. "Sorry to disappoint."

"So, what, are you staying in a hostel or something?"

There he hesitated. "Something like that." After all, the bed was the only thing in the place that felt like his. "Is that where you're staying? A hostel?" It would be the most logical choice, if she were worried about money.

"Yes."

"Which one?"

She actually rolled her eyes. "Like I'm telling you that."

"Fine. I'll just wait to find out when I walk you home."

"Is that a threat?"

"An offer. One I hope you'll accept." He leaned in closer and caught a whiff of her hair. Vanilla and rose. Sweet and warm. It drew him in, awakening something in his blood. "Because I would love to"—his lips brushed her ear—"see you home tonight."

She gave a full-body shiver. Flexed her hands at her sides so her knuckles brushed his thigh. Inside, he crowed.

Then she crossed her arms over her chest and took half a step to the side. A twitch of disappointment squeezed at him. But he wasn't fooled.

He laughed as he let her have her space. Resistant though she might be, she was warming up to the idea. He didn't have any worries.

He bumped his shoulder against hers. "And what about you? What's your 'deal'?"

"Not much to tell." It was a clear imitation of his own response, and she narrowed her eyes for a second before shrugging. "I'm from Ohio, but I went to school in New York. My mom sends me paranoid e-mails, asking me if I've gotten mugged yet once a week."

He winced. "At least you'll have something to say to her this week, then?"

"Yeah." She frowned, patting her side as if to touch the purse that wasn't there. "Four years living in this sketchy part of Brooklyn, and I come to Paris to get robbed." She dropped her gaze away from his. "Mom warned me about it, too, you know. Told me Paris was full of thieves."

Her expression was growing more and more unhappy. God. She really didn't know how to guard her emotions at all, did she? Nothing like the people he'd once surrounded himself with. The ones who would've looked at such naïveté with contempt. Here and now, it sparked a tenderness inside him that was new. He wanted to wipe the frown from her lips—or better, kiss it off. He wanted to know what had put it there in the first place. Neither reaction made sense.

So instead of touching or pressing, he steered the conversation onto safer ground. "Is it just you and your mom?"

"Pretty much. My dad's...out of the picture." And oh, but there was a minefield under there, based on the tone of her voice. She crossed her arms over her chest. "How about you?"

Speaking of minefields...

Before he could try to find a way around talking about the train wreck that was his family, they rounded a corner, and he let out a breath in relief. He craned his neck and pointed. "Look. Those banners up ahead?"

Kate followed his gaze, rising up onto tiptoes. Easily distracted, thank God. "Yeah?"

He reached out to grab hold of her hand and nearly got lost in the softness of her skin. He licked his lips and swallowed. "Come on. We're nearly there."

The crowds of tourists were more overwhelming right around

the museum, though not as bad as they would be once July hit. Letting him interlace their fingers, she quickened her pace, falling into step as they weaved their way along the sidewalk. The great walls of the place finally gave, and he dragged her along through the archway.

"Don't we have to go in through the Pyramid?" she asked, sounding breathless, evoking the famous entrance to the museum.

He twisted to look at her and winked. "Would I lead you any other way?"

They emerged out into the stone courtyard. He let go of her hand to throw his arms out wide. Ta-da. "Your Pyramid, madame."

Pei's Pyramid. It was a glass and metal structure, located at the center of the courtyard, housing the main entrance of the museum. His mother had always hated it, but he'd never really minded the thing. Besides, it was in all the guidebooks, and in high school French textbooks. Tourists typically wanted to see it.

She stood there staring at the monument for a long moment before scrunching her face up. "That is both so much cooler and so much less impressive than I expected."

Well, at least she was honest. He threw his head back and laughed. "Welcome to international travel, my dear." He dug in his pocket for his phone. "You want a picture?"

"Actually, kinda. Yeah."

"Stand over there." He motioned her to stand where he had a good view of her and the Pyramid. The sky was a bright, perfect blue, and it brought out the red in her hair. Her photo smile wasn't as arresting as her real one, but he'd take it anyway. "Say 'fromage.'"

He snapped the shot, then held it out so she could see. He expected the requisite look of embarrassment all girls gave him when he showed them images of themselves, but instead she simply nodded. "Nice composition."

It made him pause. She had been planning to spend her day sketching, had been swayed by his offer to take her here of all places, so the comment shouldn't have surprised him. But his estimation of her rose. When she looked at something, she looked deeper. Saw more.

The idea of wandering around a museum with her suddenly took on a whole new kind of charm.

He glanced at the picture again before flicking back to the camera app. "Easy when there's a pretty lady in the frame."

She cast her gaze skyward and was just starting to move away when he caught her arm.

"What?"

"One more."

"The one is plenty," she argued.

"One more for me." With that, he reeled her in, wrapping his arm around her shoulder. It was a cheap ploy, but he couldn't resist the chance to get her close. Her scent wafted over him again. He took a second to breathe her in, to really feel her against his side before he held his arm out for the selfie, shooting his own best lady-killer grin at the lens.

Her laughter sounded more indulgent than charmed, but he could work with that. "Does this move usually work for you?" she asked.

He pressed the button on the screen to take the shot. "Better than the tour guide offer, even." He snapped his teeth playfully near her ear. "Because this one gives me an excuse to touch you."

Making a show of mock-growling at her, he gave her one rough squeeze and let her go. She took only a half step away, but the loss of her left his ribs cold. He mentally shook his head at himself.

Before he could give in to the urge to tug her back in, and without a pretext this time, he turned his attention to the screen. A pang fired off inside him. They looked good together. Like a real, happy couple—the kind he'd been taught didn't exist. Her eyes positively danced, her smile as wide as her face.

And so was his. Not a thing about his expression was forced or fake. The contrast alone made his throat tighten. This wasn't one of the usual selfies he took with girls. Not one of the awful pictures snapped on the courthouse steps. Or the others. The ones from before.

His hands curled into fists, and he had to forcibly relax them.

Shutting that line of thought right down, he turned off the screen of his phone. "You'll have to tell me where to send them later."

Oblivious to where his mind had gone, she raised a brow. "Ah, now I see your game. You want my e-mail address."

"Yes," he said dryly. "It's all been a clever little ploy so I could subscribe you to all sorts of mailing lists for natural male enhancement."

She arched a brow. "Am I going to need that?"

Nicely played. "Not if you take me home tonight." He threaded his arm through hers. "Come on. The masterpieces await."

* * *

"Are you sure we're still even in the museum?" Kate spun in a circle, looking around in awe. "How can this place be so huge?"

The vaulted archways seemed to soar above her, and the ceilings were almost as gorgeous as the paintings. The whole place smelled of art somehow, even though the works were all hundreds of years old, the oils dry and the varnishes cracking. The figures within the canvases glowed with how masterfully they'd been rendered, and something inside of her felt like it was glowing as well.

She'd thought the Met had been amazing the first time she'd been there. But she'd had no idea. No clue.

She finished her slow circle, coming around again to face the center of the room. To face Rylan. He stood there, arms crossed over the expanse of his chest, gaze hot and heavy on hers, and a tremor coursed its way down her spine.

Then again, she'd also never wandered around the Met with a man like him by her side.

To think she'd been worried when she agreed to let him take her here. She hated being rushed through museums, and she'd been resolved to take her time. But Rylan had stood by patiently as she looked her fill, had been waiting to take her hand at the end of each set of paintings. Big, strong fingers curled firmly around her palm, and the warm, male scent of him mingled with the wood and polish of the gallery, making her head spin.

Swallowing hard, she checked herself. He was practically a stranger—it shouldn't be so easy to fall into step with him like this. And yet she felt more comfortable with him than she had doing this with any of her other friends. Definitely more comfortable than she ever had with Aaron. Maybe because he was a stranger. There was no point pretending to be anything she wasn't. She never had to see him again if she didn't want to. So she had nothing to lose.

Catching her eye, he tilted his head toward the next room, a silent invitation, asking her if she was ready to continue. She nodded, moving into his space again. The heat of his hand seeped into the base of her spine, but she didn't flinch. Ridiculous how quickly she was getting used to how much he liked to touch her. What had it been? A couple of hours?

A couple of amazing hours.

They'd seen a bunch of the highlights already. The sweeping statuary of *Winged Victory*, which had been so much bigger and more imposing than she'd expected. Tiny, lovely *Venus de Milo*. And much to Rylan's frustration, they'd even stood in line to see the *Mona Lisa* nice and close. She'd shoved him when he'd asked with that odd mixture of amusement and derision if she was satisfied. She'd known going into it that that particular piece had a tendency to underwhelm, but she hadn't cared. She'd seen it. In real life.

In her head, she was rearranging all her plans for the week she had left in Paris. She had to come back and spend a whole day here alone with her sketchbook and her pencils and pastels.

"You are having a total art-geek-gasm, aren't you?" he asked, releasing her so she could get closer to one of the paintings.

At this point, they were in one of the more remote galleries, one he'd insisted they make the time to visit, full of big, classic pieces done in vivid colors, depicting scenes from legends and myths. None of it was what she'd really come here to see, but she found herself getting lost in them all the same.

She was about to tell him as much when she glanced over at him, and he had that expression on his face again. It made her pause.

She didn't have any illusions that he was here for any reason other than to humor her. He was going above and beyond as far as the amount of time and energy she expected any guy to put into a pickup, but it was still a pickup.

Only, he kept looking at her like this. Like somehow, despite his worst intentions, he was seeing more than just her breasts.

She let a grin curl her lips as she turned her attention back to the walls. "It's amazing."

"It gets even better."

Hard to believe, but how could she resist?

"So the thing that really gets me," he said over his shoulder as he meandered into the next gallery, "about European museums is the scale."

She followed, craning her neck as she passed through the archway and—wow. He wasn't kidding. The whole room was full of paintings that stretched from floor to ceiling. The canvases must have been twenty feet tall, some of them maybe double that in width.

"Holy crap." In awe, she turned, trying to take in everything. She pointed to a painting at the end of the room. "That one is bigger than my apartment back in New York."

It might have been a tiny studio apartment, but still.

"Don't see this kind of thing in museums in the States, huh?" he asked.

He was standing behind her now, his breath warm against her ear. It felt . . . nice. But not nice enough to distract her from trying to memorize the images surrounding her.

"I've never seen anything like it, anywhere."

She stepped forward, away from his heat and toward the painting on the opposite wall. He let her go, walking backward to perch on the bench in the center of the room. He sat with his knees spread, his elbows on his thighs. She turned her back to him, but she couldn't help but be aware of him—his presence that felt so unreasonably large in such an enormous room.

"That used to be one of my favorites," he said, gesturing at the canvas she'd been drawn to.

"Oh?" It was arresting, the composition and the arrangement of the figures drawing the eye in. Bringing her hand to her mouth, she read the placard beside it. "Zeus and Hera?" She took a step back and tilted her head.

The two figures were seated in a garden, staring into each other's eyes. A smile colored the edge of Zeus's lips.

"They look happy." His shrug came through in his voice.

Really? The king and queen of the Roman gods weren't exactly known for their perfect marriage. How many people had died on account of their fits of jealousy and pique? She furrowed her brow. "Not exactly how I usually think of them."

From behind her, he chuckled. "No. Not usually." He paused, then added, "I think maybe that's why I liked it so much."

She hummed, asking him to elaborate.

"It was just a reminder. No matter how awful things were between them most of the time, they still had their moments. Their good times."

A sour taste rose in her throat. "Doesn't change the fact that he'd knocked up half the pantheon."

If her mother hadn't fallen for all the good times with her father...if the good times with Aaron hadn't blinded Kate...

"And the better part of the mortal realm, too," Rylan agreed, a wry twist to his tone. "But still. I always used to imagine that at one point they were like this."

"Used to?"

He chuckled wryly. "We all have to grow up sometime."

They were silent for a minute as she tried to take the whole thing in.

When he spoke again, it echoed in the space. "The first time I ever came here, I was...maybe eight? Nine?" A shade of memory colored his voice. "A few years before my parents got divorced." He cleared the roughness from his throat. "My mother brought me to this room, and I remember finding this picture and not being able to look away from it." He gave a little rueful laugh. "My sister gave me so much shit for ignoring all the giant battle scenes to look at two people who weren't even naked or anything."

Kate glanced over her shoulder at him. That was...kind of a lot of information, actually, considering how evasive he'd been while they'd been trading histories earlier. Turning back to the painting, she cast about for something to ask him more about. Not the divorce—not with the way that topic always brought her own hurts to the surface—though she tucked that away for later. After a moment's indecision, she landed on, "You came to Paris when you were a kid?"

"The whole family did. My dad's work had us doing a bunch of travel."

"What did he do?"

"Finance stuff. Very boring. And a very, very long time ago."

She frowned. "It can't have been that long ago. How old are you?"

"Twenty-seven. Don't try to tell me nineteen years isn't a long time."

He made it sound like a lifetime. For her it nearly was.

"Believe me, it's a long time. I'm only twenty-two."

"That's not so young."

She considered for a moment. "It's old enough."

"Old enough for what?" Suggestion rolled off his tongue.

His flirtation made her bold. "For knowing better than to be taken in by men like you?"

"Men like me?" His tone dripped with mock offense. "Men who take you to beautiful museums." He was off the bench and at her side again, pushing her hair from her face. "Men who want nothing more than to show you their big, huge—"

She made a noise of half laughter, half disgust and shoved him off.

"Paintings! I was going to say paintings."

"I'll bet you were."

"I was." He held his arms out to indicate the whole of the room. "Do you like them?"

And she couldn't lie, not even a bit. She spun around another time, nice and slow, taking in everything. As she twisted back toward him, something inside of her softened. All the innuendo and playfulness had fallen from his lips, and he was simply standing there, waiting for her opinion.

Looking for all the world like he actually cared what it would be.

Impulsiveness took her close to him. "I do." And this was stupid. But she did it anyway—leaned in and pressed the quickest, lightest kiss to his cheek. "I love it. Thank you."

He grinned as she danced away before he could reel her the rest of the way in. "Does that mean you're ready to agree for me to walk you home?"

A little thrill shot through her. How nice would that be? He'd been trying so hard, and she'd enjoyed every minute of it. After months of being on her guard, nursing her bitterness, it was tempting to just let go. To say yes for once. He was funny and smart, charming and gorgeous. She could do a lot worse. But she wasn't entirely sure she couldn't do better.

And besides, she'd never known it could be so much fun to watch a guy work for it.

She started toward the exit from the gallery, a little bounce in her step. "Let's start with you walking me to dinner." Glancing back at him, she smiled at the look of smug satisfaction on his face. "No promises for after."

"I would never dare to assume."

"And it had better be something good." She slowed down so he could catch up, and she didn't bother to stop him when he moved to interlace their fingers. She'd already let enough of her inhibitions go, lulled by the ease of his smile and his touch. Why not accept this, too? Especially when it felt so good. "Off the beaten path. Nothing I could find in a tour guide."

"Don't you worry." A sly grin made his eyes sparkle, and his hand squeezed hers. "I have just the thing in mind."

About the Author

Jeanette Grey started out with degrees in physics and painting, which she dutifully applied to stunted careers in teaching, technical support, and advertising. When she isn't writing, Jeanette enjoys making pottery, playing board games, and spending time with her husband and her pet frog. She lives, loves, and writes in upstate New York.

Learn more at:
JeanetteGrey.com
Twitter, @JeanetteLGrey
Facebook.com/JeanetteLGrey

CPSIA information can be obtained
at www.ICGtesting.com
Printed in the USA
LVOW12s1815201217
560400LV00001B/138/P